SHADES OF PROPHECY

LELA TRILOGY BOOK THREE

TESSONJA ODETTE

To my readers—you are amazing and capable of magical things.

To Nova—my sunshine, my baby bear, my goofball. ALWAYS follow your dreams.

To Dustin—my alpha reader, my love, my biggest fan, reacher of tall things, and opener of jars.

To Harlow—the unicorn girl—and her loving family. Love moves through the veil and beyond, existing forever in our hearts.

And to Ghost, my dog, who allows me to read my books aloud to him—in their entirety—during editing.

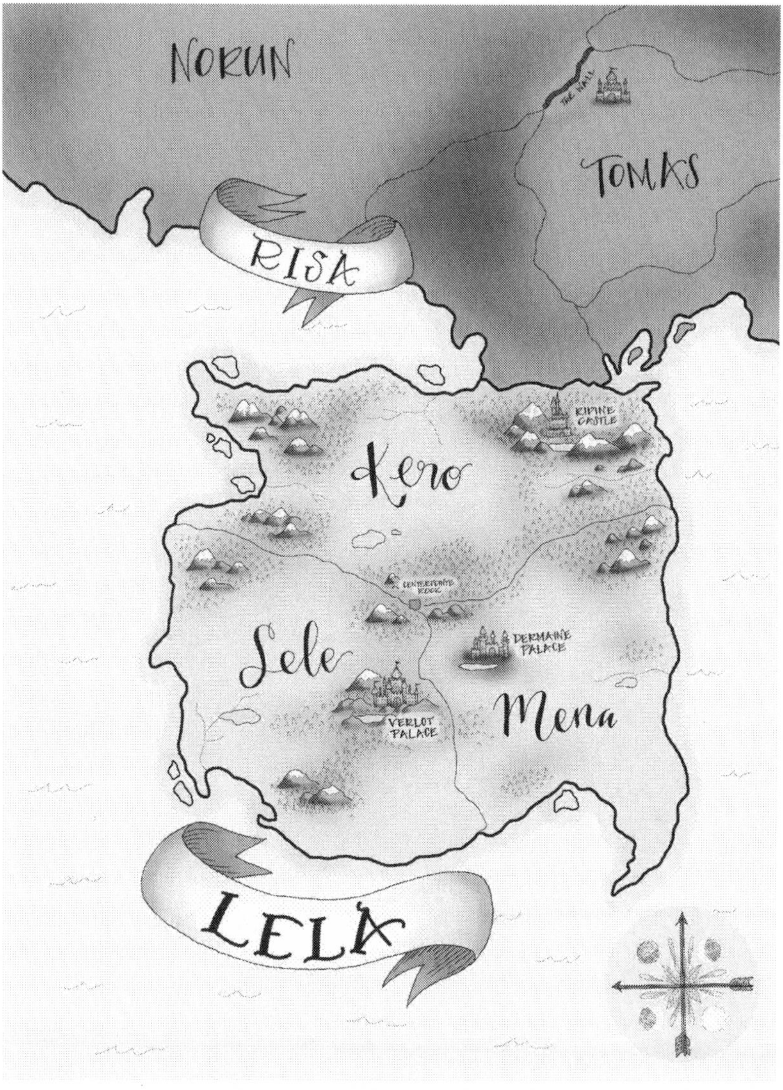
NORUN
TOMAS
RISA
Kero
RIPINE CASTLE
DERMAINE PALACE
Sele
VERLOT PALACE
Mena
LELA

CELEBRATION

Teryn

Cora paced in front of the closed doors inside our bedroom, nibbling a nail. The elegant hem of her pale blue and silver dress trailed behind her on the floor. I walked over to her. "Relax, my love."

She paused and met my eyes with a smile, hands wrapping around my waist as I brought her face between my palms and planted a kiss on her lips. "Do we really want to do this?" she asked.

I laughed. "Do we have a choice? We've been planning this for months."

She brought her nail back between her teeth. "I know, I know. Our people deserve this. The people of Kero deserve to see their king and queen with their own eyes." Her words sounded cold and rehearsed.

"They do deserve it," I said. "We promised we'd open court and hold an official coronation ceremony once

Ridine was settled. After years of uncertainty followed by war, our people deserve a celebration."

Cora nodded, but she didn't meet my eyes.

"It's not just that. *We* deserve this." I lifted her chin, and a smile melted over her lips, making my heart leap as strongly as it had the day I fell in love with her. "We've been through so much together, things our people don't even know about. It's time to celebrate *us*."

A corner of her mouth lifted as she raised her eyebrows in mock surprise. "You're just eager for me to make good on my promise, aren't you? To finally live as husband and wife on the night of our coronation?"

My cheeks felt warm. "It would be a lie if I said that hasn't been on my mind. We may be husband and wife by law, but..."

"But you let me wait."

I shook my head. "I didn't *let* you wait. I waited *with* you. We've had many urgent needs to attend to, and neither of us counts the document you signed with Morkai as the beginning of our marriage."

Cora closed her eyes with a sigh. "I've been waiting for this a long time too. I'm ready for that...but I might not be ready for everything else."

"For all the people waiting in the Godskeep?"

"Exactly. All those strangers, all those eyes on me." She turned her head, eyes unfocused. "It may be my coronation, but I feel far from a true queen. I'm not like my mother or Linette. I'm not like *your* mother or Queen Mother Helena. I'm not even like Queen Mareleau. At least *she* seems to relish the attention."

I took her hand in mine and gave it a squeeze. "What makes a true queen? A woman who defends her kingdom at whatever cost? A woman who is willing to do anything to protect her people? A woman who slaves away month after month to put her kingdom back in order?"

She rolled her eyes. "You sound like Salinda."

"I'll take that as a compliment."

"I wish she were here today. And my brother." She paled. I knew our minds went to the same place—the field where bodies of man and animal burned to ash before our eyes.

"I know he'd be proud of you," I said.

A flicker of a smile tugged her lips as her eyes glazed with tears. "So would your father."

A lump rose in my throat. "We both have some big shoes to fill."

"But we will fill them, no matter how big or uncomfortable they are."

"And we will do it together."

A knock sounded on the other side of the door, followed by the face of one of Cora's newly appointed queensmaids. "They're waiting, Your Majesties. Are you ready?"

Cora's eyes went wide as she froze. I squeezed her hand again, and she took a deep breath. "As ready as I'll ever be."

$\sim$

Cora

It wasn't until we left the Godskeep that I felt I could finally breathe freely. We'd said our vows as rulers of Kero and now wore the crowns that matched our titles.

Ice-cold air brushed my cheeks as we walked from the Godskeep to the main hall, our silent retinue following behind. Once we were within the walls of Ridine, it was as if a spell had been lifted, and everyone had voices again.

My heart quickened as the voices rose behind us, and I caught whispers of my name and snippets of giddy conversation. Thoughts of others threatened to invade my consciousness as I tried to ignore the feeling of countless eyes boring into me, seeking my favor. Teryn turned his face toward mine, and at the sight of his glowing smile, I remembered how to breathe again.

Master Arther stood at the door to the throne room, bowing low as we entered. My anxiety was stilled as we walked toward the set of ornate chairs at the other end of the elegant room. It was the first time I'd laid eyes on the newly finished throne room, and I was overwhelmed with awe at its beauty. Our thrones were made of a rich, dark wood carved with intricate floral designs twining up the legs to the mountains carved at the top. The cushions were made of plush, burgundy velvet with gold stitching.

With my head held high, I lowered into my seat alongside Teryn and watched as bodies began to fill the room. Most were strangers—nobles eager to meet their new king and queen, highborn members of our household whom I'd yet to meet, and visitors from other kingdoms. Many were desperate to gain a place at court, something that hadn't been possible during Morkai's reign.

From the crowd, a familiar set of blue eyes and golden hair caught my attention and brought a smile to my lips. Queen Mareleau, in a yellow gown that somehow made her bulging belly look like a fashionable accessory, walked toward us, arm-in-arm with King Larylis. Just looking at Mareleau made me want to sit up straighter if it meant I could emulate even half her easy grace. Behind them followed Queen Mother Helena, outfitted in an elegant black dress. *Still mourning her husband.* The thought sent a ripple of pain to my heart.

The three bowed low before us. I wanted so badly to greet Mareleau and Larylis with hugs, but Mareleau's regal countenance made it easier to keep my composure. The air sizzled between us, not with tension, but with the weight of our shared secret. No one outside the four of us knew what had happened on the field beneath the cliff. No one else had watched monsters burn to ash.

Larylis greeted Teryn while Mareleau approached me. "We offer you our congratulations," she said with a deep curtsy.

My gaze hovered over the pale, pink scar above her cheekbone, reminding me of a similar one on my forearm. While mine was hidden beneath my flowing, silver sleeves, she seemed to wear hers with pride. "We have our own congratulations to offer the two of you. Not only have you successfully merged Sele and Mena into the new kingdom of Vera, but you seem to be days away from meeting your first heir."

"More like weeks away, but we are excited just the same."

Helena turned her chin up and looked down her nose at her daughter. "Too near, if you ask me. I told her she shouldn't forgo the traditional confinement, much less travel so late in her pregnancy. It isn't safe."

"I have plenty of time, Mother," Mareleau said

between her teeth, then returned her attention to me. "I traveled by coach and have all my ladies and midwives in attendance. We're taking every precaution in order to celebrate with you. Besides, I have a feeling my child will come much later than everyone expects."

Her words seemed to be hinting at something, but I refrained from probing further. "We appreciate you attending this celebration."

Mareleau looked at the painted ceiling and the tapestries lining the walls. "The fact that Ridine no longer looks like a home for rats is worth celebrating on its own."

"Very true," Larylis said, joining our conversation. His expression faltered as he looked around. "It almost makes it possible to forget."

"Almost," Mareleau said under her breath. Her face still glowed with her smile, but her eyes seemed to have lost some of their sheen. "We'll get a chance to speak more later. We won't keep you from the rest of your guests."

Oh, please do, I said to myself, but already the three had bowed and were moving away from us. My shoulders sank as soon as they were out of sight.

The line of guests waiting to greet us had grown while I'd been talking to Mareleau. It now extended to the back of the throne room and out the door. I took a deep breath as our next guest approached.

"Your Majesties." Lord Jonston, our new Head of Council, bowed before us. He had a strong build, long, brown hair and a heavy beard. He reminded me of a bear. Yet, despite his gruff appearance, I'd already come to like him. He was honest, kind, and dedicated to Teryn's and my vision for Ridine. It was a far cry from Lord Kevan and Lord Ulrich.

Beside Jonston, a woman with graying brown hair coiled in a tight bun curtsied. "This must be your wife, Lord Jonston," I said as the couple rose.

"Yes, Your Majesties," Jonston said. "This is my wife, Lady Mary."

She smiled as she studied me. "You remind me of your mother, Your Majesty."

I flushed. "You knew my mother?"

Mary nodded. "Not personally, Your Majesty, but I spent time at court when your parents were alive. I remember you as a child."

My heart squeezed at the mention of my childhood. Of my parents. "Lady Mary, I didn't know you were originally from Kero."

"I was, Your Majesty, until this man," she placed an affectionate hand on Jonston's arm, "stole my heart and whisked me away to his home in Mena. When I heard he was offered the position as your Head of Council, I have to say I was conflicted. I didn't know how it would feel to be back after learning what had happened here. But seeing the two of you on the throne, the children of two sets of monarchs I've admired, I can't help but feel safe. Kero needs you, Your Majesty. I can't say how grateful I am for how you've turned this kingdom around."

My mouth fell open, but I didn't have the words to match what I was feeling inside. Pride swelled inside me, pushing away the anxiety, the fear that I wasn't good enough to be queen. She was right. Kero needed me.

"Thank you for saying that, Lady Mary," I said. "I hope to be everything Kero needs and more."

With my confidence renewed, I greeted our next guests with ease, learning new names, meeting new faces, and plastering on a fresh smile for each one. It only began to wear on me when the hour passed and still there was no sign that our line of guests was anywhere near its end.

With a deep breath, I forced my scowl into a smile and prepared to greet yet another stranger. But our next guest wasn't a stranger after all.

"Lex!" Teryn and I threw formality to the wind as we sprang from our thrones and took our turns hugging him.

A wide grin spread between his ruddy cheeks. "You remember me after all."

"How could I forget?" Teryn said. "You were a pain in my side for many weeks."

"How have you been since we last saw you?" I asked, ignoring the shocked stares of those nearby.

"I've managed to stay out of trouble. No quests, no battles." Lex puffed his chest. "Plus, I'm a married man now."

My eyes went wide as I clasped my hands over my heart. "Is it Lily?"

He nodded and stepped aside, revealing a short, plump woman with auburn hair and cheeks nearly as pink as Lex's. "Let me introduce Princess Lily, my wife."

Lily curtsied, keeping her eyes on the ground. "Your Majesties, Lex has told me so much about you. It's an honor to meet you, King Teryn and Queen Coralaine."

I wanted nothing more than to squeeze her in my arms and thank her for bringing joy to an old friend, but I maintained my distance with much effort. "I remember hearing much about you, as well. I can't tell you how pleased I am to meet you."

"I almost couldn't believe my eyes when I read the coronation invitation," Lex said, looking from me to Teryn. "The two of you...married! And now you're king and queen of the very place we were held captive. I'm just glad this castle looks nothing like it did last time I was here."

Teryn turned to me and smiled. "It's taken a lot of work to make Ridine feel new."

"When did this happen, anyway?" Lex pointed from Teryn to me and back again. "Last I heard, you were going to marry you-know-who." He made a face of disgust and lowered his voice. "I can at least say you made the right choice."

We laughed, and I glanced around to make sure Mareleau hadn't been nearby. "It's a long story," Teryn said. "I'd love to tell it to you. Will you be our guest for a few days longer?"

"Of course we will," Lex said. "That way you can fill me in on your latest adventures."

Teryn and I exchanged a glance. "We've had all the adventure we could ever need," Teryn said, "and certainly aren't seeking more."

Lex laughed, then cleared his throat. "I almost forgot! Where are my manners?" He stood straight and forced a regal expression, then folded into a bow. "Your Majesties. Congratulations on your coronation, King Teryn and Queen Coralaine. Tomas is forever your ally."

I smiled. "And we are forever yours."

2

VOWS

Cora

Within the quiet solitude of our bedroom, I closed my eyes and released a heavy sigh.

Teryn came up behind me and wrapped his arms around my waist. "That wasn't so bad, was it?"

I grinned. "Some guests were more enjoyable than others, but for the most part, no. It wasn't so bad."

His heart beat a rhythm on my back, reminding me we were alone. I'd dismissed my queensmaids after they'd helped me undress and brush out my hair. While it was common for them to leave me alone in my room with the man they considered my husband, Teryn had yet to spend the night in our bed. Night after night, we'd part with a kiss, and he'd retire to sleep in the adjoining room. Tonight, that would change.

As if he'd read my thoughts, he brought his lips to my ear. "Do you want me to stay?"

My heart quickened, and my hands began to tremble, but not in a bad way. Despite how tired I was from our overlong evening, I found myself growing alert as I turned to face him. "Yes. I'm ready."

Teryn took my hand and led me to the middle of the room. We stood across from each other and clasped our hands together. His chest heaved, and I could tell he was trembling as much as I was. "The real question is, am I ready?"

I felt some of the tension between us fade. "You better be. I've been waiting forever."

He laughed. "*You've* been waiting? Well, it would be treason to make a queen wait any longer." He took a deep breath, and his expression turned serious. "Queen Coralaine, daughter of—"

I shook my head. "Please, just Cora. We've had a night full of meaningless formalities. Let our own vows come from our hearts."

His lips turned up at the corners. "Just Cora, then. Cora, the unicorn girl, who shot two arrows at me and nearly killed me. Cora, the fierce warrior who could likely best me in any battle. Cora, the woman who needs no rescuing, even though I would risk my life for her time and time again. Cora, the woman I fell in love with and continue to love more and more every day. Cora, the queen at my side who I wish to grow old and gray with. Do you vow to be my wife? I need no other promises from you, no requests, no demands. Do you simply agree to share your heart with me from this day forth?"

My bottom lip trembled as tears ran down my cheeks. "I do." He slid a simple circlet of gold around my shaking finger. It was my turn, but I found it hard to speak past the lump in my throat. "I don't know if I can be as eloquent as you, Teryn. Your words bring me more joy than you could ever know. Your presence in my life has been a greater blessing than I ever imagined. Your love for me is a warmth that steadies me in the darkest of places. There is nothing I want more than to have you at my side as my king, my best human friend, and my husband. Do you vow to love me for who I am as we grow and change?"

His eyes were as wet as mine. "I do."

I slid his ring on his finger, and his hands moved to my face. Our lips met as I wrapped my arms around his waist and pressed his body to mine. With that, an eager passion began to bloom. Our kisses grew stronger, our breathing heavier.

He stepped back to remove his shirt, revealing only one scar—the one he received from Morkai—on his bare torso. The place he'd been stabbed by Valorre had been healed without a hint of scarring. I put my hand there, then moved it over his rapidly beating heart.

He placed his hand over mine. "I love you, Cora."

I lifted my hand and brushed it over his cheek, as he'd done to me many times. "I love you too, Teryn."

His lips crushed against mine, the pressure between our lips like the sealing of our vows and the signature of our hearts. We lost ourselves in each other's limbs, hearts hammering as we explored the new, previously undiscovered landscape of our love.

WITH MY HEAD ON TERYN'S CHEST, I CLOSED MY EYES AND

reflected on how much had changed in less than a year. Just a year ago, I thought I'd live the rest of my life in peace with the Forest People. I never imagined I'd fall in love, much less marry, and I never could have expected I'd reclaim my title and kingdom. Now here I was, Queen of Kero, married to a man I loved. My heart swelled with gratitude, but it didn't fill completely; I couldn't help but regret that the road to my current joy had been paved with so much blood.

Not to mention, my kingdom isn't even mine.

I lifted my head and looked at Teryn. His eyes were closed, a contented grin on his lips as he stroked my hair. "Do you ever feel guilty that we're ruling a land that doesn't belong to us?"

His eyes fluttered open. "What do you mean?"

"Don't get me wrong, I will do whatever it takes to keep Kero safe, but our kingdom is only ours because Lela got separated from El'Ara."

Teryn furrowed his brow, staring at the ceiling as he considered my words. "That's true. However, Lela was discovered as a new and unpopulated land in our world, and our forefathers settled here. No one knew any better."

"I know they didn't. But *we* know the truth. Lela belongs to another realm. A realm that is dying without it. Doesn't that bother you?"

"It does, I suppose, even though the beings of that realm tried to kill you. That bothers me more."

I remembered Etrix and how he'd tried to help me in his own way. And Garot, with his love for storytelling. "It's strange. Even though they did what they did to me, I don't feel anger over it. I'd grown up hearing stories about the Ancient Realm, about the Elvan and the Faeran. I pictured them as these perfect beings of pure love and generosity. While they *are* incredible beings, they are far from perfect. They still feel fear and judgment. When they found me, someone they considered a threat to their world, they did what they thought was best."

"If only they knew they were convicting the mother of a prophecy meant to save them."

A hollow feeling struck my gut. "It wouldn't have helped if they'd known about the prophecy. Without me being able to fulfill it, they would have considered me worse than an invader."

"You really don't think they knew about the prophecy?"

"I don't think so. They seemed resigned to their fate and didn't seem to know any way to stop what was happening."

Teryn brushed the tangled hair away from my forehead. "Is that why you feel so guilty?"

A lump rose in my throat as I pulled myself to sitting, pulling a blanket over my bare chest. "My child was supposed to be their hope. Somehow, he was supposed to make El'Ara whole again. He was supposed to stop the Blood of Darius."

"We don't even know if the Blood of Darius is still a threat. And if he were, how could a baby stop him?"

I shook my head. "Prophecies are strange. While I don't have much experience with them, I do know that they never tell the full story."

"Whatever the case, there's nothing we can do to help them," Teryn said. "Besides, you said time passed differently in El'Ara. A day passed there while weeks passed here. That means they may have centuries to find another solution. Perhaps another prophecy will emerge. This time, Morkai won't be around to stop it."

"I hope you're right." I bit my lip before my eyes locked on his. "What about us? What are we going to do about our side of the unfulfilled prophecy?"

"Our side?"

"An heir? If I prove to be truly barren…"

Teryn lifted his hand and pressed it to my cheek. "We will figure that out in time. No need to worry about that yet." One corner of his mouth lifted. "For all we know you may be with child now. And if not, we can always try again…and again."

I felt my heart stir at the mischievous glint in his eye. "Is now too soon?"

His hand moved down my face, fingers trailing down my neck until he reached the sheet that covered me. With a gentle tug, it fell away. My breath quickened as his eyes drank me in. Even though my first instinct was to curl forward and hide myself, I sat taller, shoulders back, while my cheeks burned from his gaze.

"You are so beautiful," he whispered.

I leaned forward to claim his lips with my own, when the moment was shattered by a knock at the door. We froze and turned toward the sound.

"Your Majesty," said the muffled female voice on the other side, a frantic quality to her tone.

I quickly wrapped the sheet around me as I answered, my voice a breathless croak, "Yes? What is it?"

"It's me, Breah. Queen Mareleau…her baby. She's asking for you."

3

BIRTH

Mareleau

"I told you not to travel," Mother said as she looked down at me. "You should have listened. Now you have to give birth *here*."

I breathed through the pain as my queensmaids rushed about, waking my midwives and gathering supplies. "It will pass. There's nothing to worry about." I'd already said as much about a hundred times, but no one listened.

"How could you think it will pass? Your child is due any day now." Mother paced along the length of the bed.

"He isn't due yet. It's too early."

Mother threw her hands in the air. "How can you argue with the calculations of the midwives? He is due *now*."

The pain passed, and I narrowed my eyes at Mother. "No, he isn't. It's too early."

Mother pressed her hand to her mouth and sat beside

me on the bed. "Mareleau, I want to be here for you, but you are making it difficult." Her voice shook, likely from the effort not to yell. "Your words make no sense. How can you fail to see reason yet again?"

The pain on my mother's face made me feel empty. I'd seen her fierce power drained, pouring out in rivers of tears too many times over the past few months to count. My father's death had broken her, while I continued to stress her as much as I ever had before. I reached my hand toward hers. She turned to me, brows knit together as if she couldn't comprehend the meaning of the gentle touch. Her eyes studied my face.

"Mother, I have to tell you something." I kept my voice low so the women flitting about the room couldn't hear. "I lied about being pregnant when Father tried to marry me to Teryn. I didn't conceive until my wedding night." The words felt like fire as they moved over the lump in my throat, but once they were freed, I felt as if a weight had lifted from my chest.

Her eyes went wide, but she said no word of reproach.

"I only said what I thought would convince Father to allow me to marry Larylis. I'm so sorry. I shouldn't have —" Another wave of pain rippled through my abdomen, hips, and back, unlike anything I'd ever felt before. When it passed, I found Mother still watching me.

"You weren't already pregnant the day you married Larylis?"

I shook my head. "I'm sorry, Mother. It's my fault. If Father hadn't sent me here...if he hadn't allowed me to marry Larylis..."

"Don't." Mother's voice was stern as her eyes overflowed. "Don't you dare blame yourself for his death."

"But it's my fault." My face twisted as I heaved a sob.

"It isn't your fault, and I don't want to hear another word about it. What matters now is you and your baby." She looked from my face to my belly. "He isn't due now after all."

"No. He's early. Dangerously early."

Mother squeezed my hand. "You are both going to get through this."

"Your Majesty, Queen Coralaine is here," Breah said as Cora raced to the side of the bed.

Cora looked around the busy room. "What can I do?"

I reached toward her. "Just stay with me. Please?"

Her eyes widened at my extended hand, then grasped it in hers with a nod.

Somehow, her presence set my nerves at ease. My shoulders relaxed, and my breathing steadied. "Thank you, Cora. I just need a friend right now."

Cora

The sun was beginning to rise by the time Mareleau was ready to give her final push. I held her hand in mine, wiping sweat from her brow and offering calm words of encouragement. Her mother stayed at her other side, wordless.

"This is it, Mare. You can do this," I whispered. "The baby is so close."

Her face turned red as she pushed, and her midwives waited with bated breath at the end of the bed. My eyes remained locked on Mareleau's face to keep my mind from slipping to memories of the last woman who'd attempted to give birth within the walls of Ridine Castle. *Those dark times are over,* I reminded myself.

"We can see his head," said one of the midwives. "One more push."

She took a deep breath, lifted her head, and pushed again. With a groan of relief, she threw her head back and sank into the pillows behind her. The gasps on the other end told me the baby had come.

I smiled and squeezed her hand. "You did it, Mare."

She smiled back, eyes closed. "Where is he?"

I cast a glance at the midwives and sensed a tremor of alarm. My eyes returned to Mareleau. "Him?" I asked, trying to keep the worry from my voice. "Do you think it's a boy?"

She opened her eyes and smirked. "Every queen says *him* when she's with child. I almost want it to be a girl just out of spite." She tried to pull herself to sitting, and I helped by propping pillows behind her. She looked at me and grinned. "But yes, I really think it's a boy."

Her mother joined the midwives and tossed us an anxious glance.

Mareleau tried to sit straighter to see over the fluttering hands and shuffling bodies. "Where is he? Bring him to me."

One of the women turned around, eyes wide and lips pressed into a tight line. "He isn't breathing, Your Majesty. And he's...so tiny."

No, not again. Images of Linette lying pale and limp amongst bloodstained sheets flashed through my mind. I shook my head to clear the visions and blinked at the bundle in the woman's arms.

"Bring him here," Mareleau demanded.

"Your Majesty—"

"Bring him to me now." Her voice was powerful, despite her weak condition. Without further argument, the woman brought the bundle and placed it in Mareleau's arms.

I stepped away, my breathing becoming more and more shallow while Mareleau stared down at her baby. My heart felt as if it were torn in two as pain surged through me. *Not again. This can't happen again.*

Mareleau appeared calm yet focused as she held her baby close, his tiny, pink cheek against her pale, bare chest. She lowered her face to his and placed her lips over his head. I was transfixed as I watched, feeling as if time had become slowed.

That's when I saw it.

Or rather, *felt* it. A subtle light flowing from mother to child, pouring out of her hands, her chest, and her lips as it wrapped around the baby like a cloak. As it grew brighter around the baby, it illuminated Mareleau as well.

The baby began to cry, and time seemed to flow once again. Sound erupted as the women cheered and returned to their work. I remained still against the wall, contemplating what I'd witnessed.

"Cora, come see him! I knew it was a boy."

Mareleau's voice shook me from my stupor. The midwives stepped aside and allowed me to approach. An impossibly tiny baby boy moved against her chest, making my heart flutter at the sight. "He's beautiful, Mareleau."

"He's the most amazing thing I've ever seen in my

life." Her face glowed as she stared at him, reminding me of the illumination I'd witness not a moment before. Her eyes lifted to mine. "Thank you for staying with me."

"You're welcome." I could find no other words to say when all I wanted to do was ask her about what I'd seen. She'd used the Arts. There was no mistaking it.

"Will you find Larylis? And Teryn, too. I want them to meet him."

I forced a smile. "Of course."

By the time I returned with Teryn and Larylis, the room was calm and quiet. As we stepped through the doorway, Mareleau lifted her eyes from her nursing baby. A wide grin spread over her face when her eyes fell on her husband. "Larylis! Come see our son."

Helena rose from the edge of the bed, eying Teryn and Larylis with a glare, making them pause. "You shouldn't be here. Men should never attend a birthing bed until the mother has rested and healed."

"Mother, don't be so old-fashioned. Let them in."

Helena grumbled before stepping aside and allowing Larylis to approach. I stood at Teryn's side by the door while we watched Larylis greet his wife and baby.

"What will we name him?" Larylis asked, voice trembling and tears streaming down his face.

Mareleau studied her baby for a moment. "How about Liam?"

"Liam. I like that." He kissed Mareleau on the cheek, then leaned forward to kiss the back of Liam's head.

Teryn brought his lips to my ear. "If we can't...you know...make our own baby, we could always make little Liam our heir."

I looked at him and smiled. "You think so?"

"Why not?"

My eyes moved back at Liam, and my heart felt calm. In that moment it seemed as if the answer to all my worries had been before me all along. Why had I ever worried about being barren? Why had I ever worried Teryn wouldn't have me as his wife? Of course we'd find a way. There'd *always* been a way.

"We could unite our kingdoms," Teryn said, "like Larylis and Mareleau did with Sele and Mena to form Vera. He'd be heir to—"

"All of Lela." My throat went dry as the words left my mouth. Other words that I'd believed had become meaningless rushed through my mind.

The Blood of Ailan will unite the land by royal birth and magic right and return El'Ara's heart.

My head began to spin as threads of the prophecy swirled around me, as bright and solid as a tapestry.

Where the veil abandoned its heart, one will be born that will stop the Blood of Darius. Only then will the veil be torn.

I stared at Mareleau, heart hammering in my chest.

Beauty of Satsara. Right by magic and blood. The unicorn will signify her awakening. Foreigners will flood the land. The heart of El'Ara will unite as one.

Could it be? But how?

Her son will be born under the house of the black mountain.

My eyes darted around the room. Everywhere I looked, Kero's sigil was carved into furniture, painted on the walls, and stitched into tapestries.

Morkai had it wrong. I was never meant to be the Mother of Prophecy.

Visions of El'Ara flooded my mind. I saw the colorless

veil and heard lightning ripping through it. In the center of the veil, a crack was forming.

I shuddered as my attention returned to Mareleau's room, the happy voices in stark contrast to the terror running through me.

"What's wrong?" Teryn asked. "You've gone pale."

I took a deep breath. "The Blood of Ailan lives."

4

PROPHECY

Teryn

I followed Cora from Mareleau's room and into the hall where she began to pace. The way her eyes glazed over as she muttered under her breath sent a chill down my spine. I took hold of her elbow and gently turned her to face me. "What do you mean the Blood of Ailan lives?"

Her eyes snapped to mine, her bottom lip trembling. "Mareleau is the Mother of Prophecy. It was never me. Morkai was wrong all along." She took a gasping breath as tears pooled in her eyes. "Everything he did to me...it was never meant to be me."

"It's over. It's in the past. You're safe." Those were words she'd made me promise to say if I ever saw her fall apart like this over what had been done to her. It was a promise I'd had to keep many times over the previous months.

She closed her eyes and deepened her breathing, and

I watched as calm fell over her. Her shoulders relaxed, her hands unclenched, and her body ceased trembling. "Thank you," she whispered.

I took her hand and led her down the hall. Walking seemed to help ease her even more, and only once she was breathing evenly did I speak again. "Why do you think Mareleau is the Mother of Prophecy?"

She took a deep breath. "Everything makes sense. I don't know why I didn't see it before."

"Tell me."

She paused mid-step and faced me. "I saw her use the Arts. Just before I came to find you and Larylis. Liam wasn't breathing, so she demanded her midwives let her hold him. When she did, I could...see it. This web of light surrounded him, then moved back into her. It was as if using the Arts made her stronger."

Her words sent my mind reeling. How could Mareleau use magic? *Mareleau?* She was nothing like Cora or the Forest People I'd heard so much about. Yet, if Cora thought she saw her use magic, I had to believe it was true. "You've said your own powers are made stronger when you use them to protect yourself."

We began to walk again as Cora considered my words. "My powers grow stronger when I protect myself because that is part of my challenge. As an empath, I naturally try to protect others, to absorb their pain and thoughts. When I use the Arts to protect myself, I conquer my challenge."

"Why would the Arts appear to make Mareleau stronger when she used them with Liam?"

"She was protecting him, saving his life. That act must have overcome her own challenge."

"But what about the prophecy itself? There's no doubt it had been about you."

"Are you sure about that?" Cora glanced up at me.

I ran the words of the prophecy through my head. "*Beauty of Satsara.* Emylia channeled that Satsara had dark hair—"

"The prophecy never stated the Mother *looked* like Satsara, only that she held her beauty. It was Desmond who concluded that the two must look alike. Satsara was considered a great beauty amongst the Elvan people, much like Mareleau is considered beautiful amongst ours." Her voice held a hint of bitterness.

"If you say so," I said with a shrug. Out of the corner of my eye, I saw her lips curl into a satisfied smile.

"Now that I've seen her use the Arts, I know she fulfills the line about *right by magic and blood*."

"What about *the unicorn will signify her awakening*? That couldn't be about anyone but you."

Her brows furrowed, eyes unfocused. "She was the one who created the Quest, demanding three unicorns as the goal. *Foreigners will flood the land.* The poetry contest brought princes from near and far to Lela. *The heart of El'Ara will unite as one.* That could be about the Tri-Kingdom Peace Pact, or it could be...Liam. Making him our heir unites all of Lela as one."

I felt the blood leave my face. "Her son was born here. The house of the black mountain."

"Morkai came to the wrong conclusions," Cora said. "He assumed the Mother of Prophecy would give birth to the Blood of Ailan in her own kingdom. He assumed she would look like Satsara. He assumed making me barren would keep the prophecy from coming true." Her lips pressed into a tight line.

We came to the end of the hall, and our eyes flashed to the staircase looming at our right—the stairs to the high tower. Even though we'd finished ridding it of Morkai's things months ago, my skin still crawled whenever we came near it. No amount of cleaning could dissolve the memories of what had happened there—the death of Cora's chambermaid, the crystal, my possession. We exchanged a glance before we began to walk the other way.

"If Mareleau is the Mother of Prophecy, if Liam is the Blood of Ailan, what does that mean?" I asked.

Cora shook her head. "I don't know. I've been so wrapped in guilt over not being able to fulfill my role as Mother of Prophecy, I hadn't considered what I would do if I *were* able to fulfill it."

"Is there anything we can do?"

She looked down the hall toward Mareleau's room. "For now, let's keep this to ourselves. I'll talk to Mareleau tonight."

∾

Mareleau

I stared down at the sleeping face in my arms, unable to blink as I took in Liam's pink, puffy cheeks, his tiny eyelids, his long, golden eyelashes, and his round head covered in soft, golden down. It was almost eighth bell, but no matter how overcome with exhaustion I was, I found it impossible to bring myself to set him in his bassinet so I could sleep.

Larylis, on the other hand, had been celebrating Liam's birth with endless goblets of wine amongst the court in the great hall all day and had already retired to sleep in Teryn's old room.

Mother walked over to me, a tearful smile on her face. "I remember what my first night with you was like. I couldn't part with you, either."

I returned my mother's smile, feeling a warmth between us that had been steadily growing since I'd made my confession. "I never knew a child could be such an amazing thing."

"He looks just like you as a baby." She sat next to me on the bed and brought her head close to mine to get a closer look. After a few moments, she faced me. "As much as I understand what you are feeling right now, I know you need sleep. Life with a newborn is a beautiful thing, but you will soon learn how precious sleep can be."

My face fell. "It hurts my heart to think of him sleeping away from me. I want to watch his every breath."

"I know you do, my sweet." There was laughter in her voice. "How about I stay with you tonight. I'll hold him while he sleeps, and you can sleep as well. When he wakes, I'll rouse you, and then I'll sleep."

The tenderness in her tone brought tears to my eyes. For so many years there had been nothing but sharp words and secrets between us, keeping each other at arm's length. Would things have been different if I'd told her the truth long ago? If I'd told her about my feelings for Larylis, and how Father's pressure to marry a crown prince had made me feel? What would it have been like if

I'd told her the truth about my false pregnancy from the start? Would she have supported me? Or was it the bond of motherhood that finally brought us together?

I sighed, accepting that I'd never know. "Thank you, Mother. I'd like that."

She kissed me on the forehead and reached for Liam. My heart sank as his comforting weight left my arms to fill hers. I nearly begged her to return him to me when a quiet knock sounded on the door. Mother opened it to reveal the tentative face of Cora.

"Am I interrupting anything?" she asked.

I took one last wistful look at my son, then turned toward my friend. "No, come in."

Her eyes passed over the room, lighting upon my sleeping ladies sprawled over the furniture, then resting on my mother. "Would you mind if I spoke to Queen Mareleau alone for a few moments?"

"Not at all, Your Majesty." Mother turned to me. "I'll walk with Liam for a bit so you can talk. But make sure you get some rest as well."

Cora smiled at my mother. "I promise I won't keep her long."

I watched Mother and Liam leave the room, feeling as if all the warmth had left with them. My eyes met Cora's as she approached the bed. "Thank you again for staying with me through the birth."

"Of course. I was happy to be there." Her tone didn't match her words, sending a ripple of suspicion through me.

"Why are you here?" I asked, trying to keep the irritation from my voice. Now that Liam was gone, I could feel the weight of my exhaustion.

Cora sat at the edge of the bed. "What happened this morning when you first held Liam? When you found he wasn't breathing?"

The terror of the moment struck me with a sharp pain to my chest as I recalled his blue-tinted skin, his open mouth that produced no air. I shuddered, trying to shake the vision from my mind as I reminded myself he was alive and healthy. "Why would you even mention that? It was the most terrifying moment of my life."

Cora seemed unaffected by the bite in my words. "You didn't act that way. You remained calm and collected, as if you knew exactly what to do. When you held him close, he started breathing. How did that happen?"

"How should I know?" I said with a shrug, yet her words brought to mind the calm that had accompanied my terror, overriding it. "It was...like an instinct. I just felt I had to hold him, to pour all my love into him."

"What did that feel like?"

I raised an eyebrow, wondering why I felt like I was on trial. With a sigh, I closed my eyes and tried to summon an explanation. "It felt...warm. Tingling. At first, I felt like all my blood, breath, and energy were pouring out of me. The only thing I could think was that I'd give anything— my life, even—to give him breath."

"And after that?"

A smile tugged my lips. "He started breathing, and my body felt more awake than it had ever been. It was the greatest sense of relief I've ever felt."

"You've never felt that way before?"

I opened my eyes. "Never."

Cora chewed her bottom lip, frowning at the wall. "Can I ask you something else?"

"Something tells me you will ask no matter what I say."

She ignored my sass, making me wonder what had her in such a somber mood. "Have you ever been able to do anything that was hard to explain? Have you ever been able to make surprising things happen?"

I pondered her words, finding no significance in what she was asking. "I've always had a knack for getting my way."

She studied my face for a moment. "Tell me about that. How have you gotten your way in the past? Have you ever done anything that shocked others?" At a raised brow from me, she continued. "I'm not talking about the choices you've made or the things you've said. I'm talking about things that had no reasonable explanation."

A sinking hit my gut, mostly from guilt, but also from a deep sense of foreboding. I had a feeling I was about to reveal something I shouldn't. "I was able to end numerous engagements before the Quest. My mother and father were at their wit's end trying to figure out how it had happened over and over. They blamed me, but since it was always my betrothed who'd ended things, they never could figure out how I'd been responsible."

"How *did* you do it?"

I thought back to every man I'd been forced to entertain, forced to allow to court me. I remembered their false promises, their lustful expressions when they assessed their prize, the lies they spoke in an attempt to woo me. I clenched my teeth, hands balling into fists as a burning fury roared inside me. My voice came out cool and empty. "I found ways to convince them it would be in their best interest to seek another bride.

Sometimes I used clever words. Other times I would repel them."

"How did you repel them?"

Again, the memories of those engagements flooded my mind, keeping the molten center of anger boiling within. "It was easy for me to know what repelled them. Each man judged me by my beauty and reputation, then shaped some ideal version of me with their minds. They could never see the real me, only whom they wanted or expected me to be. Once I saw what they saw, I could easily make them see the opposite. If one man wanted a calm, detached wife who spoke little and always obeyed, I would whine and cling. If one man wanted a beautiful bride to wear on his arm, I made him see me as ugly."

Cora's eyes went wide. "You actually made them see you as ugly?"

"It isn't hard. You just think about being ugly, about being repulsive, and you sink into that, let it pull at your features."

"You realize not everyone can do that, right?"

I shrugged. "I'd always figured anyone could do it if they'd tried."

She cast a glance at my sleeping ladies, then scooted closer to me on the bed and lowered her voice. "What you are talking about is called a glamour. It's a form of the Arts."

My heart raced at her words. "What are you saying?"

Her face paled, flashing between terror and awe. "Mareleau, you have magic. You're the Mother of Prophecy."

5

GLAMOUR

Larylis

I swung my sword at Teryn. His eyes widened as he dodged the dull blade by a hair's breadth, then he lunged toward my ribs.

"Do you seriously do this every day?" Teryn asked, his words coming out between labored breaths.

"Without fail." Our training swords clashed as I blinked a bead of sweat from my lashes. Despite the layer of frost covering the courtyard and the icy morning air, I was sweating profusely. "However, I don't always drink so much the night before."

Teryn came in for an attack. "I thought the benefit of being king is no longer having to train all the time."

I parried his blow. "Yeah, if you're a lazy king."

"Are you calling me lazy?"

"You're the one panting like a dog," I said with a teasing sneer, "when *I'm* the one who drank my weight in ale last night."

Teryn laughed and knocked my sword to the side. "You're right. I need a break already."

"If you insist." I kept my voice nonchalant, yet the churning in my stomach was much relieved at the thought of rest. We exchanged our training swords for skins of water and sat on a bench at the edge of the courtyard.

"Why do you do it?" Teryn asked.

"Do what?"

"Train every day. You were always more invested in your training than I was, but I never knew you were *this* determined."

I leaned forward, forearms resting on my thighs as sweat dripped from my brow to the ground below. "When we were younger, I always had to use my speed as an asset when training, since the other boys were usually bigger and stronger than I was. Training with the Black Force, using my speed, made me feel like I had a worthy skill. Even during the Battle at Centerpointe Rock, it was enough to keep me alive. But after last summer…"

Teryn put a hand on my shoulder. "I know."

My eyes met Teryn's, and I could almost see the dark cloud of memory settle between us. "When I saw Mareleau tied up, cut, and nearly sacrificed by Morkai, I hated myself for not being stronger. I hated myself for not being able to overtake the guards he'd sent after us when we discovered who he was. I hated myself for not being able to do what you'd asked me to do—what Cora had done without hesitation. And I hated myself most of all because I nearly *did*. I had the dagger in my hand. I almost killed you."

Teryn paled. "Even if you had, I wouldn't blame you."

"You wouldn't be alive to blame me," I said.

"If there's one thing I've learned from all of this, it's that there aren't easy answers to what's right and what's wrong. Had I been in your position, I don't know what I would have done. And if there's one thing I've learned from Cora, it's that the past has no place in our present. We can't let it eat us alive."

I let out a heavy sigh. "You're right. Yet, that won't stop me from trying to do what I can to protect my future. To protect Mareleau and baby Liam." My heart felt warm at the mention of my son, and I couldn't keep the grin off my lips.

"I know what you mean. I'd do anything to protect Cora, even though she's usually the one saving me."

I laughed. "She's a fierce one. I'm glad the two of you found each other."

"So am I." Our eyes locked in a moment of awkward silence—a moment where I could feel a hug was near.

I stood up. "Should we go again?"

Teryn shook his head. "You inspire me, brother, but I've had my share of training for the day. Besides, I've got plans to entertain an old friend over breakfast. You're welcome to join us, but I assume you'll be spending your morning with your wife and child."

My shoulders fell as I looked toward the great keep. "I wish. Helena nearly took my head off the first time I tried to see my son, remember? She says it isn't proper."

"Forget proper," Teryn said with a mischievous grin. "I'm King of Kero, Lord of Ridine Castle, and I order you to visit your wife."

A corner of my mouth pulled up as I recalled a similar order I'd once given him. "Thank you, brother."

Mareleau

Magic. You have magic. You're the Mother of Prophecy. The words had echoed through my mind all night while I slept, while I dreamed. They were laced into Liam's cries and pitched into my mother's tone when she spoke.

I tried to clear my head as I nursed Liam, tried to enjoy the rush of tenderness that flooded my body as he quietly suckled. But no matter what I did, what I thought about, the words were there, haunting me.

What does it mean? Can it be true?

A knock sounded on the door, and Mother stood from the lounge. Her steps were slow and uneven as she made her way across the room, eyes rimmed with red from her wakeful night. Even taking turns sleeping had only given us an hour or two at a time. Oddly enough, the lack of sleep didn't bother me as much as I'd thought it would.

Mother opened the door a crack and whispered furiously at whoever was on the other side.

"King Teryn has ordered me to visit my wife." I leaned forward at the sound of Larylis' voice.

"Lare! Mother, let him in."

"You're still in recovery." Mother put her hands on her hips, seeming much more like her usual self.

I rolled my eyes. "I don't care about these old rules. Let him in!"

With a grumbling huff, she opened the door, revealing the smiling face of my husband. He came to my side and pressed his lips against my forehead. I closed my eyes at the calming warmth that filled my heart. As he pulled away, I reached my free hand to his cheek and guided his face back to mine, bringing our lips to meet. "I missed you."

"And I missed the two of you." His eyes fell on Liam, his face nearly glowing from his smile. "How has he been doing?"

"He's perfect. He seems to nurse well, but I can't say the same for how he sleeps at night."

"I'm sorry I haven't been here to help you."

My eyes flashed over Larylis' shoulder and met my mother's gaze. "I doubt you'd have been allowed to do much," I said under my breath.

"Well, I'm here now. Tell me anything you want from me, and I will give it to you."

I thought about what Cora had said and bit my lip. I needed to tell him—to tell *someone*. Liam's suckling slowed to a stop, his breathing even against my breast. "Would you like to hold him?"

Larylis' eyes glazed as he nodded. "Please."

I gently pulled Liam away from me and set him in his father's arms. Larylis trembled as he accepted the sleeping bundle. I adjusted the top of my nursing gown and looked at my mother. "Will you give us some privacy, Mother?"

She pursed her lips. "You need rest."

"Mother, I feel fine," I said with a sigh. "I know you said it normally takes weeks to recover, but honestly, I feel as good as new already. Ever since..." I swallowed my words as Cora's revelation came back to me. *You have magic.* Did using the Arts to save Liam somehow heal me from the strain of birth? I shook the questions from my head and fixed Mother with a pleading stare. "Please trust me."

Her face softened as she gave me a reluctant nod, then swept out of the room.

We sat in silence while I debated what to say. As much as I relished the peace of the moment, I knew I had to tell him what was weighing on my mind. My heart raced as I finally said, "Lare, why do you love me?"

He turned his head toward mine, brows knit together as his lips twitched between a smile and a frown. "What do you mean? I love you because I love you."

"But why? For so many years, you loved me for the girl you imagined me to be. When you found out I wasn't everything you thought I was, you still loved me. Why?"

His eyes unfocused for a moment. "Even though there were many things about you I hadn't known before, I still loved you once I learned the truth. It made my love stronger to know the real you. Accepting you as you are is what made our love real."

"What about when we were younger? When you first realized you loved me? Did I do something to make that happen?"

"What is this about, Mare?"

I folded my hands to keep them from shaking. "There's something I need to tell you. It's about Liam's birth. I need you to know the truth."

His face paled, lips pressing into a tight line. "What?"

"When he was born, he wasn't breathing. He...wasn't going to make it. Then I held him and..." My eyes locked on his. "I used magic to heal him."

Larylis stared back at me, frozen, until he threw his

head back with laughter. My eyes darted from him to Liam, worried the noise would wake the baby.

I elbowed Larylis gently in the arm. "It's not funny, Lare! I'm serious."

He sobered and brought his forehead to mine, letting out a deep breath. "I thought you were going to tell me something else. We were talking about truth and love, and then suddenly you said you had to tell me the truth about Liam's birth. I thought you were about to say... something else."

"What were you expecting me to say?"

"That I wasn't the father."

My mouth fell open, and I felt my cheeks burn. "How could you think that of me?"

He laughed, making my blood boil even more. "My love, I would never think that of you. My mind simply went to the worst possible scenario."

I forced my anger to cool as I considered the conversation from his perspective. "I'm sorry, Lare. I didn't mean to worry you."

"Perhaps it was for the best. After what I'd been thinking, the truth couldn't possibly be any worse than that. Now, what's this talk about magic?"

I stared down at my hands. "Cora saw me do it. She calls it the Arts. I still don't fully understand it, but she thinks I've been able to use the Arts my entire life. The more I think about it, the more I think she's right."

"Are you saying you think you used the Arts to make me fall in love with you?"

I shrugged. "I've done worse. Cora thinks it was how I was able to end all my engagements. She says I used something called a glamour."

"Mare, my love for you is entirely my own. Besides, all those years I was pining for you, you didn't even *want* me to love you."

"I don't think that's true. It may have hurt me to know we couldn't be together, but at the same time, I was selfish. Your love for me sustained me. Never once did I hope you'd move on and love someone else." Fire filled my veins just thinking about it. "I wanted you all to myself, even if you were unable to know the truth."

"I understand that more than you know," he said. "It nearly killed me to think of you with my brother. If I'd been under some devious love spell, I probably would have killed Teryn to have you as my own. But I didn't. Instead, I let you go."

"Until I convinced you otherwise." I remembered the night I confessed my feelings, the truth of my past, and all the obstacles that forbade us from being together. Had I used the Arts that night? Had I carried magic on my words, held a glamour over my body?

"You didn't convince me of anything," Larylis said. "You told me the truth. I made the choice to pursue you."

His words did nothing to ease my suspicion, but at that point, did it matter? Our love felt real, and perhaps it was. It was the best thing that had ever happened to me, and I knew without a doubt that I would do anything to keep it...even use the Arts. That fact sent a pang of guilt through me. *Why am I so terrible?*

"There's something else you should know," I said in a rush before I could hold the words in any longer.

"You can tell me anything."

My gaze fell on Liam, still sleeping peacefully in his father's arms. Pools of tears welled in my eyes and began to trail down my cheeks. "When I found out I was pregnant...I didn't want him." My words tightened my chest, crushing my heart as my breath caught on a sob. "I even considered ending it."

Larylis seemed to be holding his breath as my eyes lifted to meet his. I pulled back any power I could possibly have, let my shoulders drop, let the skin of my face sag. *Truth. Let him see the truth. Let him see the real me.*

He blinked a few times to clear the moisture that glazed his eyes. When he spoke, his voice was raw. "Thank you for being honest with me. I don't judge you for what you considered. You were scared and alone."

"Knowing that...do you still love me?" *The real me. The selfish me. The me who thinks only of herself.*

He let out an exasperated sigh. "Of course I do. It doesn't matter what you do or what you say. I am going to love you until the day I die."

It felt as if another weight had been lifted from my shoulders. First, I'd been honest with my mother. Now, Larylis knew a truth that had been eating me alive for months. And he still loved me.

Whether that was real or magic, I didn't care. He was mine, and I was his. Our son was alive, healthy, and beautiful. *And the child of a prophecy.* The reminder threatened to shatter my tranquility, but I pushed it away. *Not now. Let me have this peace.*

Cora

I pushed my fork across my plate, moving through islands of egg, meat, and torn pieces of bread. Yet in all its wanderings, it had managed to bring no more than three bites to my mouth since the start of breakfast.

A hand fell over mine, stilling my fork's scraping. "Isn't that right, Cora?"

My eyes shot from my plate to Teryn, then darted toward Lex and Lily. "I'm sorry. What were you saying?"

Lex took a bite of pastry and spoke through his mouthful. "Teryn was telling me how you scolded him the night he proposed to you."

I shook my head to clear it and forced a smile. "Yes, that's right. Of course I scolded him. I thought he was a married man sneaking into my bedroom. It didn't help that he laughed when I confronted him about it."

"I suppose I could have been more tactful about that," Teryn said.

"I know all about making my beloved angry, don't I, Lilylove?" Lex turned to Lily, and she blushed under his adoring stare. "She nearly took off my head when I returned home from Centerpointe Rock."

Lily gave us a shy smile, making it impossible to imagine her angry. "I was upset at him for joining the Quest, and even more upset that he went to war without seeing me first." Her eyes met her husband's. "But I forgave him when he asked for my hand."

Lex and Lily brought their noses together, nuzzling into each other. My cheeks grew warm, and I turned my attention to Teryn, who met my eyes with a smile.

Teryn leaned toward me. "I never could have imagined this side of Lex existed," he whispered.

My eyes flashed toward the happy couple who were now feeding each other bites of apple tart. I couldn't help but laugh. "It is both a strange and heartwarming sight."

When my eyes returned to Teryn's, he held them with a furrowed brow. "Is something wrong? You seem distracted this morning."

I shrugged. "My mind was wandering. I'm here now, though."

"Is it the prophecy? Mareleau?"

My stomach began to churn, reminding me why I'd found it hard to eat more than three bites of breakfast. No matter how much I tried to keep my mind off what I'd learned, I found my thoughts returning to it over and over, leaving me with more questions than I knew what to do with.

"Eat more, Lilylove." Lex's voice pulled me back to the present, which I was grateful for. I turned from Teryn's concerned expression to watch Lex pile Lily's plate with fruit and sausages.

"I told you, Lex, I'm full."

"You won't be saying that by next bell. I know how you get these days. Eat as much as you can now." Lex caught me watching him and paused as he reached for a piece of bread. His cheeks flushed pink, and Lily brought her hand to her lips to hide her grin.

"He worries about my appetite," she said, "because of the baby."

Pain tugged at my heart, but I kept my expression even. "Oh, are the two of you expecting?"

Lily nodded while Lex's face stretched into the biggest smile I'd ever seen him wear. "My first heir," he said.

"What about the two of you?" Lily asked. "You must be excited to have children."

My hand tightened around my fork as a fire ignited in my gut. *No, we will not be having children*, I said to myself, forcing the words to hide behind my sealed lips when all I wanted to do was shout. *All because I was mistaken for someone else*.

Teryn touched my shoulder, and I let out a breath I hadn't realized I'd been holding. The fork fell from my grasp, clanging onto the plate as pain radiated through my palm. I breathed the fire away and let my eyes rest on the center of the table while I recovered my wits.

I was grateful when Teryn took the lead to answer. "We have yet to be blessed as you have. In the meantime, my newborn nephew will be our heir, and that's all the reassurance we need."

I nodded along with Teryn's words and brought my attention back to Lex and Lily.

"*Mareleau's* baby will be your heir?" Lex grimaced. "Wouldn't you rather—" Lily elbowed him in the ribs, her eyes locked on my face.

"That's a wonderful plan," Lily said.

Her sympathy touched my heart, but my fury was stronger. "Excuse me." I stood from the table and went to a window at the other end of the great hall. My eyes glazed with tears as the view of Ridine's grounds swam before them. Footsteps approached, followed by the warmth of Teryn's arm draped over my shoulders.

"I wonder if that question will ever get easier to answer." His voice sounded raw.

"I think it's only going to get more difficult." *Especially now that I know it was all a cruel mistake.*

"It's over. It's in the past. You're safe." His words sounded genuine as always, yet this time they felt meaningless, mocking. My hands clenched into fists as I turned to face him.

"Your Majesties." Master Arther approached, stealing my attention. His face was pale as he wrung his hands. "There's something you need to see."

～

Teryn

"What is it?" I asked.

"It's really better if you see for yourselves." Arther's eyes darted toward Lex and Lily, who had turned to watch us. "And it's better if we keep this private."

Cora and I exchanged a glance and excused ourselves

from our guests. My mouth felt dry as Master Arther led us through the halls to the great keep.

"Where are we going?" Cora asked as we passed door after door with no sign of stopping. We both knew where the end of the hall led.

Arther sighed. "You won't like it."

We reached the end of the corridor, and Arther turned toward the staircase to the high tower. "Please, no," Cora said under her breath.

My hand trembled as I took hold of hers. Arther didn't pause to wait for us as he made his way up the stairs. With careful steps, we followed.

As we entered the tower room, we were met with nervous glances of guards and a few of our councilmen. Lord Jonston turned away from one of the windows and gave a hasty bow. "Your Majesties, there is something urgent you must be made aware of."

"What is it?" I looked around the tower room, expecting the threat to spring forth at any moment, but all I saw was the freshly polished stone walls illuminated by new lanterns and the light of the morning sun. It was impossible to tell this room had once been the darkest, most dangerous place in Ridine, yet the memories remained, superimposed in my mind's eye, making me search for threat in every shadow of every man surrounding me. I squeezed Cora's hand, knowing she must feel the same.

Lord Jonston nodded toward one of the windows. "Come."

With bated breath, I followed. The glass had been pushed open, sending icy air into my nostrils as I approached. Silence wrapped around us as Cora and I looked out at the scenery below. From this high in Ridine, we could see the castle grounds all the way to Lake Ridine and the snowcapped mountains beyond. The sun did little to provide warmth, yet it had burned away the morning mist, leaving nothing but a clear, winter sky.

"I don't see anything," Cora said, her brow furrowed as she squinted into the distance.

I turned back to Lord Jonston. "What are we looking for?"

His face was grave as his eyes remained on the sky. "Keep watching. Look toward the mountains."

My gaze returned to the scenery, trying to pierce beyond what I saw to the danger Lord Jonston was hinting at. Moments passed, and I nearly turned away when a flash of movement caught my eye—a dark streak in the cloudless blue above the mountains. Just as quickly as it had appeared, it moved beyond view.

Cora stiffened beside me. "Did you see that?"

I craned my neck to look in the direction it had gone, but movement at the opposite range of view appeared. This time, it continued across the sky before returning the other way. We continued to watch, the shadow returning again and again, darting across the sky, soaring over the mountains. After a while, it was clear that there was not one shadow but two, and they were circling over the land like birds of prey. However, they looked too large to be ordinary birds.

Cora faced Lord Jonston. "What are they?"

He swallowed hard. "We aren't certain, but we've had reports coming in all morning from scouts and messengers claiming they've seen dragons."

My mouth fell open. "*Dragons?* That isn't possible."

Cora met my eyes, and I knew what she was thinking. *Not impossible.* After everything we'd seen and experienced, nothing was truly impossible. "Have they caused anyone harm?" she asked.

Jonston scratched at his massive beard. "The first reports we've received have claimed scorched fields and missing livestock."

Cora's chest heaved as her eyes returned to the window, knuckles white as she gripped the ledge. I followed her line of vision to the forest beyond Ridine's grounds. "Valorre."

"What's wrong?" I whispered.

"He isn't close. I have to..." She turned away and rushed from the room.

Lord Jonston gaped after her. "Where is she going?"

I knew the answer but kept it to myself as I raced to the other side of the room. "I'll be back."

"What do we do about this, Your Majesty?" Lord Jonston's tone held an edge that stopped me in my tracks. He had a way of reminding me of my place as king. While he wasn't condescending like Lord Kevan had been, he carried himself with a similar confidence. Instead of making me feel small, he made me feel like I had an important standard to live up to.

I turned on my heel and met his narrowed eyes. "Secure the castle. Set archers on the roof." Lord Jonston nodded and began to bark orders at the guards and messengers. The room erupted in a flurry of action, and I took my chance to follow in Cora's wake.

I ran down the stairs and through the corridors, ignoring Lex and Lily's startled exclamations as I passed them. I came to the door that led to the charred field and flung it open. My eyes darted toward the line of trees where Cora was running. I called after her, but she paid me no heed as she made her way into the forest. My legs flew beneath me, screaming in protest after my morning's grueling training session with Larylis. I forced them faster until I caught up to Cora and took hold of her elbow.

She spun around to face me, cheeks flushed, eyes wide and angry. "Teryn, let go. I need to find Valorre."

"You need to slow down and not put yourself in danger. Are you trying to get yourself killed?"

"Valorre could be in danger. I can't...feel him. If it's because he isn't close, then he could be too near those *things*. And if it's because he's in danger..." She swallowed hard.

"What are you going to do about either of those things? Do you know how to fight a dragon? You can't save everyone—"

She burned me with a seething glare. "How many times do you have to remind me of that? I know I can't save everyone, but too many people have been hurt around me already. I won't ever stop trying to protect the ones I love, no matter how much danger that puts me in. You can't change that, so you can either come with me or let me go."

I released her arm. "That's all I wanted—for you to wait one damn moment so I can come with you."

She rubbed her arm, and although she remained silent, her glare lessened.

I let out a deep breath to calm my pounding heart. "I was trying to say you can't save everyone *on your own*. Do you have any idea how much it kills me to watch you run away from me? To leave me behind while you endanger yourself? You may feel the need to protect Valorre, but I can't live without trying to protect you, no matter how many times I fail at it. Don't push me away, even if you're hurting. Please."

Her face fell but she didn't meet my eyes. "All right. Let's go together, then."

Tension was still heavy in the silence between us, but we made our way through the trees side by side. Cora led the way, eyes flashing toward every sound and sign of movement.

Finally, she stopped, holding out a hand for me to stop as well. Her body sagged with relief. "I can feel him. He isn't close, but he's safe. I told him to stay hidden."

I sighed, my relief reflecting hers. "Good."

Cora turned toward me, eyes lowered. "I'm sorry for leaving you behind. I wasn't thinking clearly."

I repressed my urge to reach for her, wishing she would come to me and fold into my arms the way she usually did. "I'm sorry too."

She lifted her head, giving me a hesitant glance. "Arguing never feels right, no matter how many times we do it."

"I suppose it's what helps us learn more about each other," I said.

She nodded. "There's something my brother once told me. He said, 'When you begin to share your life with another person, you meet both the shadows of yourself and the other.' It was the first time I realized two people could love each other and still end up arguing."

"Does that mean you still love me?" A corner of my mouth pulled into a smile.

Cora rolled her eyes and pressed her forehead into my chest. "Of course I do."

The tension melted away as I wrapped my arms around her and kissed the top her head. When we parted, both our cheeks held trails of shimmering moisture. I opened my mouth to speak when the forest dimmed as if it had suddenly turned to night. We looked above the forest trees at the shadow that loomed high above, blocking the sunlight. An ear-shattering screech rang out around us before the sunlight returned and the shadow was gone.

Cora stared after it, trembling from head to toe. "It went toward the castle."

7

FIRE

Cora

"What do we do?" Teryn asked.

My first instinct was to chase after it and run directly to Ridine, but Teryn's earlier words gave me pause. He'd been right; I knew nothing about fighting a dragon. I knew nothing about them at all. My feet shifted below me, eager to run. "I don't know, but we can't do nothing."

Teryn ran a hand over his face. "You're right. We may not be able to defend against dragons, but we can't hide while our people are in danger."

That was all the confirmation I needed before my feet propelled me forward. *Valorre. Where are you now?*

Still safe. Images filled my mind, similar to the view before me—branches whipping by with blue sky peeking over the trees. I could feel him getting nearer, although he was still too far away for my comfort.

Good. Stay hidden. Don't enter any clearings.

Danger. I sensed his equal concern for me.

I know.

"Look." Teryn stole my attention back to our present surroundings as he pointed at the sky where tendrils of gray began to dance higher and higher. "Is that smoke?"

I nearly tripped when I picked up speed, feeling the sting of branches tear at my skin and tug at my skirt as I continued forward. Finally, the peaks of Ridine's tallest towers could be seen above the tree line, and we began to slow our pace. The stench of burning filled my nostrils as I searched the sky. I was surprised to find the smoke wasn't hovering above Ridine like I'd expected it to—it was rising from the left.

Teryn put a hand on my arm as we neared the edge of the forest, and we stilled. "We need to be careful."

I nodded, and we took slow steps between the trees and out onto the castle grounds. Movement caught my eye at the left near the source of the smoke, and I froze. Teryn's hand tightened around my arm.

At the center of the charred field stood an enormous, white dragon. Its body was long and snake-like with white, opalescent scales. Feathers lined huge wings that were tucked up tight against its body. The dragon circled the field, nostrils flaring and tongue flicking as it nudged the blackened earth with its nose. With a screech, it pulled its head back, opened its tooth-filled maw, and sent a stream of fire onto the ground, creating a shimmering patch of glowing, orange embers.

It began to circle the field once again, clawing at the ground, turning up black ash with immense claws. Tremors shook me from head to toe as I debated what to do. Run for the castle? Stay still? Retreat beneath the trees? Before I could take a step, the dragon stopped its circling, raised its head, and narrowed its eyes at me and Teryn. Its tongue darted in and out of its mouth as it extended its neck in our direction. We were too far for it to reach us from its place on the field, but I wasn't as certain about the reach of its flame.

"What do we do?" Teryn whispered.

"I don't know. For now, let's hold still." I pulled Teryn close to me and closed my eyes. With deep breaths, I fought the anxiety that pounded in my chest and thought about the surrounding trees. My body felt as sturdy as a tree trunk, my hair blowing like leaves in a breeze. Teryn was a tree at my side, strong and steady. I opened my eyes and saw the dragon tilt its head, then return to its circling.

What are you? I closed my eyes again, holding tight to my inner calm as I extended my consciousness toward the creature, letting it creep slowly past the flames, claws, and scales, past the unfamiliar features of bone, blood, and scale until I found the being within.

Confusion. Anger. Tired. Fury.

A roaring screech forced my eyes open to see the dragon whip its long neck toward the sky. Arrows rained down from Ridine's nearest towers but glanced off the creature's scales. The dragon hissed as it brought its head back toward its shoulders, and then snapped forward, sending a stream of flame toward the towers. Shouts erupted from the castle as the stone turned black. With another screech, the dragon extended its wings, beating the ground, sending ash, smoke, and dirt tumbling away as it lifted itself into the air. As it raised itself high above the trees, its shadow again fell upon us, blocking out the light. Not a moment later, it was gone.

My breaths came out in ragged gasps as I dropped to my knees and let the glamour fall. *Valorre?*

Still safe. You?

I could feel him much nearer now and let out a sigh of relief. *I'm safe too. Do you know what those things are? The dragons?*

Home.

That was all I needed to know. The dragons had come from El'Ara. The veil was torn. And we were all in danger.

~

Mareleau

"What was that flash of light? And why is there smoke outside?" I slid off the bed and went to the window but couldn't see past the clouds of smoke.

Larylis followed, holding Liam. "I don't know, but I didn't like the sound of it. It felt like the entire castle was coming down."

The door flew open, and I whirled around to meet my mother's pale face. Our eyes locked, but she remained silent.

"What is it, Mother? What's going on?"

Mother closed the door on the shouts and pounding footsteps that echoed through the hall. "I'm so glad you're safe. Whatever you do, don't open the windows or go outside."

"Why? What's happening?"

Mother dropped onto the lounge as if her body were suddenly too heavy to bear. She stared, eyes unfocused. The fear on her pale face sent a shiver down my spine. "There was a—"

The door flew open again, making me jump. Ann, Sera, and Breah rushed in, eyes wet as they mumbled in unison.

"Quiet, you fools," I hissed. "You'll wake the baby, and I can't hear a word you're saying." Ann and Sera traded sobs for whimpers, and Breah seemed to hold her breath. "Will someone please tell me what's going on in a rational manner?"

"There was a dragon," Ann wailed. "It set fire to the old field and then blasted the castle. Men have been burned!"

I put my hands on my hips. "You're speaking nonsense. Since when is there such a thing as dragons?"

"Maybe when there became such a thing as unicorns," Larylis said under his breath, eyes still fixed on the window. I turned toward him, surprised to see his face so grave. He didn't really believe there had been a dragon, did he?

"I knew I shouldn't have agreed to come here again," Sera whined. "This place is the worst."

My eyes snapped back to my ladies. "Speak sensibly. What really happened?"

"Lady Ann is right." Mother's voice was toneless but firm. "There was a dragon. I saw it from one of the windows."

My breath caught in my throat. "You're serious."

Larylis darted toward the door. "I need to speak to my brother."

"Wait, I want to come with you." I caught up to him, and he paused. He opened his mouth as if he were about to argue but nodded with a sigh. I turned to Mother. "Will you take Liam?"

Her eyes went wide, and she looked me up and down, as if suddenly remembering where—and who— she was. "You can't go anywhere. You are still in recovery."

I let out an irritated groan as I lifted my sleeping son from Larylis' arms and placed him in my mother's. "You can't expect me to lie in bed all day after hearing a dragon has been here. I refuse to be useless."

Mother's face turned red, and I prepared for a scolding. Yet, the fire extinguished from her eyes faster than it had been ignited. Her cheeks returned to a colorless pallor as she cradled Liam close to her breast. "Do what you will, then. Just don't go outside."

Oddly enough, her resignation made my heart sink. For one moment, she'd almost seemed like her old self. I forced a comforting smile and nodded, then Larylis and I were out the door.

"What do you think is happening?" I asked as we sped down the hall, hearing wails and shouts both above and below us. "This can't have anything to do with..." I couldn't bring myself to say his name out loud. Morkai. *No, it can't be. He's gone.*

Larylis clenched his jaw as he took my hand. "I don't know."

We moved past armed guards and concerned courtiers and made our way down the stairs toward the great hall. At the bottom of the stairs stood a man with a vaguely familiar face next to a short woman with pink cheeks and a heavy bosom. He straightened when his eyes fell on my husband.

"Lex," Larylis said to the man. "Have you seen my brother?"

"Not since breakfast," Lex said. "They were called away on some urgent business."

"Do you know where they went?"

Lex shook his head. "We've been looking—"

"There they are." The woman next to Lex pointed down the hall. I turned and saw Teryn and Cora sprinting toward us. Both were covered in a layer of filth and what appeared to be tiny cuts. The hem of Cora's dress was torn and nearly black with dirt.

Larylis rushed to meet them. "What happened to you? Was it the dragon?"

Teryn looked down at his clothing as if he were surprised to find himself so unkempt. "No, it wasn't that. We were running through the woods—"

"But there *was* a dragon?" I looked from Teryn to Cora, and Cora nodded.

"What does this mean?" Larylis asked, keeping his voice low. "Does it have anything to do with Morkai?"

"Morkai?" Lex echoed from behind me, making me suppress a jump. "Dragons? Am I going crazy, or did you just say what I think you said?"

Teryn pressed his lips tight, eyes darting from Lex to the woman at his side. "It's nothing. You and Princess Lily need not concern yourselves—"

Lex narrowed his eyes. "If something is going on, you should tell me. You know what I've seen and the dangers we've faced together. We both know a threat to your land is a threat to mine."

Teryn squeezed his eyes shut and rubbed his temples. "Fine. We should talk. But not here."

"Let's go to the study," Cora said.

Teryn nodded and broke away from our group to speak with some men nearby. They nodded at his orders, and he returned to us. "I'm meeting with the council at next bell. We have until then."

Hardly anyone paid us much heed as we scurried down the hall and into a room I'd never seen before. It was modest in size and lined with bookcases, most of which were empty. Chairs were interspersed throughout next to small tables, and at the far end of the room sat a wide desk and a high-backed chair lined with red velvet.

Cora closed the door, shutting out the chaos in the hall. She brought a nail between her teeth as she stood before the desk, while Teryn took his place next to her, leaning his backside against the desk. Larylis and I exchanged a wary glance before we sat in a set of chairs.

"Prince Lex," Teryn said, voice flat and eyes unfocused, "you remember my brother, King Larylis, and his wife, Queen Mareleau." He waved an unenthusiastic hand from us to Lex. "Princess Lily—"

"It's all right," the woman named Lily said with a hushed voice as she and Lex took their seats. "We can exchange formalities later."

I was taken aback at her nerve to interrupt a king but appreciated the sentiment. "Yes," I said. "Let's talk about this nonsense about a dragon instead. What in Lela is going on? Are we being attacked with dark magic again?"

Cora shook her head. "The dragons don't seem evil. At least, not the one that landed in the field. I connected with it just before it was shot by our archers. It was confused, scared, and filled with fury, but not necessarily seeking an attack. However, that doesn't make them any less dangerous. Its mind wasn't soft or welcoming like Valorre's, or any other animal, for that matter, so I don't imagine they can be tamed."

"Were you able to sense why they are here?" Teryn asked.

"No," Cora said, "but I think it has to do with the prophecy. The veil between our world and El'Ara has been torn."

Larylis leaned back in his chair and let out a heavy sigh. "I suppose that's better than what I had been thinking. I was sure it had something to do with Morkai."

"Morkai is gone," Cora said, "but he may have been the least of our worries."

"Wait, wait, wait." Lex held up a hand. "Why would any of you consider this had something to do with Morkai? Morkai died on the battlefield, as we all know." Silence answered, and I could almost feel his confusion, remembering what it had been like when *I'd* been the least aware of the group.

Teryn finally spoke. "Yes, Morkai died at Centerpointe Rock, but he had tethered his soul to the crystal he carried on his staff. Cora found that crystal and brought it back here. He was later...unleashed."

My stomach churned as I recalled how Teryn had been during his possession by Morkai. The unwanted attention, the lingering touch. It was still hard for me to see Teryn and *not* think of him as Morkai. I suppressed a shudder and reached for Larylis' hand.

Teryn continued. "We were able to defeat him and destroy the crystal. You wouldn't have heard about it because no one outside this room knows it happened. All our people know is that Mareleau's uncles rebelled and caused the deaths of her father and King Dimetreus."

Lex nodded. "That's all I'd heard."

"That is only partially true," Cora said. "We hoped that would be the end of it, but there's something else at work that we can't ignore."

"The prophecy." The word felt dry on my tongue. "What does any of it mean?"

"What is it in the first place?" Lex asked.

Teryn took a step away from the desk. "When Morkai returned last year, I learned much about his past. I learned Morkai had come to Lela following clues from a prophecy he'd channeled from a woman named Emylia. The prophecy was meant to help his father, who claimed to be the rightful heir to a realm called El'Ara."

"El'Ara," Cora said, "is the realm of the Ancient Ones, the Elvan and Faeran. Long ago, a half-Elvan named Darius was passed over as heir to the realm in favor of his younger sister, Ailan. He was banished from El'Ara, only to return in an attempt to conquer it. War erupted, and in the end, he killed his mother, who was Morkara—the ruler—of El'Ara. Before she died, she created a veil between our worlds, meant to keep them separate so no one would ever be able to move between them again. But she died before it was fully complete. With her dying breath, she secured the veil as it was, which pushed the land that had been left outside the veil into our world. That land is Lela."

Heat flooded my cheeks. "How do I not know any of this? You've told me about this prophecy that lead Morkai here, but why is this the first I'm hearing about Lela being some remnant of an ancient realm? I thought we were bearing our secrets together, not keeping more from each other."

A flicker of guilt crossed Cora's face before it was replaced with a stony mask. "I didn't think what I knew mattered because I thought *I* was the Mother of Prophecy. I thought *I* was the reason El'Ara could never be whole again. Now we know differently."

I swallowed hard. Of course she hadn't wanted to share what she thought were the repercussions of her forced barrenness. If it *had* been her, it wouldn't have mattered; the prophecy would be dead. But it wasn't her —*I* was the one with the burden now. "So what does El'Ara and the prophecy have to do with dragons?"

Teryn furrowed his brow. "The prophecy stated, *where the veil abandoned its heart, one will be born that will stop the Blood of Darius. Only then will the veil be torn.*"

Cora's eyes were still on me. "And if we believe you are the Mother of Prophecy, then Liam's birth may have torn the veil immediately."

My hands began to tremble. *My baby. My tiny, innocent baby.* How could his fate be so huge? It was one thing to think of myself as the mother of some ancient prophecy, but it was another to consider what it meant for my son. *He* was the true focus of the prophecy; I was merely the force that brought him into the world. "What does that mean for Liam? How can he stop the Blood of Darius, whoever that is?"

"We don't know," Cora said. "All we know is that the dragons came from El'Ara, which confirms the veil has been torn. Before now, unicorns were the only creatures to have moved through the veil, and Valorre was the only one ever to return. If the veil is torn, it's possible that more creatures could get out. But we might be more concerned with what wants to get in."

Her words sent a ripple of confusion through me. "Wait, your unicorn returned to El'Ara? When?"

She wouldn't meet my eye. "We both did."

I looked from her to Teryn, who did not seem surprised by her confession. "You have a lot of explaining to do," I said through clenched teeth.

Finally, she met my gaze. "I know. I'll tell you every-thing. I'll tell *all* of you everything I know. Just not today."

"Then when?" I asked.

Bells sounded to mark the hour, and Teryn moved to the door. "I have to meet with the council. They may not know about this prophecy, but perhaps we can find a solution to keep these dragons at bay."

"I doubt that," Larylis said. "No one could possibly know what to do with a dragon."

"You should come too, Lare," Teryn said. "Lex, you are welcome as well. Just don't mention anything you've heard in this room. As you can imagine, talk of magic doesn't do well with the council." Lex nodded, and he and Larylis stood to join Teryn at the door.

I rose to my feet and put my hands on my hips, standing at my full height as I let my voice fill the room with my urgency. "Is anyone going to listen to me? When are we meeting again?" The room went still as all eyes moved to me. Cora raised an eyebrow, and my cheeks began to burn. Had I just used my power? I let my arms drop to my sides and lowered my voice. "I would like to hear more of what Cora has to say."

Cora came to my side. "Tomorrow. We'll meet back

here in the morning." A rumble of agreement came from our companions, then they began to file out into the hall. I stayed where I was while Cora paused in the doorway. "You should consider training your gifts in the Arts. I can tell yours are strong, but you have no conscious control."

I bristled. "Who are you to tell me whether I have control?"

She gave me a soft smile, ignoring the bite in my tone. "If you're ever interested, I know some people who could help."

I crossed my arms and popped my hip to the side. "And who would that be?"

"The Forest People. Or, as you once called them, *the wolves who raised me*." She left with a smirk, leaving me alone with my storm of thoughts.

8

DREAMS

Cora

Smoke filled my lungs, heart racing with every breath I took. I whirled around but all I saw was black sky and flames rising high above my head. The sound of wings pounded the air, the force of them driving the flames dangerously close to my body. I spun again, seeking an exit through the fire as the smoke stung my eyes, and finally spotted a space between two pillars of flame. I ran forward, feeling the heat sear my skin. I was almost through when the shadow of a man blocked my path. He came forward, and I stepped back. The light of the fire illuminated his face, revealing the features of a man I would never forget.

Morkai smirked as he walked between the flames, showing no sign that they affected him in any way. I fled back to the center of the ring of fire and narrowed my eyes, lips pulled into a snarl. He reached out a hand, and I felt pain deep below my abdomen. I doubled over, screaming. When the pain ceased, I straightened, hands over my aching womb. Though he stood dangerously close now, I kept my chin high. "You were wrong, Morkai. You had it wrong the entire time."

He threw his head back and laughed, and in the blink of an eye, Mareleau stood at his side, whimpering as his hand gripped the back of her neck. "You're right. It was her, not you. Should I have done it to her instead?"

My eyes darted from Mareleau to Morkai, but I could form no words with my trembling lips.

"Should it have been her?" Still gripping Mareleau by the neck, he pushed her toward one of the pillars of flame while she clawed at his arm. She screamed as fire seared the ends of her golden hair. "Say it!" My eyes snapped back to Morkai, whose face had been replaced by someone I'd never seen before. As unfamiliar as this new face was, his features tugged at my memory. But every time I tried to focus on his features, they shifted beneath my gaze. "Should it have been her?"

Tears streamed down my cheeks, burning my skin as they trailed down to my neck. "Yes!"

He pushed Mareleau into the fire.

I bolted upright, gasping for breath as I looked around the dark room and pushed at the covers surrounding me, still feeling the heat of the inferno in the warmth of the blankets. Hands found mine, and I stilled my thrashing. Teryn's soothing voice whispered in my ear, and I pressed my face into his chest. Tremors wracked my body as I sobbed, trying to shake the blinding colors of flame from my mind, the hiss of Morkai's voice, and the terror in Mareleau's eyes when I failed to save her.

Why would I dream of such a thing? I'm not like that. That's not me.

Teryn held me in silence until my breathing began to calm. I forced the dream from my mind, pushing it deep into the shadows of my consciousness where it belonged.

"I still have them too," Teryn said. "Almost every night. My dreams will never let me forget what it was like to see my body doing terrible things or the sensation of losing my sense of touch. I often dream that I reach out to hold you, but you can't feel me no matter what I do."

I looked up at him, barely able to make out his features in the dark. "I'm sorry I woke you."

He kissed me on the forehead. "I'm not. I want to be here for you. Don't ever be afraid to wake me."

I pressed my head back to his chest, and we settled under the covers. The sound of his steady breathing set me further at ease, and after a few moments, I could tell he'd fallen back to sleep. *I wish I could fall asleep that easily.*

I tossed and turned, refusing to return to thoughts of my nightmare, but it was easier said than done. With a frustrated moan, I rose from the bed and moved to the window. A starry night sky welcomed me as I stared out toward the mountains. I watched the space above them, looking for signs of movement flickering over the stars. Even though archers were ordered to stand guard night and day, I didn't feel at ease. *What can an arrow do against a dragon?*

I became aware of a shimmering light flickering at the corner of my eye and jumped away from the window to face it. Colors of white, blue, and gray undulated before me until they took on a familiar form.

"Emylia?" My mouth fell open at the sight of the wraith. "What are you doing here? I thought you moved on."

She frowned, eyes turned down at the corners. "I tried."

"What happened?" I kept my voice low and glanced beyond her shimmering form where Teryn still slept. With a wave of my hand, I motioned her to follow me to the far end of the room.

Emylia wrung her hands. "When I went to move to the otherlife, I was granted knowledge I hadn't had neither while living nor while trapped in the crystal. I had a glimpse of great mysteries, secrets of the soil and stars, like I'd always craved. However, that wasn't all I was granted. I saw deep into the timeline of my life, saw the repercussions of the actions I'd taken while living. Some were good, others were...not so much. I gained insight into how those repercussions were playing in the lives of others at that very moment." She lowered her head. "And I saw you. Cora, I'm so sorry. It's my fault Morkai did what he did to you."

I wanted to reach out a hand to comfort her but knew she wouldn't be able to feel it. Instead, I took a step closer. "It's not your fault. You didn't know what he was capable of when he was Desmond."

"But I did it just the same. Whether I knew the weight of my actions or not, I am responsible for them. I channeled the prophecy. I provided him the clues that led him to believe you were the Mother we'd learned about. I am the reason he made you barren, and you weren't even the woman he was seeking."

Mareleau's face from my nightmare flooded my mind,

but I shook it away. *No, it shouldn't have been her. Of course not. I would never think that.*

Emylia continued. "After learning what I know now, my ethera became too heavy with my ties to this world. I need to shed them to move to the otherlife."

"How will you shed them?"

She lifted her head, her face resolute. "I am going to do what I can to make this right, to use the knowledge I have to end what I've begun."

My heart quickened. "Do you know things that could help us?"

"At this point, I don't know how much it will help, but I am going to try regardless."

Inside my core, I felt the flame of hope begin to burn. "What do you know?"

THE NEXT MORNING, WE GATHERED IN THE STUDY. MY EYES burned from lack of sleep, but my mind was clear. There was so much to say, and I was ready for it.

Teryn and I again stood before the desk while Mareleau, Larylis, Lex, and Lily took their previous seats. Every set of eyes that met mine looked as tired as I felt. I froze as I met Mareleau's eyes, and the nightmare seized my mind, replacing her face with a face seared by fire while my angry outburst sealed her fate. I breathed the memory away and moved my gaze to Teryn. He nodded.

Teryn and I began to explain the prophecy, alternating details with what he'd learned from Emylia and what I'd learned in El'Ara. It was exhilarating and terrifying at once to relive my time there, recalling the stories

Etrix and Garot had shared with me about Satsara, Darius, Ailan, and the veil, and comparing them to what we knew about the prophecy.

The faces of our friends were pale, filled with wonder and shock and horror—as they should be. There was no detail that wasn't a mixture of all those things. My cheeks burned as I explained my escape from the tribunal. When I was done, I was met with silence and hesitated to see the expressions of my friends.

"So, you are a witch," Lex said with a sly smile, breaking the tension in the room. "I knew it all along."

I shot him a playful glare. "It's called the Arts, you know that."

"You can...travel? With your mind?" Larylis asked.

I looked at my feet. "I'm still not exactly sure what it is. The first couple times it happened, I thought I was having a vivid imagining, or—at most—a mental projection into a real time and space. However, in El'Ara I learned that my body followed me where I mentally went."

"Do you think that's how you went to El'Ara in the first place?" Mareleau asked.

"No, I still believe that was Valorre's accidental doing. Before the veil was torn, I believe unicorns were the only creatures able to move through it one way or the other, perhaps because of their horns. Once Valorre came to our world, he became confused about home. I think that's why none of the unicorns ever made it back."

"Is this special kind of *Traveling* part of the Arts? Of being what you are? An empath?" Mareleau shifted anxiously in her seat at the word.

I shook my head. "I don't know. Being an empath

allows me to feel what others are feeling and thinking. It allows me to tune into the energy of many things, and I'm even able to manipulate that energy at times. But Traveling was never something I was taught by the Forest People. Anyhow, I'm not sure this new power of mine will help us. But if it can, I will use it."

"Does any of this help us with dragons?" Lex asked. He put his hand on Lily's. "I can't put my wife and unborn child in danger by traveling home while those creatures are on the loose."

"You are welcome to stay as our guest as long as you need," Teryn said. "We have scouts tracking the dragons' movements, trying to see if any routes are safe. Until we know more, I suppose all we can do is consider the facts we have—"

"There's more," I said, "that even you don't know."

He frowned. "You haven't told me something? I thought—"

"I found out last night and figured I'd tell everyone at once," I said in a rush.

Teryn nodded and sat at the edge of the desk, facing me. My heart raced as all eyes were locked on me. It was one thing to retell a story, but quite another to share something unbelievable for the first time.

I took a deep breath. "Emylia came to me last night."

Teryn's eyes widened. "Emylia?"

"The wraith from the crystal?" Larylis asked.

Lex grimaced. "Morkai's ex-lover?"

I nodded. "She is unable to move on and remains a wraith in our world. However, before she turned away from the otherlife, she was able to glean important information. She shared that information with me. We all know Morkai was the Blood of Darius. Emylia has learned that Darius was, in fact, Morkai's father. And he's still alive."

A rumble of gasps filled the room. Teryn ran a hand over his face, eyes bulging as he rubbed his jaw. "Darius is still alive? *The* Darius who caused a war amongst the Ancient Ones in El'Ara?"

"Yes. Five-hundred years ago, in our time," I said. "He's been ruling as King of Syrus ever since."

"Are you saying Morkai was...a prince?" Lex asked.

Mareleau raised an eyebrow. "And this Darius has been alive for five-hundred years? How is that possible?"

"Darius was half human, half Elvan," I said. "The Elvan live indefinitely, until they choose to take what they call Last Breath. It's possible Darius has the same immortal powers and can't die from age the same way we do."

"How has an immortal being from another realm not conquered half the world by now?" Teryn asked.

"He may be immortal, but he is old and weak, which likely has to do with the veil." I closed my eyes, trying to recall everything Emylia had told me, wishing I'd written it down as she'd spoken. "When Emylia was alive, she'd known him only as the Ageless King of Syrus. Syrus is a small, isolated kingdom in the Northern Islands. Being from the Southern Islands, she never paid much heed to the stories of the withering, old king who refused to die."

"So, Darius is still alive but is a decrepit, old man who lives on the other side of the ocean," Larylis said. "Does that mean we don't need to worry about him?"

"I wish I could say yes to that," I said. "But the veil was meant to keep Darius out. Morkai had described his father's condition as being under a curse that made him forget. Darius couldn't even remember the name of the realm he was looking for. What if the tear in the veil breaks that curse and allows Darius to find El'Ara?"

"Should we care?" Mareleau lifted a shoulder in a shrug. "El'Ara has nothing to do with us. Why should we care if some old man wreaks havoc on an Ancient Realm?"

I gritted my teeth. "Lela is the missing heart of El'Ara. If Darius invades the realm and conquers it and the veil falls completely, then Lela returns to its rightful place, leaving us in the midst of whatever chaos he brings."

Mareleau threw her hands in the air. "And my son is supposed to stop this madness? How?"

"I wish I knew," I said. "All I know is that Darius was a powerful threat that only the strongest Elvan could stand up against. Even if he is five-hundred years old, I hate the thought of facing him, of what he could do to this land or El'Ara."

"That still doesn't help us with the dragons," Larylis said. "Darius is probably the only one in our world that knows a thing about them, and I don't suppose we can ask him for help. In fact, we don't even know that he isn't the one responsible for them, sending them here to destroy us."

I brought my thumbnail between my teeth as I considered his words. He was right. For all we knew, Darius may have summoned them from El'Ara, knowing the veil had been torn. But what if there was still hope for finding out what to do about them? "What if he isn't the only Elvan left in our world?"

"What do you mean?" Teryn asked.

I turned to face him. "Darius and Ailan were both trapped here, along with anyone and anything else that remained when the veil was sealed. If Darius is still alive..."

Teryn's face paled. "Ailan might be too. But how do we find her? We've already had one immortal carrying on without us even knowing he existed. How do we find a second?"

"What about that book?" Lex said. We turned to face him, and he blushed beneath our gaze.

"What book?" Teryn and I said in unison.

"The book about Lela that I read at Dermaine," Lex said, as if it should be obvious. "Don't you remember, Teryn? *The Once and Former Magic of Ancient Lela*, or something like that. It had that big map, remember? The map of some place called Le'Lana. You said I was reading the wrong book—"

My breath caught in my throat. "Did you say, Le'Lana?"

Lex nodded. "It was huge and looked nothing like Lela. I had no idea it was referring to some magical realm."

Teryn and I exchanged a glance. My heart beat high in my chest. "Someone wrote about El'Ara, or at least the kingdom of Le'Lana," I said under my breath. "If we can find the person who wrote it..."

Teryn's eyes sparkled with realization. "We might be able to find information about Ailan, Darius...maybe even the dragons."

I nodded. "I must find that book. Now."

9

READY

Mareleau

I pushed open my bedroom door and found my mother standing at the window, bouncing Liam in her arms. She turned to me, creases between her brows as her lips lifted into a weak smile. "He barely fussed while you were gone, but I'm sure he's hungry now."

I felt my heart melt like butter as I took Liam in my arms. He let out a mewling cry, mouth eagerly turning toward my chest as I sat on the bed and pressed my back against the plush pillows. I undid the top of my gown and began to nurse him, eyes fixated on his fluttering eyelids and tiny lips.

Mother returned to the window.

"Any signs of the dragons?" I asked.

"Now and then, over the mountains." Her voice sounded hollow. "None have come near the castle again though."

"Good." Silence stretched between us.

She sighed and faced me. "How are we ever going to get home? It isn't safe to travel until these dragons have been dealt with."

My words wouldn't come. *Do I tell her the truth? Or do I lie?*

A year ago, the choice would have been easy. I would have pushed her away like I'd done many times before. A harsh word would have been enough to widen the chasm and keep her at the distance I wanted her. But now that I'd opened up to her, now that I was beginning to enjoy the newfound ease between us, I was pulled toward another choice.

The conflict must have been clear on my face because Mother stepped closer, frowning. "What is it, Mareleau?"

My heart raced. "I'm going home tomorrow."

She put her hands on her hips. "That isn't possible. Did you not hear a word I said? It's too dangerous."

I met her eyes. "It's so much more dangerous than you know, and you won't be able to come with me."

Fury swept over her face, and for a moment she looked as if she would shout. Instead, she sat at the edge of the bed, shoulders hunched, eyes locked on mine. "Don't shut me out, Mareleau. Please, tell me what you're talking about."

I bit my lip and began to tremble. "There's more I need to tell you. So much more. About Father. My uncles. Morkai. Cora."

She nodded and reached for my hand. "I'm listening."

~

Teryn

"Are you sure you can do this?" I asked.

Cora paused brushing her hair and met my eyes in the mirror above her vanity, lips lifting into a slight smile. "Would it make you feel better if I said yes?"

"Are you sure you have to go?" My voice caught on my words, throat painfully tight.

She set the brush down and turned to face me. "You know I have to. I'm the only one who can travel quickly and safely between our kingdoms. It would take too long to wait for anyone else to find and deliver that book. Besides, Larylis and Mareleau need to return home to warn their council about the dragons."

"You're really going to try to take them with you? All at once?"

She nodded. "I have to try."

"You're sure I can't come too?"

Her face fell. "You know I want nothing more than to have you at my side, but you are needed here as King of Kero. We may know nothing about these dragons until we find that book, but someone needs to stay here and at least *try* to come up with a solution. It's the only way our people will feel even the slightest bit safe."

I heaved a sigh. "You're right. I also need to investigate further into Darius and any threat he could pose from Syrus."

"How will you do that?"

I rubbed my jaw. "I've planted an idea with the council that rumors have reached Lela about dragons being spotted in the Northern Islands and that the King of Syrus could be responsible for them. It was a stretch, but the councilmen seemed to believe the possibility. They agreed to send scouts north to Risa to gather more information about the Northern Islands and Darius. I thought it was a good way to spread awareness about the possible threat without revealing anything about magic or El'Ara."

Cora regarded me with a look of pride, making me blush. "I love it when you talk like a king."

I tried to keep the guilt off my face. How would she respond if I told her I was emulating a sorcerer, not a king? While trapped in the crystal, I had witnessed Morkai's carefully crafted manipulations and saw how he'd gotten others to do his dirty work for him. It was he who inspired the idea to plant my rumors with the council.

I decided to change the subject. "How will *you* do it? How will you get to Dermaine?"

She furrowed her brow, deep in thought. "Since I've never been to Dermaine, I don't think I can Travel there directly. As far as I know, I can only Travel to a place or person I am familiar with. The first time, I Traveled to Salinda. Next, I Traveled to you. When I escaped El'Ara, I Traveled to the cliff where you told me you loved me."

"Then how will you get there?" I asked.

"I'll take us somewhere I've already been first. My only options that are close enough to Dermaine are either Verlot Palace or Centerpointe Rock. Since the dragons have only been reported in northern Kero, we should be safe to travel the rest of the way to Dermaine by horse or coach from either location."

I bristled at the mention of Centerpointe Rock.

"Verlot would be safer, wouldn't it? You could bring guards to guide you—"

"And welcome plenty of prying eyes and unwanted questions," Cora said. "I don't want to risk stalling our journey to Dermaine, which makes me favor Centerpointe Rock."

I pressed my lips together to keep from begging her not to go there.

Cora raised an eyebrow and laughed. "Don't tell me you're superstitious. The Rock itself poses no threat, other than the memories of what happened there. It's harmless. Besides, Centerpointe Rock is closer to Dermaine than Verlot is. We can get a traveling coach for Mare and the baby at the nearest village and make it to the palace in just a few days."

"You're sure it's safe?"

Her face fell. "Nowhere is truly safe until we figure out what we're up against. We need that book."

"What if it tells us nothing?"

She rose from the chair at the vanity and stood in front of me. "What if it tells us everything? What if it answers all our questions? What if it leads us to Ailan and shows us how to use the prophecy to protect Lela?"

I sighed. "I'll never understand how you continue to be the bravest person I know after all you've faced."

She took my hands in hers. "It helps me be brave when I have someone I love at my side. Even though we are forced to part, I will continue to be brave, knowing I'm doing what I'm doing to protect our kingdom, our land, and our future together."

Our eyes locked, and I searched for words to match the pain that seared my heart. "Over the past few months,

I was starting to think I'd never have to say goodbye to you again."

Cora gave me a sad smile. "You should know by now that goodbye between us is only temporary. I'll be back as soon as I find the book."

"So, this is our last night together, isn't it?"

"It is." She let go of my hands and brought her arms around my waist, tilting her head to keep her eyes on mine. "We should make this a night to remember then, shouldn't we?"

As heavy as my heart felt, the glint in her eyes sent a ripple of lightness through my chest. I could forget about my worries for one night, couldn't I?

With a sly smile that matched Cora's, I shook the dark thoughts from my mind, reached for Cora's legs, and pulled them around my waist. She squealed with surprise as I lifted her, and her arms went around my neck. She was so small, her weight felt like nothing in my arms. "I can give you a night to remember, all right."

Her fingers stroked the back of my neck and tangled in my hair. "Then show me."

My lips met hers, her breath melded with mine, and nothing—neither dragons, nor Darius, nor goodbye—seemed to matter.

Cora

By the first light of dawn, I crept from the castle and into the stables. My quiver of arrows hung over my shoulder, its weight as comforting as an old friend. In one hand I carried my bow; in the other I held a lantern. I came to the stall I was looking for and set the lantern down. Hara whinnied and tossed her mane as I approached her.

"Hello, dear one," I said. "I think we're due for an adventure like old times." I stroked the side of her neck, regretting how seldom I'd been taking her for rides. We'd only been on a few rides over the previous months, either to strengthen our relationships with the council or to entertain nobles and allies. But my favorite rides—no cares, no worries, no agendas—had been reserved for Valorre. Hara didn't seem to hold it against me.

I got to work saddling her, not bothering to wake the stablemaster for assistance. My mission required secrecy anyway. Once Hara's saddle was secured, I began to stuff her saddlebags with supplies. At the sound of approaching footsteps, I whirled around and saw Teryn strolling into the stables.

He eyed me from head to toe, smiling. "You almost look the way you did when I first met you. Same braid. Same beautiful, determined face. Same weapons. New cloak, though."

"And no pants this time," I said, tugging at the skirt of my dark blue riding gown with a grin. "Who knew I'd need them again?"

Our eyes locked, our smiles diminished, and I looked away from him before my eyes could well with tears. It wouldn't help to start my journey with red, puffy eyes. Teryn came to my side, and together we finished readying Hara in silence. When our preparations were complete, we made our way out of the stables toward the forest. I peered at the windows of the castle as we passed, finding no prying eyes or curious stares following. It was still too early for most to be awake.

I closed my eyes and slowed my step as we entered the cover of the trees, feeling for Valorre.

I'm here, he said, and I could sense his closeness.

Hara tossed her mane as a flash of white appeared between tree trunks, and a moment later Valorre was beside me, rippling with a mix of excitement and apprehension.

Time to go? Valorre asked.

Yes, and we'll be taking a few others as well. How many can you hold at once on your back? Could you possibly carry two adults and one baby?

Valorre seemed slightly offended. *I am strong. I carried you and your friend long ago, didn't I? I was weak then.*

The memory moved through my mind, showing me a glimpse of Valorre carrying me and Maiya to safety from the cave I'd found him in. *You're right. I know you're strong.*

I can do it.

"They're here," Teryn said.

I turned as Mareleau and Larylis came toward us from the field, Liam bundled in Mareleau's arms. I jumped, seeing Queen Mother Helena trailing behind.

Mareleau followed my line of vision to glance at her mother. When she returned to face me, she kept her chin held high. "I told Mother everything. She deserved to know the truth before I disappeared without a reasonable explanation."

"And I insisted on seeing her off," Helena said. Her eyes darted from me to my companions. When her gaze fell on Valorre, it was her turn to jump.

Mareleau froze mid-step, as if noticing Valorre for the

first time as well. Her mouth fell open, but all she produced was a gasp.

I looked from Mareleau to Valorre and remembered she had only seen him once before, and it hadn't been under the best circumstances. "Mareleau, you remember Valorre. Queen Mother Helena, this is Valorre the unicorn." I blushed, realizing how absurd it was to formally introduce a unicorn.

Helena nodded. "I'd heard the stories about the unicorns on the battlefield at Centerpointe Rock, but I never thought I'd see one myself."

Mareleau's eyes were locked on Valorre as if she couldn't look away. "I'd barely given him more than a glance when I first saw him. I'd forgotten how beautiful he is."

Larylis put his arm over his wife's shoulders. "I feel the same way every time I see him."

Valorre watched Mareleau, still as stone. *I know her.*

Yes, I told him, *she was there when we destroyed the crystal.*

No, something else. Something before...

I cocked my head, sensing his struggle to grasp at memory. *What do you mean, something before? Before what?*

He shook his mane, and I could tell the memory was gone. *Mistaken. Or forgotten.*

"So, what's the plan?" Larylis asked, bringing my attention back to him and Mareleau. "Are we really going to do this crazy thing?"

Teryn's fingers laced through mine, and he gave my hand a squeeze. Warmth flooded my chest as my eyes met his. "Are you ready?" he asked.

I nodded. "I am."

10

TRAVEL

Cora

My throat felt tight as I sat upon Hara's back, looking down at Teryn. "Are you prepared with something to tell Lord Jonston and the council?" I asked.

"Yes," Teryn said. "I'll tell them King Larylis and Queen Mareleau insisted on returning home and hired a private guard to take them safely there under the cover of night. You went to formally name Liam our heir."

Helena narrowed her eyes at Teryn, as if considering the strength of his story, then nodded. She turned her attention to her daughter, who sat in front of Larylis on Valorre's back. "I'll follow as soon as I can, once the roads south are declared safe. Keep my grandson warm."

Mareleau could barely croak a goodbye, face pale and eyes wide as she trembled in her seat. Even Larylis seemed unsettled. The gently cooing Liam appeared to be the only one unperturbed by being on a unicorn.

Teryn placed his hand on mine, bringing my gaze to him. "I love you."

I swallowed the lump in my throat. We'd already said our goodbyes the night before, but it didn't make parting any easier. "I love you too."

With a shuddering sigh, he took a few steps back, which Helena mirrored. I brought Hara closer to Valorre, until their sides were almost touching.

"You really think you can do this?" Mareleau asked through chattering teeth. She pulled her riding cloak tighter around her and Liam, but I knew she wasn't shivering from the cold.

"We'll find out." I cringed at the trepidation in my voice. While I'd Traveled with Valorre once before, it had been a gamble and consisted of just the two of us. I had no idea if I would be able to include Hara, not to mention Mareleau, Larylis, and Liam. Even something as simple as a glamour had proved difficult in the past when I'd tried to include other people.

I shook the concerns from my head and turned to my companions. "You need to clear your minds as much as possible. Close your eyes and focus only on your breath."

"Easier said than done," Mareleau snapped.

"Just try." With a deep breath, I put one hand on Hara's neck and the other on Valorre's side, connecting them. Through Valorre, I sensed his riders. It was my intention to focus most of my power on Hara and Valorre, therefore including Valorre's riders with less effort. That was my theory, at least. Now it was time to see if I was right.

Breathe in. Breathe out.

I steadied my breath and pushed all thought from

my mind. I searched the energy around Valorre, probing it, drawing it in, until his riders seemed as if they were one with him, with me, with Hara. Still feeling the heat of Hara and Valorre beneath my palms, I shifted my focus to an expanse of field within a valley. At the center of the valley sat an old, weathered rock. Centerpointe Rock. Flashes of dark memories tugged at my mind, but I breathed them away, thinking only of the Rock. The valley was covered in a layer of frost, the light of the morning sun just beginning to touch the outer edges of the valley. Birds circled overhead beneath a clear sky. Icy air filled my nostrils. It was colder in the valley without the shelter of the forest trees.

I opened my eyes. The valley spread out before me within a ring of rolling hills. Centerpointe Rock loomed to my left. To my right stood Valorre with his three riders. I let out a deep breath. "We did it."

As the words left my mouth, my blood drained from my face, leaving me disoriented. My mind spun, the field swirling into a haze before my eyes as I slipped from Hara's saddle and onto the frosty field below.

~

Mareleau

I heard a thud and opened my eyes with a gasp. The forest was gone, replaced with an unfamiliar valley. I brought my attention to the feel of Larylis' arms, still strong about my waist, then looked down at Liam, who remained content and bundled in my arms.

Larylis let out a sigh of relief, his breath stirring my hair with its warmth. "She really did it."

"I almost can't believe it. Cora—" I looked to the side and found Hara's saddle empty. "Wait, where is she?"

Larylis sprang from Valorre's back, while Valorre stomped at the grass. I shifted side to side, wondering how to dismount from an unsaddled unicorn with an infant in my arms. Valorre circled Hara until I saw Cora lying limp on the ground. She mumbled as Larylis placed a hand on her shoulder.

"She's breathing," Larylis said. "I think she fainted."

I bit my lip. "She did warn us she may drain her strength if she succeeded at all."

Larylis nodded and lifted her into his arms. I ignored the squeeze I felt on my heart as I watched him carry her closer to the Rock. Once he laid her back down and covered her with her cloak, he returned to me and extended his arms. "I'll take Liam and help you down."

I placed our baby gently in Larylis' arms and slid from Valorre's back. Larylis placed a steadying hand on my waist as I stumbled to right myself. Once my feet were firmly planted, I turned in a slow circle and took in our surroundings. The wide expanse of field suddenly felt like a threat. There were no guards, no houses or villages in sight. Nothing but an old battlefield covered in frost where there once was blood. Or so I'd been told. "Are we crazy for doing this?"

"Yes," Larylis said, looking up from Liam to follow my gaze. "But we already made our choice. Cora needs to find that book and we need to be there for our people. Word of the dragons has likely already reached them. Besides, baby Liam deserves to be safe in his own home."

I looked up at the sky. "You don't think it will snow, do you?"

Larylis shook his head. "It rarely snows this late in the winter in Lela. Still, you and Liam need to keep warm. I'll start a fire while we wait for Cora to wake up. As soon as she wakes, we need to move to the nearest village."

Larylis kissed Liam with a tender smile before returning him to my arms. I sat down at the base of the Rock next to a sleeping Cora and watched Larylis start a fire, studying the determination in his eyes as he prodded sparks into flame. It was a look I'd seen on his face nearly every day since our confrontation with Morkai and the crystal. It was a look that told me he'd stop at nothing to protect me. Oddly enough, I found it unsettling.

We sat in silence as the warmth of the fire and the rising sun kept us safe from the chill in the air. Larylis' eyes kept darting around the field, hand on the hilt of his sword as if he were ready to spring at the slightest sign of movement.

By the time the sun was high in the sky, Cora began to stir. Her eyes fluttered open, and she pushed herself to sitting. With a hand pressed to her forehead, she looked from me to Larylis, then up at the sky, squinting under the sunlight. "I'm sorry. I hoped I wouldn't be out too long."

"It's all right," Larylis said. "Rest as long as you need. The nearest village is no more than an hour's ride from here. There we can get a traveling coach and make decent progress toward Dermaine before nightfall."

Cora looked around. "Where are Valorre and Hara?"

"Grazing at the edge of the field," Larylis said, pointing.

Cora turned to follow his direction, then sighed when she spotted the two creatures in the distance. "Give me a few more moments, then I'll call them back. After that, I'll be well enough to ride again."

"Very well." Larylis stood to repack our belongings while I got to my feet.

It felt good to stretch my legs, cramped from sitting on the cold earth so long. I took a few steps away from the Rock, eyes drawn to the legendary valley. Even under the full illumination of the sun, it made me shudder to think how many men had died here. I stole a glance at Larylis, wondering what it was like for him to be back in a place where he'd once seen such terrors.

A distant sound stole my attention, and I returned to face the expanse of field. The sound was a rhythmic beating, slowly growing louder, closer. A shadow crept over the sun, and I lifted my eyes toward the source. An enormous pair of wings beat the sky above, soaring from one end of the valley to the other. I shivered at the sight, knowing it could only be one thing. *Dragon.* As the creature reached the far end over the hills, it slowly turned until it faced our direction. Its white wings spread out and stilled as the dragon drifted lower and landed at the far end of the valley.

My heart hammered in my chest as I stood frozen. My legs quaked, but I couldn't get them to run as the dragon took a step forward. Even from far away, I could see its tongue flicking in and out of its mouth, head bobbing on its long, sinuous neck.

Larylis darted in front of me, sword drawn in one hand and a shield in the other. The dragon opened its maw and erupted with a loud screech. Cora rushed to my other side, arrow nocked into her bow.

"Get back, Mare!" Larylis shouted.

I looked from him to the dragon, wondering how he expected to face the creature with nothing but a sword and shield. My eyes darted toward Cora, her daring bow seeming more like a toy as I compared it to the size of our foe.

The dragon took a few hesitant steps forward, head weaving side to side. I eyed its opalescent scales, blindingly bright where they reflected the light of the sun. Long, pointed teeth filled its open mouth, appearing more threatening with every step it took.

Larylis slashed the air with his sword, as if that would deter it from coming closer.

"Your sword won't stop it," Cora said under her breath. I knew she was right. How could pathetic human weapons stop creatures from a magical realm?

Then it dawned on me. *They came from a magical realm. Perhaps* magic *can stop them...magic that I supposedly have.*

Again, the dragon moved forward, faster now, taking one lurching step after another. I searched within myself, trying to summon whatever powers I had. *What do I do? What do I do?* I'd never consciously used my powers before. How was I supposed to use them in the face of a towering beast? This wasn't some unwanted engagement; I couldn't simply glamour myself to be ugly.

Then I remembered what Cora had said about me using the Arts to save Liam. *How did I do it? Can I do it again? Can I protect us all?* I closed my eyes and focused on Liam, feeling the weight of him in my arms. Warmth spread through my heart and radiated outward. A smile tugged at my lips as I lifted my chin. *Of course I can. I'm the Mother of Prophecy.*

The ground rumbled beneath me, and I opened my eyes to see the dragon surge forward with increasing speed. I tried to keep my focus on the warmth of my power, on Liam, on protection, but the dragon was growing dangerously near.

The warmth was gone. I felt nothing. My power was useless.

With a shriek, I retreated until I felt the Rock against my back. Cora and Larylis followed, standing just before me. Cora pulled her arrow back and released it. It looked as if the arrow would strike the dragon's eye, but before it could meet its mark, the dragon blinked. The arrow glanced off its shield of scales and fell to the ground. With a screech, the dragon opened its mouth, a fiery glow illuminated from within. Larylis crouched, ready to spring forward with his sword.

"Get down, both of you!" Cora shouted. Before I realized what was happening, Cora dropped her bow and rolled to the ground. I folded my body over Liam and sank to the base of the Rock. A hand found my ankle and grasped it tight as heat seared overhead. A screech echoed through the valley as rumbling steps came near. Just when I was certain the dragon would be upon us, the sound of its steps passed behind and began to grow fainter. After a moment, the sound of wings beating air pulsed at the other end of the field, then rose overhead. I refused to lift my eyes until the field had returned to silence.

"What happened?" I muttered, meeting Cora's eyes as

she lifted her head. Behind her, Larylis was on his hands and knees with Cora's hand on his shoulder.

Cora looked at the sky before she removed her hands from me and Larylis. "Our weapons weren't going to work on the creature," she said, "so I glamoured us at the last moment."

"How do you know they wouldn't work?" Larylis' cheeks were red, eyes burning with fury as he got to his feet. "I could have tried."

"The archers couldn't bring it down," Cora said. "An arrow to the eye did nothing. I doubt your sword would have done more than tickle it."

Larylis threw his shield down with a scowl and rammed his sword into its sheath. "Why did I bring these things then, if not to protect the woman I love?"

I then understood the source of his anger. He'd been prevented from protecting me, from following his strongest driving force. I could relate. I'd tried to protect us all. And failed.

"What did you glamour us as?" I asked, to change the subject. Liam whimpered in my arms, and I brought my lips to his head to soothe him.

"I glamoured us as part of Centerpointe Rock."

I raised an eyebrow. "A rock? What would stop the dragon from burning a rock?"

Cora shrugged. "What would stop the dragon from doing *anything*? At least I did something...and it worked. It's gone."

She was right. *She* did something—exactly what I couldn't do. If she hadn't acted, if she'd still been asleep when the dragon came, we likely wouldn't be alive. I looked down at Liam and shuddered. *I'm just as useless as ever before.* It took all the willpower I had to force myself to mutter, "Thank you."

"Are Valorre and Hara safe?" Larylis asked, scanning the field.

Cora nodded. "As soon as I saw the dragon, I told Valorre to take Hara up the hill to hide beneath the trees. They were gone before the dragon even landed."

Larylis sighed. "We need to do the same. The sooner we get to the village, the better."

I swallowed the lump in my throat. "Will we be any safer in a village? In a traveling coach? The dragons weren't supposed to be this far south in the first place."

"I know." Cora's eyes locked on mine, then fell on Liam. "It's almost like it followed us."

Silence grew heavy around us, and I tried to ignore the terrifying questions that pounded through my head. *How did it find us? Who is it following? Is it...Liam?*

Cora turned away and began to walk toward the surrounding hills. "Stay close to me. If you hear even a hint of wings, crouch down and grab hold of me."

I wanted to scoff at her order, to argue that I didn't need her protection. I wanted to tell her that Larylis' sword was enough. I wanted to demand she show me how to use my powers then and there, so I never had to rely on her—or anyone—again. But the memory of wings, of gnashing teeth, of scales, of flame, crept into my mind, and I kept my retorts to myself. With a heavy heart, I followed close on Cora's heels and ascended the hill.

11

SEEKING

Teryn

"Do you think they made it yet?" Queen Mother Helena asked in a quiet voice as she stared out the window of my study.

I jumped, having forgotten her presence. She'd asked to sit with me that morning, and although she did nothing more than stare out a window while I tended to my duties, she seemed comforted by my company. *I suppose that's what sharing a secret will do.*

I turned to her. "They should be close, if not there already. Larylis said he'd send a messenger when they arrived, but that message could still be days away from reaching us."

"Couldn't Queen Coralaine simply...do what she does? Use her magic to show up here and tell us they made it safe?" She wrinkled her nose, as if talk of magic left an unsavory taste in her mouth.

"I suppose she could," I said, rubbing my brow. "But it

isn't what we discussed. She has work to do at Dermaine, and she still doesn't fully understand her power to Travel. I'd never ask her to use it more than necessary."

Helena drummed her fingers on the windowsill. "What if something went wrong? What if it didn't work? What if the magic...failed?" She spun toward me. "Am I crazy for agreeing to such a plan? Just a few days ago, I knew of magic only from what I'd heard about the Battle at Centerpointe Rock. Now I discover Queen Coralaine has magic. Even my own daughter...Then I saw a unicorn..."

I stood and went to her, extending my hand toward an empty chair. "Come, sit. Staring out that window isn't going to bring her back any sooner."

Helena glared, then gave in, sinking into the chair as I poured her some tea. "Thank you," Helena mumbled, then brought the cup to her lips. "Sometimes I think I'd be better off if Mareleau had left me in the dark. But I asked for this."

"I know it's a lot to take in. Even Queen Bethaeny..." My chest felt tight as I thought of my mother. She'd grown so tired since my father's death. It was as if she'd managed to remain strong only long enough to see me and my brother secured in our futures before retiring. My heart ached, wondering if Mother might not be far from joining Father in the otherlife.

"She doesn't know, does she?" Helena asked. "About what Mareleau told me?"

I shook my head. "I don't think she'd want to know either. My father's death was hard on her."

Helena nodded. "I know. Our pains have been much the same. It's been a comfort to have her living at Verlot with me, even though we spend most of our time in silence when she isn't feeling ill. I'd say it's a shame she didn't come to your coronation, but I believe she's much safer at Verlot."

A knock sounded at the door, offering a welcome distraction from the lump in my throat. I turned toward the door as a messenger entered.

"I have the day's reports, Your Majesty," the messenger said.

I nodded, prompting him to deliver his news.

"It's been more of the same, Your Majesty," he began. "The scouts have followed the dragons' movements. They seem to remain mostly in northern Kero. More crops have been burned, more livestock taken. In addition, two dragon sightings were reported in Vera."

I paled and forced my voice to remain steady. "Where in Vera?"

"One sighting was reported near Borden. Another to the northeast, near the Vera-Kero border. The sightings were likely regarding the same dragon, Your Majesty."

Borden. That's near Centerpointe Rock. "Were any casualties reported?"

"Cattle, sheep, and crops, Your Majesty."

"No...people?"

"No, Your Majesty."

I let out a heavy sigh. Out of the corner of my eye, I caught Helena doing the same. "Anything else? Any word about the King of Syrus?"

"No, Your Majesty, but the scouts should be reaching Risa any day now. If there is any information to gain about the Northern Islands, we should receive word shortly."

"Very well. Thank you," I said, dismissing him. I returned to my desk, but my eyes refused to focus on my work. *A dragon in Vera. Near Centerpointe Rock. Could it be a coincidence?*

"By the Gods, they better make it to Dermaine safely," Helena muttered.

"Make it there safe," I said, my stomach sinking. "And find that book."

∿

Cora

After arriving at Dermaine without further encounters with the dragon, I thought the hardest of my trials were over. But as I stepped into the enormous palace library, I was hit with a sense of dread and felt immediately over-whelmed. How was I supposed to find a book I'd never seen before amongst the endless shelves before me?

"I hope Lex was right about that book," Larylis said, eyes scanning the shelves as if he were thinking the same thing.

"He was." The confidence in my tone didn't match the worry in my mind. What if Lex had, in fact, been wrong? What if the book was nowhere to be found? What if Lex had remembered the title wrong? I shook the questions away. "Even Teryn said he recalled the book Lex mentioned."

"Well, let us hope it's still here then," Larylis said. "I can't imagine why a book like that would be here in the first place."

Looking around at the pristine tables, the bright light

streaming in through the tall windows, and the clean, straight spines of the books on the shelves, I could see why he would doubt such a thing. Dermaine's library had the feel of a purely academic environment. There was nothing mystical about the place. *Perhaps that will make the book easier to find.*

Larylis faced me. "I must meet with the council. I've made sure you will have the library to yourself, but if you need help, don't hesitate to send a guard to fetch a scribe. Also, I'm sure Mareleau would be happy to assist if you need her."

I nodded, although I wasn't sure he was right about Mareleau. She'd barely said a word to me since our encounter with the dragon.

He gave me a bow and left for his meeting, leaving me to the quiet of the empty library. I walked along the perimeter of the room, scanning titles, and looking for anything that stood out. *But what am I looking for? History? Mythology? There certainly won't be a section on magic.*

A sense of panic crushed my chest, making my breathing grow shallow. Just as my head began to spin, I closed my eyes and breathed in deeply. *I can do this...a different way.*

Keeping my eyes closed, I ran my hand along the shelves, reaching toward different books, sensing, seeking. *Where are you?* I thought of El'Ara, of the stories I'd been told. I thought about Satsara, Ailan, and Darius, seeking their resonance amongst the pages around me.

Finally, I felt a pull. I opened my eyes and turned toward one of the bookcases along the far wall. The air felt as if it were sizzling around me the nearer I came. As

I approached it, my eyes were drawn toward the top. *It's there.*

I whirled around, seeking one of the long, rolling ladders, and pushed it in front of the bookcase. With hands gripped tight around the rungs, I pulled myself up, feeling my inner fire burning brighter and brighter. Then I stopped.

A row of books spread before me with seemingly unrelated titles. They appeared to be works of fiction. I ran my finger along the spines until I found what I was looking for. *The Once and Former Magic of Ancient Lela.*

My hands trembled as I retrieved the book, and I had to force my legs to remain steady as I descended the ladder. Once my feet were planted on the ground, I sank to my bottom and curled my legs beneath me.

I stared at the plain, brown leather cover etched with a simple, gold script that formed the title. There was no further annotation, not even an author name. I thumbed open the cover to the pages within. I gently turned the thin paper until I reached the inner title page. *The Once and Former Magic of Ancient Lela. By A.I. Lan.*

My heart raced. *A.I. Lan. Ailan.*

In my hands was a book written by Ailan herself. My face broke into a grin, and I was barely able to contain the excitement flooding my chest. *I've found you. Now, let's see what secrets you have for me.*

12

THE BOOK

Mareleau

The library was dark, lit by a flickering lantern as I slowly circled the table, gently bouncing Liam to sleep in my arms. My eyes darted to Cora, brow furrowed as she scanned a page in the book. I'd been watching her read for over an hour, yet not once did she look up to share any revelations with me. I felt bored and unproductive, yet anything was better than sitting alone, waiting for Larylis to return from his meeting while I forced myself not to think about dragons. "Anything yet?"

Cora shook her head, and my stomach sank. I passed behind her chair and saw she was nearing the final pages. My heart hammered in my chest. *The book is almost done! How has she found nothing useful to share?* I suppressed a grumble and took a seat across from her. *Perhaps she just doesn't want to talk about it yet.*

I watched as Cora turned the final page, eyes

lingering longer than it should have taken her to read the few short paragraphs. Then, with a slam, she closed the book.

My eyes widened. "What? What is it?"

She leaned back in her chair and crossed her arms. "Why would Ailan write this?"

"Cora, you have to tell me *something*. What did you learn?"

Her eyes slowly slid to meet mine. "Nothing."

I felt the blood leave my face. "Nothing? Literally nothing?"

"Nothing useful whatsoever," she said. "The entire book was nothing but a mundane story describing Le'Lana in the barest of terms. It was presented as a tale of fiction, but there was no plot and not one character was introduced. There was no mention of Satsara, Ailan, or Darius. Not even the words Morkara, Elvan, or Faeran were used. The last page was the only thing that held even the slightest relevance, and even it told me nothing useful."

"What did it say?" I asked. Cora pushed the book toward me, and I eagerly flipped to the end. I turned to the final page.

However, the kingdom of Le'Lana couldn't last forever. A devastating battle swept the land. The queen of the land cast a spell to put an end to the fight and keep the magic safe forevermore. Yet, the spell could not be completed as planned. Once the spell was ended, a small part of Le'Lana remained. The former kingdom of Le'Lana and the magic land surrounding it disappeared into the mists, while Lela was born into a new world.

The survivors from Le'Lana who now resided in Lela continued on with their Ancient traditions. Some say you can still catch glimpses of them. Some say you can still feel their Ancient magic. Some say their descendants live on today in groups called the Forest People.

Thus ends the tale of the Once and Former Magic of Ancient Lela.

I flipped to the next page, finding nothing but blank paper. "That can't be all. Are you sure there was nothing else?"

Cora rubbed her temples and sighed. "I'll read it again tomorrow and see if I can glean any further meaning. Perhaps there was truth between the lines, and I was just too tired to see it."

I refused to accept I'd faced death to get to Dermaine for nothing. "Are you sure there wasn't something? What about the part about the Forest People? Is it not strange that she mentioned the very people who raised you?"

"It isn't news to me," she said. "I was raised with tales about how the Ancient Faeran were the ancestors of the Forest People. Once I learned about the veil, it finally made sense how that came to be. When the veil was completed, whoever remained in the central part of Le'Lana was left behind and forced into our world. The Faeran of Lela eventually became the Forest People."

"But Ailan was Elvan, wasn't she?" I asked. "If she wrote this, then she obviously knew of the Forest People, who you say once were Faeran. Did the Forest People never mention what happened to the Elvan people? If Ailan knew of them, they should have known about her—"

"That's it!" Cora's eyes grew wide as she shot to her feet. "She knew about *them*. The Forest People have been living in secret for hundreds of years. Hardly anyone knows of them, but *she* did. She may have even lived amongst them, at least for a time."

"Then why have you never heard of her?"

Cora paced along the length of the table. "She hid her identity in writing this book, calling herself A.I. Lan. Perhaps she hid her identity amongst the Forest People too. They may have heard of her without even realizing it."

"How will you find out? If she hid her identity, she probably didn't want to be known."

Cora's face fell for a moment, then her eyes slid to the book. "Why else write that? Why else write something so bland unless it contained a fragment of truth that she wanted someone to discover? Perhaps she *wants* to be found, but only by the right people. We have one clue, and I'm going to follow it."

The determination in her eyes and in the set of her shoulders made me feel small. I could never be brave like her. Could I? "You're going to the Forest People, aren't you?"

She brought a nail between her teeth and returned to pacing. "I must go immediately."

"What about the dragons?" Fear seized my mind as an enormous shadow danced in my memory.

"I won't need to worry about them," she said with a shrug. "If I can find Salinda in my heart and mind, I can find the Forest People and Travel straight there."

I looked down at Liam, sleeping peacefully, yet all I

could see was fire. "What about me? And Liam? What if the dragon comes for us here at Dermaine?"

Cora paused and studied my face, and I was sure she could see the terror that shattered my core. "You'll be safe here," she said, although her tone was unconvincing.

I blinked away the tears that threatened to spill from my eyes and stood from my seat, shoulders back and chin high in an attempt to emulate her brave composure. "Of course."

It seemed to convince Cora. Her eyes left my face, and she went to retrieve the book from the table. "I'll leave first thing tomorrow."

As she swept across the room toward the door, I felt something stirring in my chest. A fire, but not the fire of fear. It rose to my throat, and my shoulders trembled with the effort to keep it at bay. Before Cora could reach the door, I released it. "Wait."

She turned to face me, brow raised.

Within me, two forces raged at one another. One was a flame of calm determination that compelled my legs to move toward Cora, certain of what I had to do. The other was a shadow of fear, shouting and screaming at me to stay silent, stay safe. I followed the force of calm, of truth, and stood before Cora. "Did you mean what you said about the Forest People? That they would help me train in the Arts?"

Cora looked surprised as she nodded. "Yes."

"Then you aren't leaving without me."

Larylis

With dragging feet, I made my way up the stairs to my room. The council meeting had lasted most of the day. My mind felt like a pile of mush, and as expected, no progress had been made against the dragons. No one knew a thing about them. We could do nothing more than what Teryn was doing at Ridine—send scouts to watch the skies, ready our archers, and send word to our people to stay indoors whenever possible. At least I'd been successful at planting the rumor about the King of Syrus like Teryn had done.

Now all of Lela is aware of you, Darius. Watching. Waiting.

As I approached my chamber, I was surprised to see light flickering beneath the door. *Mareleau must still be awake.* At least I had her to look forward to.

I opened the door and found Mareleau in bed lying on her side, eyes open, facing a bassinet on a stand beside the bed. "This is the first night he's slept outside my arms," she said without looking at me.

I began to undress, pulling my tunic over my head. "You don't seem too happy about that."

"He feels so far away in that cold thing." She frowned at the bassinet.

I couldn't help but smile. Never had I imagined Mareleau would become so tender in motherhood. I was certain she'd be a good mother, but I'd figured she'd follow tradition and turn Liam over to a wet nurse for most of the day. I was reminded that there was still much to learn about the woman who was my wife.

Once undressed, I climbed into bed next to Mareleau,

feeling my muscles and bones melt into the comfort of the blankets. I put an arm around Mareleau and nestled my face into the back of her neck, breathing in the scent of her skin and hair. It was enough to lull me to sleep.

"Larylis."

My eyes shot open. Mareleau was stiff in my arms. "Yes?"

"There's something I need to tell you."

The trepidation in her voice returned my mind to wakefulness. I sat up and rubbed my eyes. "What is it?"

She rolled onto her back. "Cora found the book."

I put a hand to my forehead, surprised I'd forgotten to even ask how the search had gone. Relief flooded my chest as I leaned on my elbow. "That's great! Did she read it?"

Mareleau nodded. "It wasn't as helpful as we'd hoped, but it did give her a clue about the Forest People."

"The Forest People?"

"Ailan mentioned them in the book," she said. "So there's a chance they knew something of her."

"I suppose that's an important clue," I said, wondering why Mareleau still seemed so tense. "Is that all?"

She sat up, facing me. "She's leaving tomorrow morning to find them. I'm going with her."

Shock tore through me, followed by fear, then anger. The more her words echoed through my mind, the less sense they made. "What are you talking about? Why would you go with her?"

She lifted her chin, and her words came out firm and steady. "I want to train my powers in the Arts. Cora says the Forest People can help me."

"There's time for that later. Your place is here with me. And Liam."

Her expression faltered before returning to its stony mask. "Obviously, I'll be taking Liam with me. I have already decided. This is important to me."

The calm in her voice unsettled me, but I forced myself to counter her words with reason. "All right. Then I'll come with you. I'll tell the council—"

"No." Finally, her face fell, tears glazing her eyes. "Lare, the council needs you here. Our people need you. I can't take you away—"

"If our people need me, then they need you too. You're their queen."

She shook her head. "You are King of Vera, and they need you more."

"I don't care!" I shouted. "If you are leaving, then so am I. I've sworn to protect you, to protect Liam. I will watch this kingdom burn before I let you be in danger."

She opened her mouth, then snapped it shut along with her eyes. She lowered her head with a sigh. "There was a time when that kind of dedication to me would have filled me with joy. But something is changing. Something inside me is burning, telling me that isn't right."

Heat rose to my cheeks followed by a deep shame. Was it because she was scolding me? Or because she was right? "I don't care. It's the truth."

"Lare, I have to do this. I'm tired of being helpless. I'm tired of not knowing how to protect myself or the people I love."

I clenched my jaw. "I forbid you to leave."

Mareleau lifted her head and narrowed her eyes at me, cheeks a fiery red. Her voice came out cold. "Is that really what you want to do? Forbid me? Control me? Is that what it means to be my husband?"

My chest heaved as I stared back at her, fury burning my veins. Then my shoulders fell, and the fury melted away to reveal what it had been hiding—fear, shame, agonizing pain. "No," I croaked, tears stinging my eyes. "No, I didn't mean that."

Mareleau's posture relaxed, her face softening as tears trailed down her cheeks. "Larylis, I love you. I love how badly you want to protect me. You know I've always loved your reckless passion. But things are different now. Almost overnight, our entire world has changed. There's something happening that is bigger than me. Bigger than *us*.

"All my life I've felt useless and unimportant. I've felt stifled and unheard. To combat that, I manipulated others to get my way, acted more important than I felt. It made me selfish and cold and cruel, and not once did I regret it. When I felt small, I inflated myself so that I could feel bigger, stronger, better than others. Now that I know I'm meant for more, that I have a bigger role than I ever imagined, I feel smaller than ever. Yet, I have this feeling I can do something about that.

"I don't know what it means to be the Mother of Prophecy, but it has given me a sense of purpose. I'm not willing to let that go. I'm not willing to continue to feel powerless in the face of danger. I want to know what I'm capable of."

"I understand," I whispered. "Just let me come with you."

She reached a hand to my cheek. "I want to say yes.

You have no idea how badly I want to. But it isn't right. You have a duty to perform, and so do I."

Her words felt like lightning tearing at my heart. How could I let her leave without me? How could I let her take Liam, my son, whom I'd barely had a chance to love and hold? Yet, she was right. I couldn't leave Vera without a king when I'd only just returned. Teryn had let Cora come here on her own. Why couldn't I let Mareleau do the same?

I am no one without her.

The words came from deep within, heavy as stone as I lifted them to the surface of my mind. Were they true? Was I obsessed with protecting her for her safety? Or for mine?

Who am I without her? Am I a king? Or a fool?

I didn't know the answer, but as I searched the eyes of the woman I loved, I saw something new in them. She was growing, searching, changing. There was only one thing I could do; I had to support her.

I had to let her go.

13

FERRAH

Cora

In the shadows before dawn, I waited in Dermaine's palace gardens, listening for sounds of hoof beats and footsteps. The gardens weren't nearly as elegant and intricate as the ones at Verlot, but they provided the cover and quiet we needed for our early morning mission.

The hoof beats came first, almost too quiet to hear. Hara tossed her mane as a hint of white shone behind a high wall of shrubbery. Valorre approached and nuzzled my shoulder. I stroked the side of his neck, but my muscles remained tensed as I extended my hearing and listened for any sign that we weren't alone.

Mareleau had assured me the gardens would be secured until well after sunrise but sneaking Valorre onto unfamiliar grounds sent my heart racing. Our mission could be upended with just one set of curious eyes, one unruly maid sneaking about in the dark, one misplaced guard. I longed for the cover of trees, for the quiet of my beloved forests, but the land surrounding Dermaine was flat for miles. The gardens were the best we could manage while attracting the least amount of attention.

I pulled my cloak tighter around me, trying to ignore the icy air that stung my nostrils. After years of living in makeshift tents amongst the Forest People, all it took was a few months of living in a castle to lower my tolerance for cold. However, the Forest People were always prepared for winter and didn't tend to suffer from the season. I knew they would be settled somewhere in western Kero, where the winter was mildest. The tents would be made from skins instead of cloth, and soups and teas made with warming herbs and spices would be boiling over the cook fires.

Footsteps sounded down the garden path, pulling me from my thoughts. I held my breath as I waited for the approaching figure to be revealed.

"Cora?" Mareleau's voice came out in a loud whisper. "Are you here?"

I let out a sigh of relief and walked forward just as Mareleau's shadowed silhouette rounded the corner. "I'm here." As she came nearer, I was struck with a sudden sorrow that seemed to echo in the puffy skin around her eyes and the down-turned corners of her lips. I breathed in deeply, then exhaled, releasing the feelings that had seeped into me. "Are you all right, Mare?"

Liam squirmed in her arms, as if he too could sense his mother's pain, and Mareleau began to bounce him gently. "I'll be fine."

As eager as I was to take her words as truth and begin

our journey, I knew she was anything but fine. "What's wrong? You can tell me."

Her eyes locked on mine, and for a moment, I was certain she would snap at me to leave her alone. Then her shoulders dropped, and her eyes fell on Liam. "Leaving Larylis behind feels horrible. Yet, on the other hand, it feels like the right thing to do." She lifted her head, and I could see trails of fresh tears moving down her face. "I have no idea if I'm making the right choice. I don't know what feeling to listen to."

"You're beginning to touch on your inner guidance, aren't you?"

She shrugged. "I don't know what it is, and I'm not sure if I like it."

"I know what it is," I said. "It can feel scary and confusing at first, but it's a sign your gifts in the Arts are growing. It's hard to know what feelings to trust, but the more you follow them, the more you will learn what feelings are your true inner guidance and which ones are of fear."

She nodded but didn't seem comforted by my words.

I placed a hand on her arm. "I know what you're going through. If you aren't ready, you don't have to do this. You don't have to come with me."

She lifted her chin, her jaw set. "Yes, I do. I don't know if I'm making the right choice, but I know I have to do this anyway."

"Then we need to leave," I said, my voice gentle. I gave her a comforting smile, then turned toward Hara and Valorre and climbed into Hara's saddle. "I'll have you ride Valorre again."

She looked from me to Valorre, then down at Liam,

and I realized she was debating how to climb upon Valorre without aid. Larylis had helped her mount the first time.

Valorre, she needs help. Stand near the bench so she can climb onto your back.

You never need help, he said.

I pressed my lips together to suppress my smirk. *She isn't me.*

Valorre followed my instructions and moved alongside a nearby bench. When Mareleau saw what he was doing she turned to me and lifted Liam away from her chest. She hesitated before looking up at me. "Here, hold him."

My mouth fell open at the bundle before me. With trembling arms that seemed to move too slow, I took hold of Liam. My eyes slid down to meet his round, puffy face, tiny fists that reached out of his swaddling. Pain seared my throat as my eyes searched his, a sob fighting to escape my chest. In my arms was the very thing I'd never have.

The very thing I should have had. The very thing that was taken from me because of her.

I shuddered at my own thoughts and pushed them away, breathing deeply to keep my tears at bay. *Those thoughts are not mine. That is not me.*

When I lifted my eyes, Mareleau was on Valorre's back. As Valorre came alongside Hara, Mareleau leaned toward me and extended her arms. "Thank you," she said.

I passed Liam to her, but pain still pounded in my heart as I watched her pull him close and kiss his forehead.

"Is something wrong?" Mareleau asked, wrinkling her brow.

I started, my eyes snapping to her face. "Nothing. Let's go." I closed my eyes and breathed the pain away, draining my thoughts and worries with it. It took much longer than usual to clear my mind, but after a few moments, my heart was at ease. I extended my hand to Valorre, feeling the warmth of his smooth coat beneath my palm, sensing his presence, sensing his two riders. My other hand rested on Hara, and I felt the connection between us all. I was ready.

My mind moved to the Forest People, picking up the thoughts I'd left earlier. I saw the fur-covered tents and smelled the warming spices wafting over the pre-dawn cook fires. Some of the Forest People were awake, moving in shadows as they prepared for the day's hunt, while others still slumbered in their tents. I felt a stab of guilt, knowing I was about the shatter the peace of their morning with my arrival, but it needed to be done.

I refocused on the sights, the sounds, and the smells. I could sense Salinda's tent, almost hear her even breathing. My heart called to her.

Her eyes snapped open, and she sat upright on her cot. Wrapping a heavy cloak around her shoulders, she rose and stepped outside her tent, eyes searching.

My mind pulled away, past the clearing where the cookfires burned, to the trees that surrounded camp. I could still smell aromas of camp, still feel the warmth of the bodies in their tents, still hear the gentle sounds that hummed within, yet they were slightly muffled from my place under the trees.

I opened my eyes and found myself there, behind the

tree line at the edge of the clearing. At my side was Valorre, Mareleau and Liam safe upon his back. "We're here."

Mareleau opened her eyes and jumped. "I don't know if I'll ever get used to this," she said, taking in her new surroundings.

Moments later, we entered the camp, leaving Hara and Valorre to wait safely behind. My lids were half-closed as I led the way, searching for the pair of eyes that equally sought me in return. Then I saw her.

Salinda paused mid-step, shock and pleasure mingling in her features as she darted toward me and pulled me into a crushing embrace. As she pulled away, she scanned me from head to toe. "My dear, you have gotten so strong." Her eyes moved to Mareleau, who hovered behind me. "And this time you brought friends."

I nodded.

She grinned at Mareleau, but when her eyes returned to mine, her smile faded. "Why do I get the feeling this isn't a lighthearted visit?"

"It might not be," I said, trying to keep from wringing my hands like an anxious child in Salinda's powerful presence. She was shorter than I was, yet she held so much wisdom and calm in her demeanor, it made her seem as if she were fifty feet tall. No matter how intimidated I felt around her, I knew she would listen. "Can we talk?"

∾

INSIDE SALINDA'S TENT, I KEPT MY VOICE LOW. MARELEAU sat beside me with Liam on the cot while Salinda sat across from us, listening patiently while I spoke. For the most part, Salinda's expression remained neutral, aside from the occasional furrowed brow as I described my time in El'Ara and some of the stranger facts I shared.

When I was through, Salinda looked down at her hands and sighed. "That's a lot to take in."

My heart hammered with the effort it took not to bombard her with a flood of questions. I chose one to start with. "Have any of you encountered the dragons?"

"No, this is the first I'm hearing about them. We have been at camp since the start of winter and haven't needed to travel far. Perhaps they haven't flown this far west."

"What about the things I told you about El'Ara? Did you know about any of it?"

She stood and crossed her arms, grasping her elbows as her eyes unfocused, a haunted look on her face. "Much of what you've said has never been part of our knowledge. Do you really think this Darius, King of Syrus, is still alive?"

I nodded. "Perhaps Ailan too. Have you heard of either of them?"

She shook her head. "We learned the stories of the Ancient war, about the Morkaius versus the Morkara, but we were never told the names of those who fought. We learned that we were descendants of the Ancient Ones, carrying the legacy of the Faeran, but we were never taught that Lela was a land from another realm. I'd always thought our ancestors were from another time, not another place."

My stomach sank. Had I come to the Forest People for no reason after all? I gritted my teeth, searching for an angle to unearth the truth I sought. "What about the

Elvan? Were you taught what happened to them? If the Faeran settled as the Forest People, how did the Elvan settle? Did the Forest People ever speak of Elvan visitors or allies?"

Salinda frowned, squinting as if she were trying to access long-forgotten memories. "No," she finally said. "We were taught mostly about the Faeran. I'd always assumed the Elvan disappeared long before the Faeran became the Forest People."

Her lack of knowledge about the Elvan explained why my childhood stories about them had been so inaccurate. "What about the elders? Perhaps if I meet with them, tell them what I know, someone will remember something. Nalia must know something—"

"Nalia is not well." Salinda pressed her lips tight together and returned to sitting, her shoulders slumped and her face looking more tired than I'd ever seen. "She hasn't left her tent all week and refuses visitors and treatment. Some think she is preparing to enter the otherlife."

A sharp pain shot through my heart. Nalia had been our beloved Wise Woman since I'd arrived with the Forest People. She'd always kept a smile on her face, her bearing of wisdom and grace even more pronounced than Salinda's. Even though she'd been a woman of few words, she was the most respected and honored person amongst her people. "I'm so sorry," I whispered.

Salinda's lips pulled into a sad smile. "She has lived a full life. I'd say she has been like a mother to me, but in truth, she's been a mother to us all. There isn't a single person among us who hasn't known her all their lives."

Mareleau shifted anxiously next to me, and my eyes shot to her. She and Liam had been so quiet, I'd almost forgotten their presence, but now she seemed unable to contain her composure any longer. "What is it?" I asked.

She looked from me to Salinda, cheeks blazing, looking flustered as she searched for words. "It's just...it seems our visit has been for nothing in terms of the information we needed. Please tell me you can at least help *me*."

Salinda narrowed her eyes as if she were seeing Mareleau for the first time. "Yes, why have you brought this friend of yours?"

"It's part of the prophecy," I said. "I never fully explained—"

Shouts erupted from the camp, followed by a call to arms. We rushed out of the tent and met a flurry of commotion. A rhythmic sound came from up ahead, and I lifted my eyes to see a dark shadow descending from the pale morning sky over the camp. Archers and spearmen circled the clearing, shooting at the beast as it lowered toward the ground. Their useless weapons fell back to the ground as soon as they hit their invulnerable target.

It was the same white dragon we'd seen twice before. Its tongue flicked in and out of its mouth as it landed, its piercing gaze searching the crowd of screaming, scurrying people, scanning the camp from end to end. Then it stilled. Its eyes seemed locked straight ahead. Straight at me.

Mareleau stiffened at my side. *Or, perhaps, straight at her.*

My heart raced as I sought Valorre. *Safe. Hidden,* he assured me from his place outside the camp. I could sense his distress, his instinct to flee.

The archers continued to shoot the dragon, and a few

men ran forward with flaming torches. This caught the dragon's eye, and it arched back. The dragon screeched and hissed, pulling its neck back and opening its mouth.

No! I looked at the terrified faces around me, at the tents that would burn with ease. This was no castle. There was nowhere to hide, no way I could glamour an entire camp to keep them safe. I trembled from head to toe as I searched my mind for a solution.

There was nothing. I was about to die. My people were about to die.

The dragon lunged forward.

"Ferrah!" A loud voice boomed over the chaos, quieting the camp at once.

The dragon froze, snapping its mouth shut, while the people turned toward the source of the voice.

A tall woman with slender limbs and brown skin walked slowly toward the dragon, hand outstretched. Her feet were bare while long, black hair trailed down her back. The hem of her deerskin dress barely reached far enough to cover her hips, exposing most of her thighs as if it were meant for a much smaller person. Even though I could only see her in profile, I knew I'd never seen her before. "Who is she?" I whispered to Salinda.

Either Salinda didn't know or didn't want to say, because she gave me no answer.

The shocked crowd parted as the woman made her way closer to the dragon. The archers and spearmen kept their weapons trained on the beast but didn't loose them as their eyes locked on the approaching woman. "Ferrah," she said again, this time her voice gentle and soothing.

The dragon seemed to relax, its tail resting on the ground as it lowered its neck, almost like a bow. A thrumming sound, like a hum or a purr, reverberated from its chest.

"That's right, Ferrah," the woman said. "You're safe. I'm here."

Silence continued to envelop the camp as the dragon brought its nose to her palm, eyes closing as it continued its contented humming.

Liam cried.

The dragon lifted its head, but it remained where it was. The mysterious woman turned around and faced us. Her eyes locked on me, then focused on Mareleau, who was trying to hush her son. There was something about the woman that unsettled me as she began to walk toward us. Something familiar.

Those eyes, an unforgettable shade of gray, looking so much like ones once surrounded by layers of wrinkles...

That dress, too short and tight for the body that wore it, looking so similar to one once worn by...

"Nalia," Salinda said with a gasp.

The woman stopped before us, and I knew Salinda was right about her identity. But how? If everyone thought Nalia was dying, how was she standing here, looking younger than anyone had ever known her to be? I was suddenly struck by the calm of truth. "Ailan."

She looked at Salinda. "Yes," she said, then moved her eyes to meet mine. "And yes."

14

AILAN

Mareleau

Silence engulfed the camp, as if the two names uttered had everyone under a spell. All eyes locked on the woman who stood before us—the woman who was somehow both the Forest People Wise Woman and our mysterious Ailan. They watched her with a mixture of awe, fear, and suspicion...as did I.

Ailan seemed undaunted by the silent crowd as her face spread into a warm smile, and her attention returned to Salinda. "My dear one—"

Salinda stepped back, flinching away from Ailan as the woman reached out to embrace her.

Ailan's smile melted into an apologetic frown as she let her arms drop to her side. "I know, dear one. You do not understand right now. I have much to tell you."

Salinda's lips fluttered before she recovered herself, straightened her back, and took a bold step forward, eyes defiant as she met Ailan's. "You damn well better explain everything. *Ailan*."

Ailan's face flickered with hurt, but her smile returned, perhaps with a hint of indignation in her eyes. Her gaze moved to Cora, who watched her with distrust. Ailan only gave her a nod before moving on to me.

My arms tightened around Liam, pressing him closer to my chest as Ailan stepped toward us.

"Blood of my blood," she said, reaching a hand to graze my cheek. I flinched at her touch, my breath quickening. Her eyes moved down to Liam, and she sighed. "As is he." She took a step closer, lifting her hand toward my son.

I pulled away, teeth clenched as I watched her hand as if it were a snake.

Ailan's hand met only air, and she instead placed it on her hip as she let out a heavy sigh. "Very well," she said. "It looks like we need to talk. We should meet in the tent of the elders."

"I'll gather the other elders," Salinda said, her tone cold. She turned away, but Ailan put a hand on her shoulder before she could take a step. Salinda reeled around to face her. "What?"

"I think we should speak in private," her gaze moved to Cora, then to me and Liam, "before we call in the others."

"They deserve an explanation just as much as I do!" Salinda said.

Ailan nodded. "That they do. However, I think they need some time before they will be ready for it."

I again took in the gathering crowd, the narrowed eyes and fearful glances that surrounded us like blades.

Ailan continued speaking to Salinda. "These two came to find me. They have questions in their eyes and will never get their answers if we spend all night soothing the elders. Let me explain to you first. I'll need you on my side when we speak to the others."

"Who says I *will* be on your side?" Salinda asked with a glare.

"I understand you are hurt and confused," Ailan said. "You thought I was dying, and I'm sorry I couldn't tell you the truth then. But I'm ready to tell you now."

Salinda held her stare a moment longer, jaw shifting back and forth. "I'll be in the tent," she finally said, then stalked away.

Cora and I were left with Ailan, the woman we came to find but never expected to meet in such a way. Perhaps I was naive to expect anything less. What had I hoped to find? Some magical, immortal woman, all smiles and flowing hair, floating from the woods on gossamer wings? I certainly hadn't expected the sharp-eyed, stony-faced beauty with the ability to soothe dragons.

Ailan turned toward me and Liam. "He's beautiful, by the way."

My tongue struggled to form a reply; I wasn't sure if I wanted to thank her or scowl. I was saved from the struggle by a low reverberating, something like a growl, coming from the other side of the clearing.

Ailan whipped around, facing the men who still surrounded the dragon with their spears and arrows. "Lower your weapons."

The warriors hesitated, looking from her to the dragon.

Ailan stormed toward them, head held high. When

she spoke, her voice carried fierce authority. "Put your weapons down. Ferrah won't hurt you."

This time they did as told, taking slow steps away from the dragon as they lowered their weapons.

Ferrah extended its neck toward Ailan, who reached out and stroked its white scales. "We will need to give her this space to nest," she called out. "Everyone, move back."

The Forest People sprang away from the clearing, gathering their belongings and overturning the pots that hung over the cookfires in their attempt to get away.

Cora took a step forward. "She can't give the clearing to—"

Before she could say a word more, Ferrah turned in a circle, sending wafts of flame onto the ground beneath her while heat seared the air. Gasps of terror echoed around us. The ground beneath the dragon began to glow with shimmering, orange embers. After circling the area a few more times, Ferrah laid down, a puff of smoke trailing from her nostrils. She tucked her legs beneath her, wings folded along her back, and rested her long neck on the ground, head near her hind legs.

As terrifying as it was to see the dragon curl up on her bed of flame, there was a small part of me that felt tender at the sight.

A *very* small part of me.

Cora frowned, watching the dragon. "I think that's what it was trying to do at Ridine when Teryn and I found it on the charred field."

"You think it was making a bed?" I asked.

"Yes," said a voice beside me, making me jump. I hadn't noticed Ailan's return. "This is how dragons nest."

"You didn't need to give it our clearing," Cora said. I

noticed she used the word *our* instead of *their*. Although she was queen, it seemed she still considered herself one of the Forest People. "Where are we supposed to put the cookfires now?"

"We will find space for the cookfires," Ailan said. "Now that Ferrah has found me, she won't leave my side. If I didn't give her a proper place to make her bed, she would have made her own. That would not have fared well for our camp."

I swallowed hard at the thought of the dragon creating her own clearing amongst the towering trees. Then an even darker thought came to mind. "What does she eat?"

Ailan's mouth flickered with a smile. "Not us, my child. She will find her own food, but no harm will come to you or your kind."

"How do you explain the fact that she has tried to attack us three times now?" My voice trembled more than I intended it to.

Ailan regarded me as if I were dense. "Ferrah has been searching for you, my child. She has been trying to protect you, not harm you. It isn't her fault she has been received with fear and violence each time."

"Why would she be searching for me?" I asked.

"She was most certainly searching for *me*, originally. But since I've been dampening my powers, she was drawn to you instead, guided by my blood that lives within you."

"Were you the one who summoned the dragons from El'Ara, then?" Cora asked. "To find Mareleau?"

"No," Ailan said. "I didn't know they were here until I saw Ferrah."

Cora's brows furrowed with suspicion. "Then how do you know that Ferrah was searching for Mareleau?"

Ailan's eyes locked on Cora's. "You, my child, should know precisely how I am able to glean such information."

Cora's eyes widened before she nodded in understanding.

I pressed my lips together in annoyance. Whatever had become clear to Cora was still unknown to me. "What is it?"

Ailan faced me. "Ferrah is my *familiar*. She and I have a bond, much like your friend here and her unicorn companion."

"If you didn't summon them, why did the dragons come here?" Cora asked.

Ailan squinted as if she were trying to see something in the air between us. "Like I said, they were likely trying to find me. As to *how* they got here...I have a feeling the two of you will help me understand that."

Her steely gaze sent a shiver down my spine, and I was suddenly aware of the quiet in the camp, of the questioning stares surrounding us.

Cora seemed to sense it too as she shifted anxiously from foot to foot. "Should we find Salinda?"

"Yes," Ailan said. "There is much to discuss."

~

Cora

It felt odd being inside the tent of the elders without them, without the ritual incense burning—like an act of sacrilege. It was rare enough for even one non-elder of the Forest People to enter the tent, much less outsiders like Mare and Liam. The one time I'd called a meeting of the elders had been a bold act—unconventional, to say the least, and firmly against the rules.

But rules no longer seemed to matter now that the woman who'd taught them was the one breaking them.

Ailan folded her long, graceful, brown legs beneath her as she sat in her usual seat of the Wise Woman and motioned for us to sit as well. As if in defiance, Salinda avoided her regular seat of honor and sat next to me instead. Mareleau sat on my other side.

"For two women who have been looking for me, you don't seem happy to have found me," Ailan said, chin held high as she observed me and Mareleau.

I searched for words. "We didn't expect you to be..."

"She didn't expect to discover her Wise Woman had been a fraud," Salinda said.

Ailan said nothing in reply.

"Why did you hide your identity as Nalia, anyway?" I asked, my tone gentler than Salinda's.

"I needed to protect myself and this land," Ailan said. "If you have discovered who I am, then I assume you have also learned who I have been protecting this land from. You know how dangerous my brother is, correct?"

I nodded. "I know a little about him."

"And you've already seen what his son—someone with a fraction of Darius' power and ambition—can do here. The only reason Darius hasn't wreaked havoc on Lela is because of the work I've done to keep it safe from his knowledge. Morkai nearly destroyed that. It would have served no one to know who I was until now. For all I knew, even the whisper of my name could have led Darius here to find me."

"But why stay *here*?" Salinda asked. "Why pretend you are Faeran?"

"I never claimed to be Faeran, and I don't see that it matters." Ailan's voice held a fierce edge. "Your ancestors included me as one of their own. They invited me to take my place amongst them. Am I not one of the Ancient Ones? Who knows the truth of the Ancient ways better than I?"

"Then why is so much of what we are taught inaccurate or incomplete?" I asked. "Much of what I know about the Ancient Ones, I learned in—" I stopped short, not sure I was ready to reveal my visit to El'Ara. "—I learned on my own. And much of it conflicts with what I'd learned as a child."

Ailan let out a light laugh. "It is not my job to be record keeper or scribe for my people. As Wise Woman, I was simply to allow the Ancient ways to stay alive, to flourish with the Forest People. Tales will be distorted with time; it is the natural way. I made no move to thwart the progression of storytelling, only to steer our people back to the heart of our ways when they veered too far."

The wisdom in her words reminded me of the Nalia I'd known.

"Why did you let us believe you were dying?" Salinda said in a rush. The hurt in her voice was palpable, revealing the true source of her anger. I could feel her feelings as if they were my own. The woman she had loved and looked up to her whole life had been on the brink of death. I could feel how broken and hopeless she had felt about that. Now, a new pain had replaced it—the pain of betrayal.

"You let me—all of us—think you were dying." Salinda's voice broke on the word. "You should have told us the truth. You should have protected us from that pain."

Ailan nodded as if she too understood the source of Salinda's fury. "I'm so sorry, my child. I didn't know what else to do. I saw my body growing younger, felt a power I hadn't felt in hundreds of years returning to me. I didn't know what it meant, but I had my suspicions. It is rare for me to hear the whispers of my weaving these days, but suddenly I heard a demand telling me to wait. *Wait. Wait.* All I could do was trust it, to hide and suppress my power while I waited.

"This morning I heard another voice in my mind, a voice uttering my secret name. The source felt so close. Someone was looking for me." She eyed me, then looked at Mareleau. "I sensed my kin. Then I sensed Ferrah. I knew it was time for me to act and face whatever consequences awaited."

My mind reeled, her explanation providing me with more questions than answers.

"I never meant to hurt anyone." Ailan's gaze fell on Salinda. "Least of all, you."

Salinda stared at the ground between them and gave no reply.

"Now I have a question for you, dear Cora," Ailan said. "How is it you came to know so much about El'Ara?"

I hesitated, still uncertain I was ready to reveal such truths. "We came to ask *you* questions, not the other way around."

"I think you will be disappointed with what I know, if

I speak first," Ailan said. "Our stories are clearly entwined with the threads of my weaving, but there are pieces in your story that I must have in place before I will know the significance of my own."

Her words made little sense, but I didn't argue. I let out a heavy sigh. "Fine. I'll tell you what I know."

Ailan bowed her head with a nod. "Start with what happened after I last saw you. What followed the Battle at Centerpointe Rock?"

15

WHISPERS

Cora

I told her everything.

Ailan listened with rapt attention as I spoke, asking only a few questions here and there. I resisted the urge to pace while I talked, feeling uncomfortable beneath her unwavering stare. Yet I continued, sharing every event that seemed important, hesitating only when I came to details personal to Mareleau. That's when I would meet Mareleau's gaze, waiting for her nod of approval before proceeding.

I told Ailan about Liam's birth and my realization about the truth of the prophecy. I told her about discovering the dragons, our search for the book about Le'Lana, and ended with us Traveling to the Forest People.

Ailan nodded as I finished, then tilted her head to the side, eyes narrowed to slits. When her eyes returned to mine, amusement flickered in them. "In all these years, I never sensed you were a worldwalker. I suppose that wouldn't be something I *could* sense, anyway."

My mouth went dry. "Excuse me?"

"Your ability to Travel, as you called it. That's the power of a worldwalker, a rare human gift. My brother had it, as well as his human father."

I shuddered at the comparison to her brother. "I'm an empath, not a—"

"It's not something to be ashamed of," Ailan said gently. "You can have multiple talents."

"But I'm..." I couldn't find the words. There was no way I could share the same power as the man who'd sought to conquer El'Ara. The man who'd fathered...Morkai.

"The whispers of my weaving never told me you were involved, but clearly you are and always have been." Even though Ailan's words were directed at me, she seemed to be speaking more to herself. "Perhaps you were included to protect the blood of my blood."

Fire raged within me at her words. A shout built up in my throat, begging to be freed. *I was included to protect* her? *Mareleau? My body was damaged to spare* hers? *So she could give birth to the Child of Prophecy?*

My chest heaved as the anger coursed through my veins, beating at my temples, clawing at my lips. I closed my eyes and breathed it away, cooling the flames in my blood, forcing the words to quiet. *That isn't me. I would never think that,* I reminded myself.

Ailan didn't seem to have noticed my moment of distress as she stared at the space between me and Mareleau. "No, there's more," she said. Her eyes returned to mine. "What haven't you told me?"

I shrugged. "I told you everything—"

"No, there's something else. You are linked to my heir. What connection do you have to Mareleau or Liam?"

My brow furrowed as I glanced at Mareleau. "She's the wife of my husband's brother. I told you that." My eyes slid down to Liam, and I realized there was one detail I hadn't shared. "Also, my husband and I have made Liam our heir. Which makes Liam—"

"The heir to all Lela," Ailan finished for me, closing her eyes with a sigh.

"What is the significance of that?" Mareleau asked. "Why does the prophecy require that the Child of Prophecy unite the land through royal blood and magic right?"

Ailan opened her eyes and gave a quiet laugh. "This prophecy you speak of is merely the whispers of my weaving. Morkai would have done well not to seek these answers, as they have done nothing more than bring my weaving to fruition."

"But what does it *mean*?" I asked. "And what do you mean by *your* weaving? Wasn't it your mother who wove the veil?"

"It is time for me to tell my story now, isn't it?"

"Please," I said, trying to keep the impatience out of my voice.

"Very well," Ailan said. "It seems you know some of my history, the story of my mother, her affair with the human, and the birth of my brother, correct?"

The three of us nodded.

"I had to learn it from Cora, of course," Salinda said, her voice still rich with bitterness.

Ailan gave her a sad smile but didn't reply. She took a

deep breath. "I'll start with where it all ended, and where it all began. As you know, Darius invaded El'Ara with a human army, using his abilities as a worldwalker to bring his forces from the human world into ours, pulling them into every kingdom as if out of nowhere. We fought them, but Darius was relentless, always worldwalking away before anyone could get too close to him, using our differences in the passage of time to his advantage. He'd spend weeks gathering more troops in the human world and bringing them to El'Ara, when to us it was only days. We hardly had time to recover between battles. Mother realized there was only one thing to do—weave protection around our entire world to keep it separate and impenetrable from then on.

"To do this, we needed the veil to be completed while Darius was on the other side in the human world. Many failed at keeping him away, but I knew I was strong enough. I took it upon myself to fight him, to keep him distracted while my mother wove. I was willing to sacrifice myself, knowing I could get stuck on the other side with him, if it meant my mother and my people would carry on.

"Darius and I battled for what felt like ages. Every time he would attempt to worldwalk, I would grab hold of him, forcing him to take me everywhere he went. I wouldn't let him out of my reach.

"The veil was working. Mother was weaving it little by little from the opposite end of El'Ara toward the capital kingdom of Le'Lana. She was so close. All that remained was the very center of Le'Lana, the land that surrounded the palace where my mother did her weaving. At this point, however, Darius realized something was wrong. As we were locked into battle in the human world, Darius attempted to pull away and worldwalk into El'Ara. But he was blocked by the veil. He ran, as if to outrun the weaving, and I followed, allowing him to pull me along, worldwalking from one place in the human world to the next, cities flashing by in glimpses of color as I held tight to his arm, refusing to be shaken off. He barely put up a fight, as he was now more interested in finding a place where he could reenter El'Ara than he was in fighting me.

"Finally, he worldwalked us to one of the remaining places between our two worlds where the veil had yet to be woven. He pulled us into El'Ara, and I could see the palace just ahead. I tried to stop him from entering the palace but lost my hold on him. My mother's dragon tried to burn him, but he worldwalked into the palace as soon as he was out of my grip. That is when he found Mother and killed her. That is when she sealed the veil where it stood.

"I found Mother dead in his arms, while he wailed that he could no longer feel El'Ara. I told him it was because El'Ara was gone and we were both locked outside it forever. He didn't believe me and worldwalked away. When he finally realized the truth of what had been done, he returned to fight me. Again, we battled for what felt like an eternity, with him always managing to escape my fatal blow. But I wasn't as concerned with killing him as I was with forcing him off the land you now know as Lela. Once I got him to fight me beyond the border of this land, I was able to wound him. The wound was deep, and while it wasn't a killing blow, for some reason it stopped him from worldwalking.

"While he was distracted with his sudden loss of

power, I was able to grab him and quickly weave confusion over him. He stumbled back, clutching his head. It was only once he pulled the blade free that he was able to worldwalk away. That is when I got the idea for my weaving. If I acted fast, I knew I could weave something to keep him away. I quickly returned to where I felt my mother's veil, seeking the edges of her weaving. I could neither break nor finish her pattern, but I could add my own.

"I wove protection into the heart of El'Ara that was now part of the human world. My tapestry couldn't banish Darius like my mother's weaving could, but it could confuse him and keep him from finding Lela or remembering where it was. I sought weaknesses in my mother's weaving and strengthened them with conditions of my own. Her veil could be torn, but my weaving added the condition that it could only be torn when Darius could be stopped."

"So, your weaving created the prophecy?" Mareleau asked.

"Like I said, the prophecy you speak of simply comes from the whispers of my weaving. I created a tapestry, or —more accurately—a pattern of one to be completed. I created a vision I would have fulfilled by my weaving, a vision of peace, protection, and safety. A vision where El'Ara could be whole again. However, I did not create how or when it would come to pass, or even what that tapestry would look like in the end."

"When you speak of a tapestry and weaving," Salinda said, "you aren't speaking of a physical creation, are you?"

Ailan shook her head. "It is simply the closest word in your language that I can find to describe it."

"The Elvan I met in El'Ara described it the same way," I said. "Except I had to interpret their words through sensing their meaning, rather than actually hearing them."

"I wondered how you'd been able to speak with them," Ailan said. "That explains things."

I blushed, realizing I'd left out yet another detail.

"If you didn't intentionally create the prophecy," Mareleau said, "how did you know about me and Liam? You knew we were of your blood when you met us."

"The Elvan and Faeran can sense their kin through close proximity. I knew you immediately."

"How did you come to produce kin of royal lineage to begin with?" Salinda asked. "Not to mention, become the Forest People Wise Woman?"

"After I finished my weaving," Ailan explained, "I joined some of my fellow El'Arrans who were trapped in the human world with me. Most of the Elvan were killed fighting my brother, and the few who remained chose to take Last Breath before too long. Even many of the Faeran made this same choice. But those who survived learned to live a new way, creating tribes such as the Forest People. I lived amongst these groups for many years, until Lela was discovered by outsiders, and we began to see the first cities emerge.

"Following the whispers of my weaving, I entered these new societies, married into noble houses, and bore children. I took on many identities throughout the generations, always departing beneath the guise of untimely death before my agelessness could attract suspicion. I wrote the book you found, sharing only what the whispers urged me to. Then the whispers ceased, and I knew my work was done. I returned to settle with the only remaining sect of Forest People and eventually felt my youth slipping away. This is when I took on the guise of Nalia. By then, none remained from El'Ara, and my knowledge of the Ancient ways earned me the respect and position as Wise Woman."

"You still haven't explained why Liam is significant," Mareleau said. "Why did the whispers of your weaving prompt you to have an heir? How is Liam—a baby— supposed to stop an immortal madman?"

"I didn't know why the whispers wanted me to have children," Ailan said. "I just did what I felt I was guided to do. Yet, even as I did, I could feel it would someday become significant. Over the years, I'd catch echoes of the whispers here and there, similar to the words Morkai had channeled through his lover. *Right by magic and blood. Unite the land. Return the heart of El'Ara.* I knew the whispers were now working through the lives of others, bringing my tapestry closer and closer to completion. Now it is done. With Liam being heir to all Lela, the magic recognizes him. And if I name him *my* heir, he will irrefutably be the next Morkara of El'Ara."

My mind was spinning to make sense of everything she was telling us, but still more questions came to mind. "There's something I don't understand. Why didn't you ever try to harness the magic and return it to El'Ara? El'Ara began dying because of the veil, because the magic was flowing out into Lela but not returning. You were your mother's heir, which means you became Morkara when she died. You could have done something about it back then."

Ailan's eyes clouded over, showing a hint of regret. "I

didn't know what the consequences of my mother's veil had been until you told me. If I'd known that El'Ara was dying because of it, I may have done something reckless. I may have even tried to revoke my own weaving. But because my weaving was in place, I was only guided to take actions that supported the conditions my weaving created. Never did a whisper guide me to claim rule over Lela or harness the magic. Perhaps if I had, I would have died because of it, making it that much easier for Darius to inherit my right."

"So, the Morkara inherits rule through bloodline the same as human royals do?" I asked.

"Similar. The eldest child of the Morkara—regardless of gender—is typically named heir, but it's ultimately up to the Morkara to choose. The heir must be *named* as such. Any other children of the Morkara become the heir's heir until he or she can name one from their own children. This means, until I name an heir from my own blood, Darius remains my heir. All it would take is my death to strengthen his claim."

"Why must you name Liam your heir?" Mareleau asked, her voice trembling. "That will only make him a target for your brother, won't it? Why couldn't you have named your first child heir? Or any of the others of your blood that followed? Why couldn't you have birthed and trained a great warrior and named *him* heir?"

Ailan shook her head. "I only know to follow the whispers of my weaving and trust that they are true. For some reason, they need him." Her gaze held Mareleau, then me. "Perhaps it's because they need the two of you, and he is the link between you."

"What does that *mean*?" Mareleau asked, cheeks

flushed as tears glazed her eyes. "What can a baby possibly do? What can Cora and I possibly do? I thought *you* were going to have the answers for us."

"I'm sorry I have disappointed you," Ailan said. "But in putting all your faith in me, you have underestimated yourself. You wouldn't have been drawn here if not for great importance. You may not understand it yet, but you do have a role to play in what is yet to unfold. I know you can feel it."

Mareleau opened her mouth as if she wanted to argue, but then snapped it shut. "What do we do now?"

Ailan closed her eyes, inhaling deeply. "We follow the whispers of my weaving," she said, her voice soft. She opened her eyes, the beautiful gray in them as fierce as a storm as they rested on Liam. "I name this child my heir."

16

TAPESTRY

Mareleau

I expected lightning to pierce the tent, for the earth to quake beneath us, for Liam to cry at the declaration of his fate. But there was nothing. Nothing but silence as Ailan's words echoed in my mind. Once it was clear no repercussions were upon us, I let out a shaking breath. "What happens now?"

Ailan stood and began to pace. "My return to youth means my brother is experiencing the same. With my mother's veil torn, there's no telling how much good my weaving will do in keeping him away. He could remember everything now."

"You think he will invade, don't you?" Cora asked.

"Of course he will," Ailan said. "You came to the same conclusion before you even found me. It's only a matter of time."

My heart pounded in my chest. "Both King Teryn and

my husband sent scouts to uncover information about Syrus."

Cora nodded. "If he makes a move, we'll know about it."

Ailan paused her pacing and stared at us. "Is that so?" She fixed her attention on Cora. "If you were to world-walk, who would know about it? Who would sense your arrival, if you chose to be discreet?"

Cora flushed, her lips pressing into a line.

"Exactly," Ailan said. "And you are only just now discovering your worldwalking abilities. If my brother can remember even one solid detail about Lela, he could show up here. If he thinks about me the way you were able to think about Salinda..." She shuddered, eyes darting to the side as if she expected Darius to materialize beside her.

Cora and Salinda exchanged a worried glance.

"He wouldn't come here without an army," I argued. "And there's no way an army could show up in Lela undetected."

Ailan raised an eyebrow. "That gives you comfort somehow? Don't forget how much damage even an expected army can do."

I felt the blood leave my face as I considered her words.

Ailan continued. "Even if he can't remember a thing about Lela or El'Ara, his son told him what he'd learned about the prophecy. With my brother's return to health, he will easily put the pieces together and come to the same conclusions Morkai had. But, with his ability to worldwalk, he will come to them much faster."

Cora nibbled her thumbnail. "There must be a way to

prepare for him, to anticipate where he will most likely go first."

"We know he will seek the tear in the veil," Ailan said. "Whatever he does in Lela will revolve around finding it."

"Do you think he will try to do what Morkai did?" Salinda asked. "Will he try to claim rule over Lela as Morkaius?"

Ailan nodded. "I believe it is possible. If Darius thinks becoming Morkaius in Lela will give him the power to locate the tear, or even pull the veil down completely, he will do it."

Cora's eyes widened for a moment, then she shook her head. "He wouldn't be able to become Morkaius, even if he were able to conquer Lela and claim rule. *He who harnesses the magic will be destroyed by it.* Morkai spent ages trying to get that right, and never succeeded."

Salinda nodded. "Harnessing the magic itself was an act that killed him. It was Morkai's Roizan who killed him at the Battle at Centerpointe Rock, was it not?"

Cora's eyes shone with a hopeful gleam. "It was. Darius will hear of his son's folly. That will deter him."

"Just because it never worked for Morkai," Ailan said, "doesn't mean my brother won't try it. Whatever the case, Darius will invade. Whether to claim rule as Morkaius, or to seek out the veil, he will come. And he will be ready."

The cold certainty in her voice chilled me. "What do we do?" I asked.

Ailan sighed. "We continue to trust the whispers of my weaving. So far, it has brought us together. It is up to us now to work with the last threads of the tapestry. There may be war, blood, and death ahead of us—ahead of *all* of us."

Silence fell, and my mind went to Larylis. Where did he fit into all this? Would he have to face war yet again? Would he come out of it alive? My eyes glazed with tears as I recalled the night before, the look on his fallen face when I told him what I was planning to do. *Why did I leave him? Why did I do this?*

I thought my guilt would eat me alive until a small, quiet voice came through the clamor. *There's something much bigger happening here. Bigger than me. Bigger than Larylis.*

I lowered my head, and Liam's tiny face swam before my eyes. *I have a purpose.* I didn't entirely know what it was, aside from keeping Liam safe, but I knew it was true. I was meant to do more.

Cora's voice broke the silence. "Do you have a plan?"

Ailan bowed her head, eyes closed as she considered. "I must return to El'Ara," she finally whispered. Her face snapped up, eyes locking on me. "*We* must return—you, Liam, and I. I need to keep my heir safe. Even with the tear, the safest place for us is behind the veil. Darius can't worldwalk into El'Ara so long as it is in place."

"What about the tear itself?" Cora asked.

"First, we must find it," Ailan said. "That is the only way we will be able to enter. Then I will gather the Elvan, prepare them for what is to come."

"And what about the people of my world?" Cora asked. "What if he decides to conquer Lela?"

"We will have to work together," Ailan said. "We will make a plan to defend all angles Darius could have. When we go to El'Ara, you will go with us too."

Cora's face paled. "I wasn't well received or departed last time I was in El'Ara."

"I know, and I am sorry for how my people have treated you. But this time, things will be different. They will respect me as Morkara and accept you as ambassador between our peoples."

Cora hesitated for a moment. "You want me to be your ambassador?"

"Who better to relay information between Lela and El'Ara than a woman who can walk between worlds?"

Cora gave a reluctant nod. The disappointment on her face mirrored my own. Neither of us were anticipating another journey. We'd both promised to return safely to our husbands as soon as possible.

I have a purpose.

"When do we leave?" I found myself saying, surprised at the calm in my voice.

"Tonight," Ailan said. "After nightfall. In the meantime, get some rest while you can."

"What about the elders?" Salinda asked. "When will you speak to them?"

"I will speak to them now. I will tell them the truth of what has passed and what is yet to come."

Salinda met her eyes. "I will stand at your side while you speak."

Ailan's lips melted into a smile. "Thank you, dear one." She turned to me and Cora. "The two of you should rest while Salinda and I speak with the elders."

Cora and I nodded, then rose to our feet.

"I should check on Valorre," Cora said. "He can't be too happy with that dragon near."

"And I should speak with Maiya before I gather the elders," Salinda said. "You'll see her before you go, won't you?"

Cora nodded with a wide smile. "Of course. I couldn't possibly visit without seeing her."

I cocked my head, wondering who Maiya was, and watched as Cora left the tent. Salinda left the tent as well, and I followed close on her heels. "Salinda."

The older woman whirled around, a surprised look on her face. "Yes, Mareleau. Or am I to call you Your... Highness? Majesty? As you can see, we are far removed from the royal ways you are likely used to."

In any other situation, I would have been seething. But there was something so strong about this woman that made me feel humble, as if my title meant nothing coming from her lips. "Mareleau is fine," I said, grimacing at the falseness in my voice. Being casually cordial was not something I was used to.

She put a hand to her forehead. "You need a place to rest, don't you? I'm so sorry. I should have been more considerate—"

"No, it's not that. I mean, I do, but I was hoping I could speak with you."

Salinda cocked her head to the side, brows furrowed. Then she nodded. "Ah, yes. You sought something personal when you came here, didn't you?"

"Yes. It's about my...about the Arts. Cora said I might find help here in training them. I've only just discovered them and I..." I searched for words, finding myself more flustered than I'd intended to be. "I need to learn how to consciously use them. I need to learn how to protect myself and my son."

Salinda gave me a warm smile. "Of course, child. I'll do whatever I can. You can rest in my tent. After the meeting, I'll come speak with you."

"I appreciate that. Thank you."

Salinda walked me to her tent, where we'd first spoken with her. Had it only been mere hours before? When she left, I sank onto her cot, only mildly aware of my discomfort over the lack of luxuries. I felt as if I'd already been awake for a full day, muscles tense and mind reeling. I pulled Liam close to me, letting my thoughts clear, and forgetting—just for a time—about all that lay ahead.

~

Cora

I found Valorre and Hara just outside of camp at the opposite end from Ferrah's nest. Hara didn't act like anything was amiss, but Valorre was clearly flustered. I wrapped my arms around his neck and stroked his silky coat.

"I'm so sorry, Valorre. I shouldn't have asked you to wait so close."

I remember her.

"The dragon?"

From home.

"Were you enemies?" I felt a lump rise in my throat. "Are unicorns...food for dragons?"

Valorre seemed deep in thought for a moment. *Not food. Not enemies.*

"Then why do the dragons terrify you so much?"

At home they were...temperamental. Anger. Something happened. The dragons raged. They were looking for someone who was missing...

"Ailan?" I asked.

Perhaps. I don't remember it all. The dragons were not to be controlled. We were not enemies, but no one was friend of the dragons when they were angry. Valorre paused, then seemed to remember something else. *I was sad for them.*

I recalled something one of the Elvan, Garot, had said when he'd explained the consequences of the veil in El'Ara. Something about the dragons being restless. Unicorns disappearing. "Do you think that is why you left? To get away from the dragons?"

No, Valorre said. *It was something else. I could feel something calling me. Pulling me.*

I nodded, remembering him telling me something similar before. "Perhaps it was the whispers of Ailan's weaving."

Valorre went still. *I remember.*

"What?"

I could feel it. The one they were looking for. No, not the one they were looking for. Close, but not her. I could find her. I knew I could. The dragons couldn't leave, but I could. Many others of my kind had done the same, followed the calling, but hadn't returned. But I would, and the dragons would be at peace. Home would be whole again.

"Mareleau." My heart sank unexpectedly as I spoke the name. "The whispers were calling you to find Mareleau."

I turned away from Valorre, hand over my heart as my eyes unfocused. Why did it hurt so badly to know my unicorn companion—my best friend, aside from Teryn— had only met me because he'd been trying to find *her*? I took a deep breath to cool the rage that threatened to boil within me.

You're sad about that, Valorre said.

My cheeks flushed, and I couldn't ignore the deep shame that came over me. "I don't know why I should be, but for some reason I am." I felt a slight ease as I confessed those words, but I could feel many more words clawing at my lips—words I was not willing to allow to be true.

I shrugged and forced a smile. "It's silly. Mareleau is my friend too. I have no reason to be upset about that."

It's fine to be upset.

I returned to my place at his side and buried my face in his neck. "I know, Valorre."

Why am I remembering now? Valorre asked.

"Maybe it's because of the tear."

I think I can feel it. Home.

My eyes widened. "You can? Maybe you can help us find the tear."

Valorre stiffened, and I looked up to see his ears twitching back and forth. *We're going back?*

He clearly thought it was as bad of an idea as I did. Hopefully Ailan was right about her sway over her people. She was Morkara after all, wasn't she? The tribunal wouldn't insist on carrying out my death sentence with her around...would they? I breathed away my worries and closed my eyes. *Give me any reason not to go. Any reason at all.*

I remained still as I listened to the small voices within me, the voices of fear, reason, courage, and truth. All I found was calm silence.

I let out a heavy sigh. "Yes, Valorre. We are going back."

17

NARCUSS

Cora

The sun was high in the sky by the time I reentered camp. I knew I should get some sleep in preparation for our night's travels, but I couldn't still my mind long enough to even consider rest. Instead, I searched for whom my heart needed to find.

I found Maiya almost as easily as I'd found Salinda. She was as close to me as a sister. A bond like that could never be broken.

Maiya stood outside a large tent, unhooking laundry from a line. I stood behind her, a smile stretching across my face as I took in her long, raven-black hair and her plain, blue dress. Aside from the fur-lined boots and heavy shawl, she looked exactly as I'd last seen her.

She whirled around and met my eyes, a smile playing on her lips. I ran to embrace her and found something firm and round between us as we collided. My eyes fell to her swollen belly. *So, not exactly as I'd last seen her...*

Maiya giggled as she followed my gaze, then pulled me back into a hug. "Cora, it's been so long."

"I know." I found tears pooling in my eyes as I wrapped my arms around her. "I'm sorry it took me so long to come back."

Maiya tensed for a moment, then released me. She continued to smile, but there was something forced about it as she returned to her laundry.

I stepped beside her and helped her take down the remaining pieces, which appeared to belong to her husband, Roije. "I see you're doing well. You're already married to the man you love, and now it appears you're soon to be a mother." I ignored the dryness in my throat as I swallowed the words I couldn't say. *Am I the only wife in Lela not having a baby?* I cursed myself for the anger that quickened yet again. What was wrong with me lately? "You must be so happy."

"I am, Cora. I really am." Her smile stretched wide for a moment, then faded completely.

"What's wrong?" I asked.

Maiya stuffed the rest of the laundry in her woven basket, not meeting my eyes. "It's nothing. I'm happy to see you. Let's just leave it at that."

I was surprised by the sharpness in her tone. I put my hand on her arm and steered her to face me. "You can tell me anything, Maiya. No matter how much time has passed, you're still my sister—"

"That's just it, Cora," Maiya said, finally letting her full frustration show. "It *has* been a long time since I've seen you. Last time, you came with tidings of war. Our peaceful world was thrown into chaos. My husband went to battle, and I didn't know if I'd ever see him again. Now, you show up out of nowhere. Not to visit, but with dark tidings yet again. Another call to war. Another instance to take my husband—the father of my unborn child—away from me."

I stared, stunned. I'd sensed something was wrong, though I'd assumed she'd been having trouble with Roije —a recent argument, perhaps. I hadn't anticipated her trouble was with me. "Salinda must have told you."

"Yes. It sounds just like last time. Except this time, I truly can't see what it has to do with us."

I was torn between guilt and annoyance. "It is like last time, Maiya. And it has *everything* to do with us. It has to do with everyone in Lela."

"According to Mother, this evil Elvan sorcerer isn't going after Lela at all."

"That's not entirely true," I argued. "He may not want Lela itself, but he will invade to get to El'Ara."

"Then the solution is simple," Maiya said. "Give him El'Ara in exchange for leaving our land in peace."

"What do you mean, *give him El'Ara*? El'Ara isn't ours to give, nor is Lela ours to keep. Lela was never our land to begin with. It came from El'Ara."

Maiya put her hands on her hips. "I don't care where it came from. Lela is *my* home. This is where I belong. Lela is home to my husband, my family, my people. This is where my child will be born. This is where I will stay."

I stammered, searching for words. "But...but what about El'Ara? How can you even consider letting the Ancient Realm go to Darius? What do you think he will do to the Elvan and the Faeran?"

"I honestly don't care, Cora. They started this war. They should end it amongst themselves and leave us at peace. Their bickering has nothing to do with us. Nothing!"

"If Darius takes over El'Ara, what will stop him from also taking over our world?"

Maiya paused for a moment. When she spoke, her tone was empty. "If we help fight in this Ancient war, what happens to *us*? What happens to the people of Lela? Where do we go when the El'Arrans take Lela back?"

I opened my mouth, but no words came forth. The blood drained from my face. "I don't know."

Silence stretched between us. My heart hammered as I deliberated what to say. There had to be a way to mend the rift between us. In all our years growing up together, we'd never had an argument like this.

"I'm so sorry, Maiya," I finally said, my voice cracking. "I understand why you are upset with me, and I don't have all the answers. All I know is that Darius must be stopped. He's more dangerous than Morkai was. I don't know what will happen to Lela, but as Queen of Kero, I will do what I can to defend this land *and* its people. I will do whatever it takes to keep all of you safe, to make sure we all have a home at the end of this. But I can't allow another realm to be destroyed in the process. If war comes, we must fight."

"What will we be fighting for?" Maiya asked. "Our home? Or our eventual exile?"

"Our *lives*."

Maiya sighed, her gaze falling to her feet. "I hope you're right about all this."

"So do I." My voice was barely above a whisper.

Maiya's eyes returned to mine, and her face crumbled. She gathered me into a tight hug and sobbed into my hair. "I really am happy to see you. Please believe me. It's just—"

It felt as if my insides had cracked wide open as I began to sob in turn. "I know, Maiya. I understand."

We stood like that until our tears had dried. When we finally parted ways, all I could think about was Maiya's question. *What happens to the people of Lela?*

Then another set of words came to mind, words Teryn once said to me on a bloody field of ash and smoke. *You can't save everyone.*

I know I can't. But I will never stop trying.

∾

Mareleau

"Show me what you can do," Salinda said.

Her tent was dark, lit by a single lantern. I sat on her cot, and Salinda sat on a blanket across from me, while Liam slumbered in a woven bassinet. With a deep breath, I closed my eyes and tried to remember the times I'd wanted to be ugly.

The forced engagements. My terrible suitors. Father's anger.

My shoulders sagged along with my chest as my lips turned down. One word repeated over and over in my mind. *Ugly. Ugly. Ugly.*

I caught Salinda's eye, and my cheeks flushed. It occurred to me what a foolish thing I was doing. *This couldn't possibly be magic. I'm just a silly girl who knows how to frown. Idiot.*

"That was quite the glamour," Salinda said.

I cocked my head. "It was?"

She nodded. "It wasn't made for me, so I couldn't fully see what you were creating, but I could see the Arts surrounding you."

My heart fluttered. "You mean, Cora was right? I really have been creating glamours all along?"

"Yes. Now try to make one specifically for me."

"I don't know how to do that."

"Sure you do." Salinda gave me an encouraging smile. "Why do you usually create a glamour?"

I thought for a moment. "To create a favorable outcome for myself."

"Try that with me. Think about what you would desire from me. Then try to make me see that which would encourage it to happen."

I felt sweat bead at my brow as I began to ponder. What could I want from Salinda? What would be favorable to me? I supposed I desired her to see me as powerful and capable.

"Go deeper," Salinda said, as if she could read my mind.

I followed my train of thought until I unburied a childish yearning. Somewhere deep down was a part of me that wanted Salinda to deem me a true sorceress, capable of great magics beyond any she'd encountered before. I contrasted that to how she saw me now—struggling, confused, and weak.

I pulled my secret desire from my core and let it surround me. My chest lifted, shoulders back, hair flowing around me like a golden halo of power. I sat tall —taller than even Ailan had sat, towering over Salinda like I was the teacher, and she my meek student. "This is what *real* Art looks like," I said, my voice filling the tent.

Liam squirmed at the sound of my voice, and I felt the glamour disappear. I turned to him, placing my hand gently over his tiny belly until he settled back into restful sleep.

When I turned back to Salinda, she clasped her hands before her, like a gesture of silent applause. "Very good, Mareleau. This time I saw it fully. Beautifully done."

My eyes fell to the ground. "Thank you."

Salinda studied me for a moment. "Have you always used the Arts for personal gain?"

"I suppose so," I said. "Except for when I somehow used the Arts to help save my son. I had no idea I'd done such a thing. All I knew was that I was willing to give my life to give him breath."

Salinda nodded. "But using the Arts for your own favor has come most naturally, hasn't it?"

It sounded terrible when she put it that way, but she was right. "Yes."

"You have the power of the narcuss," Salinda said.

My eyes widened with excitement. "What does that mean?"

"A narcuss uses power for personal gain, manipulating what other people see, do, feel, and perceive to achieve an outcome in their favor."

I frowned. "That doesn't sound nearly as honorable as Cora's power as an empath."

Salinda sighed. "You came to me for the truth, so I won't lie to you. The Art of the narcuss can be easily used in dark ways. You have confronted the dark deeds of one powerful narcuss already."

I froze. "Are you talking about Morkai?"

"Yes."

Terror and anger surged through me. "You're telling me my power is the same as Morkai's?"

"It is the same Art, but it does not have to be used the same way," Salinda said. "You told me you wanted to control your gifts so you could protect your son. That is a good step in overcoming your challenge."

"My challenge?" I asked. "What does that mean?"

"Everyone gifted in the Arts faces a challenge. Some are easier to identify than others. As an empath, Cora gains strength when she uses her powers to protect herself. Since she most easily uses the Arts to help others, to hear them, to understand them, she overcomes a great challenge when she uses the Arts for herself alone. Her powers grow exponentially each time she filters out the voices and feelings of others, each time she protects her own safety.

"As a narcuss, your challenge will be to use the Arts without personal gain. Protecting others, putting another's safety before your own, will grow your power."

"Like how I saved my son," I said, feeling some of the terror begin to lift. "And how I want to use my power to protect him."

"Partially, yes," Salinda said. "But even that kind of thinking is a slippery slope. As a narcuss, it will be easy to convince yourself that what you do for personal gain is for another's sake. What Cora said about Morkai's past only proves this point. He thought he was being selfless in trying to bring his mother back, and again when he became obsessed with being Morkaius to bring back his lover. It's clear as day that everything he did was for his own gain, but he didn't see it that way."

"Am I being selfish for wanting to protect my son?" I couldn't keep the icy tone from my words. "All I want is for him to be safe."

"Why?"

Heat rose to my cheeks. "Because I love him, that's why. Because I want him to live a long, healthy life. Because I want to see him grow up—" I froze, feeling the weight of my words. As much as I wanted to protect my son, I equally wanted to protect myself so I could always remain at his side. I wanted to watch him become a toddler, a youth, a man. His health and safety were most important, but just below that was a frenzied determination to maintain my own.

"Do you see now?" Salinda asked.

My shoulders sank as I nodded. "What do I do? I don't want to be like Morkai."

"Seek the truth as often as you can, then simply bring it to light. When you feel those selfish undercurrents running through you, admit them, then let them be. You cannot try to outrun your nature. Just don't let it control you. Work to rise above it."

I imagined the work it would take to constantly identify my darkest aspects and felt a sudden rise of anxiety, followed by a burning hatred for myself. I'd always been this way and had never known. No wonder I was selfish. No wonder I had trouble making friends. I was a narcuss —a disgusting, awful, manipulative narcuss.

"What are you feeling right now?" Salinda asked with a wary tone.

I didn't answer.

"Hating yourself will do you no good. Even the strongest, most powerful Art is extinguished by hate—especially hate for one's self."

"What else am I supposed to do? Love myself for being naturally rotten? Won't that just make me even more selfish?"

Salinda gave me a gentle smile. "Not at all, my child."

"How can I love myself, knowing there's bad inside?"

"The same way I do," Salinda said.

I raised an eyebrow. "You? I can't believe you have even a pinch of darkness in you."

"None of us are perfect, my child," Salinda said with a laugh. "I am no exception. You saw how quickly I turned to anger when Nalia revealed herself as Ailan. I was ready to forsake her, to turn my back on decades of love and trust built between us."

"That's understandable," I said. "Of course you were angry. Anyone would have been."

"Perhaps, perhaps not. What matters is I saw my dark feelings, my hate, my anger, and I called them into the light. I revealed them and released them. I'm still angry and confused. I'm also hopeful and forgiving. It is a choice to follow the path of hope and love, even when dark feelings remain. Remember we are *all* shades of good and bad, dark and light. Just work on bringing your darkness into the light and loving yourself regardless."

"You make it sound so simple."

Salinda laughed. "It isn't. It's a lifelong task, and all you can do is try a little at a time."

I closed my eyes, reflecting on what she'd said. Now that I knew the truth of what I really was, could I love myself? I'd demanded Larylis do exactly that, and he'd accepted me, flaws and all. Could I do the same?

I'll try.

My shoulders trembled as I sought the darkness within—my selfishness, the ways I'd manipulated my parents during my youth, the way I let Larylis pine for me year after year. Tears trailed down my cheeks as I attempted to love those parts of me. At first, it felt ridiculous, forced, and absurd. Then I imagined the wounded girl I was when I'd done those terrible things, the girl who felt powerless, the girl who reacted in the only ways she knew how. The girl who survived.

I poured my love into *that* version of me and felt my body relax.

When I opened my eyes, Salinda was staring back with a wide smile. "You're making progress."

"Where do I go from here? How can I continue to grow my powers?"

"The Arts are found in love and light," Salinda said. "What you did just now was a way to connect to that force within you. I am not a teacher in the Arts like you expected me to be. I am only a guide to help you see what is already there. Keep going, my child. Keep seeking truth. Keep following love. You will find your strength has been there all along."

I tried to keep the disappointment off my face. I'd hoped by the end of our lesson I'd be able to use the Arts on command, to draw upon some untapped power to do things I'd never dreamed of doing. Yet, here I was, having accomplished not even half of what I'd expected.

Then again, I'd succeeded in ways I hadn't anticipated. I'd created a glamour with more ease than I'd thought possible. I'd gained an awareness and knowledge I hadn't had before. And I'd faced a terrible truth about myself and still managed to find love.

Perhaps Salinda was right. Perhaps my strength was already inside me.

18

THE TEAR

Cora

We made our way through the forest beneath the moonlit trees. An immense shadow passed overhead, bringing my eyes skyward to watch the silhouette until the beating wings passed from view. Valorre tensed beneath me as we rode but quickly regained his composure. *Are you starting to get used to them?* I asked.

Yes. I keep remembering they are not enemy. They aren't angry, now that they've found her.

Mareleau's gaze had followed mine, and she was still staring at the sky from her place upon Hara's back. "Is that why we are traveling at night?" she asked with a shudder, one hand resting protectively over Liam, who was nestled into a swath of thick fabric that hung over her shoulder and across her torso—a gift from one of the Forest People mothers.

Ailan nodded from atop a gift of her own—one of the

few horses the Forest People kept. When we'd left the camp, I'd been surprised at how many tearful goodbyes there had been for Ailan. It seemed not everyone regarded her with suspicion after truth had spread throughout camp. While many had watched our departure with stony expressions and crossed arms, many more had insisted on seeing us off with as many gifts and provisions as possible.

"We don't know where my brother is," Ailan said. "He could know about the dragons. He could be watching the skies for clues as to where they are coming from. I will not have the dragons give us away. We will travel at night and rest during the day."

Another set of wings beat overhead. "How many are there?" I asked. We'd only been riding an hour or two, but it seemed like hundreds of dragons had already flown overhead.

Ailan smiled up at the creature's soaring form. "Four, as of now. They are circling around us to keep pace. Hopefully we can find the tear before any more of them come through the veil."

Four dragons, I thought with a mixture of terror and relief. Four was far less than the hundreds I'd been imagining, but since the first time the dragons had been spotted in Lela, we'd only been able to confirm two. If there had actually been four all along...how much more damage had we yet to be informed about? I halted my anxious calculations, realizing burnt crops and missing sheep would soon be the least of my people's worries if Darius invaded. *Or is it only a matter of* when *he invades?*

"How are we going to find the tear?" Mareleau asked. "Do you think we are close?"

Ailan's jaw shifted side to side. "I don't know. I'd hoped once we began our travels I would be able to sense the tear. Perhaps I will once we get to closer to the veil."

Mareleau cocked her head. "You know where the veil is, then?"

"That's the easy part," Ailan said. "The veil surrounds all that is known as Lela. What we think of as the border of the land is actually where the veil begins."

Mareleau blushed. "I suppose that should have been obvious."

"Where will we start looking for the tear?" I asked.

Ailan continued. "We will head to the border north of here, between Lela and Risa. From there we will ride along the border each night, searching for the tear. I *must* be able to sense it once we are near."

That could take forever, I thought. The frown Ailan wore told me she had similar doubts. *There must be another way.*

I stroked Valorre's mane. *Anything yet?*

Maybe. Valorre seemed deep in concentration. I closed my eyes and let his thoughts pour into me. Flashes of color moved through my mind—the greens too vibrant to be of this world, the flowers too strange and majestic. The vision continued in disjointed scenes until it finally stilled, and I saw a familiar willow grove.

I remember. We rested there, Valorre said.

I remember too. I let the vision fill my mind, my body, my senses. I imagined I was there again, the forever-warm air circling my calves as I—nothing. The vision disappeared. I knew it was a foolish hope that I could worldwalk us there, but I had to try. *At least we know the veil still holds, regardless of the tear.*

Valorre, however, seemed still focused on the memory. It was up to him now. *That's when I knew I'd made a mistake*, he said. *I brought us home.*

What about before? Do you remember how we got there? I released control over my sight and again joined with Valorre's. The willow grove reappeared, bathed in sunlight. It remained as it was, the only movement being the breeze on the sea-like waves of grass. Then the vision seemed to grow smaller, slowly showing the grove growing further and further away, until it was nothing more than a hint on the horizon. Then it was gone, and new surroundings swept by. Again, the other-worldly colors filled my mind as birds with jewel-toned feathers swooped overhead in reverse. Foliage rustled as the scenery stretched away, growing more and more distant.

Then there was a sense of stillness. The scenery continued to pass, but no more did the leaves blow. No more did animals scurry. Color failed to reach the tips of the leaves as the ground became drab and dry. Finally, there was nothing but gnarled, rotting roots and bare branches.

Then came a sudden blinding, white light, followed by the darkness of night.

Familiar sounds of a nighttime forest filled my ears as the moon shone overhead. I opened my eyes and saw a similar scene around me—different from what Valorre had shown me, and distant too, but still similar.

Valorre quivered with excitement beneath me. *I remember. I found it.*

My face stretched into a smile. *Good job.*

I turned my attention to Ailan, who rode ahead with a determined expression, then Mareleau, whose eyes fluttered sleepily as she swayed in her saddle. "I have a change of plans," I said.

"What is it, dear one?" Ailan said.

"Valorre found the tear in the veil. I'm taking us straight there."

THE FIRST BLUSH OF MORNING BEGAN TO ILLUMINATE THE tips of the trees as the fourth dragon landed. I let out a sigh of relief and leaned my back against the trunk of a tree. With wary eyes, I watched as the dragon—a deep green, from what I could see in the dappled light of the clearing—slithered between the trees and out of sight. Moments later, wafts of smoke began to rise in the near distance, indicating where it had made its bed. Three other pillars of smoke rose around us.

My heart ached for the four patches of burnt earth, wondering how El'Ara could accommodate an entire world filled with dragons and still have such lush forests to show for it. *There is still much I don't know about El'Ara.*

I shifted my gaze away from the smoke, resting instead on Mareleau, who slept soundly by our small campfire. She'd insisted on staying up with me and Ailan while we waited for the dragons to find us, but we argued with her until she agreed to get some rest with Liam.

"You should do the same," Ailan said, following my gaze as she settled down beside me. "The dragons have flown long tonight. They will be sound asleep for a few hours, which means we still have a time to wait before we attempt to enter the tear."

I sighed and let my muscles relax, my back pressing

into the tree trunk behind me. Even without Ailan's prompting, I knew I needed to rest. While worldwalking with others had become much easier than it had been the first time, after two trips—one to take Mareleau, Liam, and Hara, and another to take Ailan and her horse—I was feeling thoroughly drained.

She's right, Valorre said, resting on the other side of the tree. *Sleep.*

I tried to form the words, *I know,* as I curled up at the base of the tree, but I was asleep before I knew it.

~

Mareleau

I awoke with a start, as I had every time I'd awoken since giving birth to Liam. My first thought was of him. *Where is he? How is he? Is he breathing? Crying? Hungry? Warm enough?*

He was exactly where he'd been last—in the crook of my arm beside my chest, swaddled in the blankets the Forest People had given me. I myself hadn't moved an inch and felt like I'd barely slept a wink. It continued to amaze me how I could sleep so lightly, almost as if part of me remained awake to watch over my son. Did all new mothers feel that way? Or was it just me?

I took in his face, his eyes blinking open as he began to stir. I kissed his cheeks, and my lips confirmed he was still warm from the fire blazing gently before us. On the other side of the fire, Cora was asleep next to Valorre. It took me a moment longer to spot Ailan.

She stood between two trees, hand outstretched and

eyes closed. I got to my feet, pulling my heavy cloak around me and Liam. Ailan remained still as I approached her.

"It's here," she said.

I furrowed my brow. "What is? The tear?"

"Yes. I can feel it now."

Relief flooded through me. "Will we be able to enter?"

"I haven't tried yet," Ailan said. "But I think so. I can feel the opening. I can feel where my weaving begins." She opened her eyes and looked at me. "This is the weakness I'd found long ago, when I realized my mother's veil could be torn. This is where I filled conditions of my own, weaving that it could only be torn when Darius could be defeated. In essence, this is where I wove you and Liam into all of this."

I looked at the empty space between the trees, seeing nothing out of the ordinary.

Ailan continued staring at me, her brows beginning to knit together. "It's odd, though. I feel a strand or two of my weaving is missing."

"What does that mean?"

She cocked her head to the side, her gaze sliding down to Liam. "I don't know, but for some reason, I think it belongs to him now."

I wanted her to say more, but footsteps approached behind us.

"Is that it?" Cora asked, her voice thick with sleep.

We turned to face her, and Ailan nodded. "This is the tear." Her eyes went unfocused for a moment as sounds quietly rumbled in the near distance. "The dragons wake. Gather your things. It's time."

Once the campfire had been extinguished and our

belongings had been repacked, we gathered again in front of the invisible veil. I tried to access the Arts to sense what Ailan had found but couldn't feel anything different in the space before us. I turned to Cora and whispered, "Can you see—or feel—the veil?"

She shook her head. "No, but Valorre can. Through him I can tell it's here."

I returned my attention to the seemingly innocent space. "So this is the border between Lela and Risa? I never expected it to be so...mundane." Risa was the only other land connected to Lela, and that connection was only at the border along the northern edge of Kero. The eastern and western edges, along with the borders surrounding what was now called Vera, touched the sea. "I've only ever seen the sea as a border. I always thought the border here would be something else. Perhaps with a wall or guards."

"There is a guarded wall where the main roads run through," Cora said, "but not here."

How oddly disappointing. It made me wonder how kings and queens kept track of which land was which, before I reminded myself that *I* was, in fact, a queen and should know such a thing. *Never mind such trivial matters. I'm about to enter another realm. A realm my son is heir to.* Suddenly, kings, queens, and the division of land seemed meaningless.

Ailan made her way between me and Cora, eyes closed and hand outstretched like earlier. "Are you ready?"

Cora and I exchanged a glance before nodding.

"Follow me closely," Ailan said. She began walking

forward, and Cora waved for me to follow as she and Valorre filed behind me.

I wrapped my arms around Liam as I took one trembling step after the other. Too terrified to look elsewhere, I kept my eyes trained on Ailan's back, my ears focused on the sound of Cora's footsteps and the beating of our horses' hooves behind me.

One step. Another. Then a sudden flash of light.

By the next step, the light was gone, replaced with a dull gray, like a fog. As we continued forward, I took in our surroundings. The fog-like mist had cleared to reveal colorless earth beneath our feet. Although it was bare here, the scenery seemed to grow denser—though still gray—further ahead.

Ailan let out a strangled cry and sank to her knees, hand pressed to her heart. "This is so much worse than I imagined. I can feel it. I can...feel it dying."

Cora knelt at her side, putting a hand on her shoulder. "It gets better," she said gently. "It is worse closest to the veil."

Ailan nodded and shakily rose to her feet. Rumbling steps surged behind us, followed by the beating of wings as the four dragons rose into the sky. While three of the dragons soared away and out of sight, Ferrah remained above us, making wide circles through the gray skies ahead.

We continued on in the silent, dead woods—if you could call them woods—until Ailan froze. Cora and I stopped, following her gaze. Straight ahead stood three tall figures, shrouded beneath the gloom of a towering, gnarled row of trees. As they came near, I began to make out their features. They appeared to be males wearing long, flowing robes in bold colors and intricate patterns. One had black hair, another had bronze, and the one in the middle hand long, silver hair.

The silver-haired figure stepped forward, his face even more striking and beautiful than Ailan's.

In fact, Ailan seemed to have grown taller and more beautiful since we'd entered the tear. Her skin was now more of a shimmering, dark caramel, where it had once looked merely golden-brown. Her hair was black as onyx, with hints of blue swimming in its waves. I wondered how much more beautiful she would be if it weren't for the gray dampening the colors around us.

Ailan lifted her chin, shoulders relaxing as the silver-haired man stood before her. Her full lips pulled into a slight smile. "Hello, Fanon. It's been awhile."

19

MORKARA

Cora

Fanon froze, chest heaving as his eyes drank in Ailan as if she were the only thing standing in the dead woods. His face seemed to flicker between inhuman beauty and monstrous rage. Finally, he composed himself, his expression stony. He began to speak in the Elvan language, and it took me a moment to remember how to interpret his words. His disgusted tone, however, made it easy for me to catch on. "That's all you have to say to me? And you say it in that...that human language?"

Ailan shook her head as if to clear it. "I'm sorry," she said slowly in Elvan. "I haven't spoken anything else in many, many years."

Fanon glared, giving no reply.

She took a slow step toward him, then another, until they were nearly touching. She lifted a tentative hand, fingers meeting his cheek, then sliding along his angled jaw as she stared into his pale, blue eyes. "I never thought I'd see you again," she said, her voice strangled.

To my surprise, Fanon's face crumpled in a way I never could have imagined. Sorrow pulled at his lips as he hung his head, crystalline tears trailing down his ivory cheeks. "I've...waited. You have no idea how long."

Ailan wrapped her arms around his neck, bringing their foreheads to meet. "I have a feeling it's been even longer for me."

I blushed, looking away from the couple and instead focusing on the two figures behind them. There Garot and Etrix stood, exchanging an awkward glance.

Mareleau trembled beside me. "Who are they? And what are they saying?"

"I've met them," I whispered. "I—"

"You!" Fanon shouted, eyes narrowed above his tear-stained cheeks as he moved away from Ailan and stormed over to me with long strides.

"Leave her alone, Fanon," Ailan called after him, her tone firm.

Fanon froze and shot her a wide-eyed look. "This human is an invader. What is she doing with you?"

Ailan came to my side and faced Fanon, meeting his eyes with a fierce expression. "Cora is my ambassador, not to mention the one responsible for finding me. As Morkara of El'Ara, I forbid any harm to come to her."

Fanon's jaw shifted side to side as his eyes darted from Ailan to me. "Very well, Morkara," he said stiffly. It was hard to imagine the unexpected intimacy I'd witnessed just moments before. Now there seemed to be nothing but tense formality between them. "What are your orders?"

"Take us to the..." Ailan frowned, her confident demeanor faltering. "Where is the seat of the Morkara now that the palace of Le'Lana is gone?"

Fanon's face flickered with a hint of sympathy. "We have built a new palace north of here."

Ailan nodded. "Take us there, please."

Fanon took in our retinue, nose wrinkling as he assessed our horses. Then his eyes fell on Mareleau and Liam. "All of you?"

"Yes. Me, my ambassador, my blood, and my heir," Ailan said.

Fanon sucked in a sharp breath. "Your...heir?"

"Yes."

"I see waiting for me has been hard on you indeed," Fanon said, voice dripping with sarcasm.

Ailan put a gentle hand on his shoulder, the tenderness returning to her face as if it had never left. "We will talk tonight, Fanon. There is so much I need to tell you." Her voice was barely above a whisper.

He continued to sneer at Mareleau, but his hand fell softly on Ailan's. "Very well, Morkara. Garot, weave us the fastest way back to the palace."

Garot and Etrix came forward, meeting my eyes for the first time since our arrival. Etrix gave me a subtle nod, expression neutral as ever, although I could almost swear I saw a hint of shock in his eyes. Garot's lips twitched into a half-smile when no one else was looking, then faced the direction they had come.

A tunnel of swirling gray opened before us, causing Mareleau to jump and grab my arm. "What's happening?" she asked.

"This is Garot's talent as a weaver," I said. "He's the

bronze-haired one. I don't know much about his talent, but I know it helps him move from place to place quickly."

"Like you?"

I shook my head. "No. They don't see this as anything close to what a worldwalker can do."

The three Elvan men walked into the tunnel, followed by Ailan. I heard Ferrah screeching somewhere in the distance, to which Ailan whispered a *hush* in response.

Mareleau and I followed Ailan, and the two horses and Valorre followed us. Ailan slowed her pace until we caught up with her.

"I'm sorry about Fanon," she said. "I'll work on him and the tribunal as soon as I can. Once they know my story..." Her words were swallowed up in a sigh. "I feel like all I've done for days is explain, and yet I still have so much more to do. *We* have so much more to do."

"I know what you mean," I said. "It seems like I've said little else aside from repeating the same explanation to one person or another." I turned to Mareleau. "It seems like ages ago that we were in the study at Ridine, discussing everything for the first time."

Mareleau had nothing to say in reply as she watched the swirling colors turn from gray to brown, then green.

"We've moved away from the veil," I said, as shades of blue and purple began to mix with the green. My gaze fell on the three Elvan figures walking quickly ahead of us. I turned to Ailan. "How is it they found us? The first time I came to El'Ara, the three of them found me as well, although it wasn't until I dismounted Valorre. I thought it was just a coincidence then."

"Triggers have been woven into the land throughout El'Ara," Ailan said. "They have been here long before even my mother's time. The strands from the weavings are attached to a select few protectors in each kingdom. These protectors can then sense when and where someone enters who is not of our kind. They are responsible for investigating any invasions that occur in their territory. If they are not able to take care of the threat themselves, they are to report it to the Morkara. That is how my mother met my brother's father."

"You said he was a worldwalker like Darius." *And me,* I didn't add.

"He was," Ailan said. "It was by accident he came to El'Ara, or so my mother always said. She relished telling stories of her first love, Prince Tristaine of Syrus. He was barely more than a boy when he was caught wandering around the kingdom of Sa'Derel in awe and won my mother's heart when she'd been sent to banish him.

"My mother was young too, newly appointed as Morkara, and fell madly in love with the strange young man. She kept their love affair secret, weaving a special place where they could meet and not set off the triggers to warn the others."

I looked ahead, realizing Garot had slowed his pace and was watching us. Etrix strolled on without interest, while Fanon had walked so far ahead, he could hardly be seen.

"That's the part of the story no one likes to tell anymore," Garot said with a sentimental sigh.

Ailan let out a small laugh. "I see you aren't as offended by the human language as dear Fanon is."

Garot shrugged. "I love any language that tells a story."

"You would make a great bard in the human world," Ailan said.

"I probably shouldn't, but I'll take that as a compliment." Garot smiled wide. "I'm glad you are back, Morkara."

Ailan returned the smile, although it didn't reach her eyes. "You may not be glad for long. I fear the stories I bring with me herald dark times ahead."

Garot's glowing smile didn't falter. "Then we should make haste so I can hear them."

~

Teryn

A knock sounded on the door of my study. I lifted my eyes from my desk as a messenger entered. My heart raced as it did each time a messenger approached, hoping beyond hope that this would be the day I'd finally hear from Cora. "What news do you have?"

Before the man could speak, Queen Mother Helena swept into the room as if she'd been hard on the messenger's heels. "Do you have word from my daughter?"

"Message from King Larylis, Your Majesties," the messenger said, eliciting a gasp from Helena. He handed me a folded and sealed letter, bearing the new rose and eagle sigil of Vera.

Helena rushed to stand over my shoulder as I scanned the short note from Larylis. "They made it," I said with a sigh of relief. "And they found the book."

Before I could hand the letter to Helena, the messenger passed me another. "Two messages were delivered from King Larylis, Your Majesty."

I furrowed my brow as I opened the second, unsure if I should expect good news or bad. Why send two letters at once?

"This was sent the morning after the first letter, Your Majesty," the messenger explained. "The second messenger was able to catch up with the first so they could be delivered together."

My heart sank as I scanned the words.

Seeing my fallen expression, Helena grabbed the second letter from my hand, then let out a short cry. "They left Dermaine?"

Remembering the presence of the messenger, I attempted to compose myself. "Any other news?"

"No new reports of dragons, Your Majesty. In fact, there have been no sightings for at least a day."

I cocked my head. "Not a single sighting in all of Lela?"

"Not one, Your Majesty."

I dismissed the messenger and moved to the window, brow furrowed as I reflected on Larylis' second note. *Cora and Mareleau departed this morning,* it had said. *The book didn't contain as much help as we'd wanted. Cora thinks the Forest People might have a clue about how to find Ailan. Mareleau insists on going with her. They have said they will return once they speak to the Forest People.*

I could almost hear Larylis' empty tone through his sparse words. It was clear he felt just as disappointed as I did. What could the Forest People possibly know about finding Ailan or stopping the dragons? Regret coursed through me, making me wish I'd gone with her. *At least then I'd understand what is going on.*

"No dragons," Helena muttered, shaking me from my thoughts. "Do you think that means anything?"

"Maybe," I said, considering the news under a different light. I thought about how many days it would have been since the message had been sent. If Cora had used her powers to Travel, they would already have arrived with the Forest People by now. I hesitated before voicing the hope that rose within me. "Perhaps they've already found what they were looking for. Maybe the Forest People had the answer all along." I met Helena's eyes, seeing a reflection of my hope in them. "They could have taken care of the dragon problem already. Maybe even found Ailan herself."

"Then they will be back soon. We should hear word again in a few days, right?" Helena's tone was confident, but she trembled, wringing her hands. The gesture seemed appropriate, considering her worry, until I realized she wasn't trembling but shivering.

My eyes darted to the hearth, and I was surprised to find it had yet to be lit for the day. "I'm so sorry, Helena. I hadn't realized how cold it is in here. I'll call for the hearth maid at once." How had I not noticed the lack of a fire until now? *Too much on my mind,* I realized with a shake of my head.

"Don't bother," Helena said. "The hearth maid seems to have run off."

I paused. "Run off?"

"She is supposedly missing. I haven't had a fire in my room all morning and no one seems to know where the girl is."

I let out an irritated grumble. "Then someone should have been appointed to replace her." I opened the door and ordered the hearths be tended to immediately, beginning with my study.

When I returned to my seat, I sank back and rubbed my brow. "How did I lose a hearth maid? How did an entire set of daily duties go uncared for all day?"

Helena came to my side. "These things happen, Teryn. You must remember, your household is still considered new. You will soon learn that even the most established households make mistakes. Sometimes your help runs away. Sometimes they fall ill and forget proper protocol to inform their superiors. Other times, they steal from you and have to be banished. Trust me, I've seen it all."

"Even so. The issue should have been dealt with much earlier."

Helena smiled. "Like I said, your household is still new. They will learn."

My thoughts were interrupted by another knock— rapid, this time—at the door. Was the new hearth maid here already? Before I could tell the caller to come in, a messenger rushed in, different from the one I'd already dismissed. His face was flushed, his breathing heavy as he gave me an unsteady bow.

I paled. "Do you have a message from the queen?"

"No, Your Majesty," he said through gasping breaths. "Urgent message from the scouts in Risa. They've gathered information about Syrus."

I took the letter from his sweating hands and pulled it open. My throat went dry as I read the words.

"What is it?" Helena asked.

My hands began to shake furiously, my knees growing weak. *Be strong,* I reminded myself. *You are king.* I closed my eyes and loosed a quivering breath. "The King of Syrus is in Norun. They have allied and are preparing for war."

Mareleau

I thought I would vomit before the swirling colors ceased. To my relief, the strange tunnel ended, and the colors spread out around us, revealing a clear, blue sky above, a plush green lawn below, and an immense, opalescent palace before us. Swaying on my feet as our companions paused, I stared up at the heights of the climbing, gold-tipped turrets. I never thought I'd see any palace more beautiful than Verlot, but compared with the Elvan palace, Verlot seemed like a peasant's shack.

The silver-haired Elvan named Fanon spoke to Ailan with a terse tone in his language, eyes darting to me and Cora. Ailan responded, and after a reluctant nod from Fanon, our retinue continued toward the palace.

"Ailan has ordered us time to bathe and rest before meeting with the tribunal," Cora whispered.

I resisted the urge to grind my teeth. How was it fair

that *she* could understand them when I could not? *Probably because she's a sweet, little empath while I'm an evil narcuss.* I closed my eyes, feeling my heart sink at the harshness of my own thoughts. I remembered what Salinda had told me and even avoided chastising myself for my slip-up. *Love myself. Love myself.*

I decided to choose a more productive route. "How do you understand them? Is it something that can be taught?"

Cora tilted her head as she considered. "You have access to the Arts, so it's possible."

"What can I do to try?"

"Well, start by focusing on their tone when they speak," she said. "You know how you told me you were able to see what your suitors expected you to be? Start there. Try to feel into what the Elvan speaker expects to get across to the listener. From there, try to release more and more control over what you hear, and instead focus on what you feel. Let the words shape themselves within you. Allow a word in our language to express it to you."

I nodded, trying not to feel overwhelmed by what she seemed to do so naturally, and instead shifted my focus to the conversation happening between Ailan and the black-haired Elvan. Their words were hushed, but I focused on the tone, loosening my grip on my expectations as I focused on the intentions behind their words. Nothing became clear, but I got the impression Ailan was giving some sort of order to the Elvan man.

"What is she saying to him?" I asked.

Cora hesitated for a moment, eyes unfocused as she listened. "She is telling Etrix what accommodations she expects for us. Now she's telling him when to gather the tribunal and what to tell them."

"So she's giving him orders." I pressed my lips together to hide my smirk of satisfaction. While I hadn't gathered nearly as much insight as Cora had, it was a good start.

The closer we got to the palace, the more of the intricate details I could see—white walls draped with gilded vines of ivy and rose, elegant statues that towered overhead, and an overall sense that everything shimmered like the sun over the sea. "This place is beautiful."

Cora pulled her arms tight around her, hugging herself as her shoulders hunched. "Yes. Beautiful."

Her empty eyes expressed the opposite of the awe I felt, and I remembered what she'd said about her time in El'Ara. She'd been a prisoner. She'd been...sentenced to death.

My eyes flickered to Ailan, then to Fanon, who continued to keep a fair distance ahead of us. I didn't need the Arts to tell me how he felt about me. His icy glare told me enough. The other two Elvan had barely looked my way, but I imagined they felt same. If these three were cold to me, how would the tribunal respond? Not just to me, but to...Liam.

I pulled Liam closer to my chest and kissed his cheek, feeling as if we were no longer entering the walls of a majestic palace but the mouth of a beast.

~

Cora

I kept my face passive as Etrix opened the door to a familiar room. The room looked exactly as I'd seen it last —narrow, plush cot near an open balcony strewn with hay, elegant tapestries lining the white walls. I turned to face Etrix, who lingered in the doorway, and raised an eyebrow.

"Fanon told me to bring you here." Etrix's neutral expression remained unchanged, but there was a hint of apology in his tone.

I let out a bitter laugh and stepped further into the room, followed by Valorre. Valorre paused by the balcony, then, with a lowered head, strode outside. Anger flooded my veins. "He isn't a horse, you know."

Etrix hesitated for a moment. "He has been living in the human world for a long time."

"Even there, he was never stabled," I said. "You allowed our horses to remain outside, where *he* belongs. He should be free in the forests. Or are we prisoners again?"

"You shouldn't have come back. It isn't safe for you. I tried to help you once—"

"You tried to have me kill myself." As soon as the words were out, I regretted their bitter edge. Etrix had never acted out of cruelty toward me. He simply didn't see things the way I did. None of the Elvan did, yet he and Garot had shown me the closest thing to kindness out of any of them. Still, I found it hard to summon my gratitude.

Fortunately, Etrix didn't seem to expect any. "Your

friend and her child have been given comfortable accommodations."

I nodded, wondering where in the palace Garot had been instructed to send them. Perhaps Ailan's blood and heir would be shown more respect than a former criminal. I sat at the edge of the cot, shoulders hunched with fatigue. I'd known it would be hard to come back here, but it didn't make it any easier. Especially being in this room. *How much worse will it be meeting with the tribunal?*

I looked back at the doorway, surprised to see Etrix still standing there. "I'm not going to disappear this time," I said with a sigh. "If there had been a better way, I wouldn't even be here."

"You found Morkara Ailan." Etrix's voice came out flat, but it almost seemed like a question. He studied me with his onyx eyes.

"Yes," I said.

"She brought you here."

I nodded. "She wanted me to be her ambassador between my world and El'Ara."

"Why?"

I tilted my head. "Why did she make me her ambassador?"

Etrix's face flickered with a hint of confusion. "Why does she need one?"

I considered his question for a moment. "I think it's because our worlds are going to find it necessary to work together in the coming days."

"Why?" For the first time, I heard fear in his voice, reverberating through that single word.

I opened my mouth to speak but thought better of it. "You should hear it from your Morkara, not me."

Etrix touched his hand to his forehead, then dropped it to his side, regaining his composure. "Is that why we are meeting with the tribunal?"

"I imagine so."

He let out a sigh and turned to leave. Before he was out of sight, he paused. "Thank you for finding her. For bringing her home. Fanon should be the one to thank you, but I know he won't."

If only you knew I didn't find her purely for the sake of El'Ara, I thought to myself. However, that truth wouldn't help my cause. "You're welcome."

I AWOKE TO A KNOCK AT THE DOOR AND SAT UP ON THE COT with a start. The windows and balcony showed the indigo sky of night with starlight that illuminated the room nearly as bright as if it were still day. "Come in," I said as I stood, straightening the violet, robe-like gown I wore. After Etrix had left, I'd been given a bath and a change of clothes. My dress wasn't nearly as regal as the ones I'd seen the other Elvan wearing, but it was still elegant. More importantly, it was clean, comfortable, and perfectly suited to the summer-like air of the palace.

The door opened to reveal a smiling Garot. "Ambassador, it is time to meet with the Morkara and the tribunal."

I moved toward the door, then stopped to look at Valorre, still lying on the balcony. "Is Valorre to stay?" Part of me hoped he wouldn't be forced to face the tribunal again, but another part of me longed to bring him anywhere, so long as he was able to stretch his legs.

"Actually," Garot said, "I am to see he goes outside."

"You're letting him go free?"

"Orders of the Morkara." Garot leaned forward, a conspiratorial smirk on his face as he lowered his voice. "She was not pleased when word got around where Fanon had put the two of you."

I couldn't help but smile.

"Come, unicorn," Garot said.

It's all right, I told him. *I think it's safe.* While I couldn't say I trusted any of the Elvan, I had the feeling Garot was being truthful.

Valorre stood and came to me, nuzzling my shoulder. I could sense his relief to return to the outdoors.

"Wait right here for a moment, Ambassador," Garot said. He held out a hand, and a swirling tunnel of light emerged where the hallway had been. The Elvan walked into it, waving a hand for Valorre to follow.

I will wait nearby with my friends, Valorre said. I smiled, realizing he'd referred to Hara and Ailan's horse as his friends. Before I could say anything in reply, he followed Garot into the tunnel.

It wasn't long before Garot returned alone. My heart sank, feeling Valorre's distance. But at least I *could* still feel him. He was close. He was safe.

"Shall we continue to the tribunal, Ambassador?" Garot asked.

I let out a sigh, wondering if it really were necessary for me to attend. Shouldn't Ailan address her people on her own before bringing a criminal in their midst? "If we must."

∾

SILENCE.

All I could hear was my racing heart as the tribunal processed all Ailan had said. She remained on the floor —in the exact place I'd once been condemned to death— while Mareleau and I sat at the front row, facing her, with rows and rows of the tribunal spanning behind us. Out of the corner of my eye, I saw Fanon clench and unclench his fists on his armrest a few seats down.

My heart continued to pound.

I knew they wouldn't react as harshly to Ailan as they had to me, but I couldn't shake the memories of the last time I'd been in that room. It didn't help that the tension felt the same as it had that day—which spoke louder than any Elvan word could.

Or so I thought.

The silence in the room turned out to be the calm before the storm. It began with one voice shouting a question, followed by another. Before long, a wave of voices called out, echoing through the room, then clashing with others. Questions became arguments, and arguments became a thrashing tempest.

"They're angry. Confused," Mareleau whispered as she leaned toward me. She'd been testing her attempts at interpreting the Elvan language throughout Ailan's speech, although to me her interpretations seemed more like obvious guesses. This one was no exception.

I rubbed my temples, pushing away thoughts that were not my own—ones that bore down upon my mind, adding to the pressure of the rising volume of voices. I could no longer understand the words that were being thrown throughout the room. *Breathe in. Breathe out.*

Mareleau inched closer to me as a few of the Elvan

stood to make their shouts heard over the rest. "Why are they upset?"

Fanon stood and shouted back at some of the others. I closed my eyes, ignoring Mareleau, ignoring the voices, focusing only on my breath.

A clear yet powerful voice rang out, and the shouting began to subside. I opened my eyes and saw fury in Ailan's expression as she stepped forward and repeated what she'd said. The standing Elvan returned to their seats. I breathed away the cacophony of thoughts and let my focus settle on Ailan.

"I am your Morkara," she said with undeniable authority, her tone sending a chill down my spine. "You have forgotten your place since I've been gone. Everything I've done has been for the good of our world, and my word is final. You may have your say, you may guide my hand, but you will do it with respect if you want mine in turn. Do we all agree in the ultimate power of our weavings, whatever our talent?"

The tribunal mumbled their agreement.

"Do we agree that the whispers of our weavings are the ultimate truth?"

Again, the Elvan agreed.

"Then speak not another word against the whispers of mine."

The silence returned.

"Darius will come for us," Ailan said, "and I care not whom you blame for that. We must partner with the humans, and I care not how much you'd prefer we sacrifice their world for ours. My heir is of the human world, and I care not how much that disgusts you. He is of my blood. I have named him. His place is not up for discussion. It is final."

Fanon stood and bowed his head to Ailan, eliciting quiet gasps. Then he faced the tribunal and spoke with a sense of authority almost equal to Ailan's. "Let us discuss one thing at a time, one voice at a time, with patience and decorum."

"He's showing his respect to Ailan," Mareleau whispered as Fanon returned to his seat.

I ground my teeth. Another obvious interpretation.

She leaned in closer. "The tribunal can no longer rally behind him, right?"

My eyes widened at her surprising insight, and suddenly the storm of shouting that had erupted made sense. I felt the shift in the room's energy and knew Mareleau was right. Half the tribunal didn't want to accept Ailan as Morkara. They didn't trust her as belonging to them, in the same way many of the Forest People no longer trusted her. Some of the tribunal wanted Fanon to remain steward. He wouldn't lead them to war. He wouldn't partner with humans. He wouldn't allow a criminal to enter El'Ara. But with Fanon's acquiescence to Ailan, none of them had a choice. She *was* Morkara.

Debate continued, but in a much calmer manner than before. War was discussed. Plans for protecting the tear in the veil were made. Mareleau continued to whisper her interpretations, and I was able to respond to them with more patience, now that I no longer felt like the room was closing in on me.

Conversation eventually shifted from war and safety to Ailan's heir. The energy in the room grew tense yet again, but the voices of the speakers remained civil.

"They're talking about Liam now," I whispered to Mareleau.

Her breath caught, but she said nothing.

Ailan spoke forcefully while a few Elvan argued against her. Their debate moved back and forth until the tribunal bowed their heads to Ailan's final word.

"They have accepted Liam as Ailan's heir," I said.

Mareleau let out a long breath.

But the debate wasn't quite over. It began to shift yet again as voices spoke out about the mother of the heir. The *human* mother. Disgust and fear filled their words as the tribunal argued in favor of sending her away, or worse —making her take Last Breath.

My hands trembled as I gripped the arms of my seat, listening with bated breath as Ailan argued against them, trying to appease their fears while allowing them a fair say.

Mareleau gripped my hand, and I found that hers was shaking as well.

Again, the tribunal fell to silence as a decision was agreed upon. I opened my mouth to whisper to Mareleau, to tell her what had been decided, but another argument came forth.

Sweat dripped down my neck. Another agreement was made.

Ailan's eyes flicked toward Mareleau, filled with apology.

"They said..." My mouth went dry, and I couldn't find the words to continue. Mareleau's eyes met mine, her face drained of all color. I swallowed hard and summoned the strength to speak. "They said, as heir, Liam must remain in El'Ara. They have accepted you as Liam's mother and will allow you to stay in El'Ara with him if you choose to do so. But—"

"I know." Mareleau closed her eyes, tears streaming down her cheeks. Her hand went to her heart as she sank back in her chair. "Larylis can't come. I have to choose between my husband and my son."

21

PROMISE

Mareleau

S tupid. So stupid.

"Mareleau, wait," Cora called after me.

I ignored her as I stormed down the hallway. Liam cried in my arms, as if my distress were his own. "Hush," I whispered gently, my heart breaking as I looked down at his twisted-up face, pink with agitation. I knew he must be hungry, but I refused to nurse him in front of the tribunal and their judging, condemning eyes.

Why did I do this? Why did I come here?

I arrived at my room and pushed open the door. Cora was fast on my heels, entering the doorway as I sank onto my bed. My eyes unfocused as I undid the top of my Elvan robe to nurse Liam, tears falling like rain down my cheeks.

Cora approached me with hesitant steps, then sat next to me on the bed. "I'm sorry."

"I never should have come here." My voice sounded raw.

"You did what you felt was best."

I met Cora's eyes with a scowl. "Why did I ever think I could trust my own judgment in the first place? Why did I ever believe the Arts could be useful to me? You told me I'd learn which feelings were of fear and which were my inner guidance. Now I know I should have listened to my fear. If I had, I'd be safe at Dermaine Palace with my husband, not trapped in a world that needs my son, yet hates him." I choked on my words, and my voice grew small. "How could I have put him in danger like this? I thought I was protecting him."

Cora edged closer to me. "If you hadn't found Ailan with me, I'm sure she would have eventually found you. These things have a way of working out like that."

"What do you mean *these things*?"

"Things that are bigger than we are."

There's something happening that is bigger than me. Bigger than us. That's what I'd said to Larylis the last night I'd spent with him. Now, I regretted ever saying that. "I don't care. I still wish I'd stayed at home."

"Let's pretend you did," Cora said. "Let's pretend you'd stayed at home and Ailan never found you. Then what would have happened?"

I shrugged. "I'm sure you'd have figured everything out on your own and found Ailan anyway."

"What do you think would have happened after that?"

"This is pointless," I said with a grumble.

"Just humor me."

I sighed. "Fine. I'm guessing you'd have told Ailan

pretty much everything she now knows. Aside from about me and Liam, I suppose."

"And then what?"

I shrugged. "You'd still have become her ambassador. You would likely both be here now."

"You think everything would just continue on exactly the same without you and Liam?"

I wanted to say yes, but a sinking feeling hit my gut. "Mostly the same."

Cora nodded. "Mostly. Except Ailan wouldn't have an heir. Without Liam, Darius need only find Ailan and kill her to rule El'Ara."

"I'm starting to feel like that wouldn't be the worst option."

Cora frowned.

"I know it sounds horrible," I said through my teeth. "But after that meeting, I'm finding it even more difficult than before to care about the fate of these people."

"You're forgetting two things," Cora said. "For one, there's a good chance Darius will invade Lela to find the tear in the veil. What then? Sure, you and Liam could have stayed home. But can you honestly say you'd feel content staying safe at home while the rest of us fought to defend our land? And if we'd failed, would you have been content doing nothing while you watched Lela crumble around you?"

Not long ago, I would have said yes in a heartbeat. I knew I couldn't do that this time. Still, I wasn't willing to accept her words so easily. "We don't even know if any of that *will* happen. We don't even know if Darius is alive—"

"Emylia was certain he is still alive."

My mouth hung open as I searched for another argument. "So what if he's still alive? What if he never invades Lela? What if he kills Ailan and takes over El'Ara without even a second glance at our world?"

Cora let out an impatient sigh. "That's the second thing you're forgetting. Lela is the heart of El'Ara. We know he never wanted to be Morkara, Steward of Magic. He was never content to simply watch over the magic of El'Ara and distribute it according to their Ancient ways. We know, from Morkai, that Darius wanted to become Morkaius—High King of Magic. He wanted to rule the magic and use it for himself. Who knows what power Darius would have as Morkaius? He could pull down the veil completely, bringing Lela straight into the world you are so willing to sacrifice."

My stomach sank. She was right.

She leaned closer to me. "You *can* trust yourself, Mare. I know it's hard sometimes. The Arts, our inner guidance—even what Ailan calls the *whispers of her weavings*—can take us into scary places. Ever since I found Valorre, I feel like I've moved from one scary place to the next. But that doesn't make it wrong. When I look inside, I know I'm on the right path. It might not be the most comfortable path, but I know I have a purpose. Your purpose, it seems, is even bigger than mine."

I could almost hear an edge of bitterness in her voice.

She continued. "I know it hurts to choose what you are being forced to choose. But you can trust yourself to make the right decision, no matter how painful it is."

I hated that she was right. I hated how calm and solid I felt after she said those words. The fear still clawed at me, but it no longer held sway. *It would be so much easier to give in to that fear. To run away, back to Dermaine and live in ignorant bliss.* That is, until Lela became the heart of a world run by a power-hungry Morkaius.

I looked down at Liam, who had fallen asleep at my breast. "He's the one who's important," I said. "The people here may not see it, but I do."

"They will learn," said a strong voice from the doorway.

My eyes shot up to see Ailan, and resentment swelled within me. It was her fault this was happening, after all. She was the one who unwittingly dragged us all into this with her weaving. However, my anger fizzled out as quickly as it had come. What was the point of being angry? What was done was done. I let out a heavy sigh.

"I'm sorry how you were received today," Ailan said. "They have forgotten what it is like to have a true Morkara. There is also much they don't understand about humans. I never realized how much fear and judgment reside in my people."

I nodded but didn't meet her eyes. A lump rose in my throat. "Can I at least say goodbye to them? To my mother? My husband?"

Ailan's face fell. "My child, you are no prisoner here. If you wish to leave with Cora when she reports to—"

"No. I am well aware that I am not a prisoner, but my son is. I will not leave him for a single moment."

Ailan hesitated before she walked toward me. "Liam is my heir, not my prisoner."

"But he can't leave."

She sighed, stepping closer. "We need to keep him safe here."

"I need you to promise I can say goodbye to them, and that they can see Liam one last time before all of this is over." *Before I'm stuck in this cruel, beautiful world forever. Before I never see Larylis again. Before...*

It was too much for me to even imagine. Fresh tears streamed down my face.

"Of course," Ailan said, placing a light hand on my shoulder. "I will do whatever it takes to make it so."

Cora

I followed Ailan out of the room, leaving Mareleau curled up on her bed with Liam. Her pain had been palpable, nearly impossible for me to avoid absorbing as I'd sat with her. It was a relief to feel the weight of her closed door between us.

"I've changed so much since I've been gone," Ailan said. "I never realized how much the Forest People were influencing me."

I walked beside her down the hall. "Is that a bad thing?"

"The other Elvan would think so. They don't trust me, just like the Forest People. I've lost the trust of both my peoples in a matter of days."

"It's not all of them," I said, unsure why I felt the need to comfort her after expending so much energy consoling Mareleau. Perhaps it was because the words felt like truth. "Salinda began to trust you again. And I saw many others hugging you goodbye as you left camp, as if your identity was nothing of concern."

"Probably because I told them I wouldn't ask them to fight for me," Ailan said, eyes on the floor.

Surprise and relief hit me at once. Maiya came to mind, her worries over her husband being forced to go to war. "I think that was the right thing to do."

Ailan nodded. "Fighting against Morkai was one thing. You needed allies and asked the Forest People to help you. They gave you their support of their own free will. It was wrong for me to expect their aid simply for being their Wise Woman. Salinda helped me see that when we met with the elders."

"Some of the Forest People will still fight for you," I said, "if it comes down to it. I'm sure of it. Just like I'm sure the Elvan will warm up to you. Did you know any of them before the veil?"

"Some," Ailan said. "The tribunal changes members regularly to allow new El'Arrans to have a turn with our government. Fanon was the only one I knew well, though."

I remembered their heated reunion and blushed as I debated how far I wanted to pry. "How well *did* you know him?"

She smiled. "He was—*is*—my consort."

"You mean...the two of you are married?"

Ailan pondered the question before answering. "None of us marry the same way you do in the human world. Each may choose their own partner at will. The Morkara may partner with whomever he or she desires, and any children born from any union are considered valid heirs, unlike in your world. It is only the blood of the Morkara that matters when naming an heir.

"However, the Morkara is paired with one partner as chosen by the tribunal. This pairing is a way to make alliances and reward certain families—similar to many noble marriages in Lela. The consort of the Morkara bears the additional burden of sharing in the Morkara's duties and can act as steward if the Morkara is unable to meet certain tasks. Hence, Fanon's position. As soon as Mother died, the Mora transferred to me. But when I became locked beyond the veil, Fanon was appointed steward. Unfortunately, even as steward, the consort has no ties to the Mora and can't direct its flow or make any drastic decisions. The Mora simply won't accept such orders from anyone but the Morkara."

I reflected on her words, puzzling over such an odd form of government. "What if you'd never returned?" I asked. "What if both you and Darius had died before either of you named an heir?"

"The Mora would eventually select a new Morkara, in the case that a current Morkara and all his or her children had perished without a new heir being named," Ailan explained. "It is clear the Mora knew my brother and I were still alive, as no one had been selected since the veil was cast." She began to slow her pace and paused outside an open door, extending her hand toward it. "I have provided a more suitable bedroom for you. I'm sorry Fanon had you put in the holding quarters. You aren't a prisoner here."

That explained why I'd felt like one; the room's purpose was specifically *for* prisoners. I didn't mention that the dungeons I'd been held in had been far worse, however.

"Valorre has been allowed outside, correct?"

I nodded. "Thank you for that. I know Fanon doesn't like me."

She let out a bitter laugh. "He doesn't like anyone. It's

been hard on him since I've been gone, and learning what I've done without him hasn't made my return easy for either of us. There is love between us, though."

I remembered Fanon's unexpected tears when he first saw Ailan. With a shake of my head, I cleared my mind and entered the room. It was elegant, decorated in shades of gold, violet, and opal. Best of all, it had a proper bed, instead of a cot on the floor.

Ailan turned to leave, but I spoke before she could take a step. "What happens now?"

"Hmm?" Her eyes met mine with a furrowed brow, as if she had been distracted by her thoughts.

"What is our next step?"

"Ah, yes." She sighed and entered my new room. "I am going to speak to the Faeran tomorrow and see if I can reconcile our races and work together like we did before the veil. Their kind welcomed me with open arms in Lela, so I'm hoping I can at least begin to make amends for what they blame Fanon for. They don't understand that he's had no power over the return of the Mora to *either* of our races, and—as you well know—he isn't the best at communicating with others."

"What about the tear in the veil? How will you protect it?" I asked.

"Now that we know where it is, it will be guarded at all times. I've already dispatched guards to stand watch on El'Ara's side. I don't want to risk relying on the triggers to warn us of invasion."

"Do you have a next step for me?" I twisted my hands to keep from nibbling my thumbnail. I was eager to know what lay ahead, yet terrified at the same time.

"Tomorrow you will return to your kingdom and

share what you have learned," Ailan said. "Send your own guards to the other side of the veil in Lela but keep them discreet. The last thing we need is for a group of guards to give away the location of the tear."

"When do I report back to you?"

"You said your husband has sent scouts to learn more about Darius, correct? See if he has learned anything and send more scouts if you must. If you hear anything about Darius and his potential plans, report back to me immediately. Otherwise, return here once you have assured Lela's forces will support us. Once I have that peace of mind, I can begin to come up with a plan."

I nodded, and she again turned away. Words bubbled up in my throat and came out in a rush. "What will happen to Lela when this is all over?"

Ailan paused and cocked her head.

"When Darius is destroyed and both Lela and El'Ara are safe...what happens to me? To my husband and all the people in our kingdom? To the people of Kero and Vera?"

"Ah," she said with a sigh. "I see the true question in your eyes, and the answer is yes, El'Ara must have its heart again. Once the threat from Darius is gone, I will need to find a way to undo my mother's veil and bring Lela home where it belongs. When it returns, the Mora will return as well. The strength of my people's talents will be like they were before the veil. Another weaving will be made, protecting El'Ara from others for good. This time, it won't be made under the pressure of time and war. This time it will last."

"I figured as much," Cora said, "but that doesn't explain what will happen to my people. Where will we go? Will we be forced to leave our land and make new homes elsewhere? Or will we become citizens of El'Ara?"

"I wish I had an easy answer, my child." Ailan's face was full of sympathy. "That is not something I am thinking about right now, as we have much more pressing matters to attend. However, I promise you I will do whatever it takes to protect *both* our peoples. I won't rest until our two worlds are safe and every person in Lela has a home."

I could sense the conviction in her words. She really did intend to protect us all—human, Elvan, and Faeran alike.

Still, I couldn't shake the sinking in my gut. I let her walk away, swallowing my lingering question. *What happens if you are no longer around to bring that promise to fruition?*

22

TRUTH

Cora

The wall of mist hovered in the distance as we walked amongst the dead, gray trees and crumbling soil. Ferrah swooped overhead now and then, blocking out the meager, gray light as her wings spread out like a moving canopy. Valorre stayed close to me but no longer seemed startled by the dragon.

I glanced at Mareleau walking silent and pale-faced at my side, then at Ailan, who followed closely behind. Ailan's lips were pressed into a tight line as she stared grimly ahead at the growing wall of white. She met my gaze and seemed to relax slightly. "The sight of the veil is unnerving," she said. "Not to mention the decaying land."

Ferrah flew over us again, and my eyes followed her graceful arc until she was out of sight. There was no sign of any other dragon in the sky. In fact, I hadn't seen even a hint of any other dragon since we'd been in El'Ara. I returned my attention to Ailan. "Where did the other dragons go when they returned with us? It seems only Ferrah has stayed close by."

"Ferrah's place is at my side, so she lives in the caves beneath the palace," Ailan said, surprising me. I hadn't noticed any caves beneath the palace. Then again, why would I have noticed such a thing? I'd hardly seen much of the palace itself, aside from a few rooms. Ailan continued. "The other dragons have homes of their own. Most prefer the Fire Mountains in De'Nah. Others live in the Charcoal Plains of Ce'Len. There are many other places dragons frequent that even I have yet to visit."

It was hard to imagine how vast El'Ara was. All I'd seen firsthand was the plush, eternal summer of what was left of Le'Lana. That and the dead land near the veil. I had no idea what the other kingdoms were like.

A mass of figures ahead caught my eye, shaking me from my thoughts. Rows and rows of Elvan soldiers stood before the veil, flanking the invisible tear. I was taken aback at seeing the Elvan dressed in anything other than their customary decadent robes, then equally fascinated by their iridescent armor—plates of shimmering metal over opalescent chainmail. As we approached them, Ailan stepped in front of me and nodded to the guards, prompting them to take a wide step back to create a modest walkway.

The soldiers eyed me with suspicion as we continued closer. I resisted the urge to scowl at them, knowing I could have easily avoided this unnecessary ceremony if I'd simply worldwalked to Ridine from my room at the Elvan palace. However, Ailan had made me promise not to do so. She'd said it would build trust if her people saw me leave on my own two feet.

As Valorre and I stood before the white void, Ailan put her hand on my shoulder. "You know what to do?"

I nodded. "I'll world—" I paused, remembering the glares of the soldiers that surrounded me. "I'll *Travel* home to Ridine once I'm on the other side. As soon as I'm home, I'll seek my husband and tell him what I've learned. We will immediately send guards from our Black Force to stand watch in the shadows around the veil. After that, I'll hold a formal meeting with our council as well as send word to King Larylis." My eyes flashed toward Mareleau, who took a sharp intake of breath at the mention of her husband. "Once I have secured the support of Lela's forces, I'll return to the tear and report to you here."

"Very good," Ailan said, giving my shoulder a gentle squeeze. She turned to face the small retinue that had followed us, nodding at two Elvan attendants that held the reigns of Hara and Ailan's horse. Now that she was home, Ailan had no need for a horse. The attendants led the two horses forward, then quickly retreated as if they were eager to distance themselves from the creatures.

They will follow me into the tear, Valorre said as he circled the horses. *I will keep them close.*

Thank you, I said.

As Ailan stepped back, Mareleau took her place. She wore the carrier gifted to her by the Forest People, with Liam nestled inside. The rustic cloth and earthy tones of the carrier stood in stark contrast to the pale, shimmering blue of the Elvan robe she wore. Her eyes were rimmed with red, but her face was composed as she regarded me.

I waited for her to speak, sensing she was in the process of deciding something.

Finally, she pulled a trembling hand from the pocket of her robe and brought out a scroll of delicate parchment tied with a violet ribbon. "Please," she said, her voice cracking, "give this letter to Larylis."

I accepted the scroll, feeling the burden fall into my hand, its weight crushing my lungs. With a deep breath, I forced Mareleau's pain away and tucked the scroll into my pocket.

Mareleau didn't give me a second glance as she turned and began to walk away, her shoulders heaving with quiet sobs.

Ailan sighed as she watched Mareleau's retreat, then faced me. A nod.

Time to go.

I reached a hand toward the veil, feeling for the tear. Despite its appearance of swirling mist, the veil felt solid, impenetrable, and without give. I continued to move my hand along the wall, seeking any hint of opening. It had seemed so much easier for Ailan.

I can find it, Valorre said.

I considered his offer, then shook my head. *No. The soldiers should see me do it. Let them see me as a feeble, fumbling, harmless human, like Ailan wants.*

My fingertips suddenly slipped forward into the mist, cold air biting them. The chill was uncomfortable yet wonderfully familiar. *My* world. *My* winter air.

I found the tear.

Arms outstretched, I pulled aside the tear and stepped through, Valorre and the horses following close behind. A cloudless, midday sky shone through the trees overhead. Behind me, there was no hint of the veil, nothing but endless forest.

I took a cautious step forward, checking my surroundings. There was no way to measure the passage of time in Lela while I'd been in El'Ara. Anything could have happened since I'd been gone. *Darius could be watching this very spot.*

A quiet sound came from my right, almost too subtle to hear. With silent feet, I crept over to Hara and retrieved my bow, swinging my quiver over my shoulder and swiftly knocking an arrow into place.

The sound came closer.

I moved forward, then stood behind the wide trunk of a tree, angling my body so my arrow was between the veil and whoever approached.

A flash of movement between the trees. Then another.

Two of them.

I pulled my arrow to my cheek just as the two forms cleared the trees. I froze.

My kind, Valorre said with elated surprise, as two unicorns appeared before us.

I let down my bow and released a heavy breath. A medium-sized, brown unicorn trotted toward the invisible veil, followed by a smaller, gray unicorn. They halted when they spotted Valorre and the horses, still not realizing I'd been poised to shoot them.

Valorre tossed his mane with excitement. *My kind have been finding their way home. They are not the first. Many have come already.*

The two mirrored Valorre's joy, then continued forward. I watched until they disappeared between the tear, hoping the Elvan guards would allow the unicorns to return without issue.

I looked around the now-quiet forest, a new sense of dread filling me. *Let's hope Darius knows nothing about unicorns,* I told Valorre. *The last thing we need is for him to realize all he needs to do is follow one home to find the tear.*

Getting to Ridine seemed even more urgent then it had before. I went to Valorre, pulling myself onto his back, then clicked my tongue at the horses until they stood at either side of Valorre. With a deep breath, I rested a hand on each of the horses, feeling their warmth beneath my palms.

I closed my eyes and thought of home.

Teryn

"How do we know this isn't a ploy to distract us from the southern seas?" Lord Jonston asked from his place next to me at the meeting table. "With our attention on the border between Kero and Risa, we could be missing an attack on Vera." The men at the table muttered their agreement.

My face grew warm beneath the stares of not only my own councilmen, but my brother's as well. Larylis' retinue had arrived an hour ago, aching from their hurried travels to Ridine. Despite many protests, I'd insisted our meeting begin without delay. It was clear only Lex and Larylis understood the weight of this meeting.

I cleared my throat. "There is no way to know for sure what King Darius' plans are, but his alliance with Norun makes it obvious he will invade from the north. Still, King

Larylis has sent scouts to watch the southern ports in Vera."

"Your Majesty, tell me again why you are so certain King Darius *will* invade," Jonston said with a raised brow. "Rumor first claimed he was responsible for the dragons, which was the only reason we sent scouts looking for him. Not a single dragon has been seen in almost two weeks, and all we know of King Darius is that he now resides in Norun."

I clenched my jaw. "Norun has been reported to be planning for war."

"Then I agree our attention should be on Norun, Your Majesty," Jonston said. "But for all we know, they are simply planning on adding another kingdom in Risa to their list of conquests."

Lex cleared his throat, and the eyes of the councilmen found him at the other end of the table. "Lord Jonston, as Prince of Tomas and neighbor to Norun, I have seen what it looks like when Norun is preparing for a *simple conquest*, as you called it. The reports from your scouts dwarf any efforts I've seen...aside from when they allied with Morkai. You remember that, right? Does that not give you at least a *tiny* reason to be alarmed?"

I pressed my lips together to hide my smile. Lex certainly had grown bold as of late. "He's right. When Norun allied with Morkai during the Battle at Center-pointe Rock, they became our enemies. After their retreat, they never sent any word of armistice, nor have they responded to any of our inquiries. The fact that they are prepared for war and are slowly making their way south is enough for me to gather our defenses."

Jonston nodded, but his brow was furrowed. "Still,

what does this have to do with King Darius, Your Majesty?"

I met his eyes, considering my response. There was so much he didn't know. So much I wasn't sure I could tell him—or the rest of the council. How would they respond if I told them *everything*? About the prophecy and Morkai's father. The Ancient Realm. The truth about Lela's origins.

Jonston narrowed his eyes, as if trying to read what was behind my hesitation. "Your Majesty, if there's something you aren't telling us, now would be the time."

Maybe he was right. Perhaps it was time. If the council knew what we suspected we were up against, perhaps they would give their full support and stop questioning my motives. Or...perhaps they would think I'd gone mad.

My father had believed when Lex delivered Morkai's ultimatum. Then again, that had been a direct message from someone who had witnessed the threat firsthand. All I had was the word of a wraith no one could see and memories of a prophecy I'd learned about from inside a crystal. I let out a deep sigh. *No, that sounds ridiculous. I need more proof before I bring up magic...*

I met Jonston's eyes. "You'll just have to take my word—"

The doors to the great hall opened behind me, and everyone at the table rose to their feet and bowed. I spun around to find Cora approaching, dressed in a strange robe of black silk overlaid with sheer fabric in iridescent tones. Her cheeks and nose were tinged with pink, as if she'd just come in from the cold.

My first instinct was to run to her, pull her to my

chest, and shower her with eager kisses, but propriety before the councilmen kept me frozen in place. They didn't know she'd left on an urgent mission, leaving me without any idea of her recent whereabouts or plans to return. They had no idea how badly I'd missed her, how I'd worried over her safety day after day.

Heart racing, I gave her a smile and received her with a chaste kiss on the cheek. My lips burned where they brushed her skin, wishing they could have lingered. "My dear wife, you've returned from your travels."

"I have." Her eyes rested on mine, expressing what our words could not. She was safe. She had news. And she could not wait to be alone with me too. *Later,* I promised, hoping she could see it written on my face.

Cora turned to the council and took her place at the opposite end of the table, next to Larylis and Lex. "Please, update me on current affairs."

My stomach sank. Had she not heard yet? I supposed she wouldn't have heard much if she'd just returned from her stay with the Forest People. "We've located King Darius. He is reported to be in Norun, which appears to be preparing for war. A large force has slowly been making its way south from the capital."

Cora's face went pale, and I could tell she was struggling to maintain her composure. "Then we were right. He's invading Lela."

The councilmen wore looks of confusion as they regarded her. "You believe this too?" Lord Jonston asked. "You think some king from the Northern Islands will invade us?"

"King Darius of Syrus isn't just some king," Cora said.

"He's Morkai's father and the very reason Morkai had become obsessed with Lela to begin with."

Gasps and whispers were uttered across the table, and even I couldn't suppress my shock at her sudden admission. *I guess it's time for the truth after all.*

"Councilmen," Cora said, her voice firm. The table quieted. "There is much to discuss. First, let me tell you what really happened after Centerpointe Rock."

23

TAKEN

Cora

"This is preposterous," one of the councilmen said, throwing his hands in the air. "Elves and fairies?"

Lex let out a sudden laugh. "I once thought as you did, Lord Samisch. Ancient Realms used to sound like things of children's tales. Then I was captured by a sorcerer, and all that changed. It changed even more when I fought that sorcerer, his army of wraiths, and a monstrous beast called a Roizan. You fought with us on that field, right? So, you'll remember that beast well. Oh, and there were unicorns. Everywhere. You're finding it hard to believe in the Elvan and Faeran after all *that*?"

Samisch paled, but his expression remained suspicious. "Where's the proof? I believed what I saw on the battlefield. But how am I to agree to sending members of our Black Force to guard an invisible space that is supposedly a portal to another realm when there is no proof?"

Lord Jonston turned to me. "He has a point, Your Majesty. Besides, you must understand how hard this is for all of us to believe, especially when you admit to withholding information about what happened last year."

Samisch nodded vigorously. "Why didn't you tell us the truth when we were first assembled as your council?"

I met Teryn's eyes for a moment before I took in the faces of our councilmen, wondering how best to explain why we'd kept the truth behind my brother's and King Verdian's deaths a secret from them. How could we explain that, after what had happened with our previous council, we didn't know if we could trust them? *These men aren't vile men like Lord Kevan and Lord Ulrich. They aren't even like King Verdian,* I reminded myself. It was true. They didn't scorn me for my position or fear me for my magic. *Perhaps we underestimated them back then.*

"My lords," I began, "we kept the truth to ourselves because we believed the threat of dark magic had ended when Morkai was destroyed for good. We saw no reason to alarm our people—even our councilmen—with something that would be both unbelievable and disturbing."

"We were wrong," Teryn said. "And we apologize for our mistake. We should have told you, and we promise never to withhold such information again in the future. If you are to trust us as the rulers you support, then we should trust you to accept the truth, no matter how disturbing we might consider it to be."

"That's what we are doing now," Cora said. "We are trusting you to process what I've said as truth and reflect on what it could mean for Lela. We are asking you to trust *us*."

"Is there any proof you can give us?" Jonston asked, his tone more hopeful than accusing.

My eyes locked on his. "Fail to believe me, and you will have your proof soon enough. King Darius comes for Lela. If he has allied with Norun, then they come for us as well. If we don't protect our land and the tear in the veil, we will find ourselves at his mercy."

"You're sure we can't bargain?" Samisch asked. "Give him access to the veil in exchange for leaving Lela alone?"

I clenched my jaw. "I've already told you what will happen if Darius gains power. Lela will return—"

"—to the Ancient Realm with all of us in it," Jonston finished for me. He ran a hand over his face and began rubbing his stubbled jaw. "It sounds crazy. However, I too fought at Centerpointe Rock. I saw nightmares come to life. There isn't a thing I wouldn't do to protect this land from experiencing that again."

"Then we have to be ready now," I said. "We need to stand against him *before* we have proof. We need to anticipate his moves and keep him from finding that tear."

Jonston hesitated before nodding in agreement. "What then? If we promise to protect the tear and defend Lela against invasion, how do we win? How do we destroy an immortal king?"

My shoulders fell. I wished I had an answer. "That, I do not yet know. But I know Morkara Ailan will come up with a plan. As her ambassador, I will be delivering messages and plans between our two worlds."

I waited for further argument, but only silence hung in the air.

"Are we in agreement then?" Teryn asked. "Our first step is to dispatch members of the Black Force. They will patrol this area along the border, where the tear is." Teryn tapped his finger on a map, marking the area I'd shown him.

The men at the table spoke their agreement, and I let out a breath of relief.

"Right then," Teryn said. "Meeting adjourned." He rose to his feet, while most of the council remained seated. Some reclined in their seats, eyes unfocused. Others called for messengers as they prepared to execute their orders.

As I stood, a hand fell on mine. I met Larylis' concerned expression. "How is she? And Liam?"

My heart sank, yet I forced a smile. "They both are well. They are being kept safe and comfortable in El'Ara while we make our plans."

He nodded, but his eyes seemed suddenly glazed.

Mareleau's letter came to mind. My fingers twitched as I considered reaching for it, but I wasn't sure I was ready to deliver him the pain I was sure it would cause. *Better wait until I can give it to him in private.*

Teryn approached us. "Are you going to retire, brother?"

"I have a few messengers to dispatch first," Larylis said, his previous concern now covered in a mask of cold determination. "Also, I want to lead the Black Force to guard the tear."

Teryn studied Larylis for a moment. "Are you sure your time wouldn't be better spent returning to Vera and leading your people through their preparations?"

Larylis glanced at the table where his councilmen

chatted with the others. "I'll give my council everything they need to proceed without me."

"But you're their king—"

"She's there, Teryn." Emotion choked his voice. "Right behind that tear. If I can't protect her myself, then I want to be as close as possible."

Teryn frowned, then gently grasped Larylis by the shoulder. "Of course. Make whatever preparations you need to make. You'll lead the Black Force to the veil as soon as possible."

"I will," Larylis said, then turned to his men.

Teryn faced me, running a hand along my cheek. "I'm glad you're home."

I smiled. "So am I." I linked my arm through his, and we made our way to the other side of the room and out the door.

I felt Teryn's eyes on my face as we entered the dark, lantern-lit hallway. "You won't be here for long, though, will you?"

"No," I said with a sigh. "Now that I know Darius is on his way, I must report back to Ailan. Weeks could pass before he and his army arrive, but for El'Ara, it will be merely days. They need as much notice as possible so they can be ready to help us defend Lela and the tear."

"Here's what I don't understand," Teryn said. "If Darius can worldwalk, why hasn't he brought the entire army here already?"

I shrugged. "While I'm sure he can worldwalk with others like I can, I doubt he can worldwalk an entire army at once. He'd have to bring them in a little at a time. And since he isn't running against any time restraints, he doesn't need to hurry to get here. Besides, if he's anything like me, he needs to be familiar with a place before he can worldwalk there. We know the veil has kept him away from Lela so far."

"So far."

We paused in the hallway, and I faced him. "I know, Teryn. I'm worried too."

"When do you leave?"

I had to struggle to form the words. "In the morning."

Teryn's face fell, eyes unfocused. "Too soon. I just got you back."

"It's only been days for me. But for you..."

"Weeks." He let out a heavy sigh and met my eyes. "The last time I saw you, I was saying goodbye. I can't believe we have to do it again."

"I know. But we handled it well last time. Don't you remember?" My lips pulled into a sly smile as I stepped closer to him. It felt good to smile, to see Teryn's eyes widen with realization as I pressed my hand to his chest and lifted my chin. My mind screamed at me that I had too much to worry about to let myself get distracted with things like flirting. But I needed a distraction.

Teryn leaned in and lighted a kiss on my lips, and in a glorious rush, my worries melted away. I tried to pull him closer, but he pulled away, instead reaching for my hand. Now it was his turn to smile mischievously. I suppressed a squeal of surprise as he pulled me down the hallway and through the nearest doorway into the throne room. The room was dark, aside from the dying fire glowing in the hearth. We were alone.

Teryn closed the door quietly behind us and pulled me toward the wall. My lips found his in the dark, my breath quickening as our kisses grew more and more eager. I wrapped my arms around his back, pressing his chest against mine as his lips moved down my neck. My hands slid to the hem of his tunic, and I pulled it over his torso. His fingers fumbled with my Elvan robe, searching for the intricate ties at the front that would allow it to unravel. The lowest tie came loose, exposing my leg above the knee. My back pressed against the wall behind me, and I gasped as Teryn pulled my leg around his hip as he began to work on the text tie at my upper thigh.

"Am I interrupting?"

The unfamiliar voice came from the opposite end of the room. Teryn whirled around, and I quickly covered my exposed leg, heat rising to my cheeks. My eyes searched the dark room, barely able to make out a shadowed figure on the other side.

The fire in the hearth came to a sudden roar, filling the room with an orange glow. A man sat on Teryn's throne. His skin was pale, his hair slick and black, falling to the nape of his neck. His face was long and angular with high cheekbones and a pointed chin. I'd never seen him before, yet somewhere in his features came subtle hints of two familiar faces—Morkai and Ailan.

"Darius," I said. The firelight flickering over his face brought to mind another image—my nightmare. This was the man whose face I hadn't been able to make out in my dream. This was the man who'd thrown Mareleau into a pillar of flame. *No. That wasn't real.*

Teryn took a protective stance in front of me. "What do you want?"

Darius rose to his feet and took slow steps down the dais. He paused at the base. "I've been waiting for this one for days now." He inclined his head toward me.

"Why were you waiting for me?" I asked, glaring. More importantly, how long had he been there? Had he listened in on the council meeting? Sweat beaded at my forehead as the questions pounded my mind, yet I forced myself to remain calm.

"I wanted to see the woman who had turned my son into an idiot." He shook his head with a false laugh. "Well, perhaps he was an idiot before he went looking for you, but," he clicked his tongue, "look at the mess he made of himself."

Teryn opened and closed his fists, as if willing a weapon to appear in his hands.

Darius took a few steps forward. "I never paid his reports much heed back then, when he came to tell me of the prophecy he'd learned that would supposedly return my powers. Now that my mind is clear, they make much more sense. It wasn't hard to find the black mountain over a field of violets. The woman with the beauty of Satsara."

My eyes darted toward the door, just a few strides away from us. *We must get away.* But first, I needed answers. If he'd listened in on the council, all our plans were destroyed. If he somehow saw the map...

"You said you were waiting for me. Have you been sitting there all day? All week? How have you not been caught?"

"Oh, I was caught," Darius said. "I first came here weeks ago to investigate my newfound realizations and learn what had become of my son. It wasn't hard to sneak into the palace, under the guise of a merchant. I couldn't very well come as myself. It appeared some were looking for me." His eyes locked on Teryn for a moment before returning to me. "Unfortunately, the one I sought was no longer home."

"So you've been waiting here ever since?"

Darius laughed. "Goodness, no. I managed to sneak into this room and weave a trigger on your throne before I was found by a servant. Come to tend the hearth only to have the wits scared out of her! Had to take care of that one."

"The missing hearth maid," Teryn said under his breath as his stance faltered. "What did you do to her?"

Darius' mouth fell open in mock surprise. "My good man, I didn't kill her, if that's what you're thinking. I'm not like my idiot son, you know. Good help is hard to come by."

"Then where is she?" Teryn said through his teeth.

"Doing her job like always. But in Syrus."

I furrowed my brow as I took in the new information. The missing hearth maid was news to me, but the fact that he took her to Syrus meant...

I needed confirmation that my suspicions were correct. "You wove a trigger on my throne...and world-walked away with the girl?"

"You do know of my power then. Yes, you are correct. The trigger alerted me of your presence just now. Had no idea I was about to walk in on such a priceless scene, though."

That meant he hadn't been listening in on the meeting. That is, if he was telling the truth. I wasn't likely to get any more confirmation than that. *Time to run.* I stepped closer to Teryn, ducking slightly behind his arm to obscure my face as if I were frightened. I didn't have to act. I *was* frightened. "What do you want with me?"

Darius made his reply, but I ignored him, instead placing my hand on Teryn's lower back and whispering, "Door on three."

Teryn stiffened, showing he'd heard me.

Darius, on the other hand, didn't seem to have noticed as he continued his speech. "—now I think you might be able to help me."

"What makes you think that?" I said. This time, when Darius spoke, I pressed lightly into Teryn's back. Once. Twice. Three times.

Teryn and I darted for the door. Just as Teryn's fingers touched the handle, he was thrown to the side. Darius was before me as if out of nowhere, a smile on his face. *Two can play at this game,* I thought as I focused on the space at the other end of the room. I didn't have a weapon, but I could...I could...

Why was my vision suddenly swimming? Pain seared my shoulder. I looked to the side, finding the black hilt of a knife protruding from me.

My knees buckled as Teryn rose to his feet with a shout. He ran toward us, hand reaching for me. Darius snickered. Then Teryn was gone.

Teryn

My feet shuffled across the stone floor of the hallway, my eyes filled with visions of Cora's blood running down her arm. *I should have screamed. I should have called for help. I should have fought him instead of running for the door. I should have saved her. I should have seen his blade.*

"Your Majesty?"

I looked up, surprised to find myself in the great hall. *Did I really walk here? Was this where I was trying to go?*

Half of my councilmen were still at the table, as well as my brother and his council. Lex had already retired. The room went silent as all eyes fell on me. It was then I realized I wasn't wearing a shirt.

Larylis sprang from his seat and came to me. He grabbed me by the shoulders, eyes burning into mine. "What's wrong?"

"She's gone." The voice didn't sound like my own.

"Who? Cora?" Larylis shook my shoulders when I didn't respond. "Teryn, snap out of it, what happened? Where is Cora?"

It felt as if a dam suddenly broke inside me and all the rage and terror and pain came tumbling out. I fell to my knees with a shout that was more feral than human. It sent a chill down my spine, helping to clear the remaining fog from my head. My cheeks grew red as I took in the stunned faces of the council and Larylis' wide eyes.

I stood, taking a deep, trembling breath, and made my way to my seat. "Darius was here. He found us in the throne room."

Larylis fell into the seat next to me. "What happened to Cora?"

"He stabbed her and worldwalked away with her."

Lord Jonston ran a hand over his bloodless face. "How badly do you think she was injured?"

"I don't know," I said. *She could be dying. She could be...*

The rage continued to boil within me, igniting a fire of blood and fury. It burned the fog from my mind, showing me the only clear course of action. "All I know is we can forget what we've planned tonight." I met Lord Jonston's eyes, and those of every other man at the table. "We will send our Black Force to guard the tear, but we aren't going to prepare our defenses and wait for Darius to invade us. If he wants war, we will give him war. In fact, we will bring it to him."

24

DARIUS

Cora

I woke, finding nothing but darkness all around. I tried to move, but pain surged through my shoulder. My heart raced faster and faster as I tried to calm my breathing, but the darkness was too unnerving.

Where am I? Where am I? I asked myself over and over, but no answer came, save for the pounding of my heart, the pressure rising and crashing like waves against my skull. Words and thoughts that weren't my own began to creep upon my awareness, let in by my growing anxiety.

Wait, I can use this, I reminded myself. Thoughts and words meant there were people nearby, at least somewhere in my general vicinity. The realization allowed my breathing to slow, and my heart ceased racing. *Breathe in. Breathe out.*

Once I regained my composure, I closed my eyes and turned my focus to the sensations surrounding my body. Aside from the agonizing pain in my arm, I felt something solid beneath my back and bottom. *I'm in a chair.* I moved my hands only slightly, enough to notice resistance at my wrists. I did the same with my legs, finding my ankles bound to the legs of the chair. My mouth seemed to be covered with a tight cloth.

I let out a heavy sigh, the cloth forcing my breath to return and warm my cheeks. Relief settled over me. *I may be in darkness, but at least I know something of my surroundings.*

I extended my hearing, searching for the thoughts and voices of those I'd sensed during my moment of panic. In the distance, I heard numerous pairs of muffled steps, thoughts of mundane tasks, and the whistling of some unfamiliar tune. Servants. Did that mean he'd taken me to his castle? Or was I somewhere else?

Without a second thought, I filled my mind with images of Ridine castle. I thought of the forest surrounding it, the field beneath the cliff. I thought of Teryn's face. Salinda. Valorre. Nothing. No image remained long enough for me to worldwalk to it. What was wrong? Dread filled me, and I did the only other thing I could think to do. I screamed.

Footsteps sounded from the other side of what must have been a wall. Then the creaking of a door. "She wakes."

My heart sank as I recognized the voice. I blinked into the blinding light of the lantern Darius carried. As he approached, my eyes began to adjust to the light, and I took in my surroundings. No windows. One door.

I was surrounded neither by dungeon walls nor the deceptive beauty of the Elvan holding quarters. I was in a closet.

Darius stared down at me, tendrils of slick, black hair falling over his eyes. He lifted a hand toward me, making me jump, which in turn sent another shock of pain through my shoulder.

I followed his fingers with my eyes, watching as they lightly grazed my arm. It was then I realized the black hilt of the knife was still protruding from my flesh. The sleeve of my robe appeared to have been torn off and tied into crude bandages around the blade. I tried to keep myself from flinching again as Darius lifted one of the strips of cloth and peaked underneath.

"You'll live," he said, bringing his hands clasped before him.

I tried to speak, but my words were mumbled behind the cloth. With a roll of his eyes, Darius slid the cloth under my jaw, leaving a trail of moisture on my chin. "Why is there a blade in my shoulder?" My words came out raspy and slow, my mouth feeling like sandpaper.

"Because I stabbed you."

I narrowed my eyes. "Why is it still in my shoulder? I take it from the bandages that you aren't trying to kill me. Yet."

He ignored my question and tapped a finger under his chin. "Mother of Prophecy. Blood of Ailan," he said under his breath as he scrutinized me with narrowed eyes.

I was taken aback for a moment. *Then he doesn't know about Mareleau. Good. The truth is safe.*

"I believe my son lost his mind trying to find you," Darius said. "All to fulfill his reckless infatuations. First, there was his dead mother. I let that infatuation serve me well. Until he found that young woman, another infatuation. I knew I'd lost him to her the last time he came to visit. It was only a matter of time before he then realized he could take my mission on as his own. But you already know this story, don't you?"

I glared but didn't reply. *Tired. I'm so tired.*

"Yes, because you became the next part in the story. I know some of what happened. My son continued to send me updates here and there, to keep up appearances that he was still following my will. Last I'd heard from him, he'd sent me a message claiming he'd found the Blood of Ailan and had *taken care of it*. What does that mean?"

My mind felt slow to register all he was saying. When I realized what he was referring to, I clenched my teeth. "Your son made me barren. That way I could provide no heir and fulfill no prophecy."

Darius laughed, but it wasn't the wild laugh of his son. It was more restrained, calculated. "I'm sure he convinced himself he was terrible indeed. Yet, if he'd been even remotely capable, he'd have killed you."

I wanted to shrug, but reminded myself to keep still, lest I aggravate my wound again.

"When my mind returned and my body grew young, do you know what my first thought was? *He's done it! My son has succeeded!* I figured all I needed to do was find him and wrest his ill-earned power away from him. Didn't take long to figure out where he had gone, and all it took was a night at a tavern in Kero to hear the stories about the fearsome Morkai and the beloved princess who had destroyed him. How did you do it, anyway?"

"He destroyed himself." It was basically true. I thought about how Morkai had been eaten by his Roizan, the very creature he'd expected to aid him in his conquest. "He thought he'd found a way to get around the prophecy. As clever as he tried to be, he still sought to harness the magic, and that killed him."

Darius frowned as he studied me, black brows furrowed over piercing, gray eyes—the same gray as Ailan's. His angled features held a similar ageless beauty to Ailan's, but where Ailan's beauty was elegant, Darius' was terrifying. That's where his similarities to Morkai began.

I sneered under his gaze. "What do you want with me?"

He smiled. "You're going to help me get what is rightfully mine."

So predictable, just like his son. "I'm really not."

"Why is that? You've barely heard me out yet."

"I don't need to hear a word from you to know I won't help you. I know who you are, I know what you've done, and I know what you want. There's nothing you could say to make me do anything but stand against you."

"How will you stand against me when all you can do is sit?" he said with an innocent tilt of his head.

I deepened my glare.

He laughed again, turning away from me. "Ah, I imagine you must have already found my sister. You've heard her speak of what a monster I am, correct? How I need to be stopped. How I want what isn't mine." He whirled back around, bending over me as his hands clamped around the arms of the chair, wrapping around my wrists in turn. "But it *is* mine."

I closed my eyes at the pain that shot up my wounded arm, biting back a whimper. Darius released the chair and my wrists and took a few steps away. When

I opened my eyes, he was staring at the black hilt of the knife.

"I didn't mean to hurt you just now," he said, his face and tone without emotion. "I know what it is like to be struck by that blade. Did she tell you about that? How she nearly killed me with that very knife?"

Slowly, I nodded.

"Made with a rare Elvan metal, that one is. It is what allowed my sister to outsmart me and is what keeps you here with me now."

"What does that mean?"

"Try to worldwalk away," he said. "You won't be able to."

My heart stilled as I realized he knew of my abilities. I'd been on the brink of worldwalking just before—or as —he'd stabbed me. That meant he'd been prepared. "How did you know?"

"About you being a worldwalker? I didn't. Not until I found you in your throne room." His answer didn't make sense. I opened my mouth to speak but he held up a hand to quiet me. "Let's not get off topic. You want to know why it is I deserve to be Morkaius—"

"No, I don't."

"—and how you are going to help me. It's simple. I'm going to give you Lela."

I froze. "What?"

"You are going to help me by securing Lela's Royal Force in my favor, and I am going to reclaim my rightful place as Morkaius of El'Ara. As a reward, I'm going to leave Lela in the human realm under your rule."

My mouth hung open. "That's...impossible."

"Nothing is impossible for the Morkaius." Darius

paused, studying me again. "You worked hard to defend Lela against my son. You risked your life. Would you not do anything to protect your people? Wouldn't you prefer to avoid bloodshed if you could?"

"Yes, and that means stopping you."

"So quick to judge, so slow to listen," he said with a roll of his eyes. "What do you think will happen to Lela if I am defeated and my pathetic sister is able to reclaim her place as Morkara?"

"She *is* Morkara."

He ignored my comment. "If the Mora is seeping from El'Ara like the prophecy of the Morkaius suggested, then El'Ara is losing power. The people of El'Ara will want Lela to return where it belongs. The tribunal will never let Ailan leave Lela in the human world, even if there was a way to safely do so. What do you think will happen to you and all those you care so much about?"

I paled. How did he know? How could he read the fear that weighed heaviest on my heart? I shook my head and forced a mask of confidence. "Ailan cares just as much as I do. She will do what it takes to make sure we have homes. To make sure we will be cared—"

"Slaves, Queen Coralaine. The Elvan will make slaves of you. Sure, they will call you citizens, but you will never be one of them. You will be considered beneath even the animals. And your animals! They will be killed, along with the majority of your human population. Few of you will be allowed to live. You'll either be slaves, dead, or exiled."

His words seemed so certain. *He's just trying to get into my head.* "Ailan has promised otherwise. She gave me her word."

He laughed, this time throwing his head back as Morkai would have done. The resemblance made me shudder. "That's just it! You can't trust them. They say one thing, then do another. Ailan may be speaking honestly, I'll give you that. But she isn't the only power in El'Ara. The tribunal will never allow fair treatment of humans. Once the threat is over, they would turn her mind against your kind as they once did with my mother's."

"It sounds more like you're bitter, if you ask me."

His eyes went steely as they cut into me like daggers. He stepped closer, and when he spoke, his voice was quiet, filled with icy calm. "I am bitter. I was raised to be the next Morkara from the day I was born. They knew from the beginning that my father was human, yet they allowed me to believe I'd been accepted. Do you know what my mother used to call me?"

I shook my head.

"*Min'Elle Morkai.* My little King of Magic. You see, my father was Prince Tristaine of Syrus, heir to his father's crown. Mother told me how I was, in a way, a prince of two worlds, and how I would one day be something like a king in El'Ara. I remember how she looked at me back then, like I was the only thing that could make her smile. She'd look at me and remember *him*.

"Then my sister was born. The light in her eyes that she once reserved only for me and my father's memory now belonged to her consort and her daughter. Tales of kings and princes and the human realm dried from Mother's lips. Suspicion replaced the love I once saw in her eyes when she looked at me. The tribunal began to watch me with eyes that burned with fear—there was so much fear in them. They feared me when I used the term

Morkaius. My own mother taught me the term! I was simply trying to fill the role she'd made for me!"

His voice had risen to a shout, startling me.

He seemed to notice and closed his eyes for a moment. When he opened them, he put his hands behind his back, regaining his composure. His voice returned to its quiet tone. "Most of all, they feared my power. No, not my power as a weaver. They feared my human power, the power to walk between worlds.

"It was quite by accident, on my part, that I even learned I had such a power. You should have seen the look on my father's face when I showed up in front of him one morning! Took me a bit of trial and error to understand what I'd done, even more so to learn how to return home. Once I did return, rumors of my shameful power quickly spread, alarming the tribunal, my tutors, even those I'd considered my friends. Despite this, I refused to be shamed for what was naturally mine. In fact, I took pride in what I could do. I grew stronger in my powers, and dare I say a little arrogant.

"That's when they turned Mother against me. The tribunal convinced her I wasn't fit to rule, and she agreed with them. All because of my power—a power that could have done so much for El'Ara, could have made it a realm far greater than anything we could have imagined. But I was the only one who saw it that way."

His eyes grew unfocused as his lips pulled into a sneer. "Mother then attempted to banish me, did you know that? With the same weaving she'd used on my father, no less. As if I wouldn't have known! Do you know how she did it?"

I opened my mouth to reply but stopped myself. The

tears welling in his angry eyes stripped me of words. Not because of pity, but because of something else. Fear. His fervor was terrifying.

"She hugged me," he said, without so much as a tremble in his voice, though a single tear streamed down his cheek. "Just as she had done with my father. She took me to a glade under the pretense of showing me where she'd met him. Then, with a hug, she told me she loved me. That's when I felt the weaving begin to wrap around me, and I remembered what she had done to my father. It was the exact same thing. I pulled away from her and looked into her cold eyes. There was no love for me there. I worldwalked away before she could weave another strand."

My stomach sank, as if I could feel the full weight of the betrayal. None of that had been mentioned in Garot's stories. Still, I knew there had to have been a good reason why he'd been banished in the first place. Of course, there was little chance I'd get that fact from Darius.

He went on. "I returned to my father with the intention to stay for good, to take my place at his side as his eldest son. He was a very old man by then, but he accepted me into his home and named me heir. When he died, I was prepared to inherit his crown, not knowing my siblings had other plans. They enlightened me about many things, primarily the fact that Father hadn't named me *the* heir, but one of *many* heirs, to follow my seven brothers and two sisters in the line of succession. They thought they could bully me into submission, seeing me as the youngest sibling, despite me being born before any of them. Worse yet, they saw me as nothing other than an illegitimate bastard, born of their father's youthful dalliances.

"They were wrong about me. Again, I was set aside as inconsequential because of my parentage, but this time, I wouldn't be cowed. I bided my time. I waited until all my brothers and sisters were dead, then claimed what was rightfully mine."

Did you kill them? I wanted to ask. I frowned in suspicion but remained quiet. I didn't need to hear his answer to know the truth he'd left unsaid. Besides, I knew what happened next. Next he invaded El'Ara.

Darius must have taken my frown for sympathy. "Do you see now how I have suffered?"

I bit back a laugh. While I was surprised to learn his side of the story, I was far from convinced he was the innocent party. If anything, he was blind to his own flaws. "Is pity supposed to convince me to help you?" I finally said. "It isn't working."

He seemed unaffected by my spiteful tone. "I don't expect you to pity me. I expect you to understand. Being of two worlds, I have seen injustices that no one should tolerate. I seek to make them right here *and* in El'Ara. Both worlds are corrupt. Both worlds favor bloodline yet retract their own rules when it suits them. Tell me, how many times have the rules of your world seemed unfair to you? How many wars have been fought over crowns? How many cold marriages have been forced to gain alliances? How many capable citizens have been suppressed based on class and bloodline?"

I opened my mouth to argue against him, but I came up speechless yet again. *It's just the way things are,* was the only excuse I could find. And I hated that it was true.

Darius raised an eyebrow as if he saw the conflict on my face. "As a woman, I'm certain you've been slighted, whether princess, queen, or peasant. Here, a woman is nothing without a husband. I don't say that as a taunt, I say that to put injustice on display. From what I've heard, you weren't allowed to inherit your place as queen until you married your husband, correct? Due to some suspicion about you?"

I clenched my jaw. "What's your point?"

"My point is that you weren't respected for your gender, and you were feared for your power. That's what both our worlds are missing—respect for power. Blood and birth order are nothing compared to power, am I wrong? If you'd been measured by your power, you'd have been queen without a second thought for whom you married. Likewise, if I'd been assessed by power, I would have been named heir of El'Ara without a glance at my sister. In Syrus, I would have had my father's crown as soon as he breathed his last breath."

"You dream of a world run by power?" I shook my head with disbelief. "That would mean chaos. Each man would be constantly at war with another to prove who was most powerful."

"I'm not proposing an end to all the rules and order we know," Darius said. "All I'm saying is in my new world, power will be the deciding factor."

I rolled my eyes. "I thought you said you weren't like your idiot son. You sound just like him."

"He was an idiot because he failed to see what was right in front of him. You have a power no one should deny. My son saw it, but he interpreted it wrong. He was drawn to you, obsessed even. He made mistakes because of his fascination with you, all along never guessing the truth."

I swallowed hard, not sure I wanted to rise to the bait. "What's the truth?"

"That he wasn't drawn to you because of your place in some prophecy. He was drawn to you because you were his kin."

"His...kin?"

Darius nodded. "The Elvan can sense their kin when in close proximity. As soon as I saw you in your throne room, I felt it. I knew who and what you were right away. You are a worldwalker, like I am. Like my father was. Your blood is a distant line from his. You and I are kin.

"In fact, you could almost be my heir."

25

HEIR

Teryn

I stared at the ceiling of my bedroom, watching the morning light slowly spread from one corner to the other. Had I even slept a wink? Every time I'd closed my eyes, I saw nothing but Cora's blood. My own voice echoed in my head throughout the night, declaring war on Darius, on Norun, on Syrus.

Had I really meant what I'd said? *Cora has been captured,* I reminded myself. *What else can I do but fight him?* Yet, as I listened to my shallow breathing, alone in my room, I felt too small to fight. Too small to win. *But I must get her back.*

With the morning light now fully blazing through the window, I forced myself to roll from my bed. My legs felt heavy as I made my way to the vanity and downed a glass of water. My reflection caught my eye in the mirror, showing me a haggard stranger—tousled hair, bloodshot eyes, and too much scruff on my chin. I'd probably looked better when Morkai had taken over my body and nearly killed me in the process.

No. That was a lie. I *definitely* looked better then.

At least I could still joke. *Idiot. None of this is funny.* I glared at the man in the mirror.

A knock at my door saved me from further altercations with myself. "Your Majesty," came Lord Jonston's voice.

"Come in," I said, though it sounded more like a grumble.

Jonston entered, frowning when his eyes found me.

I hadn't changed since the night before, which meant I was still shirtless. I turned and stalked toward my wardrobe, acting as if he'd caught me in the middle of my hurried morning preparations. "Yes, Lord Jonston? What is it?" I said as I pulled an undershirt over my head.

He closed the door behind him, his face apprehensive. "Your Majesty, I wanted to speak with you about what you said last night."

I donned a gray tunic, adjusting its hem to keep from having to meet his eyes. "And what is it you wish to say about it?"

"Your Majesty, the council is worried over this...plan of yours. They wonder if you should perhaps take a day or two to recover from the events of last night."

I let my eyes meet his. "They think I'm crazy."

Jonston sighed. "They think you have suffered much, Your Majesty, which you undoubtedly have." He took a few steps closer to me, his voice pitched low. "No one would blame you if you retracted last night's orders."

Heat rose to my cheeks. "Is that what you think I should do, Lord Jonston? Take back my declaration of war? Continue to wait for an attack by a man who assaulted our queen?"

Jonston's jaw shifted back and forth before he answered. "No, Your Majesty. I agree measures must be taken, and Queen Coralaine's abduction solidifies the threat you foresaw. But if you want the support of the council, you need a solid plan."

His words struck me hard, as I knew he was right. My declaration of war wasn't the calculated strategy of a king; it was the wounded cry of a boy. I swallowed the tears that stung my eyes. "Then what do we do? I must do *something*."

"And we will," Jonston said. "Let us continue with our original orders while the council considers any additional actions we can take."

I hated how right he was. I hated that I had no better plan. I hated the thought of a single moment going by that I wasn't actively fighting to get Cora back. Yet, no matter how right he was, I couldn't bring myself to voice my agreement.

"Your Majesty," a new voice said from behind the door. I nodded, and Jonston turned to open it. A guard entered, face flushed as he gave a hurried bow.

I walked toward the man. "Speak."

"Your Majesty, there's some kind of commotion on the grounds," the guard said. "A white horse was reported circling the castle all night. Ever since second bell, it has been trying to get inside through every window and doorway it can find. And now that it's daylight, we can see it's clearly not a white horse, but a..."

"Unicorn," I said, then cursed under my breath as I

darted from the room. How could I have forgotten Valorre?

Lord Jonston and the guard caught up to me as I pounded down the stairs to the main hall. "He hasn't been hurt, has he?" I asked, looking left and right. At the entrance, guards clustered in the doorway.

"No," said the guard. "Last I saw, he was trying to get into the kitchen."

I took off toward the kitchen, hearing gasps of surprise the closer I got. When I entered, I found Sadie, the cook, struggling with a broom in the doorway, while Beca, the kitchen maid, threw bits of bread. The guards had the table on its side, pushing it against the doorway so it blocked the bottom half.

"Go on, you," Beca said, tossing an entire loaf this time.

"What a nuisance," Sadie chided, giving another jab with her broom. "They sure never mentioned this in the stories."

"It's all right," I said, approaching the flustered crowd. "Let him in."

Sadie and Beca started with squeals as they attempted curtsies. The guards stood and bowed, which in turn allowed Valorre to clamber over the table. If the situation weren't so grim, I would have found his unusual lack of grace amusing.

Valorre seemed to calm when he saw me, although his teeth were bared and his breathing labored as he made his way to my side.

"Easy, Valorre. You're all right. I'm here." My audience stared with stunned faces as I stroked Valorre's neck as I'd seen Cora do many times. He tossed his mane with a whinny that sounded far too much like a cry. "I know, Val, I know. She isn't here." My voice caught in my throat, sending fresh tears to my eyes.

Valorre lowered his head and nuzzled me in the shoulder. His entire body quivered with distress.

"I'm so sorry, Val," I whispered, bringing my forehead to his soft coat. "I should have come and found you. You must have felt it as soon as she was gone. It's my fault. I didn't protect her."

Valorre whinnied again, scraping his front hoof on the stone floor with an agitated stomp.

I pulled away, a sudden idea coming to mind. "Can you sense where she is? Can you take me to her?"

Valorre lowered his head further, eyes glazed. I didn't need to know his thoughts to understand his answer.

"That's all right, Valorre. We're going to get her back. I'm going to do whatever it takes." The conviction in my voice surprised me, making me stand taller. It was as if I'd unearthed a hidden well of confidence from deep inside. *Valorre needs me. Cora needs me. I'm doing this.*

I turned to Lord Jonston, who stared wide-eyed and unblinking at Valorre. I understood his fascination. Nearly everyone knew of Cora's famed unicorn companion, but it was one thing to know about it, and another thing to see it in your kitchen. As if my gaze shook him out of his stupor, he met my eyes. "Your Majesty?"

"Gather my brother, Prince Lex, and Queen Helena. I request a meeting."

"Shall I call the council as well?" Jonston asked.

"No, this will be a private meeting of those I am closest to only."

Jonston raised an eyebrow. "Is that wise, Your

Majesty? If you are discussing our plans, you should include the council."

I furrowed my brow. "You said so yourself, I should approach them only once I have a solid plan."

"Yes, but I feel any plans of war should be made amongst your closest advisers."

"Which is why I'm inviting you, Lord Jonston. If I am being reckless, my friends will be the first to tell me so. However, they understand what we are dealing with better than anyone else. If we come up with a plan that you support, then we can bring it to the council together." I took a step toward Jonston, my voice firm as I said, "We are getting Cora back. We are taking action."

Jonston hesitated before nodding. "Yes, Your Majesty."

"Gather those I've ordered. We meet today."

Cora

"I...I can't be your heir. I'm the Blood of Ailan. I'm the—"

"Mother of Prophecy?" Darius shook his head. "That isn't possible. I can sense you are my kin, but not through my sister's blood. No, you are of my father's blood. However, I am impressed you've tried so hard to stick to the Mother of Prophecy story. Who are you trying to protect?"

I swallowed hard, lest any word betray me.

"Could it be...Queen Mareleau?" Darius pulled a crumpled scroll from his pocket, the violet ribbon gone. *Mareleau's letter.* He unrolled the parchment, scanning it.

When he was done, he flourished it with a smirk. "This looks serious. Were you supposed to deliver it? Or did you steal it?"

"That's a private correspondence," I said, cursing myself that it was my best reply.

"Private indeed. Now, why do you have it? Here you are, protecting the identity of the true Blood of Ailan, yet withholding her personal letters. Who is King Larylis to you?"

I couldn't help but laugh, although I tried to move as little as possible as the mania tore from my throat.

His face flashed with irritation and the barest hint of a blush. "Have I made a joke you enjoyed?" he said through his teeth.

"Your attempts to bait me are not only obvious, but horribly misguided."

His expression regained its calm. "Enlighten me then."

"I was given the letter to deliver and would have done exactly that if I hadn't been abducted by a madman first. It's as simple as that. I'm not withholding anything."

He studied me a moment before echoing my laugh with his own. "You can't blame me for trying, can you?" He crumpled the letter and tossed it on the floor, then took a step closer to me. Laughter still played on his lips, but his eyes took on a cruel intensity. "I thought, perhaps, there may have been something other than pure friendship between you and this Mareleau, that's all. You did protect her by taking on the whole Mother of Prophecy guise, yet I can't say you tried very hard."

My lips pressed into a tight line. "What would have been the point? You obviously figured it out already."

"You are right about that. My son wasn't nearly as thorough as he'd thought, all because of his obsession with you. It blinded him to the truth. You were the obvious answer, born the year of the great bear in the kingdom bearing the black mountain sigil. Yet, just a kingdom away, another was born in the year of the great bear. I hear she gave birth to a son recently. Born at Ridine Castle."

He met my eyes, and I shuddered beneath the anger rising on his face.

"He should have seen the possibilities. He should have *looked* for them." Just as quickly as the anger arose, it dissipated with a sigh. He replaced his scowl with a smile. "Yet, what's done is done. Mareleau has lived a safe and privileged life, all so she could give birth to the Blood of Ailan. And *you*—you should win an award for all you've done for the cause! Your childhood was filled with blood and death, your womb broken before you even knew you had one. Did you always know your suffering had such a great purpose?"

My breathing quickened as I narrowed my eyes.

"No? When did you find out? When did you learn that everything that had happened to you was done by mistake? That you were carrying a punishment that had been intended for someone else?"

I bit the inside of my lip to stifle my reply.

"Do you enjoy being Mareleau's protector? Do you enjoy watching her with her newborn baby—a baby that was only born at the cost of all the children you could ever have?"

No. Get out of my head.

His voice began to rise. "Are you glad that you lost

your parents so *she* could keep hers? Are you proud that you gave up your youth so *she* could be coddled and loved, fought over by princes and poets? Have you ever wondered what it would have been like if Morkai had left you in peace and found her instead?"

"Stop." The word came out like a growl.

"Have you ever daydreamed about what it would be like if you'd grown up with your family, instead of watching them all die one by one? Have you looked at Mareleau's son and imagined him as your own, knowing you'll never experience the joy she now feels?"

"Stop!" This time, it came out as a shout.

His voice seemed to mingle with the pounding of my heart, rising to a roar in my head. "Can you honestly say you have no regrets? That you would have chosen this path for yourself? If you could do it all over again knowing what you know now, would you still choose what has been wrongfully chosen for you? Do you deserve this punishment? Are you happy with all you've sacrificed, or do you wish the burden had been put in its rightful place? Should it really have been given to you, an innocent child born in the wrong place at the wrong time? Or should it have been her? Do you *wish* it had been her?"

"Yes." The word was deafening, erupting from my throat and leaving everything—my breathing, my racing heart, Darius—in stunned silence.

"Yes, what?" Darius prodded, his voice soft.

"Yes." Tears streamed down my cheeks, my shoulders wracked with sobs. I welcomed the pain that burned my shoulder. "I wish it would have been her."

Darius placed a hand on my arm, his touch gentle.

"You have been treated wrongly, as have I. Injustice was thrust upon you, as it was thrust upon me. You want what should have been yours, as do I. You and I aren't so different. El'Ara belongs to me. Lela belongs to you."

With that, he took the lantern and left, closing the door behind him and leaving me in darkness. All I could hear were my quiet sobs.

26

DELIRIUM

Teryn

"So, what's the verdict?" I stood before the desk in my study, hands clasped. Larylis, Lex, Lily, Queen Mother Helena, and Lord Jonston sat in the chairs before me. "Tell me the truth. Is my plan crazy?"

Larylis sat forward in his chair, eyes alight with excitement. "No, brother. It makes more sense than anything else. Of course we should bring the fight to him! Keep Darius from stepping foot in Lela altogether!"

Lord Jonston rubbed his brow. "But how do we *do* it, Your Majesty? It's one thing to say we should march for war, and another to do so and actually *win*. Even with Lela's combined forces, Norun and Syrus will have us outnumbered, not to mention, the benefit of familiar terrain."

Helena, sitting straight-backed and regal in her chair, lifted a finger. "This man, Darius, can Travel at will. If all our forces are fighting in Norun, who will stop him if he decides to leave the fight and come here?"

"We will have to keep some of our men behind," I said, "to guard the areas he would most likely target. And some of the Black Force will still go to northern Kero to guard the tear. That part of our original plan won't change."

"How will you find it?" Lex asked. "I know Cora marked the area on the map, but wasn't she supposed to show the Black Force the exact location?"

"We will have to patrol the entire area she indicated," Larylis said. "We know the veil falls on the border between Lela and Risa, and the location she gave us narrows things down to a manageable radius."

"This proves my point," Jonston said. "If we have men guarding the veil, others stationed at the ports in Vera, and everywhere else of importance, we'll be even more outnumbered."

"You're right," I said, though it made me sick to admit it. "There's no way we can win if we march north to fight their entire legion. There has to be another way. We need to weaken them somehow."

"We could wait until they are far enough south from the capital, then send the Black Force to sabotage their supplies," Larylis said.

Lex shook his head. "They'd only be replaced the next day. Every city in Norun is occupied by soldiers to keep all the conquered kingdoms in check. They ration all goods out to the citizens and can just as easily take them to the army instead."

"We could block the roads leading to them," Larylis said.

"That means we'd have to allocate even more men away from our main fighting force," Jonston said, "giving us even *less* men for the actual attack."

"We need to stir up chaos."

"We need a solid plan."

"What if we attack at night?"

I stopped listening to the ideas and arguments as I leaned against my desk. *This isn't going to work, is it?* Everything inside me burned to take action, to rush head-first into battle, to do whatever it took to get to Darius. But Jonston was right. There was no way we could be successful if we didn't have a plan. There was no way we could *win*.

If we faced Darius head on in a single battle, our forces would be decimated. The path would be clear for Darius to invade Lela.

Cora would be lost to me.

I let out a heavy sigh, my shoulders slumped. "Enough."

The arguing quieted, and all eyes fell on me.

"We can't do this," I said, eyes on the floor. "Let's stick with our original plan. Defend Lela against attack."

No one said a word against me. I was almost disappointed.

I lifted my eyes, opening my mouth to dismiss the meeting, when Lily raised a timid hand. "I have an idea," she said, her cheeks blazing.

Lex turned to regard her, looking just as perplexed as I felt. "Lilylove?"

"You are free to speak, princess," I said, although I was more curious than hopeful.

Her voice came out small. "Why don't we use the rebels?"

I furrowed my brow. "What do you mean?"

"There is a resistance in Norun," she said. "There has been for decades, but it is coming to a boiling point. The conquered kingdoms want to fight to reclaim their land and titles, but the Norun occupation makes it impossible. All weapons are forbidden to anyone but the soldiers, every forge has been seized by the capital, and anyone suspected of dissension is put to death."

"I appreciate the idea," I said, "but from what you say, I don't see how the rebels could be in any position to help us."

Lily blushed. "We would have to help them first. Provide them with weapons and an opportunity. The rebels will do the rest. Norun will crumble, leaving the army isolated and without hope for reinforcement. The unrest is there. All they need is a little help."

I looked from Lily then to Lex, who still stared aghast at his wife. "Lex, do you know what she speaks of?"

He met my eyes and smiled, face full of pride. "Yes, what she says is true."

I cocked my head. "Princess Lily, how is it you know of this?"

"My brother, Your Majesty," she said. "He's one of the resistance leaders."

"He was a lord in a wealthy kingdom in Risa," Lex said. "A kingdom that now belongs to Norun." He turned to Lily, lowering his voice. "I didn't know you remained in contact with him."

"Of course I have," she whispered back. "In secret."

Something bubbled inside me—hope, excitement,

the thrill of realizing *this could work*. My eyes flashed to Lord Jonston, looking pensive as he rubbed his chin. He caught my eye, and I raised a brow. He nodded. I turned my attention back to Lily. "Tell me more."

Cora

I wish it had been her. I wish it had been her.

How could I have said such a thing? How could I have...*meant* such a thing?

You and I aren't so different.

It wasn't true. It couldn't have been true. I was good. I was kind. I was an empath. I used my powers to help people.

I wish it had been her.

Mareleau's face, charred by flame. A pillar of fire consuming her body. *Should it have been her?*

"No!" The sound of my shout startled me, returning my awareness to the dark room, to the ropes biding my wrists and the dried tears on my cheeks. Even in the dark, I could tell my vision was swimming. The pain in my shoulder had grown to a nauseating degree, my breathing shallow just to keep myself from moving too much.

Tired. So tired.

How long had it been since Darius had left me? A strangled cry escaped my lips as thoughts of Darius brought back thoughts of my confession.

No, that was a lie. That's not me.

So much of what he'd said rang true. Growing up, I'd

often fantasized about a childhood where my parents had survived, one where Linette and her children played with me, where Dimetreus forever loved me and never turned me out of Ridine Castle.

When those fantasies seemed too outlandish for me to indulge, I would dream of discovering I truly was one of the Forest People, the blood of the Ancient Ones, a Faeran from the stories I loved. With my dark hair and small stature, it wasn't hard for me to imagine it could be true. My powers could have been handed down from a long-lost Ancient ancestor. That's what I'd told myself, anyway.

And if I'd been of Ailan's blood, it would have been true.

But no, my magic was human magic. My blood was human blood, passed down from a man who fathered a son that craved power. I wasn't related to the beautiful Elvan or the gentle Faeran. I was related to...Morkai.

Rage flooded my veins, as visions of Mareleau filled my mind—her golden hair, her crystal blue eyes. *Beauty of Satsara.* She was Elvan through and through. Darius was right about her being fought over by poets and princes. My own husband once courted her.

It should have been her.

Shame extinguished the rage, and I cried out, feeling as if I were drowning beneath a weight of impenetrable darkness. A darkness that was me.

Face the darkness. Face it. Look at it. My voice taunted me as the darkness pressed me further down.

"No. No. No!"

The door swung open, and I saw daylight illuminating the room beyond. In the doorway stood a petite, feminine figure carrying a bucket. "Your Majesty."

I blinked, letting my eyes adjust to the light as I tried to place the familiar face. "You..."

The girl curtsied and gave me a warm smile. "I'm Gerta, Your Majesty. I was hearth maid at Ridine Castle."

The girl who caught Darius in the throne room. "Gerta! He kept you alive! Thank Lela you found me."

Gerta laughed as she set the bucket on the ground and began to unwrap the strip of cloth surrounding the blade at my shoulder. "Of course he kept me alive, Your Majesty. He brought me here to be your queensmaid."

Her words were puzzling, but the pain in my shoulder tore rational thought away as Gerta continued her ministrations. Once the bloodied cloth was removed, she began to clean the area surrounding the blade. Whatever herbs were in the pungent-smelling water seemed to alleviate some of the pain. But why wasn't she removing the blade?

"Forget about the wound, Gerta. Please cut my bindings at once."

Gerta paused, not meeting my eyes, then began wrapping fresh cloths around my shoulder, blade still intact. "King Darius has ordered me to care for you yet leave you as you are for now."

My stomach sank. "Gerta, you don't serve King Darius. Your home is Kero and Ridine Castle."

"Not anymore, Your Majesty. Darius has given me a new job. Here in Syrus, anyone can be anything, if they prove they have the skill for it. In Kero, I could never be anything more than a household servant. Here, I can be queensmaid, chambermaster, councilman, merchant, artist, whatever I have the talent to be."

I let out a grumbling sigh. "Is that what he told you?"

"It is, and it is what I've seen since I've been here." Gerta's voice was full of awe. "Only those who have no merit are used as servants, Your Majesty. My low birth has no influence here. I am judged as I am, simple as that."

Irritation coursed through me. "We need to get home, Gerta. *I* need to get home. Please help me."

She ignored me as she made the final knot securing my bandages. "I don't know why you are tied up like this, Your Majesty, but King Darius wishes it so. I may not understand, but I am willing to prove my merit to him." She stood and gathered her bucket.

Anxiety coursed through me. "You aren't leaving me, are you?"

"I will be back again, Your Majesty," she said, turning toward the door.

"Please, don't go!" *Don't leave me in the dark. Not again.*

Gerta closed the door halfway, then paused. "You may scream if you wish, but no one will attend you until King Darius orders it." With that, she closed the door.

Again, the darkness pressed around me, robbing me of breath. The pain in my arm had lessened, but nausea continued to churn my stomach, my head pounding harder and harder.

"I have to get out of here." My voice was strangled, sounding so unlike my own.

This is your voice. The darkness said, coming from within.

"Get me out of here!" I shouted.

This is you.

I tried to steady my breathing, focusing on thoughts of Salinda. "I need you," I called out. "Salinda, please!" Her face formed in my mind's eye, and I nearly sobbed with relief. But the image lasted only a moment before it morphed into a reflection of my face, features twisted in a hateful scowl. Again, I tried to think of Salinda, but all I found was me.

You can't escape me. You can't escape you.

"That's not me."

This is you. Look at me. Look at me!

Finally, I relented and let myself look. I saw my face looking back at me, shrouded in darkness. My eyes were full of rage. A row of cages appeared behind the figure that was me, filled with corpses of unicorns. My shadow self shouted in anger at what had been done to them. I remembered that moment, when I first discovered what was being done to the unicorns by Morkai's hunters.

The image shifted, and I saw myself crying at Linette's bedside as the life left her eyes. I watched as I fell to my knees in the hall outside her room, saw my face turn to a scowl as Morkai approached, heard my voice as I shouted hateful things at my brother.

The image shifted again, and I watched my face as Morkai told me what he'd done to prevent me from creating any heirs. I saw the rage burn in my eyes, followed by a hollow brokenness. A new setting replaced it, and I saw a vial in my hand bearing my name. I watched the pain rip across my face.

I saw myself watching Mareleau with Liam, my expression dark with resentment. I watched as Mareleau passed Liam for me to hold, and saw the heartache pull at the corners of my lips. It was real. It had happened.

Anger. Hurt. Rage. Resentment. I'd experienced all of that, no matter how I'd tried to deny it. It *was* me.

The calm of certainty fell over me, and my breathing grew deep and easy.

"I am angry."

Truth.

"I am bitter over what was done to me."

Truth.

"I wish it had been her."

Truth.

Darkness continued to press down on me, but this time, I didn't turn away from it. *Look at it. Look at all of it. Face it. Unpack it. Embrace it.*

And so I did.

27

EDELL-MORKARA'ELLE

Teryn

I paced in front of my desk, heart racing as I soaked in Lily's information. "This could work. This could *really* work."

"It could," Jonston said, although I could hear the caution in his voice. "We still need more of a plan. How do we get the weapons to the rebels? We'd never be able to sneak weapons into each city. Besides, that could take far too long."

I ran a hand through my hair, uncaring as strands fell this way and that in disarray. "The resistance is strongest in the south," I muttered to myself. "The capital of Norun is in the north. Surely we can use that in our favor."

"We wouldn't need to distribute the weapons to each city," Lily said. "We would just need to get them to the resistance leaders, then they can distribute them."

"How would we even get weapons into any part of Norun?"

I stopped pacing and faced Lex. "Tomas borders the southern part of Norun, right?"

Lex eyed me with suspicion. "Yes."

"And our scouts have reported the army is still in the northern part of Norun, slowly making their way south." I rounded my desk and unrolled one of the maps I had scattered there, flattening it before me. "This is perfect. Lex, what if we distributed the weapons from Tomas?"

Lex frowned. "We have a wall—"

"We could meet the rebels *at* the wall."

"I don't know if my father will agree to that." Lex grimaced. "He's always tried *not* to gain the attention of Norun."

I leaned forward, hands flat on the desk. "Lex, if this works, he wouldn't need to worry about Norun ever again."

"Still," Lex said, "Father's not one to risk such a thing."

Larylis turned to Lex, scowling. "Your father allied with us against Morkai. How is this any different?"

Lex raised his hands with a shrug. "Don't get me wrong, if I had my way, we'd do this. But my father won't see it that way. He allied with you at Centerpointe Rock because what Morkai did was a direct threat to me, and I convinced Father it was the right thing to do. Even that was difficult! And he's been paranoid of a Norun backlash ever since."

"There has to be a way to convince him," I said. "He wouldn't have to provide a thing, just allow passage through the wall."

Lex nodded. "I'll try to convince him. But—"

"Is there anything we can give him to guarantee his

agreement?" Larylis asked. "Can we give him a stronger alliance? Promise him land in Norun if we succeed?"

Lex considered but didn't look convinced.

"A wife?" My heart sank as the words left my mouth. "Your father is a widower, correct?"

Lex nodded.

I hated myself for what I was about to say. "What if I sent my mother to be his bride?"

"Teryn!" Larylis shouted. "You can't!"

I ignored him. "She's queen mother of two kings with a sizable fortune. If she married your father, we'd be more than allies. We'd be family."

Lex wrinkled his nose in distaste. "He has been seeking a new wife," he mumbled.

Mother, please forgive me. "Then it will be done."

Larylis opened his mouth to argue, but another voice drowned his.

"It most certainly will not," Helena said, rising to her feet. She strolled toward me, chin held high. "Your mother doesn't have the constitution to marry again, and you know it."

"But—"

"You'll send me instead."

My eyes widened. "You?"

"Yes." She whirled around to face Lex. "I may not be queen mother to two *kings*, but I am the mother of a queen, and my fortune is far greater than Bethaeny's."

Lex shrank beneath her intense stare. "That...sounds great."

"Then it is done," Helena said. "You go on ahead to Tomas, and I'll follow behind with a caravan of my belongings." She faced me. "I'll need to borrow much from Ridine, as we don't have time to wait for my actual belongings to arrive from Verlot."

"We can send for them later," I said. "I'm sure King Carrington will provide all the comfort you require."

"No. We need my household caravan," Helena said, "because that is how we will mask the weapons we are bringing. No one will question the travels of a noble woman meeting her new husband. No suspicion will be raised over the number of guards I travel with, no rumors will be spread to alert our enemies."

My mouth hung open. It was brilliant. *This is going to work.* I looked to Lord Jonston. "Will the council accept this plan?"

He pondered for a moment, rubbing his chin. "There's still more to discuss. If we are to attack in secret, we'll need to get our forces into Tomas without detection. Also, we need more strategy for the actual attack. It will need to be synchronized alongside the rebellion." He met my eyes and grinned. "But, yes, I think the council will support this."

His words flooded me with relief. "Then let's proceed."

With that, everyone stood. As we began to file out of the study, I realized Helena had remained behind. She stood at the window, back facing me. I waited until the footsteps of our companions could no longer be heard in the hall before I approached her.

"Thank you," I said. "For what you did for my mother. You were right. A marriage would have crushed her."

Helena said nothing as she continued to stare out the window, eyes glazed. Gone was the confidence she'd shown just moments before.

I placed a hand on her shoulder. "Will you be all right?"

She lifted her chin and turned toward me. Tears welled in her eyes, but she forced a smile. "Like my daughter, I was made to be queen."

Mareleau

I stared out the golden-framed window in my beautiful room, looking out at endless summer skies as blue as the sea, emerald trees tipped with flecks of gold, and shimmering flashes of light where birds soared over the perfect landscape.

I hated all of it.

It was too perfect, too calm, too elegant. It contrasted too much with the tempest of pain roaring within me.

I squinted toward the horizon, searching for a hint of that dead gray I knew was out there. Had Cora made it home yet? Had she given Larylis my letter? She'd only left that morning, yet she'd warned me time moved differently here. There was no way of knowing how much time was passing in the human world. It could have been days, weeks. Anything could have happened there while I watched the sun rise here.

The thought made me shudder.

I turned away from the window and rested my eyes on Liam, sleeping in a bassinet made of some opalescent material that reminded me of a seashell. The sight of him helped lift some of the weight that hung over my chest. *This is all for you, my sweet one.*

A knock sounded at the door, making me sit straighter. An Elvan figure—a youthful female—entered carrying a tray of food. She didn't so much as look at me as she set it on the table in the middle of the room.

I stood, forcing her eyes to flash my way. With a smile, I breathed deeply and walked toward her, taking one slow step after the other, focusing on an image I wished her to see, feelings I wished her to feel. My power wrapped around me, and I felt myself become that image. *Respect me. Honor me.*

"Edell-Morkara'Elle," said the Elvan girl with a nod of her head.

It took me a moment to interpret her words, but I knew she was referring to me as Liam's mother—mother of the Morkara's heir. *Like a queen mother.* "Thank you for bringing my food."

The girl nodded again, then paused, studying me with a bemused expression.

Perhaps I overdid the glamour. *Too late now.* "You may leave."

The girl swept out of the room, and I immediately moved to the long mirror that stood on the wall. I turned my head this way and that, trying to see if I could catch a glimpse of the glamour I'd created. With nothing much to do inside my beautiful prison, it had become a way for me to pass my time. Create a glamour, study its effects on the Elvan I used it on, and look for evidence of what I created. So far, it seemed to work best when I focused on a glamour that improved my standing amongst the Elvan people. Beauty. Respect. Trust.

Seeing no obvious sign of my glamour, I let my eyes grow unfocused, detaching from my need to see it. There, out of the corner of my eye, I saw it. I was taller, like the Elvan. My eyes slightly more slanted, my skin with a hint of opalescence. That was likely what gave the Elvan girl pause. *Perhaps my glamour should focus more on the feelings I want to create in them and less about them seeing me as one of them.* I made some mental notes about what to try next time, then turned away from the mirror.

I jumped, finding Ailan in the doorway, lips pulled into a half smile. "What were you doing just now?"

My face flushed, and I considered creating a glamour to hide my embarrassment. Then again, what did I have to hide? All she saw was me looking in the mirror. Right? "I wanted to see whether this Elvan robe flattered my figure."

Ailan stepped into the room, her dark hair loose and flowing like a midnight river, an Elvan gown of deep gold illuminating her golden-brown skin. She walked with confidence. Like she was queen. "My child, I've been with the Forest People long enough to recognize the use of the Arts."

My blush grew deeper, and I couldn't bring myself to meet her eyes. Why was I so ashamed at being caught using the Arts? I was using them to test my abilities to glamour the Elvan people...but what was the harm in that? "I was practicing. Salinda taught me some about my powers, but I need to practice if I am ever to use them to protect myself and my son."

"Good. You should practice."

I looked up, surprised at her quick acceptance. "I've been practicing on your kind," I admitted.

She nodded. "Darius is half Elvan. I think it is wise to learn how to use your Art with human and Elvan alike."

I sat taller at that. "You must know much about the Arts yourself. Is human magic any different from what you do as a weaver?"

She looked lost in thought for a moment, considering. "Human magic has always been viewed by the Elvan as something invasive. Elvan kind have rarely encountered humans, and most knowledge of the human world comes to El'Ara from truthweavers, the Elvan who have a talent for receiving information. You could compare an Elvan truthweaver to a human channel. However, the difference lies in Elvan perception.

"The Elvan see a human channel as someone who seeks information through invasion, infiltrating hidden mysteries, finding knowledge in sacred places. On the other hand, a truthweaver creates a vessel for willing knowledge to be received. Other forms of the Arts are seen the same way. A pathweaver like Garot moves through time and space on existing paths, while a world-walker invades any place at will, private or not. A mindweaver communicates through directed thought to and from another willing source, while an empath invades the thoughts and feelings without permission."

"That's insulting," I said, crossing my arms over my chest. "Without Cora's *invasive* powers, we wouldn't have found the tear in the veil as easily as we did. If we'd followed *your* plan, we'd probably still be looking for it."

Ailan let out a light laugh. "I didn't say I agreed with this point of view, Mareleau. I was merely reporting the pervasive perception of my people."

I uncrossed my arms, feeling the flush of anger dissipate. "Well, what do you think?"

"I think human magic and Elvan magic are different,

that's all. Even Faeran magic is different from both. Weaving is a way of Elvan life. We pride ourselves on creating beauty, ease, protection, and quality of living. However, if you pored over our ways with a fine-toothed comb, I'm sure you'd find flaws."

I don't need to look nearly that deep to find the flaws, I thought.

Ailan continued. "Human magic has its own path. From what I saw during my time in the human world, the Arts are in their infancy, discovered only by a select few. The magic is there, swirling through everything, yet hardly anyone knows it. Hardly anyone is willing to admit it's there, much less touch it and use it. It's different. It isn't obvious and all-encompassing like it is in El'Ara. It's a mystery still to be discovered."

I cocked my head. "Do you mean all humans have access to the Arts?"

"I'm not sure," Ailan said. "I felt it there, all around. The Forest People felt it too, and with ease. I never understood why others could not. Like I said, human magic has its own path. I'm not sure what place the Arts have in that world, but I know it has a place, and it is growing." Her lips turned down at the corners. "I loved my time in the human world. Part of me wishes I could watch it all unfold, see what becomes of the Arts, the people, the future. But my place is here now."

My expression mirrored hers. *Mine too.*

With a shake of her head, Ailan seemed to regain her composure. "We should get you out of this room. Would you like to take a walk? There's someone I think you should get to know."

28

CLARITY

Cora

When Darius next came, I was calm.

"I've been told you stopped screaming days ago." Again, he brought a lantern, the open door revealing night had fallen in the room beyond. "Did you lose your voice, or did you decide your time was best spent on other endeavors?"

"My voice is fine." My words were smooth like honey, with not even a hint of a tremor.

Darius paused, head tilted, before he reached for my shoulder and inspected the fresh bandages. "Hmm. I take it you've had some time to think about the things we discussed?"

"I have."

"And?"

"And I know what you're trying to do," I said, my tone neutral. "You think pitting me against Mareleau will bring me to your side."

He stepped back, folding his hands before him. "I simply saw a truth that needed to be unearthed. I was right, wasn't I?"

His arrogance made me bristle. *But...* "Yes, you were right."

"Did Gerta treat you well?"

"Well enough." She'd returned daily to feed me and help me relieve myself. The latter were certainly my more humiliating moments. She refused to tell me anything about Darius' whereabouts, but I assumed his absence meant he was busy in Norun. "She seems keen on *proving her merit.*"

Darius smirked as he stepped back. "I'm sure that surprised you. Who would have thought the honorable Queen Coralaine could lose such a dedicated subject to a tyrant like me?"

I kept my voice level, my tone curious. "What is it she thinks she's getting from your approval?"

"It's not what she thinks," Darius said. "It's what she knows. This is how things work in Syrus, and she's seen it for herself. I've told you, in my new world, power will be the deciding factor. It begins here in Syrus, and it continues in El'Ara. It ends with the rest of the human world."

I furrowed my brow. "In a world run by power, what of the powerless? What power does a hearth maid have that makes her think she will rise in your favor?"

Darius shook his head. "You fail to understand my meaning of power. Yes, there are the powerful ones such as you or me, those with magic. But there are also other forms of power that deserve recognition. Intellect is power. Cunning is power. Talent is power. Physical strength is power. Emotional fortitude is power. Capability is power. Those who can prove their merit will rise in my empire, regardless of birth, education, or gender."

"And those you don't deem capable?"

"Those will serve the empire, but fairly. Come." Darius snapped his fingers, and two guards entered. As they approached, each offered a bow before kneeling on opposite sides of my chair. My bindings remained around my ankles but were unwound from the chair legs. Then, the guards secured the bindings together, creating a tether between my ankles. They did the same with my wrists, leaving only a short gap between them.

I could run, I realized as the guards stepped back. *I could reach for the blade and pull it free. I could worldwalk out of here.* The thought was fleeting. *No.*

One of the guards placed a hand beneath my uninjured arm and gently pulled me to my feet. I winced as every muscle in my body cried out at the movement. At least the pain in my shoulder was dulled and my delirium had passed.

"I'm sorry you must remain tied up like this," Darius said, although his face showed no remorse. "I know you don't trust me yet, and I can't have you running off when I feel we are just starting to understand each other."

I remained silent as Darius left my closet-prison, the guards following behind, guiding me forward with the tiny steps my bindings allowed me to take. We made our way past the outer room, giving me a glimpse of a few simple furnishings.

As we left the room, I was met with a mild breeze and

the smell of fresh, salty air. An open-walled hallway lit
with elegant lanterns stretched to the left and right. I
squinted into the surrounding dark outside and saw
moonlight reflecting off water in the distance, unfamiliar
trees with thick trunks and bushy leaves sprouting from
the top, and rows and rows of homes stretching from
what must have been the palace wall to the shoreline.
The sight made me pause; it was unlike any place I'd ever
been. I wished I could see it under daylight.

"Come along," Darius said from up ahead, and one of
the guards gave me a soft tug under my arm to prompt
me forward.

We continued down similar hallways, moving past
closed doors here and there that led to smaller buildings
that were likely bedrooms. Servants passed by on occa-
sion, their eyes meeting mine with nothing other than
curiosity. None of them hurried by with lowered heads at
the sight of their king, as I'd seen many other servants do
at Ridine or Verlot. None looked starved or beaten as I
would have expected of Darius' household staff.

We came to a staircase, and I nearly lost my composure as one of the guards lifted me into his arms and
carried me to the top. I tried to keep the heat from my
face as he set me back on my feet, and I bit my lip at the
sudden sting of pain in my shoulder. Once the pain
passed, I allowed myself to investigate my surroundings.
We were on what appeared to be a balcony, Darius at the
railing, looking out at the scenery beyond. He waved a
hand for me to come forward, and the guard led me to his
side.

I looked beyond the balcony, finding more homes,

more endless ocean, more stars. I didn't speak because I'd have to admit I found the view beautiful.

"Does this look like a kingdom run by a monster?" Darius' voice was quiet, a disturbing contrast from the man who had shouted truths to break me.

"A sleeping city tells me nothing," I said. "Those homes could be empty, for all I know. Your citizens could be dead."

Darius laughed. "The city is sleeping peacefully, and that should tell you enough. You see the lanterns flickering in the windows, do you not? Listen carefully, and you can hear sounds of merriment coming from the taverns."

I didn't need to extend my hearing to know the city was alive. I could sense it. And he was right; it was peaceful.

Darius turned his head toward me. "This is a kingdom run by power. My cities are ruled by the capable, not some noble family. Same with my advisers, guards, and officers. Positions of power are given to those who prove they deserve them through their own merit. No one is overlooked. There are no elite families, no ruling class. Everyone here earns their place and accepts it with pride."

I squinted into the night, trying to uncover things he left unsaid. "That can't be the entire story. What about those who disagree with you? What about those who define merit contrary to how you do? And what about you? You are the royal son of the former king, and you've been ruling Syrus for five-hundred years. Has anyone been given the chance to take your place?"

His face darkened. "Five-hundred years may seem long to you, but it is nothing when it comes to reshaping a society. Syrus needed me to remain king, or this never would have come to fruition. Yes, you are clever enough to know not everyone has agreed with me, and they have been dealt with."

I raised an eyebrow. "You killed them."

"Yes," he said without shame. "Creating a better world is of utmost importance. There is no room for those who threaten my vision. It is the selfish few who fail to see what I am creating, and their insignificant lives are worth the thousands I've improved."

"That is what you would do to El'Ara and the rest of the human world," I said, trying to keep my tone level. "You plan to rule by force, killing all who oppose you."

"It is the only way."

I angled my body away from the view to face him. "And that is what you would do to me, to my friends, to my loved ones. You would kill us all."

"Only if you oppose me. That is why I brought you here. You are my kin. What I create could be your inheritance. You could do in Lela what I've done in Syrus. Every kingdom, city, and territory both here and in El'Ara will be ruled by those with visions like ours, those who want to live in a fair world. Can't you see it?"

I could. His words wove images in my head, images where I wasn't feared for using the Arts, where my barrenness didn't compromise my standing as queen, where the values of the Forest People became the values held by all. They struck a yearning within me. Yet these visions were paved with blood. Decades of war. I shuddered. "Thousands—millions, even—will die. Few will support such radical change."

"That only proves how much corruption exists," Darius said.

"You will kill Ailan. Liam. Mareleau."

Darius looked amused. "You all but said so yourself that you resent Queen Mareleau."

I wish it had been her. The words moved through me without pain. *This is me.* "I know. You may have been right about my feelings toward her, but that doesn't mean I can support her murder, not to mention that of Liam and Ailan."

"Their lives are few."

"Their lives are important."

"And what of those born to inconsequential families?" Darius said. "What of those whose gender or low-ranking birth keep them from ever reaching their fullest potential? Are their lives not worth it?"

I sighed. "What if you forgot about El'Ara? Let Ailan return and seal the veil. Focus on Syrus and sharing your vision with those who would listen. You could change things *here* in this world. Slowly, yes, but things *could* change."

Darius looked back toward the ocean. "With the sealing of the veil comes my death, I am sure of it. I have only lived as long as I have because the Mora has been seeping into the human world. Besides, why should I wait? Why should I work on such a small scale when I can claim my place as Morkaius of El'Ara, using my increased power to change, not a kingdom here and there, but two entire worlds?" His eyes were wide with passion as a smile stretched his lips.

"That's it, then? Join you and watch good people die, or fight you and watch good people die?"

"No," Darius said. "Join me and see two worlds become better than you've ever imagined. Fight me and never see it. Either I die, my vision with me, or you die and forfeit everything you deserve."

My breathing grew shallow, though I tried to keep it steady. "What will you do to me if I refuse?"

He met my eyes, showing a hint of forced regret. "I suppose I'll have to kill you, after I force you to give me the location of the tear. Then I'll invade Lela with Norun's legion."

"And if I agree to support you?"

"Then I'll name you my heir. The Norun invasion will stand down and ally with you. You will call off any orders you have made against me. Your army will defend me in securing the veil and I will do what needs to be done."

I knew what he meant by that. *Killing.*

He continued. "Once I am Morkaius of El'Ara, I will easily remove any remaining opposition. I will destroy the veil while leaving Lela intact in the human world. Lela will then be yours."

I frowned, choosing my next words carefully. "How do you plan on becoming Morkaius without being destroyed by harnessing the Mora?"

He rolled his eyes with an irritated sigh. "Oh, that prophecy. My son really shouldn't have delved into such matters. Prophecy is so unreliable."

I raised my brows. "Which means..."

"The prophecy of the Morkaius has to do with using the Mora in the human world, not in El'Ara," Darius said. "My sister's weaving must have created a safeguard against the Mora being harnessed and pulled entirely from El'Ara. This safeguard was interpreted as a prophecy. My son never foresaw what becoming Morkaius in the human world would do to the Ancient Realm, since—as we know—he was an idiot. It would have destroyed El'Ara, draining the realm of life and power completely."

"But in El'Ara..."

He smiled. "There, nothing is stopping me from harnessing the Mora. That is what the Morkara does. He harnesses it and—typically—redistributes it back to the land. *Morkaius* is simply a name I have chosen to express how I will use the Mora. Not as steward, doling out power to those who aren't even worthy of it, but as High King of Magic, using it for the good of the realm as I see fit."

I tried to keep the surprise off my face. I hadn't realized the prophecy pertained only to one gaining power in the human world. Still, it made sense. We fell into silence as I reflected on the rest of our conversation. *His city. His vision. Two new worlds. The blood of my friends. The blood of millions.*

Darius turned away from the rail and nodded to his guards before meeting my eyes. "Shall we return?"

I looked at his outstretched arm and hesitated. "Perhaps you should cut my bindings if you intend on being a proper escort."

"Clever, but no," he said, taking my uninjured elbow as he guided me down the stairs. "We have yet to come to an agreement that warrants your freedom."

I bit my lip and forced my breathing to remain steady as we returned to the halls, making our way back the way we came. *Breathe in. Breath out.*

"Name me heir." My voice came out quiet but confident.

Darius turned his head toward me, eyes narrowed. "As I said, if you ally with me, I will name you heir."

I stopped and faced him. "Say it. I want to hear you name me heir right now. Say it, and I will ally with you."

His face flickered between a smirk and a frown. Then, with a roll of his eyes and a flourish of his hand, he said, "Fine. I name you my heir."

"Now what?"

Darius tugged at my elbow, prompting me to walk again. "Now, unfortunately, you return to your chair. I'll need more than your word to know I can trust you."

"And how will I know I can trust *you*?"

"I just named you my heir, did I not?"

"Well, you said it out loud, but where is the official documentation?" I infused my words with a hint of jest, my shoulders relaxed despite my restrained steps.

Darius let out an exaggerated sigh, reflecting my playful tone. "Is this what it's like having an heir? More trouble than it's worth, if you ask me."

We continued down the halls until we reached the doorway to a dark room. My prison.

Darius released my elbow and faced me. "If you meant what you said, tomorrow we can make our alliance official and arrange your return home. For now..." He gave me a bow and extended his arm toward the room.

The guards flanked me and brought me back to the chair, quickly retying my bindings. I maintained my posture as they left the room, smiling as Darius closed the door and took all the light with it. Darkness surrounded me, but I didn't mind. I allowed myself to sink back, exhaustion pulling at every muscle. *Breathe in. Breathe out.* I allowed myself to fade out of consciousness, Darius' words dancing through my dreams.

When I woke, all was clear. In the dark of my prison, I knew what had to be done.

29

BONDED

Mareleau

"Where are we going?" With Liam close to my chest in his carrier, I followed Ailan across the lawn outside the palace.

"You'll see," Ailan said.

We continued around to the backside of the palace and began to descend a steep set of stone steps. I steadied myself with one hand on the wall as we made our way further down. As we descended, the terrain around the steps became rockier, the looming palace above casting our surroundings in shadow.

Once we reached the bottom of the steps, it was hard to believe it was the middle of day. Gone were the shimmering walls and golden turrets of the palace. Here, the trees grew closer to the palace grounds, the golden-specked emerald of their leaves so high above us, all I could see were the brown trunks. Enormous crags flanked us, and it seemed the base of the palace itself was made from stone.

Ailan walked toward this alien part of the palace, and my heart sank. Ahead gaped three black caves. I froze. *The dragon caves beneath the palace.* Ailan turned when she realized I'd stopped following.

"Why are we going in there?" My arms wrapped protectively around Liam's carrier, although he seemed content as ever.

Ailan turned away from the caves and made her way back to me. "I'm sorry, my child. I didn't anticipate this would be a distressing visit. When my mother took me to visit her dragon, it was both an honor and a thrill. I'd waited my entire youth to be formally introduced to Berolla."

I lifted my chin to feign indifference. "I've met Ferrah a number of times."

She shook her head with a smile. "There is a difference between being in the same vicinity as a dragon, and being formally introduced to one. When Mother took me to be formally introduced to Berolla, it meant gaining the dragon's respect. She would listen to me after that. Not as dedicatedly as she listened to my mother, of course, but I could have my say. More importantly, the introduction meant Berolla would someday hatch my *familiar*."

"Ferrah is...the daughter of your mother's dragon?"

"Her hatchling, yes. It is tradition that the Morkara be bonded to a dragon, and that the succession of dragons follows accordingly."

An excitement I didn't want to acknowledge crept up my spine. "What does this have to do with me?"

Ailan looked down at Liam. "One day he will bond with a hatchling of his own. However, no dragon has had a hatchling since the veil was constructed. Through the work we do against my brother, we will bring back the flow of Mora. By the time Liam is old enough, there will be plenty of hatchlings again." She raised her eyes and met mine. "In the meantime, I want to be sure Ferrah feels a bond with both of you. This is essential to the future hatching process."

"You want Ferrah...to bond with *me*?"

Ailan nodded. "You are Edell-Morkara'Elle. You may not be the next Morkara, but you are my blood and mother to my heir. That gives you power here. Can you accept that?"

My eyes flashed to the caves, and I let out a trembling breath. "Yes."

Ailan smiled. "Good. Follow me."

We entered the caves, and my shoulders began to relax when torchlight shone up ahead from a sconce in the wall. More sconces lit the way.

"The first time I came here was supposed to be the most wonderful day of my life," Ailan said from her place in front of me.

"*Supposed* to be?"

"Instead, it ended up being a day that set off a chain of events that had dreadful consequences."

I suppressed a chill. "What happened?"

"Darius," Ailan said. "He let jealousy get the better of him and showed once and for all how dangerous he could be."

The air seemed colder the deeper we went into the cave. Every sound we made echoed off the walls, and my muscles again grew tense. "What did Darius do?" Part of me asked out of curiosity. Another part asked simply to have a distraction from our creepy surroundings.

"I'd just been named heir and was taken to the caves to bond with Berolla," Ailan said. Although her voice was quiet, it reverberated as if there were three of her. "She was hesitant to greet me, even though my mother stood by, coaxing her. Just as she was about to press her head to my outstretched hand, my brother worldwalked behind her, startling her. As a reflex, she clawed out in front of her, slashing me through the chest. Everyone thought I was going to die, even the skinweavers. The Elvan have innate healing abilities, but there are wounds even the strongest of us can't come back from. Luckily, and with much care, I healed. When I woke up, my brother was gone, banished from El'Ara. You know the rest."

Great. First she takes me to these dark caves, now she tells me this? Sounds came from up ahead. "So this bonding thing...can be dangerous?"

Ailan looked back at me with a smile. "No, my child. It was only Darius who made it so. Ferrah won't hurt you or Liam, I promise."

I stopped, my heart racing as the sounds ahead grew louder and louder. "How do you know?"

"Dragons may be large and potentially lethal—"

"That's not comforting."

"—but you will see how kind and wonderful they are when you get to know Ferrah. It broke Berolla's heart what she'd done to me on accident. She willingly sacrificed one of her claws in atonement."

I grimaced. "One of her...claws?"

Ailan nodded. "No dragon had ever done such a thing

before, but I accepted the gift. My father had it forged by a weaponsweaver into a blade for me."

More sounds came from ahead, followed by a grumble that made the cave walls tremble.

"Yes, Ferrah, I'm here," Ailan said with a laugh, although I could see no reason to be so lighthearted. She turned to me. "Come. I'll be right by your side."

I hesitated. "Is this really necessary?"

"You want the other Elvan to respect you." It wasn't a question. "You can create all the glamours you want, but evidence in a way they can understand will be what sways them. Being bonded to a dragon will solidify your position here."

If she was manipulating me, she was doing a good job. It was all I needed to hear to get my shoulders to pull back, my chin to lift. "Fine. Introduce me, then."

We continued forward, rounding a bend and coming to a wide cavern. Pools of fire danced over the cavern floor but didn't seem to spread. In the middle of this cavern was Ferrah, sinuous tail swishing side to side, fire-light glinting off her white scales. At the sight of Ailan, Ferrah bounded over to us, feathered wings tucked close to her body. I held my ground, struggling to maintain my composure as the dragon halted before us. My arms never moved from around Liam.

Ailan extended her arm, palm forward, and Ferrah brought her nose to meet it, a purring sound rumbling through her chest. After an exchange of purrs and pets, Ailan stepped back and edged closer to me. "Your turn," she whispered.

My heart felt as if it would leap from my throat. "What do I do?"

"Keep your eyes on her, your body relaxed, then extend your hand. Let her come to you."

Ferrah's head bobbed side to side as she regarded us, tongue flicking in and out of her scaly mouth. "You expect me to relax?"

"Just try."

I took a deep breath, then imagined a glamour. *Confident. Calm.* My power wrapped around me, making me stand even taller. Then I froze. *No. I can do this on my own. I am confident. I am calm.* The glamour fell way, but it felt as if my power remained. Slowly, I lifted my hand and raised my palm toward Ferrah.

Ferrah continued to eye me but didn't seem keen on moving closer. I remained steady. Liam made a cooing noise, and for a moment I worried it would startle her. I breathed away my fear and kept my palm raised, eyes fixed on the dragon.

Finally, Ferrah took one step, then another, her claws scratching on stone as she moved to stand in front of me. She brought her head close to my hand. I nearly jumped as her tongue tickled my skin. *Stay calm. Stay calm.*

Ferrah brought her face to my palm.

Terror and awe and joy flooded me from head to toe as I felt the warm scales touch my skin, heard her rumbling purr. I couldn't help but grin, thinking it was the widest I'd smiled in days.

Ailan put her hand on my shoulder. "She will listen to you now. Somewhat."

"What does that mean? Am I supposed to talk to her?"

"You can," Ailan said.

I swallowed hard. "Hi...Ferrah. I'm Mareleau." Something flooded my mind. Not words, not even a feeling. It was more like a knowing. *I am accepted.*

Cora

I felt strong.

The pain in my arm was beginning to return—it had been hours since Gerta had come to care for my wound. Yet, my mind was at peace, and that was all I needed. Darkness no longer pressed me down, it was part of me. Welcome. Comforting. I'd already faced what was in the dark. What else was there to fear?

Time to go.

I'd learned what I'd needed to learn. Now it was time to save myself.

I closed my eyes, breathing deeply, letting my power flood my veins, burning from head to toe. The harshness of the ropes binding my wrists filled my consciousness. I remembered what they'd looked like when I'd stood in the light—each frayed strand, each coil that formed each knot. Its color, shape, even the smell of the rope became my focus.

I thought back to its earliest composition, before it was rope, before it was fiber, before it was plant, before it was seed.

It was soil. Water. Air. Fire. It was life—growing, breathing, moving. No different from me.

The rope was *part* of me.

As if I were moving a finger, I moved the seed, the

fiber, the strand, let it uncoil. Then another. And another. And another.

With my breath, the rope moved, then fell away like a second skin.

My wrists free, I lifted my hands to my shoulder, breathing away the pain the movement caused. With trembling fingers, I searched for the knot that secured my bandages, then loosened it, gingerly unwrapping it from my shoulder until only part of it remained around the blade. Then, with one hand bracing my skin and another around the hilt, I pulled the blade from my flesh, suppressing a whimper as my shoulder seized with renewed pain. Tears streamed from my eyes as I struggled to re-wrap the bandages, careful to cover the now-bleeding gash. I was thankful for the darkness; it saved me from having to see the warm blood I felt seeping into the cloth.

With my wound bandaged, I took a few moments to catch my breath, steeling myself from the dizziness that swept over me. *Breathe in. Breathe out.*

I bent down to untie the bindings at my ankles, setting down the knife. My fingers brushed something by my feet. I reached toward it, feeling wrinkled paper, and remembered Darius tossing Mareleau's scroll when he'd first tried to bait me. I pocketed the note before returning to the ropes, my shoulder screaming with every move.

Once free, I retrieved the blade and stood on unsteady legs. *Breathe in. Breathe out.* It was all I could do not to faint.

I closed my eyes and thought of home—*No. Not home. He will look for me there.* I needed to go where I knew

Darius wouldn't follow, somewhere he wouldn't have thought to place a trigger.

I thought of Centerpointe Rock.

When I opened my eyes, early daylight shone overhead, the field around me covered in frost. I sank to my knees and another wave of exhaustion washed over me. *Water. Food.* I looked at my shoulder, unsurprised to see red blooming over the bandages.

I was surprised, however, at the sudden emptiness I felt. Leaving Darius meant leaving his vision behind. It meant solidifying him as an enemy. It meant Lela would be invaded. War. Many would die.

More will die if Darius wins.

I knew I had to stand against him. Darius may have been a visionary, but his drive was that of vengeance. When he'd spoken of peace and the citizens he'd helped, I hadn't sensed he cared about them nearly as much as he wanted me to believe. He cared about himself. His vision was a world where *he* would thrive, and those he hated would perish.

I could have thrived in his world.

I shook my head. *Not at the cost of those I love.*

You and I aren't so different. Darius' words taunted me.

But he was wrong about that. We *were* different. He'd kept the pain of his youth in shadow and allowed it to harden into hate. I faced my darkness, brought my pain to light. I was angry, resentful, bitter. But I was also hopeful, forgiving, loving. *This is me. I am both.* My pain didn't control me. My bitterness wouldn't turn to hate. My darkness wouldn't bury me.

I couldn't say the same for Darius.

With a sigh, I faced the Rock and kneeled at its base,

hand outstretched. I closed my eyes, extending my senses, letting them reach deep within the Rock, the soil, the grass. Waves of power rippled forward, subtle but distinct. There was magic there. Not the magic I felt running through my veins, not the Art of the empath or worldwalker. Similar, but different, like a familiar song in an unknown language. It was the Mora from El'Ara.

This *is the heart of El'Ara.*

I breathed deeply, feeling ripples of the Mora hesitating near my hand, feeling how I could almost touch it. As if it *wanted* me to touch it. There was but one thing standing in the way.

I smiled, even more certain of what I must do.

Darius had been right about one thing. Lela belonged to me.

30

CENTER

Cora

I closed my eyes and pictured the land surrounding the tear. I saw dappled light on the forest floor, diffused through green pine. A light breeze blew overhead while birds chirped high in the branches. I opened my eyes and found myself there.

I turned, finding the familiar space between two trees where the tear would be. Before I took a step, something tugged at my mind. I froze, extending my senses, careful to keep even my breathing quiet.

The crackling of a fire. Hushed tones.

People are near.

Keeping to the shadows of the trees, I crept toward where I sensed the activity. As I neared, I heard snippets of casual conversation. A small clearing came into view, where I saw soldiers sitting around a modest fire. But whose soldiers where they? Their clothing was neutral, with no visible sigil—

"Don't move."

The voice came from behind me, and I realized a knife was at my throat. *How did this one sneak up on...me?* I raised my hands to show I was unarmed, while my mind raced to consider the best way to retrieve the blade I'd stolen from Darius and hidden in the folds of my tattered robe.

The man made a subtle whistling sound, almost like a bird call, his arm firm around my waist. A similar call echoed nearby.

I felt the fire burn through me, filling my blood, my veins. It burned my palms, ready to explode—

"Cora?"

A figure stood next to me, one I hadn't seen approach. He was clad in black; even his head and mouth were covered. But those eyes. My heart raced when I recognized their hazel hue, and I wanted to scramble into his arms. *But, no, that's not him. The nose is just different enough.*

"Larylis!"

"Release the queen, Temberly," Larylis said, pulling the tight, black cloth from his head, revealing the rest of his face.

Temberly obliged and fell to his knee with a bow, apologizing profusely. "Please forgive me, Your Majesty."

I placed a hand on his shoulder. "At ease. You were simply doing your job. Quite the good job, in fact. I didn't see or hear either of you." I lifted my eyes toward Larylis, suppressing a start as I noticed sets of eyes in shadowed faces coming from behind the trees, some even *in* trees. "I didn't see or hear *any* of you."

Larylis grinned. "That's why we're the Black Force. But forget about that." He came toward me, taking my shoulders as he scanned me from head to toe. "You're alive."

"I am."

His eyes fell on my shoulder. "You're injured."

"It's nothing."

"Teryn has been worried sick. Did he...find you? Is that why you're here?"

I cocked my head. "No, I escaped Darius and came straight here. Why do you ask? Where is Teryn?"

Larylis frowned. "That does make more sense. He couldn't have found you so soon. He's probably only just now arriving in Tomas."

"What is he doing there?"

Larylis explained what had happened since I'd been gone—Teryn's distress, his declaration of war, his new plan with the rebellion. My eyes were wide as I took it all in, wondering how so much had happened in a matter of days. Or had it been a week? Being locked in darkness hadn't been conducive for keeping track of time.

Teryn's plan worried me. It wasn't that it was a bad plan—it was brilliant. But I hated the idea of him getting so close to the enemy with the motivation of finding me. What if he did something reckless? *I could go to him now. But then I'd have to delay what I need to do in El'Ara...*

Larylis must have seen the conflict on my face. "We'll send our fastest messenger to tell Teryn you're here and safe."

I nodded. "Good. I need to update Ailan. She has no idea what is happening here. What are your current orders?"

"We guard the tear," Larylis said. "But since we don't know the exact location of the tear, we've been patrolling the area you'd marked for us. We've decided to use this camp as a decoy, hoping it will attract anyone who seeks the veil while the rest of us watch in secret."

"It worked on me, which is saying something," I said. "Well, let's get one problem solved. Come with me. I'll show you the tear."

"THAT'S IT?" LARYLIS FROWNED AT THE INNOCUOUS SPACE between the trees. "I expected something...more magical. Maybe a shimmer in the air, at least."

"It looks more significant on the other side," I said. "Although, not in a good way." I stepped closer to the veil, hand outstretched as I tried to feel for the tear.

Larylis put a hand on my shoulder. "Tell her I'm here," he said, his voice wavering. "Tell her I love her and Liam. Tell her I'm right outside to protect them both."

I froze, remembering the note in my pocket. I didn't need to read it to know what it contained, what pain it held. My fingers moved to the pocket, brushed crumpled paper. I suddenly felt as if my lungs were being compressed by the weight of the world. I breathed it away. *No.*

"I'll tell her," I said with a reassuring smile, then returned my attention to the tear.

My fingers brushed nothingness, then sank into warm air. *Found it.* Without a second glance at Larylis, I reached through the tear and pulled myself into a world of gray.

I froze, meeting the spear tips from a dozen Elvan soldiers.

"I am Ambassador Cora," I said, raising my arms in surrender for the second time that day. "Ailan is expecting me, and there is no time to waste."

After a moment of hesitation, one of the soldiers called out, and they stepped back, righting their spears.

"I'll take her to the palace," one of the soldiers said as he approached. Without looking at me, he nodded his head, then began walking away. I sprang forward to keep up, my heart racing with impatience. *How long will this take without Garot's weaving? Every minute in El'Ara could be dozens—maybe even hours—more in the human world.*

I clenched my jaw and tried to keep my worries at bay.

A wide set of eyes in a sun-browned face regarded me from up ahead. As we neared, I recognized the features as belonging to one of the Faeran. I noticed many more as we continued, each one eying me with curiosity. It was better than the hostility I found in the eyes of the Elvan.

I wanted to stop and speak with the Faeran, but I had to nearly jog to keep up with the Elvan guard's long stride. Luckily, I didn't have to slow down to get my wish.

"I remember you," a small voice said from behind.

I turned and saw a petite figure hurrying to my side. Her eyes were large and round, her dark hair brushing her shoulders. It was the kindness in her eyes I recognized.

"Illian!"

She smiled as I said her name. "They don't try to kill you this time. I was sorry to hear that they did last time."

"You heard?"

She nodded. "I had to know what happened to our strange guest. I asked the soil, but it said you never came back to it from the palace. Had to spy on Elvan for answer."

The guard tossed an annoyed glance over his shoulder.

"Then the soil said otherwise," Illian continued. "You'd returned. Along with Morkara Ailan."

"Is that why you're out here?" I asked. "Did Ailan speak with you about an alliance?"

"She did," Illian said. "Faeran are not made to fight. We don't weave weapons or crush the soil with our houses. It is not our way."

It amused me that Illian considered building houses and forging weapons to be in the same category. "So, did you turn her down?"

"We will do what we can. We can heal the hurt, share secrets of the soil. Ailan will bring the Mora back to its strength. When she does, we will share the Mora of the soil again."

Her words stirred at something inside me. "You mean, once Darius is defeated, she will find a way to finish the veil and return the heart of El'Ara."

Illian nodded.

"You work with the Mora of the soil," I said, slowly choosing my words. "How tied to the land itself is the Mora?"

Illian frowned. "What is this *tied*? There is no tie in Mora."

"Is the Mora bonded to the land in any way? Or is it separate?"

"The Mora flows as it will," Illian said with a shrug. "It flows out to your world and gets stuck because of veil. All Mora flows to center and returns."

"You need the center for El'Ara to be whole again."

"Yes. Ailan is doing this." Illian grinned. "And you are helping. I thank you."

I returned her smile. "And I thank you for being a friendly face."

31

BARGAIN

Cora

Ailan rushed from the palace doors as the guard and I crossed the lawn. Her face flashed from a smile to a look of terror as she approached. "What happened to you?"

Despite being out of breath, I tried my best to stand tall. "We need to call a meeting immediately."

"You need to see a skinweaver," Ailan said, taking in my bloody bandages. She turned furious eyes to the soldier. "You should have summoned Garot. My ambassador is to be treated with every respect and accommodation given me."

The soldier nodded. "I didn't notice the wound, Morkara. She seemed fine."

"Humans don't heal like we do," she said through her teeth.

"It's fine," I said. "We can worry about my wounds later. Right now, we have urgent matters to discuss.

Darius is coming. I know where he is, and I have information you need."

She pursed her lips, then gave a reluctant nod. "Very well. I'll send you a skinweaver this evening. For now, at least let us get you cleaned up."

I opened my mouth to argue but thought better of it. *It will help if I look respectable for what I'm about to do.* "Fine, but we need to hurry."

Once I was bathed, robed, and had my bandages changed, I found myself once again amongst the tribunal. I stood on the floor with Ailan at my side, Garot and Etrix flanking the floor, while the rest of tribunal filed in and took their seats. Last came Mareleau, holding Liam. She met my eyes with a small smile and took her seat at the front.

My note, she mouthed. *Larylis?*

I looked away. *She'll know the answer soon enough.*

With the tribunal seated, Ailan addressed them, telling them I had important information about Darius and that everyone was expected to listen with respect. Then she took a step back, giving me the full attention of the tribunal.

Breathe in. Breathe out.

"Ailan is right. I have important information about Darius. I know where he is, and I know what his plans are. I know where he is going and who supports him. I know how to stop him from worldwalking."

Gasps escaped those before me.

"But I'm not going to give you that information without something in return."

Silence.

"You see, I've thought a lot about the fate of my

people who live in the land now called Lela. I've been offered an opportunity to save the land I love. However, I turned it down in order to help you. And I will help you...*if* you are willing to bargain for what I need."

Shouts erupted from all around, but I was prepared. I let them shout, let their eyes burn me with their scorn. Oddly enough, the only one who seemed to remain silent was Fanon. However, the heat in his face said enough.

Ailan stepped forward and raised her arms, demanding silence. It took a few moments, but the tribunal obeyed. She faced me, and my heart sank at the look of horror on her face. I wondered if she would stop me. Yet, she gave me a nod, then took a seat next to Mareleau. *It's best she remains seated, anyway.*

"Darius comes this way," I said. "He has allied with a kingdom called Norun, which lies north of Lela. Every day they march south with the intention of invading Lela and finding the tear. I discovered this because Darius abducted me and kept me from worldwalking. To do so, he used something against me which I am now in the possession of. I have the very thing we need to keep him in place long enough to kill him.

"But that's not all I learned. I also learned I am of his blood. He named me heir."

Another round of gasps emerged, and I could see Ailan pale out of the corner of my eye.

"He offered me Lela in exchange for my support. I denied him," I said over the sudden shouts. Again the room roared, then quieted. "But before that, I allowed him to name me heir. You see, I can do one of two things. I can share with you what I know, tell you how to destroy Darius, keep the orders I already have in place to thwart

Darius' alliance with Norun, and use my forces to defend the veil.

"Or I can return to Lela, call back my forces from attacking Darius, and use them to support him instead. You will determine that choice. I want to help you, but I need one thing. Lela."

I waited with patience as another wave of shouts and threats of violence came at me. Ailan was slow to rise to her feet and didn't look my way as she came to my side. For awhile, she just waited there, eyes unfocused as members of the tribunal stood, demanding I be sentenced to Last Breath. Finally, she turned her head and met my eyes. Our gaze locked as I kept my face passive, all the while hoping she could understand. *I have to do this.*

With a sigh, she nodded, then faced the tribunal. Her voice rang out over theirs, her fury cowing them back to their seats. "Don't make me say it again," she shouted. "You are to listen to Cora until she is finished. When you have questions and suggestions, you may make them one at a time." This time, she didn't go to her seat and stayed at my side instead, arms crossed as she glared at the stunned tribunal.

"I will help you defeat Darius," I continued. "When we win and it is time for Ailan to try and fix the veil, I want you to leave Lela in the human world."

This time, no one said a word, though I could see they were fuming. Ailan turned to me, her expression gentle. "Cora, I've told you before. What you ask isn't possible. We need the heart of El'Ara for the Mora to return to full strength. There is no way I can fix the veil without bringing Lela back to El'Ara."

I faced her. "There is a way. You don't need some piece of land to return the Mora. You simply need a new center. The Mora itself is the heart of El'Ara, not Lela. If we can push the Mora back to El'Ara, you wouldn't even need to construct a new veil. You would only need to fix the tear. With all the Mora on this side of the veil, the void would be no more."

Ailan furrowed her brow, studying me. "How can you know this?"

"I just do." *For the love of Lela, I hope I do.*

I turned to face the tribunal and found Fanon with his hand raised. His temples throbbed as if he were exercising great effort to maintain his calm.

"Yes, Fanon," Ailan said.

Fanon stood. "She may be right about the Mora, but how could we possibly bring the Mora back to El'Ara? If that were possible, we'd have done it long ago."

"I have a plan for that too," I said. I took a deep breath, choosing my tone with care. *The time for striking fear has passed. Now I need them to trust me.* "Darius named me heir the same way Ailan named Liam heir. I have a right to the magic seeping into Lela, and that magic recognizes me. Once Darius is defeated, I'll claim my rule over all of Lela by right of magic and blood. I'll allow the Mora to come to me—"

The word *Morkaius* hissed through the tribunal, but with one stern look from Ailan, they returned to quiet.

I tried again. "I'll allow it to come to me, but instead of harnessing the Mora, like Morkai would have done, I'll push it away from me. As it flows to me, I will push it back to El'Ara. Once it returns, Ailan will fix the tear."

Again Fanon raised his hand to speak. "How do we know you won't harness the Mora for yourself instead?"

I shrugged. "Why should that worry you? If I harness it, I'll be destroyed by it."

Another Elvan, a female, raised her hand. "Why should we agree to this at all?" she asked, eyes on Ailan. "Do we really need the human?"

"You tell me," I said. "If I left right now, you would have no way of knowing the information I've gathered on Darius. You would have no allies to warn you when he came near, no way of knowing if he found the veil. Not to mention, a way to stop him from worldwalking."

Murmurs swept through the room. My eyes found Etrix, whose face was as neutral as ever, then Garot who stood grinning. *I'm sure he's enjoying watching this story unfold.*

I turned my attention back to the tribunal before the murmurs could rise to a cacophony. "One more thing. For me to properly work with the Mora, I'll need there to be no contest to my throne. I'll need to rule Lela indisputably. This means King Larylis must stay here in El'Ara with his wife and child."

Now the murmurs did rise.

Ailan turned to me, her lips pulled down at the corners, eyes wary. "I don't like this, Cora," she said, too quietly for the others to hear. "But I understand why you are doing this. I hope you're right about everything you said."

Me too. "It's the only way I could truly protect my people, to guarantee they have a home when this is all over."

Ailan nodded. "I'll accept this bargain, then. However,

it will take me time alone with the tribunal to get them to accept as well."

"We don't have much time," I said, biting my lip. "You know how time passes here."

She sighed. "I know. Still, I need to let them feel they are part of this decision. Give me until sundown, then we will discuss strategy."

I let out a breath of relief, then left the floor. Once outside the room beyond the closed door, I heard conversation once again arise. I pressed my back against the wall, eyes closed as I fought to calm my racing heart. Exhaustion tugged at every muscle, every bone. I wanted nothing more than to sleep. *There's so much more to be done.*

The sound of the door opening made my eyes dart wide. I tried to stand straight as Mareleau stopped in front of me. Our eyes locked, neither of us saying a word, until Mareleau heaved a sob and wrapped her free arm around me, a cooing Liam between us.

"Thank you," she whispered, crying into my hair. "Thank you for finding a way for them to accept Larylis, Cora. You have no idea what this means to me."

I returned the hug, arms around the two of them, feeling warmth flood my chest. *I may resent her at times, but I love her more.*

I am both.

32

TRUST

Teryn

Lex's father, King Carrington, leaned back in his chair, arms crossed as he eyed me from across the room. "You took quite the risk coming here with nothing but a cryptic message to warn me of your arrival, King Teryn."

"I'm sorry to surprise you like this," I said, trying to form words from my travel-weary mind. Lex and I had ridden hard to arrive promptly in Tomas and hadn't wanted to wait to rest and wash before speaking with the king. Perhaps that was why Carrington had grimaced when Lex and I took our seats in his study.

"Some would call it rude," Lex's brother, Ben, drawled from his seat at his father's side. His arms were crossed to mirror his father's, but that was where the similarities ended. There was no regal bearing in the young man. He may have been close to my age, but with his lanky build and childish sneer, he seemed much younger. "Lex, why do you keep bringing strays home like this?"

Carrington's face reddened, eyes wide as he turned to his son. "Ben, Teryn is a *king*. You do not speak of kings in such a way, nor do you speak to your brother like that."

Ben shrank away from his father's scorn. "But...you were...I was just...Father, it's just like last time! They want us to fight again."

Carrington maintained his calm, although his presence was intimidating nonetheless. "Apologize."

Ben turned crimson as his eyes met mine. "Sorry, Your Majesty," he said through his teeth.

Carrington rolled his eyes and returned his attention to me. "Like I was saying. You took quite the risk assuming I would accept this new alliance. You say my bride is on her way? How do you know I won't turn her away when she arrives?"

"If you truly find her an unacceptable bride, you may turn her away," I said. "It is what she brings that is of utmost importance. Also, she travels with Princess Lily, so she must arrive here either way."

Anger flashed over Carrington's face. "You bring weapons into my kingdom without my permission."

"Father," Lex said, "it isn't that we aren't asking your permission. We are. But we didn't have time to wait for it before executing our plan."

"*Our* plan?" Carrington raised a brow. "What is this *our* you speak of?"

Lex blushed but didn't shy away. "I am allying with Lela, even if you choose not to. Lily is the one behind much of this plan with the resistance, and I will support it no matter what."

"Lily...is orchestrating a plan against Norun?" Carrington shook his head, then paused, seeming to realize something. "Ah. Her brother. I should have known."

"I know you aren't happy that I am involving you in dealings against Norun," Lex said. "I promise, if you want nothing to do with this, we will find another way to do what we need to do. But I beg you to consider how this could benefit Tomas. If the conquered kingdoms were reclaimed from Norun, Norun would no longer be a threat. We would have nothing to fear from them any longer."

"They already did it once." Ben's voice was like a whine, his face twisted in a scowl. "They conquered half of Risa! What if they do it all over again and this time take *us*?"

Lex kept his eyes on his father. "Risa was a land at peace for hundreds of years. None of the kingdoms were prepared for an invasion. *That* was why Norun succeeded. They maintain that success through force and suppression. If Norun can be put back in its place, it will lose that advantage. Norun will fall. And if it ever rises back up, the kingdoms will be ready."

I smiled. Lex really had changed since we'd first met. I remembered his fear about everything, his clumsiness, his bitterness over his situation with his brother. Now, here he was, holding his own and *fighting*.

Carrington furrowed his brow, then turned to me. "You say I need not join you in the battle. You'll need no soldiers of mine."

"Correct," I said. "All we need is passage through the wall to Norun where we can distribute the weapons to the resistance leaders. In exchange, you have a bride, her fortune, and a closer alliance with Lela than ever before."

"Not to mention," Lex said, "you'd be helping defeat a threat bigger than Norun. You know...Morkai's dad? If Morkai creeped you out, just wait until his dad takes over our entire world and kills us all with magic."

Ben groaned. "Yet another battle that has nothing to do with us."

Carrington held out a hand toward Ben to silence him. "You're sure this King of Syrus is who you think he is?"

"He's known as the Ageless King," Lex said. "How do you think he got that name?"

Carrington sighed. "I have heard the reports about Norun and Syrus joining forces. I'd be lying if I said I hadn't been worried about what they were planning. Now I know."

I leaned forward, hands clasped, elbows propped on my knees. "Aiding the rebellion is just the first step in what is to come, but it is essential. The fate of our world could depend on it."

Carrington tapped a finger on his desk, eyes unfocused. "Very well. You have my permission and protection to use the wall. I will meet this bride of mine and consider her."

I rose to my feet. "Thank you, King Carrington."

"Retire. Wash," Carrington said. "We can speak of further details. I imagine your forces are already secretly making their way to Tomas as well. They'll need accommodations."

Lex and I exchanged a glance. *Does nothing get past his father?* "Yes, my Head of Council is in charge of sending my troops north to join us here. They will begin to arrive over the coming weeks."

Carrington stood and began arranging papers on his desk. "You will have mine as well, King Teryn."

I tilted my head. "What do you mean, King Carrington?"

"My army. If we're going to hide your troops, it's best they blend in with mine. And if we're going up against Norun, we better do it right. My forces will join you in the attack on the Norun legion."

I was speechless. It was beyond anything I'd hoped from King Carrington.

Lex looked equally surprised. "Thank you, Father."

"Next time, don't hesitate," Carrington said, eyes on Lex. "Don't sit across from me, asking my permission. Stand at my side and *convince* me. This kingdom will be yours someday. Your choices are the future of Tomas. You've shown you are capable of leading. Act like it."

Lex lifted his chin, a satisfied smile on his face. "Agreed, Father."

Cora

I rose from the couch in my room, studying the seamless flesh of my shoulder. Not even a bruise remained.

The skinweaver, a waif-like Elvan woman, watched me, nose upturned. "I did good work, yes?"

I rotated my shoulder and swung my arm to test my range of motion. No pain. I couldn't say the same for what it had felt like when she'd performed the actual weaving. All she'd done was lay her hands over my wound, yet I'd felt the agony of my flesh being fused back together for what seemed like an eternity. At least that was over now, and I was grateful for the result. "Yes, you did amazing work. Thank you."

The skinweaver nodded, then left the room.

Ailan took her place, examining the former wound. "I'm glad she was able to help you," she said, not meeting my eyes.

"I am too. Thank you for sending her to me." It was hard to ignore the tension in the air between us, but I tried my best to act as if I hadn't betrayed her trust just hours before. "I'll need my shoulder in good shape if I am to fight."

"You'll be needing a bow, I assume."

I nodded, pulling my robe over my shoulder and securing the ties. "Please, if possible."

"I'll have a weaponsweaver craft one for you. In fact, we can speak about this at the war council. I'm sure they are waiting for us now. Are you ready?" Ailan finally met my eyes.

I nodded, although part of me wished I had more time to rest. I'd been allowed to nap while Ailan had finished with the tribunal, but I needed more than that to relieve the exhaustion coursing through me. Perhaps with my wound healed, my energy would return. *It must. There is so much more to do.*

"Come." Ailan made her way to my door, then paused, turning. "No more surprises, right?"

I gave an awkward smile, not wanting to expend the energy to feign confidence. "Not like earlier."

Ailan looked relieved, her shoulders relaxing. "I

meant what I said, Cora. I do understand why you are doing this. I just wish you would have trusted me. I would have done everything in my power to protect the people of Lela."

I took a deep breath, feeling the tension melt away. Certainty filled me, the kind I didn't have to fake. "It isn't that I don't trust you, it's that I trust myself more. I know you would have done everything in your power to help Lela. It just so happens, I have power too. A lot of it. And I will die before I step aside and not use it to protect the people I'm sworn to."

Ailan's eyes widened, taking me in as if seeing me for the first time. Her expression softened with a small smile. "You've come a long way from the scared little girl I found in the forest."

It was so long ago that I'd been discovered by the Forest People, I'd almost forgotten Nalia—*Ailan*—had been the one to find me. "I know."

"It's funny I never realized it until now," Ailan said, "that I didn't find you by chance. You didn't fall, starving and unconscious, near the Forest People camp by coincidence. The whispers of my weaving brought us together." She held out a hand. "So we will work together. If I am to trust the whispers, then I am to trust you."

I put my hand in hers.

33

RESISTANCE

Cora

"Let me get this straight. The *humans*," Fanon wrinkled his nose with distaste, "will warn us if Darius arrives in Lela? How can we trust them with such an important duty?"

I forced myself not to roll my eyes at him from across the table. "If your kind would suffer the indignity of patrolling in the human word, you wouldn't have to leave it to the humans. Even so, my Royal Force is perfectly capable of doing what needs to be done."

"They have to enter the tear to communicate with us," Etrix said. He didn't pose it as a question, but I could tell he was concerned, despite his neutral tone.

"Yes," I said. "Only a handful of my most secretive soldiers know about the tear and how to enter it. They are under strict orders only to enter the tear in case of emergency." I met the eyes of the members of the war council—Ailan, Fanon, Etrix, Garot, and a few others I recognized from the tribunal. "If we don't post Elvan guards on the outside, it is essential we allow human entrance through the tear. It's the only way we can know if Darius is coming."

"I agree with Cora," Ailan said. "We must allow the humans to enter to give us warning. Even if our Elvan guards would agree to a post in the human world, it is best we leave the task to Cora's Black Force. They know how to not be seen and will not draw attention like our own guards would."

"In addition to the force we have guarding the veil," I said, "my husband is making great efforts to thwart Darius' alliance with Norun and keep their army from coming to Lela."

"Our efforts will be focused on keeping Darius from entering the veil," Ailan said. "If he gets in, there will be no stopping him from worldwalking wherever he wants. Therefore we will have our soldiers stationed inside the veil near the tear. At first word that Darius has located the veil, we will enter the human world and fight him there."

"How will we kill him before he gets a chance to enter the tear?" asked one of the other Elvan, a male with thick arms and rich, midnight-black skin. "No one was able to defeat him before. Why would this time be any different?"

"Jasa is right," Ailan said. "We need to kill Darius before he gets a chance to reach the tear. That is where our secret weapon comes in. Right, Cora?"

All eyes fell on me. I was surprised at the confidence in Ailan's voice. Not even she knew the secret I'd been withholding. I reached into the folds of my robe and withdrew the knife, placing it on the table before me. "We have this."

Ailan gasped, reaching for the black hilt with trembling fingers. "I haven't seen this since..."

"Since you stabbed Darius with it?"

She met my eyes, expression uncertain. "How is this going to help us?"

"When you stabbed Darius with this blade, he wasn't able to worldwalk, right?"

"Not until he pulled it free," she said.

"The same thing happened when he stabbed *me* with it," I said. "When he abducted me, he kept me tied up, blade stuck in my shoulder. I wasn't able to worldwalk away until I pulled it from my flesh."

Ailan furrowed her brow, seeming almost disappointed.

"There's something special about this blade," I said. "Darius told me it was made of a rare Elvan metal. If we can arm our forces with weapons made from this metal—arrows, swords, spears—we can keep him from worldwalking. Without that power, he's no stronger than any of us. We can lay a killing blow on him."

"Cora..."

"I know this can work. Where can we get more weapons like this?"

Ailan turned to face me. "Cora, this is the only blade of its kind. There are no others like it."

My heart sank, but I refused to give up. "What about the metal? Can't we find more? We must have enough time to forge at least a few more weapons."

Ailan shook her head. "This isn't made from a metal.

Darius was wrong, because he didn't know the truth. I kept it from him."

I studied the knife, its iridescent blade shining through crusted blood. "What is it made from then?"

"Claw. From my mother's dragon."

My mouth hung open. *Dragon claw? How?* My mind drew up memories of the two weapons I'd once carved from unicorn horn. To make those weapons, I'd stolen horns that had been brutally cut from live unicorns. That method of removal was the only way to keep the unicorn horns from turning to dust after the creatures died. What if dragons were the same way? I shuddered, nausea churning my stomach. "We can't get more claws, can we?"

Ailan's eyes looked haunted as she turned the knife over in her hand. "Berolla nearly killed me with this very claw because of a cruel trick my brother had played. When she realized what had happened, she sacrificed this piece of herself and gifted it to me. The claw was then made into a blade. I never told Darius, because I knew he'd begin to see dragons as something to carve up and exploit."

"Is there anything else in El'Ara like this?" I asked. "Anything with properties that could stop a worldwalker?"

Ailan shrugged. "I don't even know why this blade works the way it does. Perhaps it only works against worldwalkers because that was the power Darius used against Berolla. Dragons are mysterious creatures. It's hard enough to understand my own, much less my mother's."

"And your mother's dragon..."

Ailan met Fanon's eyes across the table. He shook his

head. "Berolla took Last Breath not long after Satsara died," he said.

Ailan sighed. "I figured it was so. I saw no sign of her in the caves."

My shoulders slumped as I leaned back in my chair. "So we have one weapon. One shot."

"It can still work," Garot said with a smile, his hopeful voice and twinkling eyes in contrast to the damp mood that had fallen over the rest of us. "Someone needs to get close enough to stab him, then—as Cora said—make the killing blow."

"I'll do it," Ailan said.

Fanon glared. "No."

She didn't meet his eyes. "I'm the only one who can. I was the only one strong enough before, and I'm the only one strong enough now. Darius will *want* to fight me, to end me, so he won't try to worldwalk away until I am dead. But he won't get the chance. I will plunge this blade into his heart and take off his head with my sword."

Her tone was calm. Cold. Certain.

Ailan wrapped her hand around the hilt of her knife, knuckles white. "Darius can come. I'll be ready for him."

Teryn

"Stop pacing, Lex. You'll draw attention," I said, frowning at Lex's shadowed form. The night was dark and quiet and would have been serene, if it weren't for our nerve-wracking mission. I crossed my arms and took a seat on top of the wooden crate—a crate in which dozens of swords were hidden.

Lex froze, tossing a glance over his shoulder. "Draw attention from whom? Do you see anyone?"

Lily put a hand on Lex's shoulder, pulling him closer to the tree the three of us were clustered around. "Teryn's right. You need to stay calm. Everything is going fine; we have nothing to worry about."

Lex grumbled. "It's you I'm worried about. You shouldn't be here, Lilylove. We're on enemy grounds! What if something happens to you?"

"Nothing will happen," Lily said. "The guards said they never see anyone this close to the wall on the Norun side. Besides, me being here is the only thing securing my brother's trust in this operation."

"She's right, Lex," I said. "After tonight, we'll gain Lord Orik's trust, and Lily can stay behind for our future meetings."

Lex sighed and leaned against the trunk of the tree. "Fine, I'll relax."

With our return to silence, I scanned the field, watching for movement. Under the boughs of the nearest tree, I could just barely make out the silhouettes of our guards waiting with more crates. But beyond them...was that movement up ahead?

"I hope Father isn't smooching Helena right now." Lex's voice was heavy with disgust, startling me from my observations.

I rolled my eyes while Lily swatted Lex on the arm.

"What?" Lex shrugged. "He seems to really like her. I swear he's been waiting for me to get out of the castle just so he can fawn all over her without feeling guilty. *I'll meet my bride and consider her.* Ha! He barely laid eyes on her before he started acting like a lovesick puppy. It's gross."

"Lex, your father deserves to remarry." Lily's annoyed tone made me think this wasn't the first time they'd had this conversation. "He's been a widower for what, nine years? Just let him—"

I held out my hand to quiet them as I got to my feet. *Now that is* definitely *movement.* A group of shadowed figures emerged onto the field. In the distance, I could hear the subtle pound of horse hooves and wagon wheels.

"He's here," Lily said in an excited whisper. As she hurried toward the figures, the tallest came forward and met her in a hug, while Lex and I followed cautiously behind. Our guards left their hiding place and filed in behind us.

Lily separated from the hug and faced us, arm linked with the newcomer's. "Lex, King Teryn, please meet my brother, Lord Orik."

"Lord of nothing, she means," Orik said, bowing. He —as well as his four companions—wore a hooded cloak, keeping most of his face in shadow. From what I could see, the five men looked ragged with tired eyes. Yet their postures were of noble men—noble men who seemed unafraid of moving in the dark. *They are no strangers to dealings such as this.*

"Your brother will have his title again, princess," said the man next to Orik, "once I reclaim my land and my throne."

Lily gasped. "King Edowain!" She gave him a deep curtsy, then turned toward me and Lex. "He's done so much for the resistance. He's responsible for rallying the other conquered kingdoms."

Edowain regarded us, then smiled. "I am pleased to meet our new allies. We've spent years trying to arm the resistance, but with all the forges and weaponries in Norun being controlled by the capital, it has been a slow process. What you offer us will finally put our plans into motion."

"You can accommodate as discussed in our correspondence?" I asked. "We need to be sure the conquered kingdoms execute the rebellion simultaneously. Norun must fall and leave the legion isolated."

Edowain nodded. "You have my word. Give us two weeks."

"According to our spies," Orik said, "the legion is still in the north. Two weeks will put them well within our grasp."

Two weeks? I groaned internally, wondering what condition Cora would be in two weeks from now. That is, if I even found her. Alive. I shook darker thoughts from my mind. *This is the best I can do.* "Very well."

"We will send our master smuggler to meet you here every night for the next eight days," Edowain said, tipping his head toward the wagon that had now pulled to a stop behind them. "That should give him enough time to collect and distribute all of the weapons you've provided."

A man climbed down from the wagon and approached me and Lex. He was shorter than the men in King Edowain's retinue, and when he smiled at me, I could see he was missing at least two teeth. With an exaggerated flourish of his hands, he removed his tattered hat and folded into a bow. "Master smuggler, at yer service. You can call me Stone."

I took a step back, choking on the repulsive odor that wafted forth. When Stone righted himself, he replaced his hat and winked. A low rumble of laughter moved amongst the rebels.

Lex heaved, then covered his face with his hands. One of our guards retched behind us, while Lily hid behind her brother. "What in the name of Tomas is that smell?" Lex asked, and for once, I was glad he was less polite than I was. I needed to know too.

Stone walked to the back of the wagon and lifted a corner of the heavy burlap that covered the bed. The revolting stench filled the air around us, and even the king's rebels stepped away and turned their heads until the smuggler replaced the cover.

"Is that...manure?" I asked, breathing through my mouth to no avail.

Stone gave an innocent shrug. "Ya see, I'm just yer innocent manure merchant, my good man. Yer Majesty, I mean. No need to look in the bed of my wagon. You can clearly smell I'm up to no good."

My eyes went wide as I made the connection. "You're going to transport the weapons...in manure?"

"It's a real shit job, I know." Stone tipped his hat and winked.

I stared back at him, shocked over both the genius and the repulsiveness of the plan, while Lex burst with poorly stifled laughter.

"It's a wonderful idea," Lily said, wrinkling her nose. "But I am glad this will be my only trip to meet you like this, brother."

Orik laughed. "Once Edowain gets his kingdom back, it will be safe for us to visit again. I'm glad I got to see you now. Next time, I think you'll have a babe in your arms, won't you?"

Lily rubbed a hand over her belly, then gave her brother a final hug.

Edowain waved a hand toward the wagon. "Have your guards bring those weapons, then grab a shovel. We've got work to do." He pulled a cloth over his mouth and nose, securing it at the back of his head. "Next time, you'll want to bring one of these."

34

ARMOR

Mareleau

I crept across the gray soil, past rotting trees with curling, gnarled branches on each side of the path. The wall of mist loomed ahead, and the sun could no longer be seen in the colorless sky above. Before the veil stood rows upon rows of Elvan soldiers, perhaps ten times the amount than the last time I'd been at the veil. Half their rank faced the veil while the other half faced me. The sight of them was unnerving, but I took a deep breath and proceeded forward.

In unison, the soldiers facing me thrust their spears outward and shouted a warning for me to stop. I pulled my arms tight around Liam, then focused on the soldiers, taking in their distrust, their fear, their alarm and wrapped it around me like a new cloak. There I transformed it, allowing it to morph my bearing into one that should be respected, honored.

The soldiers didn't lower their spears as I continued forward, but they didn't tell me to stop again, either. I heard a few whispering, *Edell-Morkara'Elle.*

"Let me through," I said, authority ringing in my voice. "I am not leaving; I only wish to stand by the veil. You may guard me there, see that I am not harmed."

A few of the soldiers exchanged wary glances, and not one lowered his spear.

I wrapped my power closer around me. *Respect me. Honor me.* "Did you not hear me? If this command were coming from Ailan, would you ignore her? I am to be given the same respect as she, am I not?"

One of the soldiers grumbled, then whispered furiously to the men around him, all the while not taking his eyes off me. "You are permitted to do as you wish," he finally said, "so long as you don't leave."

"Well then," I said with a pleasant smile, walking up to their masses before they'd even had a chance to right their spears. They scrambled to make way for me, standing aside and leaving a narrow path for me to reach the veil.

I ignored the eyes I felt burning into me as I approached the wall of mist and folded my legs beneath me. Liam turned his head this way and that, as if fascinated by the gloomy gray. I couldn't help but smile. *I think you may be the only one in the entire world unaffected by all this, sweet one.*

I looked over my shoulder and found the closest soldiers nearly pressed against my back. "Some privacy, please? Five steps back will do, thank you." Before they could obey, I returned my attention to the veil, hearing grumbles behind me, followed by the shifting of feet and the clanking of armor. With a sigh, I reached my hand to the veil, feeling the cool wall of mist beneath my fingers.

"Larylis," I whispered, "I know you can't hear me, but I also know you're there." My throat became tight, and I struggled to bite back tears. "Cora says you insist on guarding the tear yourself, which doesn't surprise me. I wish I could tell you all about what she's done for us. Did she tell you when the two of you spoke? You're going to stay with me and Liam in El'Ara. Can you believe it? I'm glad she didn't give you that letter. I know it would have broken your heart. How many times have I already done that to you?

"Part of me wishes I could send a new letter to you, telling you about this news, give you something to hope for. But perhaps it's best you don't know. Who knows if any of us will even survive what is ahead. When you fight, I don't want you to fight for me. I don't want you to protect me. I want you to protect yourself. I don't want you to worry about what happens to me, because I am going to do whatever it takes to protect Liam. That might put me in danger.

"Can you accept that? Can you fight and defend yourself without wondering where I am? Without putting yourself in more danger to protect me? Knowing you will be allowed to stay here once everything is over has lifted a weight off my chest. If I die, I can be at peace knowing Liam will have you. That's why it's so important for you to protect yourself, not me."

I let my hand fall away from the veil and wiped a tear from my cheek. "I know this all sounds grim, but I can't help but have this on my mind. These preparations have made the threat feel so much more real. I'm supposed to stay under guard with Liam night and day in my room. No less than a dozen guards are posted in the hall at all times. Honestly, I'm not supposed to be here right now, but you know me. I have my way of getting what I want.

"I know what you'd say—go back to my room and stay under guard. I will. I just wanted to be close to you. I wanted *Liam* to be close to you. You know, one last time before things get crazy." I let out an irritated sigh. "I hate not knowing what's happening out there. I hate not knowing how much time has passed. Darius could be here any moment."

My words made me feel cold, and my proximity to the veil took on a new significance. Yes, I was as close to Larylis as I could possibly be, but I was also closer to the threat from outside. With Liam, no less. I stood, a sudden urgency propelling my muscles. "I'll see you again, my love." With one final brush of my hand against the veil, I turned and made my way through the sea of soldiers.

Once clear of them, I froze, finding Cora on the path ahead, arms crossed as she narrowed her eyes at me. Next to her stood Garot, a sheepish grin on his face.

I rolled my eyes. "Garot, do you not know the meaning of a secret?"

He shrugged. "Cora asked where you were. I couldn't tell her I *didn't* bring you here."

"That's precisely what it means to keep a secret."

"No," Garot said, "that would have been a lie. I don't tell lies, I tell stories."

I couldn't be mad at him. Of all the Elvan, he seemed

to be one of the only ones I didn't have to coerce with a glamour to make like me. Still, I refused to look ashamed as I approached them. "Fine. I suppose we should head back then."

Garot opened his swirling tunnel, and I walked into it, not waiting to let Cora catch up. She did anyway, of course. "What were you thinking coming out here?" she asked.

Lie? Or truth? I began to prepare a glamour, then stopped. *She's my friend,* I reminded myself, feeling my cheeks redden. *I don't need to glamour her.* Now that I'd been practicing my powers so often on the Elvan, it was almost becoming a habit. A bad habit, perhaps. I turned to her and smiled. "I'm sorry. I just wanted to be close to Lare. I know it's dangerous, and I won't do it again."

She put a hand on my shoulder. "I know you don't like being cooped up or bossed around. I don't either, but..."

"But Darius is coming to kill my son," I said. "Which could happen any day."

"You, Ailan, and Liam are all that stand between Darius and unlimited power. Since Ailan will be fighting Darius, you and Liam must be kept safe."

I sighed. "So back to my room I go. I know."

"Well, first, Ailan has something to show us."

I cocked my head, then slowed my steps. "Another dragon?"

Cora seemed confused. "I don't think so. She was asking for us both, which is why I came to find you. Luckily Garot," she smiled at the beaming Elvan, "is an honest gentleman—or gentelvan."

"Oh, I like that!" Garot said. "Though, I'm still curious to know more about this *bard* thing you have in your world. Do you think I could be one here? A bardelvan?"

Cora laughed. It felt good to hear her laugh, no matter how faint it was.

I decided to join her. "Garot, I'm sure you already are."

～

GAROT'S TUNNEL ENDED, ITS SWIRLING COLORS OF GREEN and gold going still, then spreading out before us over the lawn in front of the palace.

"Ailan will be waiting for us in the armory," Cora said.

I frowned. "The armory? Why?"

"I don't know. But I won't tell her where you went. Neither will Garot." Cora fixed him with an intense stare. "Right, Garot? It will only worry her."

Garot shrugged. "So long as she doesn't ask."

Cora met my eyes. "I found you waiting for me in my room. You wanted to get away from the guards for a bit and came to find me. Right?"

I was surprised at Cora's willingness to cover up what I'd done. Wasn't she supposed to be the perfect one? No matter, so long as I didn't have to explain myself again. Besides, she was right. It would worry Ailan to no end. "Right."

"Just don't do it again. Please?"

My heart sank at the genuine worry on her face. I nodded.

Garot took his leave of us, and I followed Cora into

the palace, up one of the immense ivory staircases, and down one of the long, towering hallways. Although I still felt like the palace was more of a prison than a paradise, I was coming to admire its beauty more and more each day. Not one wall held anything but the most breath-taking art. Each tapestry showcased the most dazzling scenes in colors I wasn't sure I'd ever witnessed before. Each stone beneath our feet was polished to a mirror-like shine. *I could get used to this. I could.*

We came to a darker hallway, one with walls of deep reds and golds rather than the ivory and opal that spanned the rest of the palace. At the end of the hallway, a wide arch led into a cavernous room where endless rows of swords and spears lined the walls. Tables were piled with chainmail and shimmering armor, the light from the lanterns casting rainbow-like patterns over the iridescent metal.

Ailan stood at one of the tables, inspecting a selection of swords with hilts set with immense jewels. She no longer wore one of her flowing Elvan robes. Instead, she wore chain and armor over what looked like thick leather leggings. Her forearms were adorned in metal gauntlets and around her waist was a swordbelt from which numerous knives and an empty scabbard hung. An Elvan man stood across from the table, one of the burliest Elvan I'd yet seen. His skin was dark, and his arms were roped with muscle.

Ailan lifted one of the swords, and Cora and I kept our distance while she took a few practice swings. "Thank you, Jasa. This is the one." Ailan sheathed the sword in the scabbard at her waist, then faced us. "Good, you're here. Come." She waved us toward another table. As we approached, I found a large metal container of some sort, plate and mail, and a bow with a quiver of arrows.

Cora's eyes widened at the sight of the arrows, her mouth falling open as she looked at Ailan. "Is this for me?"

Ailan nodded. "Weaponsweaver Jasa made them especially for you, with my recommendations. I asked him to mimic the style and feel of the set you are used to from the Forest People."

The arrows were fletched with gold feathers and the tips appeared to be of the same shimmering metal as the other plate and weapons in the room. Everything else, from the shaft of the arrows to the bow and quiver were black. I didn't know much about shooting arrows—or using any weapon, for that matter—but seeing these made me almost wish I did. *Was I going to be gifted something similar?* I frowned, seeing no other weapon on the table.

Cora strung the bow and practiced pulling it to her cheek a few times. "It's perfect."

Ailan extended her hand toward the plate and mail. "You each get a set of armor, also."

Cora seemed excited by this, but I wrinkled my nose. Armor? Me? Then again, Ailan did look stunning in hers, not to mention intimidating.

My eyes moved to the strange metal container. "What is that?"

Ailan placed her hands on one of the four thick sides. Two of the sides were longer while the ends were short, creating a rectangular shape with four, lightly rounded corners. It was almost shaped like a...

I took a step closer. "Is that a bassinet?"

"An armored bassinet, for Liam," Ailan said.

I looked from Liam to the bassinet, wondering how he would be any safer in there than in my arms.

"We will place a cushion and blankets inside, so he will be comfortable," Ailan said. "The sides will protect him from any weapon."

"What about the open top? Someone could simply grab him out."

Ailan smiled. "No one but you or I will be able to take him out of the bassinet. I've had it woven by a protectionweaver."

My heart raced, and I couldn't say the words that came to mind. *What if we both die? What if he gets stuck in there?* "Does the weaving protect against weapons too?"

Ailan's face fell. "Well, no..."

"So instead of taking out my son, Darius could just stab him through the opening."

"That won't happen," Ailan said. "I won't let him get through the veil, much less into the palace. This is only a precaution."

How was she so sure? Was I the only one willing to face the worst? I saw the concern in Ailan's eyes and realized she was doing her best to put on a brave face. She knew the dangers. She knew what could happen. Yet, she was doing her best to protect us.

I forced my lips into a smile. "It's a great idea. Thank you, Ailan."

She seemed relieved. "I'll have it brought to your room before nightfall."

I nodded and took her words as a dismissal, turning

to go. Before Cora and I could take a step, Ailan lightly took hold of my arm. "Mareleau, please don't leave your room again. If you must go, take your guards. I can't risk losing either of you."

"I will stay from now on," I said, trying not to scowl. Then back to my gilded cage I went.

35

FIRST WAVE

Teryn

I stood at the top of the wall, midday sun warming my shoulders as I stared over the land that was Norun. To the north and south, Tomas' wall expanded as far as I could see until it disappeared into shadows and trees in the far-off distance.

Stone pointed to the east. "My spies say the legion is just there, Yer Majesty, over the ridge. They'll make camp tonight, two hours' march from here."

I raised my brow. "So, not only are you a smuggler, but also a spymaster?"

Stone grinned. "A good smuggler needs good spies."

I shrugged. "I'm grateful either way. And for the fact that you no longer carry with you the scent of manure. I thought I'd never get that smell out of my nose."

That made Stone laugh. "Yer Majesty, I hate to tell you my scent hasn't changed. Was only my natural stench, you see? You simply got used to it after eight nights with a shovel."

I slapped Stone on the back. "Perhaps you're right. Now, what of the weapons? Have they been delivered to the rebels?"

"Aye, and not a speck on them." His expression hardened. "They are ready, Yer Majesty. It will be tonight. Norun will fall."

My breath caught, heart racing. After two weeks of waiting, it was finally time. *Tonight I find Cora.* "What have your spies noted about the legion's previous camps? Where can King Darius be found?"

"Aye, yer prey. King Darius' army settles at the southern end of camp, while King Isvius' legion settles north. Big tents, those kings have."

That's where my retinue will go, then. "You've already reported all this to King Carrington?"

"Aye. War council in an hour, he says. If that's all, Yer Majesty, I'll be on my way. I've got to prepare for some chaos that needs stirrin' tonight."

"Thank you, Stone. You may go." I watched the horizon for awhile after Stone left, wishing I could see the legion from here, anxious for a glimpse of what we'd be up against. *Let's just hope Norun has continued to underestimate Tomas and doesn't have spies of their own waiting on the road ahead.*

I descended the stairs of the wall to the Tomas side, moving from crisp, open air to a sea of tents that made up our war camp. Messengers wove in front of me, while servants carried weapons, armor, and plates of food, all wearing the livery of either Tomas, Kero, or Vera. The heightened activity told me word was already beginning to spread through camp.

I made my way to my private tent. Not a big tent, like Stone had reported Darius and Isvius would have, but it suited me well enough. I expected no luxury during this operation. With a sigh, I sat on my cot and closed my eyes. *I'm coming, Cora. Hold out just a little longer.*

"Teryn."

I rose to my feet, hand on the hilt of my sword as I faced the source of the voice.

A subtle light was all I found, a shimmering white, blue, and gray in the corner of my tent. The light rippled and expanded, slowly taking on human form until an ethereal woman stood before me. "Emylia?"

"I didn't mean to startle you," she said, her voice sounding as if from far away. "It's been hard to get you to see me until now. Cora was much easier."

I removed my hand from my sword hilt and took an eager step toward the wraith. "Have you seen her? Spoken to her? Is she well?"

Her expression fell. "I haven't spoken to her since Ridine Castle. I've had...other tasks."

"Can't you see everything? Cora said when you tried to move to the otherlife—"

"I *could* see everything," Emylia said. "I no longer can. I had a glimpse into everything that had happened during my lifetime and everything that was happening as a result. I turned away from the otherlife and no longer have that ability."

"What about your abilities as a wraith? You found me. I imagine you didn't walk here like a mortal. Can you... sense her? Find her?"

Emylia's pale, misty eyes seemed to stare into the distance for a moment before returning to me. "I can't sense her, Teryn, and I haven't seen her amongst the legion."

The disappointment weighed heavy on my shoulders, but I tried to focus on the other information she'd given. "You've visited the legion?"

"Yes." She almost seemed exasperated. "I lost track of Cora shortly after I spoke to her at Ridine. It was like... she just wasn't *anywhere*. So I've been checking in on you instead. But you couldn't see me, couldn't hear me. When I saw what you were doing here, I finally understood what I could do to help."

She just wasn't anywhere. The words haunted me as I tried to make sense of them. "Cora worldwalked after you last spoke to her, and eventually ended up in El'Ara. Perhaps that's why you couldn't find her."

"Perhaps," Emylia said with a shrug.

Then what did it mean that she couldn't find her *now*? Was it possible Cora had escaped Darius, or was she...

I refused to let my mind go there. *No, she's alive. She must be alive.*

"Teryn." Emylia shifted, bringing my attention back to her. "You are attacking the legion tonight, yes?"

I nodded.

"Then I want to help."

I frowned. "What do you intend to do?"

Emylia put her hand to the side, as if resting it on something invisible. A dull, gray light undulated beneath her hand until it took the shape of a man. An armed man, long sword clasped in his hand.

A warrior wraith.

I jumped back, hand flying to my sword once again, but Emylia held her free hand out to stop me. My chest heaved as the wraith watched me with his lifeless eyes. Eyes so chilling and familiar. "Is that what I think it is? One of Morkai's *wraiths*?"

"Yes," Emylia said, her voice steady, "but you have nothing to fear. Morkai's power was the only thing that made them dangerous. And I've found them, all of them. Do you know who they are? Who they once were?"

I shook my head, although something tickled the back of my mind, something Morkai once said...

"Morkai's wraiths were the souls of the humans who fought for Darius against the Elvan," Emylia said. "Some were from the army of Syrus, others were mercenaries or men recruited from other kingdoms. None stood a chance against Elvan fighters. Darius used them as lives to be expended for his personal cause. They died fighting a war they could never win, in a realm they didn't belong to. Ever since, they've been trapped in Lela, unable to move to the otherlife."

Finally, Morkai's words breached the surface of my mind. It felt as if it had been ages since I'd heard them. *Lost souls of the dead, in the world of the living. Souls of men who lost their lives in an ancient war you've never heard of...*

Emylia continued. "Morkai captured them, controlled them with his power. He promised them peace in the otherlife, but when he died, the wraiths were left behind. Their ability to kill had been taken from them, so they returned to their wanderings. I can't give them the power Morkai gave them, but I've been able to guide them back to a sort of sentience."

"How?" I studied the wraith, who continued to watch

me. His face was passive, and although his eyes were life-less, he stood at attention, not like I'd expect of a wandering, mindless wraith.

Emylia smiled. "By giving them a sense of purpose. I've shared with them what I've learned and what is happening in the lands around us. They know what you are planning tonight. We want in."

"Without Morkai's power granting them the ability to fight, what can they possibly do?"

"I heard the word chaos mentioned on the wall."

I shook my head. "Stone will be burning supplies. How can you help with that?"

Emylia and the wraith exchanged a glance, which startled me. It was the first time I'd seen the warrior wraith move. Emylia grinned. "What would you do if you woke up in the middle of the night to a camp full of armed wraiths? Never mind whether they can kill you. Would you linger long enough to find out?"

I furrowed my brow, then my lips began to turn up at the corners. "No, I suppose I wouldn't."

"You would run, right? Where would you run?"

"Away from the wraiths," I said. "Anywhere."

"What if the wraiths were everywhere, aside from one clear path away from the camp? What if enemy forces awaited at the end of that path, hidden in the dark?"

A chill ran up spine as I realized what she was proposing. "Instead of invading the legion, we could divide them, chase out portions of the camp to meet our forces at predetermined areas around the camp."

Emylia nodded. "Send an initial force to begin the attack. When the camp wakes, the wraiths will be the first thing they see to chase them out."

I ran a hand through my hair. "Not everyone will run. Some will face the wraiths."

"True, but hardly a man will have time to be fully armed. You can deal with those once the first wave is dealt with."

"None of this feels quite honorable," I said with a sigh.

"No," Emylia said. "I suppose I will judge myself for this day too, when I try to return to the otherlife."

I took a deep breath. "Let us be judged, then."

"WE'RE HERE, YOUR MAJESTIES," THE SCOUT ANNOUNCED, approaching me, Lex, and King Carrington. "The camp is just ahead. Guards posted as expected, but other than that, the camp is quiet."

Fire flooded my veins, bringing a shock of wakefulness to my tired eyes. We'd been given mere hours to rest before we began our two-hour march through the middle of the night, and I imagined I wasn't the only one who'd been unable to fall asleep. *I'll sleep when this battle is won and Cora is safe.*

I faced Lex and King Carrington. "I'll lead my forces south to Darius' end of camp."

Carrington nodded. "I'll take the west, Ben will take the north, and Lex will take the east. Your men have their orders?"

"Yes," I said. "Luck be with you."

"Luck be with you," Carrington echoed, then joined his forces.

Lex lingered, his face pale under the moonlight. He

extended his gauntleted arm. "Don't get yourself killed, all right?"

I extended my own arm, plated in the crimson armor of the Red Force, and grasped him at the elbow. "You too, Lex." I fought back the lump that rose in my throat as we parted ways, forcing my posture to remain upright as I approached my Black Force.

The men already had their faces covered, showing nothing but their eyes. For a split second, I expected my brother to be among them. But no, he was at the veil where I hoped he was safer. For now, at least.

"You know how to move like shadow," I said, voice loud enough for them to hear, yet not so loud that it carried through the quiet night. "You know how to strike like a viper. I don't need to tell you to remember your training, for it is in your blood. You proved your capabilities at Centerpointe Rock, and tonight we face a similar foe. Again, we face the Norun legion. Again, we face a man with powers unusual to this world. And again, we will win.

"You may see things that frighten you, visions of wraiths from the nightmares you've had since that horrific battle not too long ago. Tonight, I ask you to ignore these visions. Tonight, these visions will serve you. Let them terrify the legion. Let them chase our enemies out into the night, onto our waiting spears and swords. Give them not a second thought, nor a second glance. They won't hurt you.

"First wave Black Force." A section of the group saluted. "Invade the camp, retreat when they become alerted to our activity. Second wave Black Force." The remainder of the group saluted. "You will await those who come to you. Deal with them swiftly."

I turned to the other portion of my force, the men in red-painted armor. "Red Force. Once the first and second waves have begun, we invade the camp and take down those who remain." I regarded the men, looking from the Black Force to the Red, meeting the eyes of my soldiers. I saw a mixture of fear and bravery, a reflection of what I felt inside. "Ready."

Instead of a shout, the men brought their fists to their chests.

I nodded. "First wave Black Force. Go."

36

REBELLION

Lex

My sword arm was heavy, and blood splattered my face, dripping on the inside of my helm. Yet, I kept swinging, kept killing. I did it for Lily, for her brother, for the future of our unborn child. I did it for peace in a land that had known nothing but suppression. I did it so we wouldn't have to rely on a stupid wall to keep us safe from now on.

I gasped for breath as I tore my sword from a man's stomach, no longer fighting the urge to retch, as I'd become dulled to the sight of blood, to the eyes of dying men. *How much longer?*

As if in answer, a horn called out, two blasts. Then again.

"The eastern camp has been secured," said Clemence, Captain of my Princeguard. My remaining men had finished their foes and came to join us. "What are your orders?"

It took me a moment to get over the shock that the east—*my* quarter of the camp—was the first to become secured. Yet the battle wasn't over. Three quarters remained, and I could still hear the clash of swords in the distance, screams and shouts amongst the flaming tents illuminating the dark of the early morning. First light had yet to creep over the horizon, but I knew it couldn't be far off. "Let's move to the north end of camp and see how my brother's forces are doing."

With that, we took off, stepping over bodies and discarded pieces of armor, dodging wraiths that wandered, searching for people to terrorize. *At least they aren't terrorizing our side this time.*

Sounds of fighting grew closer as we approached the northern end of the camp, and before long, we fell into the melee once again. My Princeguard moved around me with the grace of dancers, while I lumbered around like a bear in armor. However, even as a bear I wasn't too bad. I mean, I *had* been working out, training each month since the Battle at Centerpointe Rock. Never mind my muscles were hard to see beneath the fat. They were *there*.

"I'll have your head on a pike."

I started at the voice; its whining, grating tone could belong to only one person. With a whirl, I saw Ben, his scrawny form sauntering up to...*is that King Isvius?*

My stomach did a flip, and I nearly missed the sword that swung near my face. At a warning shout from Clemence, I darted back and engaged my foe, blocking his sword with my own. We exchanged blows, his striking the armor over my chest. I stumbled back from the force of it, feet slipping in blood and mud. The man came at me with a shout. *This is the end,* I thought as I struggled to regain my balance.

Clemence threw himself between me and the man, his sword plunging into the enemy's neck. Without hesitation, I spun toward where I'd seen Ben, only to find him sprawled on the ground at Isvius' feet. My mind reeled at the sight. Why was Isvius even here? Father's forces were supposed to have drawn him to the western side of camp.

Don't tell me he's defeated Father.

I ran for them as Ben backed away from Isvius, hand to his bloodied cheek, his other arm limp and useless at his side. Ben's eyes flashed to the sword that lay in the mud not too far away, but Isvius kicked it out of my brother's reach. The king's sword was sheathed, but there was murder in his eyes as he squatted before my brother. "You are nothing but a little bee. Your sting only annoys me."

I was within striking distance as Isvius turned my way, and with a calm, swift step, unsheathed his sword and blocked my blow. Ben scrambled further back.

"Now the big bee wants to play," Isvius said with a smirk, reminding me too much of his despicable son, Helios.

"Where is my father?"

Isvius' face darkened. "I'd like to say King Carrington fell to my sword, but I am not a liar. However, you and your pathetic brother will do."

My heart leapt. That meant my father could still be alive. I charged Isvius again, and my Princeguard surrounded us, engaging Isvius' men. I knew it was a battle I could not win. No one bested King Isvius.

I don't have to win. I just have to hold out.

"Hey, did you know I watched your son die?"

Isvius was taken aback for a moment before he swung at me. "Don't speak about my son. I know how he died. That ally of yours murdered him."

"Nah, it was that ally of *yours* who murdered him," I said, labored breathing and all, as I blocked his blow. "I mean, Morkai did it indirectly, considering it was his Roizan that killed Helios, but it's pretty funny how he still convinced you to side with him. Even more funny that you now side with his dad!"

Isvius blinked hard, as if he were trying to make sense of my words.

"Oh, did you not know that? Yeah, the immortal King of Syrus is the father of Morkai, the evil wizard that nearly got your entire army killed. How embarrassing."

"What's embarrassing is how easily you lie," Isvius said, grinning as if our fight were a funny game. My Princeguard remained close, likely so they could step in if things looked dire. Well...things were dire, and they obviously couldn't tell.

Four horn blasts. And again. That meant the western camp was now secured.

Isvius let out a roar, his expression no longer amused, and he came at me with renewed vigor. I blocked his sword with my shield, feeling my muscles scream in protest as I struggled to maintain hold. He continued to pummel my shield, and I ducked, covering my head as I swiped out at his legs, sword crunching into his armor. That distracted him enough to allow me to back away.

Isvius heaved, teeth bared as he shouted toward the brightening sky. A battle cry. It was finally daybreak, and Isvius was preparing to come in for the kill.

"I think that's enough," I said, trying to keep the tremor from my voice.

Isvius narrowed his eyes, a dark smile pulling at his lips as he shifted from foot to foot. "Getting tired, boy? Ready to surrender?

I shook my head. "No, it's not that. I was just saying I think it's been long enough for your palace to be ransacked. You have a lot of nice things there, right?"

Isvius frowned. "What lies do you speak of now?"

I pointed my sword at the horizon, where the first rays of the sun shone behind the trees—trees shrouded in smoke. In fact, pillars of smoke rose in the distance from every direction. "Can't you see? While you've been fighting here, Norun has been falling to a mass rebellion. You'll hardly have a home by the time you get back to your palace."

A runner in Norun livery approached, spoke to one of Isvius' men. My heart sank, seeing one of my Princeguard dead at the soldier's feet. I risked a glance at the fighting still going on around us, relieved to see most of my men were still alive. Isvius' soldier approached the king and delivered a hushed message.

Isvius' face twisted. "How do we know it's true?" he muttered to his man, though his eyes remained fixed on me. "Where would they get the weapons?"

I smiled at that, and Isvius' eyes widened. My chest heaved as I struggled to catch my breath, waiting to see if Isvius would charge. Tense moments passed, the king and I locked in our stances.

Isvius took a step away. "Pull back," he shouted. "Retreat." The runner blew a horn, a single long blast, and others echoed through the camp.

"What, you don't want to finish the fight?" I called out. Isvius ignored me, fleeing with his men as arrows rained over their raised shields. "Good, me neither." I scrambled across the camp, looking for Ben. I spotted him at the edge near the trees, one of my Princeguard at his side. Where was *his* Princeguard? As I made my way toward him, stepping around bodies in Tomas yellow and green, I knew my answer.

Ben whimpered as I kneeled before him. "I could have taken him."

"No, Ben, you couldn't have. Neither could I."

"What did you say that scared him off?"

I smirked. "I said our wall isn't afraid of him anymore, so he better run home."

Ben pouted, then winced, bringing the fingers of his good hand to his cheek. "He broke my arm and...slapped me."

"You're lucky he didn't do worse." I sat next to Ben in the mud, listening to the sounds of fighting growing quieter. Where were the other horn blasts, signaling that the other sections of the camp were secure? "I hope Teryn finds Cora."

Ben cocked his head, then winced again. "Here? Why would he find her here? She's in some place called the veil."

My eyes widened, locking on Ben. "What? How do you know?"

"We had a messenger. It was days ago."

"Why didn't you deliver it to King Teryn?"

"I'm not a servant," Ben said. "I left it in Father's study."

I rubbed my temples. "If you weren't injured, I'd punch you right now. You're lucky I'm glad you're alive."

Ben had the decency to look ashamed. "I'm...sorry. I didn't know it was important."

"If you'd listened to anything we've been talking about at the war council—"

"If you included me I would! If you didn't treat me like a child, like the idiot you think I am, I would know what's going on."

"If you didn't act like a petulant turd, I would want to include you! You act like every meeting we have is beneath you!" We eyed each other, our faces red. Something rumbled in my throat, then erupted into laughter. "Petulant turd."

"It's not funny, Lex."

I sobered, rubbing my eyes. "I think we both have some things to work on. If you want me to respect you, you need to respect me too, all right? You have a lot of growing up to do. But, I admit, I haven't been warm to you...ever. Can we start over? Can we, you know, act like the princes Father wants us to be?"

"Are you only saying that because I might be crippled forever and you feel bad?"

"Yes, but I mean it." I tousled Ben's hair, which earned me a smile. I looked up at my men, who were trying to act like they weren't paying a lick of attention to our brotherly moment of insults and bonding. "Clemence, find a runner. Tell him to find King Teryn at once. Deliver the message that Cora is not here, she's behind the veil."

∿

Teryn

One short horn blast. And again. *The north.* That meant three quarters of the camp were now secure, not to mention the Norun legion had retreated. It should have given me hope, yet the fighting was still thick around me.

A wraith ran between me and my opponent, ethereal sword swinging toward the other soldier, but my enemy ignored the attack, charging through the apparition instead. I cursed and met his attack with my sword. Unfortunately, the wraiths didn't seem to have had as strong of an effect on Darius' men as they'd had on the Norun legion. Perhaps the men from Norun recognized the wraiths, remembering the power they'd had the last time they'd been on a battlefield.

Not so for Darius' soldiers. Only a small portion ran toward the Black Force's ambush, and the ones who remained fought fiercely and incessantly. My muscles screamed with every blow, every swing of my sword. The rising sun told me we'd been fighting for hours, and I still hadn't made it to Darius' tent.

Impatience made me reckless, my heart racing as I beat back my opponent, taking a few hits on my red armor. I pressed in closer and closer, forcing him back while closing the distance between us. The soldier lunged for my midsection, but I spun to the side, crunching the hilt of my sword into his helm and sending it flying to the mud. With his head exposed, I swung my blade through his neck, not waiting to see him fall before I took off deeper into the camp.

A figure jogged up alongside me—Lord Jonston, followed by a few others of my retinue. "The king's tent should be up here, in the middle of his camp," he said, leading the way as we cut down the soldiers who charged us at the sides.

I heard my name being called in the distance and turned to find a runner in Tomas livery sprinting toward us. "Your Majesty," the runner called. "Queen Cora isn't—"

A soldier sprang from behind a tent and cut down the runner. One of my men charged forward and cut him down in turn.

My heart raced, bile rising in my throat as I turned away. *What was the runner trying to say? Cora isn't what?* I shook the worry from my mind and continued deeper and deeper into the camp until I finally spotted the top of a tent, taller than the rest, flying an indigo banner. I charged ahead, swinging wildly at anyone who stood between me and that tent, my retinue finishing the job as I continued to race ahead. As I approached the tent flap, Jonston called out for me to wait for him. I turned to heed his caution, but an enemy soldier engaged him.

Without a second thought, I charged into the tent. I spun around, blinking into the darkness inside, searching for sound and motion.

It was empty.

I upturned tables, kicking aside bags and blankets. There was nothing—no sign of Cora. No hint at where she could be now. My heart sank.

A long horn blast rang out, lower than Norun's signal for retreat, but it was a retreat signal nonetheless. I let out an agitated roar and stormed out of the tent.

"Where is he? Where is Darius?"

Jonston and my surviving retinue jogged toward me.

Bodies littered the ground, belonging to both sides. "Another runner came. Darius' army is retreating into the woods outside of camp," Jonston said.

"Is the Black Force still out there?"

"Yes," Jonston said. "And some of our Red Force are pursuing the retreat."

"Then let's join them. I need to find Darius alive." I took off for the southern edge of camp, blood pumping with every stride. My throat was raw, and my legs were revolting as I pushed them harder.

We approached the edge of camp, where tents still burned. Ahead, figures retreated beyond the tree line, disappearing into shadows. I waved my men forward, their feet pounding behind me.

A figure in black armor appeared before us, as if from nowhere, and I skidded to a halt. My retinue flanked me. Darius, free of helm but with sword in hand, flashed a dangerous grin. "Looking for me?"

In a rush, my confidence fled, the heat from battle draining from my veins and leaving me in terror as I found myself frozen in place. No longer did my reckless abandon to get to Darius seem anything close to an intelligent choice. Before me was a man who could close the distance between us in the blink of an eye. He could plunge his sword into my heart before I even had a chance to see him move.

I knew I couldn't fight him. I'd never intended to in the first place. Breaking his defenses and finding Cora had been the only goals for this attack. *Now that I've succeeded at the first, all I need is the second.*

I took a deep breath to steady my nerves, then

sheathed my sword. "You've signaled your retreat, and you will have it. I'm here for Cora."

Darius laughed, but remained where he was. "You thought she was *here*?"

My stomach sank. "Where is she?"

Amusement twinkled in Darius' pale, gray eyes. "Perhaps we should bargain. You tell me where I can find the tear in the veil, and I'll tell you where Cora is."

I opened my mouth, but nothing came out. What was I supposed to do? If I gave him the location of the tear, would El'Ara be ready to face him? My heart begged me to say anything to get Cora back, but I forced myself to shake my head.

In the blink of an eye, Darius was in front of me, hand on my shoulder. "I think I can persuade you."

The shouts of my men were cut off, replaced by the sound of shuffling bodies. It took me a moment to orient myself, realizing I was now beneath the trees, facing a group of Darius' soldiers. I craned my neck to look behind me, expecting to see my retinue, but all I saw were more trees. And more soldiers. Thousands of them. *He worldwalked with me.* More surprising, though, was how still the soldiers remained. They weren't retreating after all...they were gathering.

Darius pushed me into the middle of a cluster of about a dozen soldiers, sending me sprawling at their feet. When I stood, the soldiers remained, Darius amongst them, but open sky was overhead. Where were we now?

I whirled around, trying to catch my bearings, then realized Darius had disappeared. Moments later, a new cluster of soldiers appeared beside the first, then another, and another. I caught glimpses of Darius in each cluster, only to see him disappear again. My hand flung to my sword hilt, but the narrowed eyes of the soldiers that surrounded me gave me pause. There was no fighting my way out of this.

Darius appeared beside me. "Don't try anything stupid. I'd hate for this arrangement to end badly."

"We don't have an arrangement," I said through my teeth.

"Oh, I think we do." Darius made his way forward, and his soldiers parted for him while pushing me to follow in his wake. As we breached the edge of his army, Darius pushed me in front of him, finally revealing where we were.

Ridine Castle stood before of us, the rising sun illuminating the tops of the tallest turrets as birds sang to the morning. Why had he brought me here?

Darius faced his men. "Burn it down."

His soldiers ran forward, jostling me in their haste to obey, while I stared dumbfounded ahead. "No!" I shouted, the word catching in my throat. Ridine may not have been as well-staffed as it usually was, considering our call to war, but much of our household remained. Some would still be sleeping.

Darius took me by the neck of my bloodied chest plate. "I'll call them off if you tell me where the tear is."

Out of the corner of my eye, I saw his army reach the outer gate, then heard the clash of swords. I knew our guards wouldn't last long against them. *At least the fighting might alert those within the castle.*

"Fine, I will. First, tell me where Cora is. That's all I ask of you."

His eyes locked on mine, but he said nothing.

Why? I remembered the runner trying to get my attention, Darius' laughter when I first confronted him about her whereabouts. My stomach felt hollow. "You don't know where she is, either, do you?"

Darius frowned.

That's why Emylia hadn't been able to find her. Cora had escaped and must have returned to the veil. Hope and rage coursed through me, filling me with renewed determination. I kicked Darius in the thigh, unsheathing my sword as Darius stumbled back. I lunged for his side, plunging my sword between two plates of armor.

Darius barely grimaced as I withdrew my sword and retreated a step. "Fine. Watch it burn." He came at me with his sword, and I gritted my teeth to meet it with mine, when a flash of white dashed in front of me. Valorre rammed his head into Darius' chest, horn clashing against armor, then reeled toward me. He lowered his head, and without a second thought, I pulled myself onto his back. I was barely on straight before Valorre took off.

I expected Darius to appear at my side, perhaps striking Valorre, but when I turned my head, Darius remained in place, watching us ride away. Behind Darius, plumes of smoke rose into the sky. I faced forward, heart heavy with the burden that Ridine burned behind me.

37

WORLDWALKER

Cora

I pulled the bowstring to my cheek, the gold feather at the end of the arrow brushing my skin. Then I released it, sending the arrow soaring across the emerald green lawn to land in the middle of the red and gold target—one of many that spanned the length of the lawn.

My first target had been a tree in the woods near the Elvan Palace, but at the horrified gasp of a watching Faeran, I returned to the palace to procure a less offensive alternative. Practicing on the palace lawn under the watchful eyes of guards and soldiers making their rounds was less than ideal, but so was shooting a tree, apparently. Yet, practice was what I *needed*, whatever the accommodations may be. It helped me take my mind off things I'd rather not ponder; things like Teryn. Valorre. The people of Lela. How the operations in Norun were going. How long it would be before Darius invaded.

I took a few steps to the side and sent another arrow into the next target, then the next and the next.

"You've always been good at that," I heard Ailan say behind me.

I didn't turn to watch her approach as I sent an arrow into another target.

She stood at my side, Garot and Etrix behind her. "How do you like the armor?"

I let down my bow, then flexed and relaxed my arm, rolling my shoulders. "I like it." After a few days of donning the armor day and night, aside from during sleep, I was getting used to its weight and mobility. While not nearly as bulky as the armor worn by Lela's Red Force, it was certainly heavier than my usual attire. But I felt safe in it. Strong. That's what mattered.

Ailan smiled. "Good. It makes you look like a warrior. Not that you need to look like one to be one. I know you already are."

"Thanks," I said, facing her. Ailan looked like a warrior herself, black leather beneath her shimmering armor, dark hair done in an intricate arrangement of braids set on the top of her head like a crown. In that moment, it was hard to imagine she was ever the old, gentle Nalia of the Forest People. My eyes rested on the knife she wore at her belt, reminding me of what she must do.

Her face fell, as if she knew what I was thinking. "I wish there was another way. Sometimes I wonder if things would have gone differently if Darius had been treated as an equal here."

I was torn between sympathy and worry. Was she having second thoughts? "Darius made his choices."

She nodded. "Yet, he made them from a skewed perception. He never realized how much I looked up to him. How much I adored him. Mother too. He was everything to her."

"I don't think he can be reasoned with, Ailan. He believes too strongly in his own ideals."

"I know." She sighed, then pressed her lips into a tight line, jaw set. "I'm ready to do what needs to be done, and I won't hesitate to do it. I just wonder at times."

I opened my mouth, but the words were forgotten as my eyes were drawn to Garot and Etrix. Both had shifted suddenly and were exchanging a sharp look.

"Did you feel that?" Etrix asked.

Garot nodded. "The trigger. A human has entered the tear."

Ailan whirled around and called out to a nearby soldier. "Make sure Mareleau and Liam are surrounded by two dozen guards. Now!" The soldier sprang into action, running toward the palace, while Garot held out a hand, palm forward, as a swirling vortex of color opened.

We entered the tunnel, my mind reeling as we hurried toward the veil. When the swirling stilled, the tunnel opened to reveal the soldiers guarding the tear. Ailan raced toward them, and they parted, allowing me, Etrix, and Garot to file in behind her. At the end of the rows of soldiers, Ailan paused, and I made my way to her side.

Larylis stood inside the tear, hands behind his back in a military stance, his expression stoic as half a dozen spearheads framed his neck.

"Stand down," Ailan ordered, and the soldiers drew back their spears. "Speak," she said to Larylis.

His eyes moved from Ailan to me. "Teryn is here with word from Norun. Darius has reached Lela."

Teryn

My eyes were locked on the invisible space where Larylis had gone, unable to look away, unable to blink. Not until I saw Cora. I *had* to know I'd been right.

Movement ahead, the shifting of the Black Force that guarded the two trees. My heart quickened.

Larylis emerged first, followed by a flood of towering soldiers in unusual armor, who filed out in front of the tear, spreading out before it. *Elvan*, I realized with awe. More figures came through, but the soldiers were blocking my view.

Valorre stomped his hooves beside me, tossing his mane up and down.

I placed a hand on his side. "I know, friend. Me too."

Finally, the Elvan soldiers parted, and a petite figure ran forward. I barely had time to register her face before Cora jumped into my arms. Our armor clashed, renewing my more painful battle wounds, but I ignored them, relishing the feeling of her arms around my neck, her breath on my cheek, her lips seeking mine.

When we finally parted, her cheeks were wet, and we were both out of breath. She kept her arms around my neck as she studied me, then brushed her fingers along my jaw. "Are you hurt?"

"Nothing bad," I said, finding my throat raw. "You?"

"No. An Elvan Skinweaver healed the wound Darius gave me."

"You escaped him, then?"

She nodded, and Valorre nuzzled her shoulder. Cora pressed her face into his neck. "I'm so sorry," she mumbled into his coat. "I know. I know you were worried. I was worried about you too."

After a few moments, she pulled away and met my eyes, expression hard. "Where is Darius? How close is he?"

A sharp pain struck my chest. How could I tell her? "He worldwalked with his army to...Ridine. He said if I didn't tell him where the tear was, he'd burn it down."

She closed her eyes, breathing deeply, her face twisting with pain. "So he did, didn't he?"

"Yes. Valorre intervened when Darius tried to fight me, and we came here. I didn't get to see how far the damage went."

Cora's lower lip trembled as she opened her eyes, but her breathing remained steady. "I'm glad you didn't give him the location of the tear. Your warning will give us time to prepare. He will find us, eventually. He—"

The Elvan soldiers suddenly moved in unison, startling us, and we whirled to face them. Their spears were thrust forward, at us. No, at something behind us. Valorre whinnied, sidling into Cora. She and I turned.

Darius stood alone beneath the trees a short distance away. "Thank you, Teryn. I knew our arrangement would be beneficial."

"We had no arrangement," I shouted through my teeth.

"Oh, I think we did. You wanted Cora. Obviously, you

figured out where to find her. And I wanted the veil. Win, win." He slapped the neck of his chest plate, grinning.

My own hand flew to my chest plate, remembering how he'd grabbed me there. It all began to make sense. How he'd watched me ride away with Valorre. How he'd barely seemed bothered when I'd stabbed him. He *wanted* me to get away. He knew where I'd go.

"You wove a trigger on my chest plate," I said, more to myself than to him.

"Like I said, thank you." Then he was gone.

I stared at the space where he'd been, shame flooding me. How could I have been so stupid?

Whispers from the Elvan soldiers and the Black Force alike erupted behind me. I could almost feel the terror coursing through them.

"It isn't your fault, Teryn," Cora whispered at my side. "At least you warned us."

I said nothing as I continued to watch the empty space, chest heaving. Cora stared up at me, brow furrowed with concern, then joined my watch. She knocked an arrow into her bow. I unsheathed my sword. From the corner of my eye, an unfamiliar female figure joined us, knife in one hand, sword in the other.

"It's time," the woman said.

Then, where Darius had disappeared, a cluster of soldiers materialized. Then another. Then other. And another.

"Yes," I said, shifting my feet into a fighting stance. "It is time."

∾

Larylis

Our forces clashed, Black Force fighting alongside the Elvan soldiers as the newcomers charged us. I remained with those who were entrusted to protect the tear, half Black Force, half Elvan. The Elvan guards sneered at us, but they didn't have much attention to spare as the fighting moved closer and closer to us.

I stood in the back row of guards, closest to the veil. Closest to Mare and Liam. If Darius wanted in, he'd have to cut me down first.

A blood-chilling scream came from nearby. One of the Black Force guards, it seemed. I shuddered. Then a scream came from the other end of the guard squad. Then another from a few men away.

Black Force and Elvan alike dropped one after the other, forcing our remaining squad to cluster closer together as we struggled to watch all around us at once.

"He's coming," Temberly said, standing at my side. Temberly was one of the bravest of the Black Force, yet his sword trembled in his hand. "He's killing us one by one. It's like he's playing with us."

The Elvan at my other side muttered something in his language. Although I couldn't understand him, his tone was laced with fear. It chilled me. Weren't Elvan nearly impossible to kill?

My eyes searched for the first sign of movement, for the first hint that—

Blood splashed my face, and I gasped. I swung to the side, striking at the man who'd slit Temberly's throat. All I saw was a maniacal grin and a bloody knife before the attacker—it had to be Darius—disappeared again. I had to force my eyes off Temberly's lifeless form, ignoring the lurching of my stomach. For the love of Lela, how was I going to make it out of this alive?

I just have to keep Darius from entering the tear. But how? We couldn't fight someone who could move that fast. Again and again, more screams came from nearby. There was barely any sign of actual combat before it seemed Darius had moved on to surprise another victim. Our squad filed in closer and closer.

Why was he playing with us like this? Why kill one random guard after the other?

Then a chilling realization came to me. I knew exactly why he was doing what he was doing. With every man he felled, another would take his place, narrowing our squad as we fought to remain in front of the tear. The more men he killed, the narrower our range. The better he could see where we focused our attention.

"Spread out!" I called to the soldiers around me. I repeated the order until they began to obey. It was risky leaving so much space through to the veil, but how were we benefiting by closing a gap that Darius could world-walk to, no matter what the size? We needed to keep him guessing, keep him from narrowing down his options.

As our squad spread out, it also gave us more space to watch for Darius, more visibility to defend our comrades. Even so, men continued to fall to Darius' slaughter. Some out of sight, some just out of my reach.

The clash of sword on armor rang out beside me, and I joined the Elvan who had jumped in to attack Darius as he'd tried to fell one of my men. Darius engaged the Elvan solider, but as I swung at his side, Darius disappeared, only to reappear behind the Elvan. I called out a warning, but Darius' blade swept through the Elvan's neck, cutting his head clean off.

I stumbled back, eyes wide, staring down at the disembodied head. The Elvan may be immortal, but I knew there was no coming back from that. I charged at Darius, but he disappeared. I whirled around, prepared for his ruse. Sure enough, he materialized and lunged forward with his sword. I dropped to the ground beneath his swing and rolled away.

I got to my feet, crouched in a half-squat, but all I saw was a wall of mist. *Oh no. No, no, no, this isn't good.* I'd been too close to the veil. Too close...to Mareleau and Liam. The position I'd been so determined to keep would now be my downfall.

Maybe he disappeared before he could see where I went. It was a futile hope, one that didn't have time to take root before a pale hand reached through the veil. I lifted my sword, joining the ranks of Elvan soldiers who'd been left to guard the inside of the tear. Their spears inched closer as Darius stepped through.

He seemed unperturbed by the spears as he closed his eyes and took a deep breath, as if relishing the scents around him. An Elvan soldier called out something in their language, and the squad surged forward. Darius didn't bother to open his eyes before disappearing.

"Where is the Blood of Ailan?"

I turned toward the voice and found Darius with his sword at an Elvan soldier's neck.

"No answer?" Darius swung his blade, beheading the soldier before disappearing.

"Where is the Blood of Ailan?" Again, Darius appeared amongst the squad, sword to a soldier's neck.

Dead. "Where is the Blood of Ailan?" Another dead. "Where is the Blood of Ailan?" No one could act fast enough before Darius could exact his judgment. "Where is the Blood of Ailan?"

A terrified voice called out in words I couldn't understand. I spun, finding Darius with his sword at another Elvan soldier's neck. The words were repeated, causing Darius to hesitate. "You'll tell me where to find them? Good."

The squad surged forward, but Darius—and the Elvan he'd held beneath his sword—vanished.

I stared at the empty space, eyes wide. Heat flooded my veins, boiling my blood. "Let's go! Now!"

The Elvan soldiers turned toward me, but none moved to obey.

I pointed toward what was clearly a path away from the veil. The Elvan may not have understood my words, but they had to understand what I wanted them to do. "We know where he is going. He's going to find Mareleau and Liam. We need to protect them."

"Edell-Morkara'Elle," said one of the Elvan, followed by a string of shouts from another, voice ringing with the authority of one giving an order.

Three soldiers turned toward the veil, bracing themselves before disappearing through the tear, while the rest took off down the path. I followed the latter, gritting my teeth and hoping beyond hope that we could get there in time.

38

MASSACRE

Mareleau

"**W**as that a scream?" I rose from my seat at the edge of my bed, heart racing as the guards pacing my room grew terrifyingly still. Another wail sounded, and this time I was certain it was coming from inside the palace. I scooped Liam from his place on my bed and cradled him to my chest.

More guards filed in, the last shutting the door behind him. "Edell-Morkara'Elle," he shouted, then pointed to the tall table in the middle of the room. I ran to it, setting Liam in the metal bassinet that sat atop the table. My body trembled as the guards circled me and Liam, facing away from us, swords drawn.

The screams continued, growing closer now. A shuffle in the hallway. The clash of metal.

I looked down at Liam sucking on his hands, not a hint of alarm in his wide, innocent eyes. He had no idea that danger was near. No idea what those crashing sounds in the hallway meant. No idea that my heart felt as if it would burst from my chest. My knuckles were white as I squeezed the edge of the bassinet, fighting the urge to pull Liam out of it. As clever as I knew the bassinet was, at that moment, it looked more like a coffin.

What if Ailan is already dead? What if I'm next?

I heard the door to my room burst open, and without thinking, I gave in to my instincts and took Liam from the bassinet. The sound of clashing steel erupted as I threw myself under the table, Liam pressed in close as I curled in on myself. I watched between the legs of the Elvan soldiers who surrounded me, seeing flashes of red, bodies dropping to the ground.

The protection of the table seemed suddenly inconsequential. Darius was *here*. And once he cut down the guards, he would see me. *I need to be invisible,* I thought, mind spinning. *How does Cora do it? How will I do it?*

Though my body was still wracked with tremors, I forced my breathing to steady as much as I could, closing my eyes and trying to ignore the screams. I thought of Liam, let the weight of his tiny body grow heavy against my chest plate, let the scent of him fill my nose. Warmth spread through me, and I let it wrap around me and Liam, let it cover us like a comfortable blanket.

You can't see me. No one can see me. There is nothing here. Nothing to see.

I opened my eyes and watched as pools of blood crept toward me, soaking into the hem of the blue robe I wore beneath my armor. More bodies fell, piling on top of one another. I ignored that, ignored the blood, the wails, the empty eyes that stared up from the floor, focusing only on my glamour.

A thud sounded behind me—like an armored body dropping to the ground. Then silence. Creeping footsteps came toward me, stopping just behind. With a slam, the tabletop shuddered, the ring of metal against metal echoing in my ears. A moment later, the bassinet tumbled to the ground, paired with an angry roar.

"Where are you, Mother of Prophecy? Blood of Ailan?" Footsteps circled the table until a pair of legs came into view. They were plated in black armor, splattered with dirt and blood. "Come out from hiding. I won't hurt you."

Darius stopped in front of me, then walked away from the table, stepping over bodies. His full form came into view the further he moved from the table, revealing a face stained red, black hair plastered to his head. He scanned the room, hands behind his back as if he were taking a casual stroll, the hilt of a dagger clasped in his fingers.

I held my breath as I watched him, putting all my effort into holding my glamour in place.

"Come out, come out," he called as he opened the doors of my wardrobe. "I promise I won't kill you or your son. Let's make a bargain instead." His voice was gentle, and a smile played on his lips, a disturbing contrast to what he was doing to my furnishings—slashing pillows, kicking over chairs, slicing through the curtains. He walked in front of the table again, facing away from me as he squatted down.

Liam reached a hand to my chin, and I fought to keep my concentration as Darius turned his head and stared straight at me.

Nothing to see. There is nothing to see here. Nothing. Empty.

Darius furrowed his brow as he continued to look my way. Liam began to squirm, face turning toward my chest, hungry mouth finding nothing but my chest plate. He was growing restless, and I knew what would come next. Next, he would cry.

Nothing to see. Nothing to hear. Nothing. Empty.

I pressed my lips to Liam's head, though I didn't take my eyes off Darius. Darius cocked his head.

Something flew through the air, and Darius brought a hand to his neck as he shot to his feet. He pulled an arrow from his collarbone as if it were merely a splinter.

I looked toward the other end of the room, where Cora, Ailan, and Fanon emerged from a swirling tunnel.

"Garot, get the others!" Ailan shouted, and the tunnel disappeared. Ailan and Fanon raced toward Darius while Cora shot another arrow. Before it could meet its mark, Darius worldwalked away, only to reappear behind Ailan, sword drawn. She was ready for him, spinning to meet his sword with hers, while Fanon charged from the side.

Darius swiped out with his knife, scratching Fanon's chest plate, then disappeared again. He materialized at the other end of the room. "Now, dear sister, is three against one fair?"

"It is when one of us has the advantage of world-walking."

Darius' eyes found Cora. "Only one of us? Hello, my naughty heir."

Cora sneered and trained her arrow on him.

Ailan held out her hands, one toward Cora, the other toward Fanon. "Stand down," she said, then took a step toward her brother. "Why don't we end this, one on one."

"Am I supposed to trust your two little lapdogs won't cheat?"

Ailan raised a brow. "Am I supposed to trust you won't either?"

"Very well," Darius said, sheathing his knife but keeping his sword as he began to close the distance between them on foot.

Ailan nodded at Cora and Fanon, who each took hesitant steps away from the siblings, giving them space to begin circling each other. Darius assessed Ailan with narrowed eyes, while Ailan watched Darius with a seething glare. Darius swung his sword in attack, which Ailan parried. They circled again, then exchanged blows, as if testing each other's abilities.

"Mother would be so disappointed," Ailan said.

"She always has been," Darius said through his teeth, swinging at Ailan. "I'm half human, remember?"

She blocked his attack. "Not disappointed in you. In me."

Darius let out a false laugh. "You? Her perfect daughter? How so?"

Ailan charged, spinning toward him like a dancer. "Because I have to kill you."

He met her attack without effort. "She's the one who wanted me dead."

"Dead?" Ailan shook her head, eyes filled with malice. "Everything she did was to keep you alive. Everyone *else* wanted you dead. Why do you think she tried to banish you in the first place? Her love for you was her downfall."

Darius swung for Ailan's neck, but she arched back,

barely avoiding the blade. "She betrayed me," he growled.

"She loved you. And so did I. You betrayed *us*."

"Love? When did you show me love?"

"You were too blind to see it," Ailan said, "and it's too late now. All I can do is show you death." As Darius raised his arm to swing his sword, Ailan ran closer to him instead of darting away, crushing herself against his chest. Darius froze, and for a moment, I thought Ailan was hugging him. Then I noticed her hand just beneath his armpit, the black hilt of a knife locked between her fingers.

Darius blinked, then narrowed his eyes. "So much for no cheating."

"This isn't cheating. This is justice." She kicked him in the stomach, pulling away to swing her sword at his head.

Darius was faster.

His sword cleaved through Ailan's neck, separating her head from her shoulders. A spray of blood splashed on the floor, followed by her limp body falling to the ground.

I opened my mouth, hearing screams from Cora and Fanon, not sure if my own mingled with theirs. Fanon charged Darius, but Darius spun to the side, pulling the knife from beneath his arm and tossing it to the ground. It slid on the floor, landing in a pool of blood next to the hem of my dress. My stomach heaved as I stared at it.

When I looked back up, Darius was gone. Fanon kneeled at Ailan's body, sobbing, while Cora trembled behind him. I could do nothing but stare, not even aware of Liam's cries as he squirmed in my arms. *Nothing to see. Nothing to hear.*

Cora's voice shocked me from my stupor. "Mareleau, wherever you are, stay hidden." She moved through the room, as if searching for something. She bent over, looking under my table, then turned away. I was surprised to realize my glamour still held. Cora returned her attention to the body on the ground and placed a hesitant hand on Fanon's shoulder. Just then, a clash of swords and shouts came from outside the palace. "We should go, Fanon. He's still out there."

Fanon's sobs dried to a whimper, and he rose to his feet.

"Did you see what Darius did with the blade?" Cora asked. "We need that."

Fanon shook his head, not meeting her eyes.

"He must still have it. Let's go." Cora grabbed Fanon's arm, and they disappeared.

"It's here," I said, but I knew it was too late. Why didn't I speak up earlier? Why didn't I do anything?

Heat flooded my cheeks, shame scalding me from within. I looked at the bodies littering the ground, the pools of blood, wondering how I could have let such a slaughter happen around me without lifting a single finger.

I was useless. Evil. Narcuss.

Love myself. Love myself.

I cursed that voice. How could I love myself when I'd let so many die? How could I love myself when I'd done nothing?

Liam's cries seemed louder now, breaking through my clouded thoughts. As if waking from a dream, my mind became clear. "I'm so sorry, my sweet," I said, surprised to find my voice so calm. In that moment, it was as if nothing else mattered. I could forget the gore around me, just for a time, if it meant caring for my son. I tore off my chest plate and undid the top of the robe beneath. His tiny mouth sought my breast, and I allowed him to nurse.

It was then I could admit I hadn't done nothing. I'd protected Liam. That was all I could have done, and I'd succeeded.

From what I could hear, the fighting was escalating, but I focused on my one duty. After awhile, Liam fell asleep at my chest. I sighed, fixing my robe, then rocked Liam in my arms. It was as much to calm myself as it was for him. Maybe more so.

I jumped as something barreled through the balcony doors, sending shards of glass and shattered wood to mingle with the blood. Ferrah squeezed through the broken opening in the wall, screeching, tail lashing as she dashed toward Ailan's body. I barely had time to scramble out from under the table as she knocked it to the side in her haste.

Once Ferrah found Ailan, the dragon began to make a rumbling sound, like a mournful purr, as she nudged Ailan with her snout. My heart wrenched as I watched the dragon, and I realized I now had yet another duty.

I approached Ferrah with careful steps, Liam cradled in one arm as I held my other arm out toward the dragon, palm facing her.

When Ferrah noticed my approach, her head snapped back, and she hissed. I continued forward. "I know, Ferrah. She's gone. Shhh. Shhh. I'm here, though. I'm here."

Ferrah lowered her head and resumed her mourning purr, looking from me to Ailan and back again. I stopped before her, hand outstretched. Ferrah whined, taking one last look at Ailan, then pressed her head to my hand. Her pain was so palpable, I wanted to cry.

"Mother of Prophecy!"

I froze, and Ferrah whipped her head toward the opening in the wall where the balcony once was. The voice was coming from outside, rising over the fighting.

"You'll want to come out here," Darius said. "I have your husband."

My heart leapt into my throat. *Larylis*. I took a deep breath, replacing the glamour I'd discarded when Ferrah had entered, and crept toward the opening. There, strolling across the lawn, was Darius with a knife at Larylis' throat. The armor was missing from Larylis' arm, and blood streamed down from elbow to wrist.

Darius continued to call out. "Come on out, girl. I know you're hiding somewhere. Bring me your son, I won't kill him. Let's make a bargain! Now that Ailan is dead, I will make Liam my heir. You and your husband can live happily ever after with your son."

Larylis struggled in Darius' grasp, but it was no use. Soldiers who clearly belonged to Darius surrounded them, keeping all others at bay.

"I'll give you five minutes to surrender to me," Darius said. "Bring me your son. Let me make him my heir and give you the life you deserve. Otherwise, your husband dies. Don't think I won't eventually find you too."

I shuddered, and Ferrah nudged my arm with her snout. Instinctively, I reached up and scratched her scales. "What do I do?" I whispered.

Darius continued his stroll, Larylis' face turning red in his grasp, until they were out of sight.

I looked down at Liam, taking in his content, sleeping face, then at the massacre within my room. My eyes fell on the knife with the black hilt, still where I'd left it, then at Ailan's lifeless form. I turned away and looked back through the opening to the lawn. I could still hear Darius calling for me as he rounded the palace.

With a deep breath, I closed my eyes. "I know how to save you."

39

INFERNO

Larylis

I was losing blood. A lot of it.

My vision swam as Darius tightened his grip, gauntleted arm pressing against my windpipe as he paraded me across the lawn. Swords clashed around us, though I couldn't see much of the fighting anymore. Darius' men constantly circled us, and when one was felled, another would take his place, running from the fray to join his guard.

"He's not going to last much longer," Darius called out. "Come out, come out—"

An ear-shattering screech came from above, and I struggled to crane my neck toward the source. A white dragon slithered around the lower turrets of the palace.

"Hush, you!" Darius shouted at the dragon. "If you burn me, you'll burn him too. I don't think the Mother of Prophecy would like that."

The white dragon roared again, watching Darius from its perch, but made no other move.

"Your time is up, Mother of Prophecy." Darius released his grip, then kicked the back of my legs until I fell to my knees. His knife grazed the skin at my neck.

I gasped, choking for air.

"I'm here."

My blood went cold at the sound of Mareleau's voice. "No." My mouth formed the word, yet no sound came out.

"I'm happy to see you, Mother of Prophecy," Darius said. "It seems you are intelligent after all."

Darius' guard parted to reveal the door to the palace, Mareleau standing on the top step of the stairs leading to it. Her hair was disheveled, her hem torn and soaked with blood that I hoped hadn't come from her. In her arms was a bundle held close to her chest. *My son.*

"No!" This time, my voice carried, cracking with pain. "Go back Mareleau! Don't listen to him."

"Come," Darius said, his tone oddly gentle. "Or your husband dies."

Mareleau descended the steps in front of the palace, eyes locked on me, terror twisting her pale, blood-splattered face.

I launched myself forward, letting Darius' blade cut into my skin. "Just kill me already and let her go."

"Larylis, stop!" The distress in her voice gave me pause. She continued forward, one trembling step at a time. "You have to let me make my own choice. I choose for you to live. I choose to make this bargain. Please don't make this harder than it already is."

My heart crumbled, and my shoulders slumped as I

sank further down, not caring about the fresh gash in my neck. Tears streamed from my eyes. I blinked them away, only so I could see Mareleau. And Liam. It would perhaps be my last time.

When my vision cleared, I shivered. Something about Mareleau's bearing had changed. No—not changed. I was seeing something else, something...different. She continued to make her way across the lawn, shaking, sobbing, hunched over as she held our son. Yet, at the same time, I saw her standing upright, chin held high, not a single tear on her face. She was confident. Certain.

She stopped a short distance away. "You promise you'll let us live?"

"Of course," Darius said.

"Then let Larylis go."

Darius brought a knee to my back, sending me toppling to the side. "Go on, then," he said to me. "But not to her."

I rose to my feet, hand pressed against the wound at my neck. The guards parted to my right, allowing me to pass. My eyes lingered on Mareleau, still seeing two visions of her. The calm version nodded. With a deep breath, I left the ring of guards, stopping just outside their circle.

Mareleau proceeded forward, and Darius went to meet her halfway. My eyes followed. I held my breath as Darius reached for my son.

Mareleau set the bundle in his arms, but as he touched it, the blanket unraveled, revealing nothing. In that same moment, Mareleau plunged a black-hilted knife into Darius' throat. "Now, Ferrah!" she shouted.

Fire rained down from the turrets above, engulfing

Darius, engulfing Mareleau, lapping toward his guards like a burning wave. It swallowed them all in a pillar of flame, until smoke seared my eyes and nothing else could be seen.

Mareleau

I'm dead. I know that, and it's all right.

In fact, it's more than all right. I saved them. I saved them all. My life was worth living just for that.

Memories surfaced, flashes of the first time I met Larylis when we were children, the first time we ran together, played together. The vision shifted to a secret kiss shared amidst a haystack in a stable, then to another kiss, held beneath the flickering light of a lantern in a bedroom. I smiled—perhaps not with my lips, but with whatever part of me remained. My soul? Was I a wraith now?

The visions continued, and I saw a tiny body, limp in my arms. I felt myself giving my newborn child life as I poured everything I had inside me to bring him breath. Now that I was dead, I knew I'd nearly died then too. It had been worth it, then and now.

It had also been worth it to twist that knife into Darius' throat, see his eyes widen with terror as the fire melted our flesh, burned us to puddles of ash. I poured everything into that final act, drained every inch of my power with that glamour, with that thrust of the blade, with that shout to Ferrah. I'd hardly felt any pain when the fire came.

So why did I feel pain now? And where was it coming from? The dead didn't ache, so why did I? It was a persistent ache too, growing stronger with every breath.

Wait...breath? What breath? The dead didn't need to breathe.

Yet, I was doing just that. For the love of Lela, how my lungs burned with the pain of it. It felt as if my bones were being hammered, muscles ripped apart, skin and sinew peeled away. Or perhaps not peeled way. Perhaps knit together.

My breathing grew deeper, and just as my pain reached an agonizing crescendo, it began to subside, one aching bit at a time.

Voices floated upon my awareness.

"She's healing. I can't believe it." That sounded like Cora.

"Mare! Can you hear me?" My heart leapt, knowing that voice belonged to Larylis.

"She's definitely breathing." That one was similar to Larylis' voice but was just slightly wrong. Teryn, then. "But where is Liam?"

At that, my eyes flew open, my blood pounding through my veins as I pushed myself upright. "He's safe," I tried to say, but my throat felt raw.

"Slowly, my love," Larylis said. My vision was blurry, but I knew his face was the one wavering before me. I reached a hand to his cheek and felt his arms wrap around me. There was something else around me too. Something that felt scratchy against my tender flesh. A cloak?

I swallowed and noticed my throat was far less sore. "Liam is safe in the palace," I croaked.

Larylis smiled, and my heart flipped as his face came into focus before my eyes. He was covered in soot, and sticky blood coated his neck, yet he was the most beautiful sight I could see. The anxious eyes of Teryn and Cora hovered behind him. "I thought you were dead," Larylis said, pressing his forehead to mine.

"I did too," I said. "I'm supposed to be. I...I gave *everything* to make that happen."

"You sacrificed yourself," Cora said, voice quiet. "And that, in turn, saved you somehow. Healed you."

"What about Darius?" I asked.

"Not as lucky." Teryn looked to the side. I followed his gaze to a pile of charred bones. Not far away, similar piles sat, some still smoking.

"The dragon's flame killed Darius and his guards," Larylis said. "I thought it would get me too, but I had the sense to scramble away. I'm merely seared."

I frowned, noticing the frayed ends of his hair. With a start, I reached my hand to my head, finding nothing there but tender skin. My heart sank. I pulled my hand back, then stared at the pink flesh of my hand and arm, mottled with red burns that were growing smaller and smaller before my eyes.

"I'm sure your hair will grow back," Cora said.

I would have blushed, if my skin would allow it. The heat rose to my cheeks regardless, and for a moment I was ashamed to be disappointed by such a simple vanity. Still, it *had* been beautiful hair. I shrugged with an air of nonchalance and began to rise to my feet. Larylis helped me, pulling the cloak tight around my naked body.

I stared out at the lawn. The fighting had ceased. Petite figures—the Faeran—moved amongst the injured, placing their hands on wounds, applying poultices, offering skins of some liquid or bowls of crushed herbs. A few Elvan skinweavers worked alongside them. But not everyone was lucky enough for any kind of healing. Discarded armor, weapons, blood, and bodies littered the grass and extended as far as I could see. Soldiers were gathering the dead, while others secured those who had surrendered.

So much death. Yet, somehow, not my own.

The air filling my lungs suddenly felt more luxurious than anything I could ever imagine. The breeze tickling my hairless scalp felt like a lover's caress. The pain in my muscles and the blood rushing through my veins were like a beautiful song.

I was *alive*.

The sound of wings beat overhead, and a gush of air pushed against me as Ferrah landed nearby with a screech. I smiled at her.

"What do we do now?" Teryn asked.

We all looked to Cora, who shrugged. "We continue on as planned. Return the heart of El'Ara. Seal the veil."

"How?" I asked. "Ailan is…"

Cora sighed. "Liam is Morkara now."

A slight panic rippled through me. "How is he supposed to handle the return of the Mora? He's a baby. He doesn't know how to be steward over Ancient magic, much less repair the tear in the veil."

"And you don't know how to survive dragon fire," Cora said, "but you did so anyway. Ailan wove this tapestry that brought us all together, brought us to where we are right now. We have to trust we can finish this without her."

I wanted to argue, wanted to tell her she was wrong, yet something inside me felt at peace. "I suppose we don't have any other choice, do we?"

Cora shook her head.

"All right. Let's end this." Linking my arm through Larylis', I attempted an unsteady step toward the palace. "Come, Lare. Let's go see our son."

40

MAGIC AND BLOOD

Cora

We stood at the veil, the swirling wall of mist swallowing the sky above and the dead earth below. I took it all in, knowing it would be my last time, knowing I'd never see what this place looked like without the gray void.

I faced Mareleau. "Are you ready?"

Her eyes were already filled with tears. "You brought Mother?"

"Yes." My gaze moved to Larylis, who wasn't faring much better. "And Queen Mother Bethaeny."

Mareleau let out a shuddering breath. "It's time to say goodbye."

I turned back to the veil and reached a hand through the tear. "Goodbye, El'Ara," I whispered.

On the other side stood Teryn, his wounds bandaged, his deeper injuries already tended to by skinweavers. He smiled at me, arm around his mother's shoulders. She and Helena watched the space behind me with anxious eyes. At Teryn's other side, Valorre tossed his mane.

I stood next to Valorre, face resting against his neck as I watched Mareleau step out of the veil, holding Liam. Behind her came Larylis, followed by two Elvan guards, as well as Fanon, Etrix, and Garot. I could hardly look at Fanon without feeling his anguish over Ailan's death. Surprisingly, he'd been steadfast about defending Mareleau and Liam in her absence.

Mareleau ran to her mother, while Larylis shared a tearful reunion with Bethaeny. I stepped away, giving them space to say their goodbyes. Valorre stayed close to my side.

"You will miss him." Etrix's voice startled me.

I looked from Etrix to my friends. "*Him*? Who do you mean?"

He nodded at Valorre.

It felt as if my blood had turned to ice. "Why would I miss Valorre? He isn't..." My words caught on the lump in my throat.

His face flashed with a hint of sympathy. "Unicorns belong in El'Ara. He should be with his family. All the others have returned, so should he."

"*I'm* his family."

Etrix shook his head. "It was what we agreed to with Ailan, so that you'd be allowed to proceed with your side of the bargain. Mareleau, Liam, and Larylis would be the only humans allowed to remain in El'Ara, while none from El'Ara would remain in the human world."

My mind fought to argue, to beg, to threaten.

It's all right, Valorre said, and the fight left me. In its place an overwhelming sorrow squeezed my heart. *I will stay. Do not fight. This is how it should be.*

"If he stays in the human world, he will be the last of his kind. That is no life for a unicorn." Etrix placed a hand on my shoulder. "I'm sorry."

I sobbed, wrapping my arms around Valorre's neck, feeling as if my chest was being crushed beneath a boulder.

Don't be sad for me, Valorre said. *I will be home.*

Home. He was right. Etrix was right. El'Ara was Valorre's home, and that was where he belonged. That didn't make it hurt any less.

The sun was beginning to set when we finally agreed it was time to go. Another round of hugs. Another fresh wave of tears. When I came to Mareleau, I held her tightly, and she sobbed into my hair.

"I will never forget you," she whispered.

"I love you, Mare." This time, there was no resentment, no darkness lingering between us. "Take care of Valorre for me."

Mareleau and I parted, and Helena placed Liam in her daughter's arms. Teryn released Larylis from a hug, then came to my side. Larylis planted a kiss on Bethaeny's tear-stained cheek, then made his way to the invisible tear, where Etrix, Fanon, and Garot waited with the guards.

"I will tell this story," Garot said, eyes on me. "I will tell it right. Make sure you find a bard in your world who will do the same."

"I will," I said. The guards filed into the tear. Then Garot and Etrix.

Fanon extended his arm for Mareleau and Larylis to

follow. They took one final look at us, then disappeared from view. Fanon raised a brow at Valorre who remained at my side.

I stroked his side, capturing the silky smoothness of his coat in my palm, as if I could keep it with me always. *I love you, my dear friend. Life will never be the same without you.*

Valorre faced me. *Life should never be the same. It changes, as it should.* He bowed his head, horn pointed toward me, hovering just over my midsection. Then, with a light touch, he pressed the tip of his horn below my abdomen—over my broken womb. I felt a slight pressure, then a glorious warmth.

As he pulled away, I furrowed my brow. *What was that?*

He ignored my question. *Be happy. Happy for me. Happy for you. I will be with you.*

I nodded. *You be happy too.*

Valorre turned and slowly made his way toward Fanon, toward the tear, and beyond. I watched until the last flash of white could no longer be seen. I watched until I caught my breath, dried my tears, and felt as if I could breathe again.

I would breathe. I would smile and be happy. But I knew part of me would always be in El'Ara.

AT CENTERPOINTE ROCK, THE MOON SHONE OVERHEAD, stars twinkling in the black sky. I rested at the base of the Rock, exhausted after so much worldwalking. Helena was back with her betrothed in Tomas, Bethaeny was back at Verlot, and Teryn and I were alone at Center-pointe Rock.

Teryn squatted next to me. "Do you want me to start a fire? We could sleep here for the night."

I shook my head. "No. I want to do it now." Now, before I could second guess myself. Before I could convince myself it would never work. Before I could begin to *hope* it wouldn't work.

With a deep breath I rose to my feet, clearing my mind. *Breathe in. Breathe out.* I placed my hands on the surface of the Rock, letting my senses fill with the scent of the stone, the grass around it, the harsh feel beneath my palms. I felt waves of power radiate to and from my palms, felt the Mora communicating with the Arts, Ancient magic mingling with human magic.

"I am Queen of all Lela," I whispered to the Mora. "I am the heir of Darius. My heir is the Blood of Ailan. I claim my right by magic and blood."

A surge of power roared through me, swirling around me, whipping my hair back. It filled me with an unparalleled euphoria with an equally unparalleled pain.

The Mora was mine. I could claim it, do anything with it. It was mine to have and mine to command.

I felt it tickling my insides, awaiting my order, burning me with its impatience to move.

I could use it. I *could*. Queen of Lela seemed suddenly so *small*, so unambitious. With this power, I could be queen of the world. Not only that, but I could...fly, fight, destroy, create—anything I wanted! It was all mine. I could be, do, or have *anything*. All I had to do was harness it. Give it a command. The pain and euphoria rose in tandem, spiraling up and down my body.

Breathe in. Breathe out.

I ignored the pain, ignored the euphoria, ignored the visions flashing through my mind—visions of grandeur, blood, and beauty. Instead, I focused on the veil. I saw the invisible space between two trees in a dark forest, thought of the loved ones behind that veil. Valorre, Mareleau, Liam, Larylis, the Elvan, the Faeran. Their faces replaced the visions, replaced the burning intensity inside me with a calm warmth.

I pushed the Mora away, pushed it from my palms, back down my body, down my feet.

Breathe in. Breathe out.

I pushed it away from the Rock, watching the Mora in my mind's eye, seeing it reeling away, toward the veil. As the Mora retreated from me, from the Rock, toward the edges of Lela, I watched it crash against the invisible veil. It swirled against the barrier, and I chased it away, pushing it along the veil and toward the tear.

There, I saw the Mora streaming away, felt it leaving me, felt it leaving the land I ruled by right, magic, and blood.

I pushed it away until there was nothing left to push against.

It was gone.

The Heart of El'Ara was where it belonged.

Mareleau

The veil of mist was gone.

I hardly had time to blink before the wall of white disappeared, revealing gray, dying land all around. The ground itself looked strange, as if it were patched together. I supposed it had been, in a way. With Lela no longer creating the void in the middle of El'Ara, the remaining land must have had to reshape itself.

My heart sank, knowing what all this meant. The tear had been sealed. I would never see Mother, Cora, or Teryn again. I would never see *Lela* again.

Larylis put his arm around my waist. "Cora succeeded," he said.

I looked down at Liam in my arms. "He must have succeeded as well," I said. "The Mora sealed the tear."

"We should return to the palace," Fanon said. "There is much to be repaired."

"As well as many new beginnings," Garot said with a smile. "We've never had an infant as Morkara before, much less a human."

I took in the faces of those around me, the soldiers and guards that waited to escort us back. Their eyes rested on Liam and were filled with curiosity, fear, ambition, terror, excitement. I was sure the tribunal would show more of the same.

I held my head high, chin up, shoulders back. "Garot, lead the way," I ordered, not waiting for his swirling tunnel to begin before I proceeded forward. *My son may be the ruler here, but I am still a queen. Let them remember that. If anyone wants to get to him, they'll have to go through me.*

Just before Garot opened his tunnel, something green caught my eye. I paused. A leaf was slowly unfurling from one of the dead branches to my right. In fact, everywhere I looked, tiny green buds were beginning to emerge. With a smile, I took Larylis' hand in mine and entered the swirling tunnel.

Flowers bloomed in my wake.

41

QUEEN OF LELA

Cora

I opened my eyes to the sound of birdsong, Teryn's bare chest rising and falling beneath my cheek. With a yawn, I sat, pulling a robe around my shoulders despite the warm air filling the tent.

"Not yet," Teryn mumbled, pulling me back down to our cot.

My lips met his, and heat flooded me from head to toe. We rolled amongst the blankets, not caring whether sounds of our passion traveled to the nearest tents of our makeshift camp. They were probably used to it by now. There had been much...passion...as of late.

And why not? Lela was at peace. El'Ara was safe and sealed for good. Helena had solidified Tomas' alliance with Lela through her recent wedding. Norun had fallen to the rebellion, and the conquered kingdoms had been restored. Emylia had visited to tell me she was moving on to the otherlife. Just outside our camp, a new palace was being built. A new home.

We had *a lot* to celebrate.

Once we were spent, we rolled onto our backs, and I giggled as Teryn kissed my neck. My hand rested over my stomach, and I remembered what Valorre had done, still unsure what it had meant. Was it too much to hope I'd been healed? Was it possible? *Maybe.*

Either way, the thought left a bittersweet ache in my heart.

Footsteps sounded outside the tent. "Your Majesties, messages have arrived," Lord Jonston said.

Teryn sighed. "One moment," he called out.

We dressed, then met Jonston outside. I yawned as we made our way to the meeting tent, watching carpenters and stonemasons preparing for the day's work on the palace. The bones of our new great hall had already been constructed, rising as a backdrop to our camp.

"Messages from Tomas," Jonston said, handing Teryn a few scrolls.

Teryn opened them. They were all from Lex. "He wants us to come for a visit and meet his baby daughter," Teryn said.

I planted a kiss on his cheek. "Then we will have to plan one."

Jonston passed another handful of scrolls. "Messages from Syrus. The new government is taking shape there."

I reached for the messages, eager to know how things were going without Darius. As his heir, I remained in control of the kingdom of Syrus. Yet, I wanted to see how the kingdom would proceed with Darius' ideals. Without the bloodshed, of course.

Perhaps I could learn a thing or two. Or perhaps it would crumble. Either way, I would watch it unfold. Shape it. Make it better.

I may not have unlimited power, but I will make changes here. I will do everything I can to make this a better world in my lifetime, no matter how small those efforts will be.

I knew I couldn't save everyone. I couldn't change everything wrong in the world.

But I would never stop trying.

We reached the meeting tent, and Jonston went inside. I paused outside the doorway. "Can you handle the morning meeting without me? I'd like to stretch my legs for a while longer."

Teryn squeezed my hand. "Of course, my love. But only if you'll be my date for dinner. I'm thinking we should eat in the great hall. Sadie and Becca are dying to use the new kitchen."

I followed his gaze to the unfinished building, then met his eyes with a grin. "I can accept those terms."

Teryn entered the tent, and I continued toward the new palace. I took off my shoes, feeling the soft grass beneath my feet, letting the morning sun warm my face as it peeked above the hills surrounding the valley. As I approached the new great hall, I closed my eyes, imagining what the palace would look like once finished. It wouldn't be as grand as Verlot, and it wouldn't have the same charm as Dermaine. And it would never be like Ridine, a place that held so much pain and joy in equal measure. It would be new. That's all I wanted.

I circled the construction site to what would one day be the palace gardens. There, I found Centerpointe Rock. This too, had once been a place of great suffering. It had also been a source of immense power. Now it would be our home, where Teryn and I would rule Lela together.

I pulled myself onto the Rock, then crossed my legs beneath me. There I watched the sun rise over the hills, watched the birds flit across the sky. Sometimes I'd catch myself expecting one of the birds to be the silhouette of a dragon, and I'd laugh. Would I ever forget what it was like to see a dragon in the sky? I hoped not.

A sudden tingling crawled up my spine, and I froze. Someone was near. Watching me.

I looked side to side but couldn't find the source. With a shake of my head, I tried to clear my thoughts. Had I imagined it?

No, it was there again, like a tug at the corner of my mind. I stood, then jumped from the Rock to the grass below. Eyes closed, I extended my senses.

There.

I looked toward where I sensed the presence. It was at the edge of the field where the valley met the rising hills and the trees that blanketed them. It was coming closer.

I couldn't see it, but I could feel it.

It was familiar.

A flash of white darted from the line of trees, speeding toward me across the field. My breath caught, heart racing as my eyes took in the impossible.

Valorre.

I ran to meet him, feet flying beneath me. His joy reached me before he did, filling my entire being with calm warmth, with love, with pure excitement.

"How? How is this possible?" I cried as I wrapped my arms around his neck. Dark thoughts tugged at me. Was something wrong? Had the veil fallen after all?

Valorre seemed to sense my worry. *I am here and nothing is wrong. I told you I will be home. I told you I will be with you. Were you not expecting me?*

I couldn't help but laugh as I pulled away to stare at him. "No, I was not expecting you. How did you get here?"

He tossed his mane. *Veil could never keep me out before. Why would it now?*

"Your horn. It can still pierce the veil?"

Yes. It was hard at first. At times I thought it would be impossible. But I figured it out. I followed thoughts of home.

"Home," I said, brow furrowed.

You. You are my home, and I stay with you.

"You will be the last of your kind here."

I am all right with that. We are all *the last of our kind. You are the only you. Teryn is the only Teryn. I am the only me. Why should that worry me?*

"You're right. Absolutely right." I turned to face Centerpointe Rock, the sound of hammers now ringing across the valley. I smiled, feeling peace radiating from the crown of my head to the tips of my toes that dug into the warm earth beneath my feet. "Welcome home."

ABOUT THE AUTHOR

Tessonja Odette is fantasy author living in Seattle with her family, her pets, and ample amounts of chocolate. When she isn't writing, she's watching cat videos, petting dogs, having dance parties in the kitchen with her daughter, or pursuing her many creative hobbies. Read more about Tessonja at www.tessonjaodette.com

Made in the USA
Columbia, SC
10 August 2021